HEATHER GRAHAM

SEIZE THE DAWN

ZEBRA BOOKS
KENSINGTON PUBLISHING CORP.
http://www.kensingtonbooks.com

ZEBRA BOOKS are published by

Kensington Publishing Corp.
119 West 40th Street
New York, NY 10018

All Kensington titles, imprints, and distributed lines are available at special quantity discounts for bulk purchases for sales promotion, premiums, fund-raising, educational, or institutional use.

Special book excerpts or customized printings can also be created to fit specific needs. For details, write or phone the office of the Kensington Sales Manager: Attn.: Sales Department. Kensington Publishing Corp., 119 West 40th Street, New York, NY 10018. Phone: 1-800-221-2647.

Zebra and the Z logo Reg. U.S. Pat. & TM Off.

First Zebra Books Mass-Market Paperback Printing: February 2001
ISBN-13: 978-1-4201-3817-7
ISBN-10: 1-4201-3817-0

10 9 8 7 6

Printed in the United States of America

RESCUED ... OR ENSLAVED?

Safe!

The ship tossed. Her head reeled. She was still damp from her unsuccessful escape overboard and twisting with a fever.

The door of the ship's cabin suddenly burst open.

He stood there. She saw his face, as she had in dreams.

He filled the door frame, his head taller than the clearing, his shoulders spanning it side to side. He had changed his wet clothing, and a hated woolen tartan was once again over his shoulder, held there by a silver Celtic brooch.

Was she dreaming, or was this real? There was light; morning had come. But the light was like mist, and she knew then that they still rode the storm.

"Come with me, lady. Now!" he commanded.

The devil had come, she thought. In the flesh. Older, grimmer, harder. Aye, vengeance had found her.

But she smiled, for whether he were dream or real, she could not obey. She tried to open her mouth and speak. She hadn't the strength.

"Stubborn wench!" he swore, and came to her. "I'm trying not to leave you locked here in the midst of this tempest! Is there anyone to whom you listen, any point at which you stop being such a stubborn fool?"

He reached for her, and she couldn't fight him. He swore suddenly, "You are still soaked to the bone, ice and fire in one!"

His arms wrapped around her. He lifted her, and carried her, steady despite the rock and sway of the ship.

They left the cabin. The misty light fell more fully upon them from the stairway to the upper deck.

Then a flash of lightning ripped through the fullness of the sky. It created an illumination like a burst of pure white fire. Thunder roared.

The sea meant to kill them. The wind, the rain, the thunder, the lightning. God's great hand upon them all.

Her head fell against the chest of her greatest enemy.

Darkness descended. The heavens continued to roar.

But for the time, Eleanor knew no more.

More historical romances by Heather Graham

The King's Pleasure

Come the Morning

Conquer the Night

Knight Triumphant

The Alliance Vampire novels

Beneath a Blood Red Moon

When Darkness Falls

Deep Midnight

Realm of Shadows

The Awakening

Dead by Dusk

Prologue

Falkirk, Scotland
July 22, 1298

There could be a strange beauty to war. The sight of the arrows was awesome.

They appeared suddenly in the radiant blue summer sky . . .

And they were spellbinding, an arcing rain, flying high into the sky, cresting, then falling with a strange grace back to the ground.

Then the hurling, whistling whir of them suddenly took precedence.

Along with the sounds that followed . . .

Brendan could hear screams, for those Scotsmen who had taunted the expert bowmen of the English army with their backsides discovered too late that grace and beauty were as deadly as stupidity. Arrows connected with flesh, spewing blood, breaking bone. Men shouted, staggered, fell, some wounded, some killed. Horses neighed shrilly, animals died, and knights, not hit themselves, cursed as their mounts stumbled and fell, many wheezing out a death rattle. Foot soldiers scattered; cavalry began to break; commanders shouted.

''Hold, you fools! And cover your backsides!'' John Graham, Brendan's kinsman, shouted from atop his tall black steed. They'd had a certain advantage. William Wallace, their leader, knew how to choose his ground for a fight. Though Edward had great numbers of foot soldiers and cavalry — perhaps twelve thousand of the latter and twenty-five hundred of the first — William had chosen to wage war from the flank of the Callander Wood. From there, a fiercely flowing burn, or stream, met with another from Glen Village, and because of this, the terrain the English must traverse was little but mire, soggy wet ground, a morass to wear down horses and men.

But today, the English had come on. Mired, they had rallied.

And it was the Scots now breaking.

''Hold!'' John shouted again.

Brendan saw him shake his head with disbelief, wondering what fool confidence had suggested such a show of idiocy.

Indeed! What man had not seen the arrows? They had thought to defy the deadly barrage of the English — and so life was wasted. The major assault had not even begun.

Along with the screams and shouts, he could hear the jingle of horses' harnesses, the trappings of some of the richer men's mounts. His own great dappled stallion, Achilles, stamped the ground with nervous impatience as a cloud of moist air streamed from his nostrils. More arrows were flying. Men were falling, dying. Edward of England was no fool, and surely no coward, and any of them who had taken him as such were doomed. The English king had ruthlessly destroyed the Welsh — and from them, he had gained his talented longbowmen. He had brought soldiers talented with the crossbow as well: Flemish, Germans, mercenaries — even some of the French he was so constantly fighting.

Even Scotsmen rode with him. Scotsmen who feared that Wallace, their protector, their guardian, could not hold against the forces of the Plantagenet king of England, self-proclaimed Hammer of the Scots.

Scotsmen who were perhaps now changing sides.

"Sweet Jesu, help me!"

English riders were following their bowmen. Scottish knights were breaking. Hand to hand battle came closer and closer. The Scots were experts with their schiltrons — barriers created by men arranged with rows of pikes — weapons that held well against the English knights.

But even they were failing now.

Brendan quickly dismounted, hurrying to the rugged old warrior with the arrow protruding from his thigh. He couldn't wrench out the arrow; the man would bleed to death there on the field.

"Break it!" the man commanded.

"MacCaffery, I can't — "

"You will, boy, you will." Beady blue eyes surveyed him from beneath a fine bush of snow-white brows and hair, so completely entangled, it was impossible to say where the one began, and the other gave off.

"MacCaffery — "

"Haven't you strength, boy?"

MacCaffery was taunting him on purpose. Aye, and the taunting worked. He snapped the arrow, gritted his teeth — and removed the shaft, immediately using his linen shirt to put pressure against the wound.

"Fool!" he accused his elder.

"Aye," MacCaffery said softly. The old man hadn't flinched,

hadn't let out so much as a whimper. ''A free fool. And I'll die that way, boy.''

Die that way . . .

Did the old man feel it, too? A strange sense, not so much of fear, but of unease and trepidation. They should not have fought that day! Many of the commanders had said it. They should not have fought. They should have continued their northern flight. They had left the land desolate, stripped; if they had just kept ahead of the English army, they could have starved it out!

Yet almost a year ago now, at Stirling Bridge, the forces of Scotland, forces truly of Scotland — rich men, poor men, diggers of soil, purveyors of gold — had faced the might of the English, and there, they had triumphed. And since that precious time, Scotland had been free. The great baron of the north, Andrew de Moray, had died soon after the battle, mortally wounded in the fighting. But until the very last minute, the great survivor of the struggle, Sir William Wallace, had kept his name alive in official correspondence. Wallace had reigned as the guardian of the realm. He had gained so much power that he had pushed the tide of bloodshed into England, ravaged York, and given something incredibly valuable to his followers as well: pride.

Pride.

Pride had now turned to foolishness.

''Take heed!'' Old MacCaffery warned.

Brendan turned, just in time. An armored knight, wearing the colors of the House of York, was bearing down upon him. Brendan wielded his weapon with a desperate power, aiming deliberately for the throat. His opponent went still, hovered in time and space, clutched his neck. Red seeped through his fingers, and he fell into the mire. But another knight was coming on, riding hard despite the mire, and Brendan braced to meet him.

He had first learned the hatred of the enemy at Hawk's Cairn where he'd fought with no talent and no experience, and had survived because he'd been left for dead. That now seemed a lifetime ago. He'd learned. Time had given him strength and judgment—and a well-trained sword arm. He'd learned victory . . .

And suddenly, he knew.

Here, he was about to learn defeat.

But he would never accept it. Just as old MacCaffery, who had risen to his feet despite his wound, and, though the blood drained from him, fought on. Raising his great sword, letting it fall, raising it . . .

Again and again.

And the mire beneath their feet turned red.

Brendan heard a shout and turned. His kinsman was down. John Graham was unhorsed, on the ground. His men flocked around him, tried to wrest him from the onslaught of men now decimating the Scots, riding them down.

"Go to him, lad! I'll cover your back!" MacCaffery shouted. Aye, he was a fierce old man, and half dead or nay, there was no man better to cover him. So Brendan ran, and fell to his knees where they were lifting John, and he saw the wound at his kinsman's throat, and heard the rattle of death in his lungs.

"John, for the love of God." He reached for him, would have carried him, but John placed a bloody hand on his chest. "Brendan, run, run with these fellows! They've just gotten Wallace out. Go after him—"

"I'll not leave you!" he insisted. "I'll take you from the mire to the wood—"

"Brendan! I'm a dead man, and you haven't the time to save a corpse."

"John—"

"For the love of Scotland, Brendan! Go! This battle is lost, much is lost! But hope is alive and freedom lives in your heart! Go!''

John gripped his hand tightly.

The grip failed. Brendan rose slowly, clenching his teeth. He looked around.

He stood in a field of dead men. Even as he watched, old MacCaffery wavered and fell at last. He had died a free man, defiant to the end.

The English were still coming. Hundreds of horsemen. More and more. Yet their horses stumbled over mud and corpses and blood. A knight dismounted, and came at him. Brendan let out a roar, the battle roar of the Scotsmen, a cry that sounded to heaven and earth and gave even armored and battle-hardened Englishmen pause.

Then he stepped forward, slicing, slashing, piercing, wielding his sword with the strength of madness and rage. Men dropped before him, often felled with a single blow. He walked slowly, with purpose, rage and strength growing. John was dead, old MacCaffery was dead, by God, the dead were everywhere and the hated English were coming and coming . . .

Too many of them.

Yet, he realized, he wasn't fighting alone. He glanced to the side, saw the colors and emblem of his own family, and realized his cousin Arryn had ridden in. Together they walked through the shadow of death, steel glistening in the sun, running red . . .

Blood and haze. There was so much on the field it was hard to tell who was who anymore. Hard to read the crests on tunics that covered mail, and harder still to tell the woven colors of the wool on the men who fought kilted, without armor.

There was a break, suddenly. The English before them had fallen.

More came . . .

Yet at a distance.

And like the arrows, they were spellbinding, horses and men in their armor and livery beneath the sun and sky, colors flying, great muscles moving . . .

Beautiful. Awesome. Deadly.

"To horse!" Arryn shouted. Some of the man who had fought with them ran.

Brendan shook his head, eyes narrowed. "There are more of them! John is dead, MacCaffery is dead — they're all . . . dead," he said, looking at the field. "For them, freedom — or death!"

"There will be no freedom if we don't keep the fight alive!" Arryn told him. "Damn you, Brendan, to your horse!"

At sixteen, he had known the sweet taste of victory at Stirling Bridge.

Now, at seventeen, he knew that he must swallow the bitterness of the defeat at Falkirk.

Arryn mounted his horse. Achilles loped behind him. Brendan hesitated but a second more. He mounted his horse and followed.

By John's body he paused.

"Aye, cousin! For the love of Scotland, I'll ride. And I swear to you, John, I will ride until Scotland is free forever. By God's blood, so help me, I so swear! I will never surrender — myself, or my country."

The English were almost upon him.

He waited.

And with a fierce and fiery fury he turned one last time, bringing down the first knight to attack him, and the man behind him. It seemed again that there were men all around him. They had come near the wood, near the edge of the trees. As he engaged then, still mounted, striking with his sword, he found himself fighting into the cover of the trees. He was nearly unhorsed; he dismounted of his own volition, turning to fight on foot. One man assaulted him, and he pressed back hard until his attacker was at a tree, and there he killed him.

Then he turned, covered in shadow and darkness. Someone stood in the copse, wearing a dark cape over chain mail.

Friend or foe?

He started forward.

For a moment, the figure attacked with strength and aggression, but Brendan returned each strike of the sword. The enemy fell back and cried out, "Wait!"

It was a young voice, a female voice.

The cape fell from her; she tore the mail helm from her head. Stunned, he stared at her. She was very young—his own age, perhaps? Younger still. In the shadowed light of the forest, her hair gleamed with a golden fire. Her features were as perfect as carved marble, her eyes as bright as stars, as innocent . . .

He made no move against her. He just stared.

And it was then that he heard the figure behind him. The enemy at his back.

He whirled with a split second to spare. Before the man could slice off his head, Brendan skewered him through the gullet.

Something from the rear hit his head. He fell to his knees, pain shooting through his temples, blinding him. *The girl. The girl had struck him down,* he thought, as the world began to fade.

"Brendan!" His cousin's voice brought him struggling back.

Arryn had reached him. Dismounting, he drew Brendan to his feet.

"Come on, we've got to ride harder, further, deeper, into the wood!"

Gritting his teeth, Brendan grasped his horse's saddle, and managed to pull himself up.

The pain he felt was horrible; the self-anger was worse. No enemy was ever to be trusted!

"Brendan! Hold boy, ride!"

His vision wavered.

Then he saw the host coming hard behind them, slipping into the trees.

He nudged Achilles and rode hard. Thankfully, his horse followed his kinsman's. And as they rode, and the English fell behind, he damned himself in an impotent rage and desolation. They had lost. They had fought so long, and so hard . . .

And he had been downed by a girl.

But he had survived.

He had been ready to fight to the death, but they had been right—death now would avail him nothing, nor would it serve his country. He would fight again.

Never surrender.

Never forget, never forgive.

His head pounded ferociously and he nearly fell from his mount, but he held on and stayed alive through will power alone.

He must survive now.

For the love of Scotland!

And for vengeance.

One day, by God, aye! One day he would find out who she was!

Vengeance, anger, they were strong emotions for life!

Sanctuary . . . at last they reached sanctuary in the woods. "Safety, lad, we've reached safety!" He heard Arryn's rough voice, then fell into his kinsman's arms, and as he did so, he knew he would not stay conscious long. Darkness was encroaching all around him. A deep crimson darkness, like the shadow of blood and death . . .

He would live.

For vengeance, and for Scotland.

Aye, to find her! — and for the love of his country. He would not die.

Nay . . .

He would avenge the evil done today.

And he and his country would both *live* — at peace, triumphant.

And free.

Chapter 1

The Eve of the New Century
1301–1302

"She's an outlaw!" Captain Abram cried. "A pirate ship. Full sail! Hard with the wind! We must outrun these bloody bastards!"

The white-bearded, leathered old sea captain was tense as he shouted the command.

Lady Eleanor of Clarin, Yorkshire, England, had been standing at the bow, feeling the salt spray tease her flesh and the wind whip her hair and clothing about her. She frowned at the captain's shout, not at all certain of his deduction. Despite the lookout in the crow's nest she had been the first to see the oncoming vessel, the first to bring the ship to the captain's attention. It was a very fast ship — she now watched in amazement as it bore down on them, seeming to fly over the Irish Sea.

"A pirate ship," she repeated. She wasn't sure she believed him. She'd heard of a few exploits, certain seamen ready to risk all to improve their fortunes, but they were few and far between. The days when the Vikings ruled the seas with their own brand of piracy had now faded, and though many a man living in Britain, Eire, and, aye, maybe even all of Europe, carried Viking blood, there were dire consequences for men captured in such acts. King Edward was merciless to pirates — they stole from his ships, his coffers, and he needed his money for the wars he was constantly waging.

"Pirates!" Captain Abram repeated, aggravated, his attention suddenly on her. "And you, my lady, are to get below, to my cabin."

"Captain Abram, if pirates seize this vessel, I will be no safer in your office than elsewhere," she told him.

"Lady Eleanor, I intend to hold my ship!"

"Captain, many men have *intended* many things."

"I will fight — " he began, outraged.

"I have no doubt!"

He sighed, studying her, aware he was talking to a young woman who had seen too much.

"Lady, you could be slain in the boarding of such outrageous fellows. Those who dare the seas know little of the conventions of the *civilized* world!"

The *civilized* world. If she lived within a civil world whatsoever, she had yet to see it in effect. The *civil* had sent her on this trip, and the *civility* of her concerned male relations.

"Perhaps it is not pirates at all, but one of my cousins," she murmured.

"Lady, I know the ship!" Abram insisted. "She belongs to the French rogue pirate Thomas de Longueville! My lady, I would not have you die!"

No, he would not, she thought sadly, though she wondered if the possibility of her death hadn't been a driving factor toward her presence now on the Irish Sea, heading for France. She kept such counsel to herself, however, and reminded him, "Captain, I was present at my family home north of York when the savage Scotsman, Wallace, set fire to a barn imprisoning thirty men. I was the one, sir, to defy the remnants of the butcher's army, and open the doors."

Abram didn't look pleased. "Aye, the people think you a saint, touched by God, and men of York followed you into battle at Falkirk, lady, but we are asea here! My good young woman, you could die by the accidental touch of a grappling hook! By the fall of a mast. Call your maidservant, lady. Get below."

"Captain, with all respect — "

"Girl! Is there no one to whom you will listen!" he cried.

The sound of his voice gave her the first real sense of alarm she had felt. She turned around. The ship was nearly upon them. The vessel she rode seemed a poor, creaking, groaning beast of burden now, hard put to come up with any speed. Sailors rushed about, commanded now by the captain's mate, and what she saw in their eyes was surely good warning.

She looked back to the ship coming upon them. Small, smooth, sleek, with excellent sails proudly riding the masts, she cut the water with the accuracy and precision of a knife.

"Eleanor!"

At the call of her name, she turned. "Are ye daft, child? Pirates are upon us!" Bridie, her maid, was standing at the top of the few steps that led to the captain's cabin, crossing herself over and over again. Despite the situation, Eleanor arched a delicate brow — Bridie never spoke to her in such a tone. Surely, she must believe that they were facing imminent death.

"Bridie — " she began, but Bridie came flying across the deck, dodging seamen in their desperate attempts to build speed.

Tall, slender, just three years older than Eleanor, she was a good and stalwart companion.

Now, as she had been before.

She threw her arms around Eleanor. "I was *there!* I was *there* as well that day, I *know* that you hated what you did, I know that they dragged you to the field of battle, *I know!* So don't go pretending you are as steely as any man, by the blood of the Virgin Mary, come with me, lady; come below. Would you view any more blood?"

Her courage, or determination, falted at Bridie's words. *God, yes! She had hated the bloodshed, hated the fear, hated the fighting, the watching as men died . . .*

Bridie was right. It had not been courage that had made her act as she had at Castle Clarin. It had been pure madness.

Still, she had learned. Much about battle, and much about men.

"Please!" Bridie whispered.

"All right, we'll go below."

Eleanor followed Bridie, feeling the pitch of the ship but balancing to it. She wasn't afraid of the wind or the water. A sure knowledge of their character gave an intelligent respect for the wrath of the pirates.

But nothing, nothing in the world frightened her as much as the prospect of being *locked in*.

Before they reached the door, a violent shuddering sent them both flying. It was as if the whole of the vessel let out a cry. Wounded, aye, she was wounded, rammed, run down. Sailors were abandoning their positions to draw their arms. The pirate ship had come upon them, skimmed them, taken them. Grappling hooks flew into the air like silver birds, then fell to the ship's planking like winged teeth of steel.

"My lady!" Bridie called.

She catapulted into Eleanor; they both went sprawling. By then, sailors from the assaulting ship were dropping on them like flies upon meat. Men hung from the rigging, then slid to the deck, their swords bared. Fierce battle was engaged.

Flat upon the deck, Eleanor stared into the eyes of a dying seaman, watching as they glazed over. His blood spilled upon the deck, and trickled toward them both.

"Up!" she shrieked to Bridie, and they were both on their feet. Two men, their weapons lost, went crashing behind them, plowing into the cabin. It was one of the attackers who had their first mate by the throat. Eleanor charged after them, capturing the heavy, very costly Bible from the captain's desk, and dashing it upon the head of the attacker. Dazed, he stumbled away. The grizzled first mate stared at Eleanor.

Bridie went for the Bible.

She lifted it high. "The Lord is with us!"

"Is he, now?"

They both spun around. A tall man stood at the entry to the cabin, his hand upon the door frame as he looked in. "Alas, mademoiselle, I think not." He stepped down into the cabin, sweeping his hat from his head. "Allow me to introduce myself. Thomas de Longueville. And God is with me, and against you, for the moment." He wasn't an old man, but somewhat weathered bronze by his days at sea. His breeches were a dyed dark linen, his shirt, white, his doublet, a cranberry color, his boots tall, and his eyes, sharp, narrowed, and all-assessing. A small smile curled his lips. "Ah . . . so it's true. Lady Eleanor of Castle Clarin, I do believe. You sail to France — to meet a rich man. To bring new money to coffers destroyed by the Scots — God bless their savage souls! Well, we shall see what this man is willing to pay to have you at his side."

The first mate, backed to the cabin wall, suddenly came to

life, springing forward. "You brigand! You'll not touch the lady—"

As he surged forward, the pirate drew a knife. Eleanor quickly stepped between the two men. The impetus of the mate sent her crashing into the pirate. An unnerving little fire took flight within his eyes. She pushed away from him, still between him and the mate.

"There's been enough death!" she said firmly.

Thomas de Longueville arched a brow, amused. "You will tell me when there has been enough death?"

"Do you kill for the pleasure of it?" she demanded. "You have taken the ship. There is no reason to kill this man."

"Aye, that's true. I have the ship. And as to this man . . ." Silently, he thought a moment. "Jean!" he called, and quickly a second man came running to the cabin doorway. "Throw this fellow overboard. Don't kill him, though. Whatever you do, make him hit that water alive and well!"

"Whatever you do, make sure you set him in a small boat!" Eleanor exploded, as another pirate arrived, and her would-be defender was dragged out.

"Nervy little wench, eh? But then, you are the defender of Castle Clarin. *Santa Lenora,* eh?"

"She is a lady, born and bred, a gentle maiden, mild-mannered and well-behaved!" Bridie lied, coming to put an arm around her. "And if you . . . and if you . . ."

Her words faltered. Her cheeks flushed.

"She's trying to say that if you harm me in any way, I'll not be worth nearly so much to my prospective bridegroom," Eleanor said flatly. She wondered if any of it mattered. She had been born to a battered land, and from the day her father had died, her life had become a gamble, a charade, a travesty.

"Ah, but what if it doesn't matter to me, just what kind of riches I make off you?" he inquired, eyes still alight with humor.

"What if nothing matters to me, and I throw myself into the sea?" she cross-queried.

Anger, a flash of annoyance, touched his face, and he started to retort, but suddenly the man named Jean was back.

"A ship!" he said tensely.

"A ship?"

"Aye, and flying at us!" Jean said.

Thomas de Longueville took the time to bow to the women. "You will forgive me, I beg you. Adieu, for the time. Lady Eleanor, a pity, we were just beginning to know one another. I will finish off this new enemy as quickly as I might, and be back with you. I would not want you to miss your engagement with the sea!"

The door slammed upon them. Eleanor let out a shriek of terror, flying toward the cabin door. It was bolted tight.

"My lady—" Bridie cried, coming to her.

She could not be locked in. Confined.

Yet, suddenly, she flew back, slamming against the captain's desk. The ship let out a long, terrible shudder.

Wood.

Groaning, cracking . . . giving.

And then . . .

The scent of fire.

"Fire!" she turned on Bridie.

"We were told to stay here; the fire is beyond us—"

"We'll not burn, I'd rather a swift sword through the heart!"

"Eleanor—"

"I refuse! I won't do it, I won't!" Eleanor cried, and she recklessly began searching through the cabin for a weapon, any weapon, to use against the door. At last, behind the tapestry that protected the captain's bed, she found an axe. An old battle-axe, perhaps a weapon of war, or maybe just a necessary tool. She didn't know which. She didn't care.

She gripped the axe with determination.

"Eleanor, you mustn't," Bridie told her. "Listen. Pay heed to me! The captain said that we must stay here. We could be killed by accident."

Eleanor stopped dead still and stared at her maid. "No, Bridie, pay attention to me. Don't you smell the fire? Shall we die like trapped rats?"

"But, my lady—"

"I don't care how I die, Bridie, *as long as it is not by flame*. Bridie, listen—breathe! Fire, there is fire aboard!"

Bridie took in a deep breath.

Indeed, there was fire. How serious, Eleanor did not know. But she would not be trapped.

"Fire, Bridie, fire!"

Bridie took in a breath again and seemed to come to life.

"Fire!" she gripped Eleanor's shoulders, staring at her wildly. "Fire, Eleanor! Let me help you. What can I do?"

"Stand back, Bridie. I wield such instruments well." To prove her point, she took several steps back, then hacked away with vigor and efficiency at the door.

"Can we take her?" Brendan demanded, looking through the captain's glass.

"Aye, if you're willing!" Eric Graham, a kinsman, commanding the *Wasp,* told Brendan.

"Oh, I am willing!" Brendan murmured. It was a strange sight at sea. The pirate ship had rammed an English vessel flying the colors of Edward I; they had come upon a battle scarcely completed.

Both ships had suffered damage in the scuffle. Both had surely lost men as well. The *Wasp* was of Norse design, built in the North Islands still under Norse rule. She was smooth and sleek and carried a handful of seamen with the blood of

Vikings strong in their veins — and Scotsmen, too often defeated, and too honed to battle.

"You know the pirate ship?" Eric inquired. He was a large man, Brendan's own height, but where Brendan's hair was dark as night, his kinsman sported a pate and beard the color of copper, and his eyes were a paler Nordic blue than the almost cobalt coloring of Brendan's own. They lit upon Brendan then with good humor. "Tell me, you do recognize the colors flying!"

"Cousin, I've spent most of my life fighting upon land," Brendan reminded him. Aye, he'd come to adulthood fighting. He barely remembered the time now when he had been a youth of good family, naturally learning the instruments of war, but spending nights with books as well, with language, mathematics, history, and music. "It's only of late that I've had these — opportunities? — to come to the sea." And his mind had been otherwise occupied when he had been asea, so he knew little about the flags being flown by different men.

He turned to Eric. "Eric, are you intending to share the information?"

"The ship belongs to Thomas de Longueville."

Even he knew the name. "The infamous Frenchman?" Brendan inquired.

"Aye, an intriguing fellow. Knows how to bargain when the time is right."

"And he has taken an English ship? Let's have at them then!"

"Will Wallace agree? We are on a matter of national diplomacy," Eric reminded him.

"To taking a French pirate on our way to France — and capturing a vessel flying Edward's flag? Aye, he'll agree." He turned, training the glass aft of their ship. Wallace's vessel rode somewhat behind theirs. Before they had come upon the curious sight before them, they had been prepared for battle at sea.

They always sailed prepared for battle.

Though Falkirk had been lost, William Wallace, the great defender of Scotland, had lived. And there were few men King Edward I wanted dead with a greater vengeance. Since Falkirk, Wallace had never faltered from his dream of freedom, or his ideals for Scotland. But he was an intelligent man; his only real power as a leader had lain with his success, simply because of the feudal structure of their society. Wallace wasn't a great lord or nobleman with hereditary rights over men. He did not have scores of tenants sworn to serve him in times of war. Since the Scottish loss at Falkirk, he had continued to tirelessly defend Scotland, harrying the English troops who had kept a foothold in southern Scotland, seizing supplies, fighting where speed and strategy could outweigh the forces of might and resources against him. He had traveled as well, to Norway, the Shetlands, and most important, perhaps, to France and Italy.

But no new great armies had been raised.

Still, some good had come from the defeat at Falkirk: Scotland's nobles had been forced to take some of the responsibility for Scotland. Other men were guardians now.

Edward had not released his hold upon Scotland. He'd not managed to aquire the manpower to usurp Scottish rule in the north, but he continued to swear himself the great overlord. Edward I of England would never cease his pursuit of the Scots, Brendan knew. Only his death would release the threat Edward wielded over the land. But Edward fought other battles, and he hadn't the manpower to leave Scotland at this time to subdue—nay, crush—the country! His ultimate goal. Not for now.

Brendan often wondered how William Wallace, the extraordinary warrior and leader, could accept his situation with so little resentment. The great barons had used Wallace's power, the heady potency of his nationalist eloquence, his blood, and his sweat, all for the freedom of Scotland. But they had never really stood behind him.

William still recognized John Balliol as king of Scotland; he had been the anointed king. But John Comyn, known as The Red, and Robert Bruce had the same blood of the ancient line of Scottish kings in their veins. It was often rumored now that John Comyn had taken his forces on the field at Falkirk and run, and thus caused the defeat. For awhile, both men, Comyn and Bruce, had been guardians of Scotland. They harried the English, but they did so with care. The age-old rivalries between the two had threatened to destroy what Scottish control remained to the Scotsmen, and Bruce had resigned, and then Comyn. John Soulis, a good Scotsman, sworn to hold the country in the name of their absent king, John Balliol, was Guardian of the Realm.

Wallace had watched it all, fearing the individual goals of the men, and even their affection for their own wealth and power. At any sign of being crushed, they were ready to capitulate to the English king; they feared the loss of their lands and titles.

William Wallace had fought with nothing, and without the compromise of having so much to lose. John Balliol, the anointed king, remained alive, and though few men thought he would ever return to Scotland, he was still king. A sad king, a maligned king, a cowardly king — known most often as 'Toom Tabard,' or 'Empty Shirt.' But he had now been released from the papal confinement in Italy to which Edward had condemned him, and he was in France. He was much of the reason they now hurried to the French king with whom they had been such allies on previous trips.

"Well?" Eric demanded, drawing Brendan quickly from his thought.

"Well? Will William agree? Oh, aye! That he will!"

"Then we're on to it!"

"Aye!" Brendan hurried down the length of the ship where the men in his command had gathered now, watching the helm where he and Eric had conferred. They waited expectantly; they had expected action. As the lead ship, they watched for Englishmen who would surely like to seize Wallace from the seas and deliver him unto Edward.

"We take her!" he cried, and grinned, and quoted famous words from the leader they all followed. "Not for glory, but for freedom! For Scotland!"

"For Scotland, always! And for whatever riches we may now plunder as well, eh, Brendan? Needed for our failing coffers!" Liam MacAllister, a tall man with a fine humor and flaming red hair called out.

A roar went up among the men.

"The Lord knows, Liam, we can use what riches we might seize from a sinking ship, indeed."

A roar went up again, cries of laughter — cries that were loud. Very loud.

Often enough as well, they had used such ferocity to give them courage against crushing odds.

"Full said!" Eric shouted in command to his sailors.

The chase was on.

"They outnumber us, surely," Eric warned Brendan.

Brendan grimaced. "I've never been into battle or skirmish without being outnumbered." He turned to his men. "Arrows, my friend! We'll keep them busy saving their hides from burning as we board. The best three, come forward, eh? Liam, you, Collum, Ainsley, barrage them. We've pitch and rags, set her ablaze!"

Men scrambled to obey his commands.

They had learned well from Edward's use of archers against them.

Now, they announced their arrival to the English — and the pirates.

With flame.

"Watch, Bridie, watch!"

The door was down; Eleanor and Bridie burst out upon the deck just as a cascade of burning arrows came flying across the sea and sky, colliding anew with masts and sails. She forced Bridie to duck; a savage missile whistled past them, embedding into the wall of the cabin, bringing the smell of fire before their faces. The ship was not afire, but it might as well be. The pirate crew were adept at sea. They rushed to steady the ship, prepare for the boarding attackers — and put out the flames.

Standing on the deck not far from them, cursing and shouting orders, de Longueville studied the oncoming enemy vessel.

"They've brought land battle to sea!" he roared. "Arrows! Arrows!" He raised a fist to the ship now ready to ram them. "Fight like men! Draw your swords! Scots! Mon Dieu!"

Even as he spoke the words, grappling hooks were hitting the ship anew. It was amazing that the English vessel was not completely crushed, for the pirate ship remained lashed to her port side while this new assault came from starboard.

"Aye, pirate, we've drawn our swords!" came a cry. Eleanor looked to the new ship upon the scene, caught fast to them now. The man who had spoken balanced with a grip upon the rigging that tilted toward the deck, one hand upon the ropes and one upon his weapon.

Scots.

The first thing Eleanor noted was that this invader was clad in a tartan. He wore dark leggings, skin boots, and linen shirt beneath a garment of interwoven, blue and green wool. A large Celtic brooch held the tartan at his shoulder. His sword was indeed drawn as he leaped with surprising agility from the rigging to the deck, ready to face the pirate. He was young, with pitch dark hair that fell near to his shoulders, rigid bronzed features, and sharp eyes that cast a fatal warning. He was clean shaven; he had spoken in the pirate's own tongue.

No matter.

A Scot!

He was *not* civilized; he was a madman, a savage. They were now being boarded by mountain dwellers, *animals,* men who killed one another over petty quarrels, and were as vicious as wolves against their enemies.

Ah, but the pirate was ready when his enemy fell; steel clanged against steel.

Other men began dropping from the boarding vessel. She heard ancient cries in Gaelic; she had heard them before. Curses in Norse rang out as well. The Frenchmen cried out in the civilized tongue with which most men and women of any breeding — aye, and without — were surely familiar in this day and age. A melee had broken out, and still, Eleanor stood with Bridie, outside the battered door, staring incredulously.

"This cannot be happening!" Bridie wailed. A man fell at their feet. A pirate. He looked up at the two of them, grinned, came back to his feet, and charged the burly Scot now upon him once again.

"One attack! One attack is quite rude enough — but two!" Bridie cried out, so outraged she forgot to be terrified for a moment.

"Rude! Bridie, we are in serious danger. This is not a matter of manners. We must think quickly, and act with even greater haste."

"Let's get back into the cabin!" she implored. "The fires are out, we'll not be trapped; we'll soon be skewered!"

"No!" Eleanor snapped back. Her fear of fire was paralyzing. But they were in dangerous positions, indeed, with the hand-to-hand combat going on all around them. "Bridie, to the aft!" she shouted suddenly. "Aft!"

She caught Bridie's hand, dragging her between two men just before they charged one another. They ran along the edge of the ship, heading behind the main masts and cabins to the far rear of the vessel. There, Eleanor stopped, catching her breath, staring overboard. The water churned and frothed. The Irish Sea could seldom be called a gentle pool!

Nor so was it today! It had been beautiful; the skies had been blue, blue like eternity, clear, like a promise of heaven.

Gray clouds had formed, as if summoned by the violence aboard the ship. The wind moaned, crying out at the clashing steel that pierced it.

"Eleanor!" Bridie cried out. "You're not thinking about . . ."

"Diving in? No," she said ruefully.

"Then what? We are trapped! Better the cabin—"

"I'll go to the sea before a fire!" Eleanor assured her, looking back to the churning water. Swim? Aye, she could swim. To shore? From here? Hardly likely! And what manner of beasts lived within the sea? Sharks with razor-edged teeth, sharper than any sword. Sea monsters! Creatures whispered about in poor taverns and inns. Creatures that sucked on the body, squeezed and crushed . . .

Better than fire!

"Alors!"

Eleanor spun from the sea to stare down the deck of the ship again. "The prize!"

It was one of the French pirates, a man with inky-dark, oily hair, a strange pointed beard, and sly eyes. He was racing toward them. "Get back! Come, woman!" he commanded harshly to Bridie, as he hurried toward them. "Mademoiselle!" he cried to Eleanor.

"By God, I will jump!" Eleanor muttered, fingers grasping the hull.

But before she could do so, another man came charging after the first. He did so with such impetus that they crashed into the aft together. There was no battle; the second man had a knife, worn at his calf. He drew it and slew his opponent in seconds.

The pirate's sword came flying across the deck. Instinctively, Eleanor reached down for it. The weapon was fine, honed steel. Excellent. A Frenchman's rapier, light, sharp . . .

She picked it up. Tested it in her hands. Then she saw that the enemy who had so quickly slain the Frenchman was coming toward her.

It was the dark-haired savage who had first fallen to the deck, leading the attack. There was something about him . . .

"Lay it down, lady," he told her quietly, his Norman French as well accented as any she had heard at court.

She would never be deceived. She knew these men. She had learned about them firsthand.

"Nay. Go your way, highlander. Go your way in peace. Leave me."

"You're English."

"I'm on my way to a French fiancé, and therefore, you had best take care."

His eyes were very deep blue. He showed her even more amusement than the pirate de Longueville. Yet he watched her curiously as well.

As if he recognized her.

"Drop the sword," he told her. "We'll discuss this fiancé, your journey — and your future."

"There is no future when one faces *Scots!*" she said, her loathing and contempt lacing the last.

"Give it to me, or I shall take it."

"Give it to him!" Bridie encouraged. "M'lady, for the love of God!"

Eleanor gripped the skirt of her gown, sweeping it behind her, stepping forward. *By God, she wouldn't burn. She might go to the sea, but she wouldn't burn, and she would never, ever throw herself on the mercy of a Scotsman!*

"Drop it!" He came forward with a thrust intended to ring power through the steel of her blade, and force her to drop it.

She held fast, returning the strike with a speed that caught him unaware. She nicked his arm, drawing blood. Startled, he stared at the wound. She experienced a moment's supreme satisfaction at her small victory and his amazement, but when she quickly thought to make good on the element of surprise, he was ready. She attacked, but he parried. She was backed against the hull. She saw the danger of her position, and thrust and parried in a manner intended to free her from her position, to give her leverage to fight. But each clash of steel cost her more and more. She gained new position, but lost strength. She moved down the deck, grimly fighting, parry for parry. She knew nothing at first but the sound of steel harshly shrilling against steel, over and over again.

Then she realized that no more battle sounds came from the rest of the ship. Daring to glance around, she saw that the battle had ended.

How, and in whose favor, she could not tell.

They all stood about: Scotsmen, Frenchmen, Norse sailors. Captain Abram and his English seamen had disappeared; they had either been killed or cast to sea long ago now.

Her audience was one of enemies.

Pirates.

Madmen.

Her opponent came at her with a force that first caused her

arm to shudder in a terrible reverberation, then the length of her body. Even her teeth chattered and threatened to crack.

She held fast to her weapon.

But she looked into his face and saw a look of grim determination in eyes a darker blue than the roiling sea. His lips were drawn in a tight line. One hand was held behind his back; he wielded his sword with only the other. He had not so much as drawn a sweat, though she was still glad of the blood that stained his left sleeve.

She did not drop her sword. She gasped for breath, and prayed for strength.

She flew toward him, aiming for his heart.

He watched her . . .

And retaliated at the last minute.

And this time, his blow was such that no fear of fire or flame or even eternal damnation could give her the power to hold on to her own weapon. Her steel clattered to the deck. She held herself still then, teeth clenched hard, jaw set, the length of her rigid. She stared at him.

No, she did not know him.

Yes, she did. There was that something, so familiar . . .

A hint of recall, of seeing those eyes.

Cries went up all around them. Maybe the pirates and even the Scotsmen applauded her courage — and stupidity.

But *he* was staring at her. Just staring at her, eyes narrowing. He knew it, too. Knew that he knew her . . . from somewhere.

''Who *are* you?'' he demanded softly, curiously.

''Who are *you?*'' she cross-queried.

Suddenly, she knew.

She barely choked back a gasp.

Perhaps he remembered as well, at exactly that moment, for it seemed that his entire countenance tightened and darkened. He was prepared to take a step toward her. Her heart was beating faster than a hummingbird's wings.

She dived past him, racing down the length of the ship.

When she reached the aft, she didn't hesitate. She was aware of Bridie's shriek of alarm, yet it meant nothing to her. She leaped to the wooden ship's railing, looked to the sea.

And dived.

Chapter 2

Brendan gave pause for one moment, incredulous.

She had plunged into the Irish Sea. In the middle of winter.

It was freezing, the water was churning. As could all too easily happen, the weather was changing. A beautiful day was turning into a stormy night.

The English . . . idiot!

Let her drown!

For a moment, the bitter thought flashed through his mind. He had given her mercy once, and nearly died for it. He had spent years swearing that he would find her — and avenge himself.

And now, suddenly, here she was. Time had gone by, and they had both changed, and it had taken him long moments to recognize her, though why, he could not now understand. Her blue-gray eyes were unique, as tempestuous as the threat of the storm now rising. Yet why not? He had etched her features into his memory. And still, he had never really expected to see her again. He had fought on, because the concept of surrender was not an option. She was English, lived on land fully controlled by the English king, far beyond his reach.

Yet . . .

Here she was.

A gift. On a platter. Now casting her fate to the depths!

He leaped to the rail, plunging in after her.

The Irish Sea was cold, bone-chillingly cold. The water hit him like a blow, an icy strike of lightning. The waves sucked at him, tossed him, made light of him as a man, powerless against this kind of force. Yet she had come here; she too, was rocked and tossed, with the air all but stolen from her lungs, arms flailing in an attempt to control her fate in the waves.

He broke the surface and looked around, blinking the cold salt water from his eyes, using precious breath to curse her.

Amazingly, she was ahead.

He dived below the surface once again, warming himself with powerful strokes against the cold force of the sea. He broke the surface; still, she was ahead. He dived again. *Thank God that she could swim, that she had not already been dragged downward into a spiral that would end in the darkness of the depths* . . .

He broke, treading water. He was gaining on her. Gaining, he thought, only because of the cumbersome clothing she wore, the long gown tangling around her legs . . .

She went under.

He swam harder, swearing again, feeling a sudden desperation.

A moment later, his hand touched fabric. He almost had her. Below the surface, she turned to stare at him. Her hair trailed out behind her like a golden banner, caught by sunlight, even while the gray of the coming storm threatened all illumination from above. She stared at him, at his hand where he gripped her gown.

She had a knife, he realized suddenly! A knife. The blade was flashing through the water, and he might be taken completely unaware again. But the knife didn't strike him. Either by accident or intent, it slashed through the fabric of her dress. She was free, and swimming hard again. Now the length of a long, slim, perfectly formed leg flashed before him; she was escaping again.

Yet . . .

Escaping where?

Just how far did she think she could get before she tired and perished?

He pursued her again with a new burst of speed, surfacing to gasp air, plunging below again for the speed of movement he could achieve below the waves. A second later, he grasped flesh. His fingers curled around her ankle, and he jerked her back. She faced him in the water, golden hair streaming around her like the halo on a water-angel. She waved her arms through the water; he saw the knife still in her hand, and quickly grasped her wrist, vising with such force that she had no choice but to release her hold.

The knife glittered briefly in the water, then drifted to the depths below.

He maintained his grip upon her wrist, drawing her to the surface. Rain began to pelt them, and the light that had remained in the sky was gone as the last of the clouds covered the remnants of the day's sun.

He slicked his hair back from his forehead, freeing her to tread the water. Behind him, he saw they had launched a small boat from the *Wasp,* and soon, it would be upon them.

"You incredibly stupid woman!" he charged her. "You could have killed yourself."

"Better to die by my own hand than yours," she told him.

"A suicide, my lady? A sin, by any judgment of God."

"Perhaps I didn't intend death," she told him.

"You'd never have reached the shore," he told her.

She smoothed back her long, tangled, water-darkened hair, still meeting his eyes. "Perhaps *you'd* have never reached the shore," she told him. "I fully intended to do so."

"It seems you are more impressed with your abilities than reason would allow."

"Really? And that from a Scot, a nation of mountain men always far more arrogant regarding their strength than any sense of logic would allow."

He was tempted to reach out and duck her back under the water. He'd killed in battle time and time again. It was, no matter what the call to glory, honor, or freedom, the taking of a human life. But random murder lay beyond reason, sanity, and Christianity.

The water was very, very cold. He seemed to taste nothing but salt as the waves slapped around them and the rain pelted them. They should be thinking of survival. But still, he could not allow her the last word.

"The Scots have bested a greater force many a time, lass."

Her chin inched up out of the water. "I'm not a lass, and I'm an excellent swimmer."

"Excellent — just not quite fast enough."

"Brendan!"

He turned at the call of his name. The small boat, manned by Eric and Collum, was nearly upon them. It was Eric calling out to them. In the growing squall, he and Eleanor were difficult to see, Brendan realized.

"Here!" he called.

As he turned, she started to swim again. Luckily, his reach was long. He caught an ankle again, jerking her back. She went under and came up coughing and gurgling. By then, Eric had brought the rocking boat up beside them. Strong hands reached down; he delivered her to them, then hiked himself over the edge, and landed, breathing hard, upon the bottom.

"Cold?" Eric inquired, grinning.

He looked up at his Norse kin's light blue eyes. "Aye, as a witch's tit!" he muttered, then remembered that they were carrying none other than the Lady Eleanor of Clarin with them, and she was convinced that they were uneducated peasants, ignorant, illiterate, and scarcely aware of the existence of books. He pulled himself up, hiking himself carefully into a seat. It was bitter, when a man was wet. Beyond cold.

Eleanor was seated next to Collum at the aft. He turned to see her as Eric again took up the oars, shooting them back toward the ship. In their absence, the crews had already begun dislodging the grappling hooks.

Their reluctant passenger had her arms crossed over her chest, hugging herself against the cold. She stared out over the water without expression. Yet she appeared rather blue, and her teeth were chattering ferociously.

"Lady," Collum murmured, offering her the long swathe of tartan he had unwound to wear as cape and hook. He was a big, muscle-bound, red-headed man with an eye to aim better than any other he had ever met, and his voice was low and courteous.

She seemed not to hear him, looking out over the water. Brendan turned to her. "Lady Eleanor, Collum is offering you the warmth of his wool."

"It is a garment, sir, I would much rather freeze, than wear," she said simply. She flashed Collum a glance, and he thought that she would apologize — except that he was a Scot.

Eric was about to take the fur cloak from his shoulders to offer her; Brendan stopped him, raising a hand. "Then, lady, you must freeze. Ah! Eric would offer you fur — but though he is Norse by the majority of his blood, and his inclination, he is *my* kinsman, and the Norse lands where he resides are extensions of *my* country. We understand how you would rather freeze.''

Her teeth were gritted and chattering. Still, she cast him one withering glare and sat dead still, staring into the night.

Eric rowed them to the *Wasp*. He didn't help her from the small boat, but crawled the rope ladder first himself, and was glad of the fur coat quickly cast over his shoulders by Ian Dyerson, Eric's first mate at sea, right-hand man on land. He flashed him a quick smile of gratitude, then stood back, watching while Eleanor came aboard. She did so without help — preferring to climb by her own power rather than be assisted. She couldn't have been accustomed to such a climb, and he leaned over the rail as she slipped. ''I'd aid you, my lady, but I don't want to distress you with the touch of these barbaric hands.''

''You're quite right; I will do fine on my own,'' she told him.

And she did, coming aboard deftly, dripping as she did so.

Moments later they stood on deck with a number of the Scots and Norse crew, and several of the pirates. Some of the men were still busy, disabling the attacking ships, while others simply stood still, staring at their arrival.

Eleanor stood very straight, and very wet, and made the supreme effort not to shiver. She surveyed them all and turned to him. ''You are in league with the pirates?''

''I never met de Longueville before in my life, lady,'' he said, leaning casually back against one of the masts, dripping and trying not to shiver. ''And we Scots are of one purpose, you know that. But in the midst of a clash of steel it occured to both of us, the pirate and me, that we have much to offer one another.''

''And what is that?'' she inquired.

''The terms of our agreement are really of little concern to you.''

"Since my vessel was attacked, my captain brutally murdered, and it appears that my ship's seamen have been hurled to the waves, I do consider it my concern. That the Scots have chosen to join with thieves is really no great surprise—"

"That the Scots have chosen to join with thieves!" he interrupted, his anger suddenly flaring. "Edward is the thief, the English, lady, are constantly the thieves. Wales was stolen, her nobility slaughtered. The Scots did not come to London, m'lady, the English came north. Collum, see the Lady Eleanor to her cabin, if you will."

Collum stepped forward. She backed away. "If you direct me, I will go," she told him.

Brendan tired of the game, turning to Eric. "We've sent word back to William's ship?"

"Aye, 'tis done."

"Then I will rid myself of the Irish Sea as well."

He left both the sailing and the situation to Eric's capable hands, and went below to change into dry clothing.

He had also discovered that he needed time alone. He was beginning to shake with a vengeance, and it wasn't from the cold.

Nay, not from the cold, but from memory.

Though the ship bearing the crew of Norse and Scotsmen was sleek and narrow, built for speed, it also had been designed with a certain amount of comfort in mind. She was taken directly below, and was surprised to see, as she passed, that steps led down to an even lower deck, one carrying supplies, she surmised, and probably affording quarters for some of the seamen as well. Thiws deck offered a few small private quarters — so small a man could scarcely wedge his body into the cots, but private nonetheless. At the aft itself, though, was a fairly large cabin, fitting exactly to the design of the ship, with the narrowed rear allowing space for clothing, gear, or books, the port side offering a bunk, the starboard side allowing for a navigator's desk, or for the work of whatever rich man, noble, or official might be aboard.

Someone had occupied this space, certainly. But she was surprised to see that her traveling trunk lay center in the generous, but still small space. It had been brought from her ship.

Her heart was beating loudly as she came here; she had heard them say the name Wallace, and all that she knew of the man was that he was a bitter butcher who offered no mercy to his enemies. She knew that firsthand. His brutality had changed her life, brought her to a battlefield at Falkirk, and indirectly, here now. It seemed that Wallace was the head of this party, and as fate would have it, the young soldier she had chanced upon at the end of the fighting was directing their journey.

Perhaps it was not surprising that they should join with pirates. It was true that Edward I would pay dearly to have the man in his hands. It was strange as well. Many of the Scottish barons had risen against Edward, surrendered, and been forgiven. But Edward loathed Wallace. He had stated time and again that he would never accept anything from the man other than total and unconditional surrender. And that, any man, enemy or friend knew, would never happen.

Collum, the big fellow, ducked to maneuver the ship. She almost felt guilty. He was trying to be sympathetic and gentle. He couldn't possibly understand that she had good reason to despise his kind.

He stood just outside the cabin as she entered it.

"If there is anything you need—"

"My maid," she said sharply. "Is she well?"

"Aye, lady."

"May she come to me?"

"Nay, lady. Not now."

"When?"

"I don't—"

"Ah, yes, never mind. You serve that jackanapes, and he will make the decisions."

"Aye, lady. Lady, you are all but blue. If I might suggest—"

"I'm to be locked in here?" She tried very hard to keep the fear from her voice.

"Aye."

She nodded, turning around.

She didn't look back. A minute later, she heard the door close. She winced as she heard a bolt slide into place.

She had no intention of panicking; she would fight her own demons. But it seemed that the door had scarcely closed when she smelled the smoke. She flew the few steps to the cabin door, banging hard against it. "Wait, please—"

She heard a grating sound; the door flew open. Collum was gone. It was the man from the battlefield at Falkirk again. Still sodden and dripping, he appeared irritated.

"Aye, my lady?"

She backed away.

"Something is burning. There is a fire."

His eyes held hers for a moment. "Aye, lady, the English ship is set afire."

"Are . . ."

"Are we what? I have told you, we are burning the ship. She was seized, scavenged, and now set ablaze. Are there men aboard? Nay, lady. No human or living animal will ever burn, if I am in command. Is that what you wished to ask?"

She nodded, but oddly enough, she felt slightly ashamed. It wasn't what she had been about to ask. "Are we . . . are we in any danger of catching fire here, on this ship?" There was a scratch to her voice as she queried him.

She lowered her eyes, aware that he was studying her curiously, and very much wanting to avoid his perusal.

"None whatsoever," he assured her.

She nodded. He turned away. She didn't know what caused her to call him back. "Drowning in icy waters cannot be a kind form of death either."

He paused, then turned back to her, watching her once again. "I assume not. Why did you wish it for yourself?"

"I told you; I was not suicidal."

"You would have drowned in this storm."

"I am asking about Captain Abram, a gentle enough man, brought into this service by my kin. What was done to him will rest heavily on my heart for as long as I live."

"For however long that might be," he murmured.

"You do intend then to *murder* me?"

She was startled that a smile actually curved his lips. "Nay, lady. I am not an executioner. Your life span will probably be cut short due to your own recklessness. As to your Captain Abram, I have no idea what you're talking about."

"He was thrown overboard—"

"Lady, pirates are thieves who prey upon those at sea. Although they don't hesitate at killing those in their way, they are most often after riches, not blood. Captain Abram is alive and well, over on de Longueville's ship, the *Red Rover*."

"But de Longueville said—"

"What he said, he did not mean. Aye, lady, men died in the boarding. Men die in battle, and that is the way of it. But neither your captain nor any of his men were cast upon the sea in coldblooded murder. I leave that to the English."

She shook her head, amazed at his words. "You are a liar yourself, or you know nothing about the men you serve!" she told him heatedly.

"I can't begin to tell you what horrors I have witnessed at the hands of the English!"

"And I can't begin to tell you what I know about the heinous brutality of the Scots! But I should be happy to try, if you wish!'' she informed him. Unaware of her own intent, she walked toward him. ''Castle Clarin, does it mean anything to you? Perhaps not, we are not so great or grand a castle as that at York, where your people also practiced horrid atrocities. At Clarin, men — farmers, merchants, artisans, as well as warriors — were herded like cattle into a barn and fires were set. The Scots came like cowards, when my father and kin were off to battle. They seized innocent people — ''

''Amazingly, lady, I saw the *English* practice such tactics firsthand,'' he interrupted her curtly. ''If we are cruel, we have learned our butchery from our enemies. If you'll excuse me, Lady Eleanor? I drip. And I freeze. As you surely do yourself.''

He started to close the door.

''Wait!''

He paused.

''Again?'' he inquired, annoyed.

''Aye, again!'' she said angrily. ''Must you . . .''

''What?''

''Never mind. Nothing.''

But he still paused and watched her curiously.

''Bolt the door?'' he said.

''Yes.''

''Aye, I'm sorry, I must. You are a very valuable captive, Lady Eleanor.''

''Then I am to be ransomed?''

He cocked his head slightly, musing the question. ''I've not yet decided.''

''If not ransomed, then — ''

''Ah, that's to be seen, isn't it?''

''Look! As you said, I'm worth a great deal — ''

''In many ways.''

The edge to his voice unnerved her, and she forced herself to stiffen and stand firm, and keep her eyes coolly level upon his. ''Ah, yes, that's the way of battle, isn't it? Plunder — and rape. Well, then, why wait? I assure you, I'll afford you no pleasure—''

''M'lady, I don't think that you can assure me anything regarding what I might find to be pleasure. But, alas, at the moment you resemble a drowned rat, and I am soaked, and weary, and bitter, oh, aye, bitter! Oddly enough, you're simply not appealing enough for the energy that must be expended in such a form of plunder. I bid you good night, lady. Unless you would feel better—most fully abused at our hands—if I were to give this offer of yours up to the crew?''

Madness must have set in; the icy waters had numbed her mind. She flew at him, but he was quick, expecting her reaction perhaps. He caught her by the upper arms before she could do any harm; fingers of steel seemed to wind around her, his body, beneath the wet cold of his garments, seemed as hot as any fire she might have feared. She looked up into his eyes, suddenly more afraid than she had ever felt before, so much more aware of this enemy than any man she had ever known.

At first, his expression was dark. A scowl that threatened damnation. Surely he was aware of the same discomfort, their sodden bodies so flush. His scowl slowly turned to a crooked smile. The storm-tossed darkness of his eyes lightened to a glint, and he carefully set her away from him. ''Who knows, m'lady? Maybe you clean up well and I can oblige you myself at another time.''

She fought to keep herself from making the mistake of flinging against him again. ''I should rather accept your offer of the entire crew,'' she told him, making an attempt of smoothing back her hair. The long strands seemed as if they were mortared together by sea and salt, and she doubted she managed much of a noble presence.

''That can still be arranged,'' he promised lightly.

She lowered her hand and stared at him icily. ''Get out.''

He bowed his head and reminded her, "You summoned me, lady."

"For the love of God!" she flared. "Leave! Close the door!"

"Aye, of course, I am ever willing to oblige!" he assured her.

The door closed.

And bolted.

She stood, staring at it. For the longest time, she fought the urge to throw herself against it and cry.

Instead, she cast herself upon the taut rope cot. Covered with a soft feather mattress, it offered a surprising comfort. There, she burst into tears, and exhaustion at last seemed to overwhelm her.

She was dreaming, she knew. Reliving the moments that had brought her here, now, tossing, turning, in pure misery.

She was home. At Castle Clarin. The Scots had been defeated at Falkirk. She had ridden with English troops. She had been called *Santa Lenora* — for simply acting on instinct. The enemy had come, invaded, pillaged — and yet not done so thorough a job of it, for Castle Clarin was a fortress in stone, with a stout stone wall around the immediate tower, and that protected as well by a natural moat.

The weakness of the homestead and her father's hereditary Clarin lands was that it offered little help for the villagers surrounding the castle, for the tenant farmers, the merchants, the people scrambling to eke their lives from the earth and their own talents. And so, though she had been forced to safety in the tower, she had watched as the men had been grouped into the barn beyond the walls. She had seen the fire lit. And she had seen the Scots, with their shields and siege works, stand to watch. Alone, she had refused to do nothing. She had ordered the castle defenders to the ramparts, demanded that oil be cast down upon them, that their own fires be lit. Arrows had caught the attackers with fire as well, and burning themselves, they had fled in retreat while she raced to the barn, the castle guard and wives and children in her wake, to hack down the walls for the men to escape. Burning like torches, they had thrown themselves into the moat at her command, and amazingly, they had lost but seven of their number. Ah, but those losses!

Still, rumor spread. Men at arms from the surrounding area, called by the king to fight the Scots beneath Wallace, sent out a war rally: she must come. She must ride with the family Clarin. Men would come then. Whether forced by feudal law or no, they would come, they would rally to a saint!

So it had come to pass. And the Scots had been defeated. But on the same day that she saved the men in the barn, her father was killed while protecting a supply wagon intended for the king's effort against the Scots. His death made it easy for her to ride against such a heinous enemy.

But that time had come and gone. And though she was her father's heiress, the law was such that she merely held the castle, the lands, and the revenue—until she produced "male issue." Despite her father's death, she was not alone.

She had kin; kin held responsible for her, by her father's deathbed requests.

She saw again, as if she were there, the great hall at Clarin, in the well-protected tower. That day, no threat of war tormented them. A fire burned in the hearth. New tapestries by Flemish masters, gifts from nearby merchants, hung from the walls, keeping out the dampness and cold. Battle had ended, the farmers prospered, the merchants did well. She had adored her father, a man before his time, an educated man who believed in the mind, and in the soul. But he was gone, and she would miss him until her dying day. A great deal of responsibility had become hers. Welcoming the king's men when they traveled north. Caring for the disruptions in their small village.

Looking after the sick, caring for the church, burying the dead, welcoming the new life that came to each household, just the same.

Her cousins had contemplated many a matrimonial contract on her behalf. They had paraded Europe's most illustrious — and wealthy — men before her. Castle Clarin was a beautiful place. It had also seen devastating loss at the brutal hands of war. They needed new riches in their coffers for repair, to arm the fighting men Edward was forever demanding.

To her horror, it seemed that each wealthy suitor they found her was worse than the last. Robin of Lancaster was no taller than a ten-year-old, and suffered from a strange, rotting skin disease. He was, at least, courteous and well-educated. Tibald, Lord of Hexin, was next in line to an earldom, but though a handsome man, he enjoyed drowning kittens for amusement.

And so it went. She turned down suitor after suitor. The Count Etienne Gireaux, a Frenchman, passed through, eager to meet the heiress of Clarin.

He was as bad as the rest.

He came, he left. But the following morning, just when she felt somewhat at peace with herself and her world, her cousin Alfred begged her presence in the great hall.

"There is no excuse for this procrastination!" he told her angrily, pacing behind Eleanor's chair. He gripped the back of the carved wood seat and leaned close to her ear, adding a fierce, "None! You were rude last night, quite frankly, rude. And Count Gireaux descends from one of the finest families in all Normandy!"

He straightened, a tall man, well-built, a soldier who had earned respect in battle as well as by birth. He walked away from the banquet table in the great room and strode toward the hearth where a fire burned brightly. "Eleanor, it has been as if we walk on eggshells around you. You lost your father, you were forced to the defense of your home, but the attack was years ago now. You are far past being a child in any semblance of the word. Indeed, word of your courage and grandeur has turned to speculation that there must surely be some terrible mark upon you, that you are daft, crippled, or—"

"So ugly that none with the required position and fortune will make claim to her?" Corbin inquired, the question voiced from the great chair that flanked the hearth. Corbin was two years younger than Alfred, and her kin with the greatest sense of humor regarding life and society. He, too, had fought for the king. Valiantly. It would never be said that any of the Clarins of north York shirked their duty to their country. But his attitude toward Eleanor differed greatly from Alfred's. Corbin was content to let things go on as they were; Alfred had an annoying sense of responsibility toward her late father. She wished he would realize that her father would not have forced the issue.

"Alfred, perhaps he is immensely wealthy, and respected," Eleanor said quietly, staring at her hands, folded in her lap before her, then heatedly pushing back her chair to stand and meet his eyes. "But he smells frightfully, and he's . . . he's a . . ."

"Lacking in any admirable quality whatsoever?" Corbin suggested.

His brother shot him a withering glare. "Brother, you don't help matters in the least!"

Corbin grinned, winking at Eleanor. "If she refuses to marry, and therefore produces no heir, the property reverts to you, Alfred. One would think you'd let her be."

Eleanor gave him a quick grin. "Since I, a lowly woman, hold the property in the name of my male issue only, Corbin is quite right."

Alfred's eyes, dark and damning, touched hers. He shook his head with aggravation. "Eleanor, it's my duty to see you legally wed, taking your proper place in society. It is your duty to continue your father's line. At the death of so many, how can you question this debt to the man you claim to have loved so greatly?''

''I adored him!'' she cried, distressed.

''And he left you in my care, yet you sit there and scuttle every effort I make to do justice to his name.''

She inhaled. ''Alfred,'' she said, and began to count off on her fingers. ''Listen to me. Count Gireaux is cruel to his servants. He is coarse in his speech. He is vicious in battle — ''

''That might be considered a virtue,'' Corbin said, interrupting. ''Especially by our honored king.''

His brother shot him another stern glare.

''Vicious, cruel, merciless, with no sense of justice,'' Eleanor insisted.

''You would talk of justice?'' Alfred asked softly.

She felt a weakness in her knees. It returned every so often, when she would remember the terror of the time that the Scotsmen had raided here. When the fires had burned.

''There must be some reason and sanity among men,'' she said evenly, and continued, ''Count Gireaux might well turn on a wife in the same way. And he is most unpleasant — ''

''Actually, he's a pig,'' Corbin said cheerfully. ''A swine! But a rich swine, nicely landed.''

''And there's my point. He's rude, offensive — ''

''You have met my wife, haven't you?'' Corbin teased dryly, interrupting again.

''Aye, and look where you are, and where she is,'' Eleanor reminded him. She hadn't meant to be cruel herself. Corbin had married as had been required. He had acquired his title through marriage, and a great income as well. But they despised one another. Isobel was a shrew, selfish, self-indulgent, and demanding. She was a beautiful woman, but Corbin often said that he wished he'd been blessed with a hag.

Isobel lived in London most of the time. Corbin remained at Castle Clarin.

Corbin rose, stretched, and came to her. "Alas, that's the way with marriage, my dear. It matters not if we wed the most repulsive creature in all the land—should that creature have position and wealth. Maybe you won't have to see him that often."

"Alfred, I will not marry Count Gireaux. It's not that he's a repulsive boor—it's that I believe him to be mad!"

Alfred shook his head. "There is one alternative."

"I am not going to a nunnery."

"No. You will go to France. Count Alain de Lacville has been recently widowed—without issue. He is older . . . but you have always liked him and admired him, right?"

She hesitated. Alain was a good man, and a very rich one. Intelligent, soft spoken, kind. He had a full head of rich, white hair, and despite his age, his features were still well-defined and very handsome. She liked him very much. But . . .

"He is older than my father was!" she whispered.

"I think that my wife is older than God," Corbin said cheerfully.

"Corbin, she isn't old!"

"Aye, I think she is. A witch, who keeps her beauty through her pacts with the devil!" he said, eyes wide, a rueful smile on his lips.

"Eleanor, your father died in the king's service," Alfred reminded her, impatient with both of them. "You were young, and you served him at Falkirk. But if we're not careful, sooner or later, Edward will remember that it's his right to step in on marital negotiations, and if the king decides that you should wed a warthog, you will do so. Go to Normandy, meet with him. We have been communicating since the death of his wife.

Accept his proposal; venture out as his fiancée. If you do not reach a happy agreement, we can simply let the negotiations lag.''

She was silent.

''Eleanor, Count Gireaux might take his proposition to the king.''

''I'll go to France,'' she quickly agreed.

And so . . .

She had gone asea. And she had avoided Count Gireaux and whatever petition he might put before the king.

And instead, she had sailed straight into the hands of the Scots. Not just the Scots in general. *The* Scot she had met on the field of battle. *The* Scot who had attempted to destroy everyone and everything she had known and loved for a lifetime.

She tossed and turned, sleeping, waking, dreaming, seeing the carved wood of the confines of the cabin where she lay. It seemed that, as she slept, as she dreamed, her head was spinning more and more viciously.

She was back in the forest at Falkirk. Lost in the woods as the English surged forward with the breaking of the Scottish ranks. She raced into the trees, desperate to hide.

But *he* found her. She could remember raising her sword. She'd had lessons, yes. But she had been an unwitting heroine at Castle Clarin, desperately moving on instinct alone. And now . . .

The sword beat down hard on hers, wielded by someone who had mastered the craft of warfare. She was going to die. She would be sliced to ribbons in another few seconds . . .

''Wait!''

And she had dropped her cape, pulled the mail from her head. And he had stopped, and stared with surprise. His sword had lowered.

Etched . . .

Yes, his face had been etched in her memory then. The deep blue of his eyes, the darkness of his hair, the high set of his cheekbones, the arch of each brow. Time had changed him, as it had changed her. But never enough that she shouldn't have known him.

And known that look. The way his expression had changed when he realized that an enemy had come behind him. Just before he had turned to defend himself from the Englishman about to swing his sword, and decapitate him.

She had seen that look . . .

And brought the hilt of her weapon crashing down on his head before he could turn back to her, certain that she had cried mercy just so that he might be slain from behind.

He had fallen.

And she had heard his fellow Scots coming, racing through the woods. She had melted into the trees, and in the aftermath of battle and war, she had never forgotten that moment, and yet she had convinced herself that she would never see him again. She had dreamed of him sometimes. Dreamed of his face, of the way he had looked at her. And sometimes, she had almost thought that war was as horrible for the enemy, for the youth of Scotland, striking and proud, were dying as well. But she couldn't forgive the Scots, and so she could offer them no sympathy.

Edward hadn't had the strength of arms right then to really crush Scotland as he had wanted, and in the north, Scottish barons were ruling Scottish holdings. But Falkirk had been a serious victory for Edward, and the Scots would not venture south again, and so she would be safe.

Safe!

The ship tossed. Her head reeled. She sneezed and coughed, and realized that she was still damp, and twisting with a fever.

The door suddenly burst open. She wanted to jump up. She could not. She hadn't the strength.

He stood there.

She saw his face as she had in dreams.

He filled the door frame, head taller than the clearing, shoulders spanning it side to side. He had changed his clothing, and a hated woolen tartan was once again over his shoulder, held there by a silver Celtic brooch. She saw him, then he seemed to fade.

Was she dreaming, or was this real? There was light; morning had come. But the light was like mist, and she knew then that they still rode the storm.

"Come with me, lady. Now!" he commanded.

The devil had come, she thought. In the flesh. Older, grimmer, harder.

Aye, vengeance had found her.

But she smiled, for whether he were dream or real, she could not obey. She tried to open her mouth and speak. She hadn't the strength.

"Stubborn wench!" he swore, and came to her. "I'm trying not to leave you locked here in the midst of this tempest! Is there anyone to whom you listen, any point at which you stop being such a stubborn fool?"

He reached for her, and she couldn't fight him. He swore suddenly. "You are still soaked to the bone, ice and fire in one!"

His arms wrapped around her.

He lifted her, and carried her, steady despite the rock and sway of the ship.

They left the cabin. The misty light fell more fully upon them from the stairway to the upper deck.

Then a flash of lightning ripped through the fullness of the sky. It created an illumination like a burst of pure white fire.

Thunder roared.

The sea meant to kill them. The wind, the rain, the thunder, the lightning. God's great hand upon them all.

But she couldn't care.

Her head fell against the chest of her greatest enemy.

Darkness descended. The heavens continued to roar.

But for the time, Eleanor knew no more.

Chapter 3

"Will she live?"

Margot Thorrsen looked up, startled by the sound of the deep male voice and by Brendan's presence in the cabin. She had thought she was alone with the sleeping girl, and she should have been accustomed to the silence with which men so often wary of enemies could be.

The wind had ceased to blow, the rain to fall. With the ships in control, she had been summoned to help with their English prisoner. The girl had been afire at first, damp to the bone, and in danger of a fever that could sweep her away. But—despite Brendan's protestations that she was to be kept from her English maid—Margot had sent for the woman, Bridie, for help. Between them, they had stripped away Eleanor's wet, sea-salty clothing, cooled her with fresh water, and forced mouthfuls of broth filled with rich, healing herbs down her throat. The night of the storm had ended; another day had passed, and now, night was falling again. Eleanor had yet to really open her eyes, but she lay still and sleeping. She had become Margot's charge, men having a tendency to leave the care of the injured to their womenfolk. She was surprised to find Brendan here, though it had been Brendan's cabin on this voyage before he had fished the English girl from the sea.

Margot had known Brendan for the many years she had been with Eric. Despite the wars in Scotland, kin often stayed close. Eric's father, a cousin of Brendan's, had married Ilsa, daughter of the jarl of a far northern island, land still held by the king of Norway, and so, naturally, he was more Norse now in many ways than his family name would suggest. And due to the fighting with the English, the Scots tended to get on far better with their northern brethren than they had during the early years of Viking assaults. Indeed, she had been called upon to tend him during certain of his childhood illnesses.

She had not expected to find him in the shadows of the cabin near the cot, leaning forward and looking on as she tended to the patient. His voice was deep, resonant, and brusque as he spoke to her, his eyes intent as he asked once again, ''Margot, will she live?''

''She will live, I believe.'' Margot dipped a cloth in a bowl of cool water and smoothed it over the English girl's face. She looked at Brendan, the lock of dark hair falling over his forehead, the tension locked into the lines of his face, the power in the hands that were folded idly before him. A young man, twenty-odd years, but he had known warfare — treachery, loss, victory, and defeat — for most of his life. He followed William Wallace, but he had learned to lead under circumstances of both flight and battle. The nationalists in Scotland had learned the bitter truth that freedom was not to be acquired in one great stroke against the English, but in taking their battle into time, and into the forests. Living, to fight another day, was victory in itself, even when all seemed lost.

"Is she worth a great deal?" Margot asked.

"What?" Brendan said, staring at her with a frown.

"Is she worth a great deal?"

He mused her words strangely, then said, "Aye, I'm sure she must be."

Margot started to speak again, her language Gaelic, which they spoke most frequently among themselves, though all of the men were adept at the Norman French of the English aristocracy.

He brought a finger to his lips. "Norse," he said quietly.

Margot switched to her native tongue. "Brendan, if we go to seek a French king's help against the English, how do you go about ransoming an Englishwoman?"

His voice lowered a notch with a slight irritation. "According to the woman, Bridie, she is on her way to meet with a French fiancé, Count Alain de Lacville."

"So . . . we have rescued her — or she is a prisoner?" Margot inquired.

"I've not quite decided that," he told her after a moment. "God knows, all the world is one thing this moment, another the next. King Philip detests Edward, but if necessary, fears him. When an alliance with the English become expedient, there will be an alliance."

"Are we safe then?"

"Aye, though it may well be soon enough, there is no alliance as of this moment, and if there were, Philip of France would still relish the idea of welcoming William Wallace, the one man who has stood against Edward's tyranny, never capitulating. We have sailed as we have knowing that Edward has offered a fortune to any man capturing Scottish leaders on the sea," he told her, "so he is aware as well that he will not be seizing us as prisoners, once we reach France." He rose impatiently. "Whatever she may be, she needs to live, Margot. Beyond a doubt, she has value."

"Aye, Brendan," Margot said, confused as she watched him leave. Then she turned her attention back to the girl, touching her forehead, her cheeks with the cool cloth once again. The girl's eyes began to flutter. "Ah, there, you come among us!" Margot said.

The girl's eyes opened, but she studied Margot with confusion.

"It's all right, you're doing very well."

The girl still didn't respond. Margot realized she had still been speaking Norse. She switched smoothly to French. "You are with us again. How do you feel?"

"Thirsty," the girl said.

Margot smiled and poured water for her from an intricately carved Norse horn on the table. She accepted it with a grateful nod, drank quickly at first, then slowly as Margot gave her a warning to take care.

"Thank you," she said, handing back the horn, sinking weakly back into the pillows. She still studied Margot with perplexity. "Who are you?" she asked softly. Then she hiked up on an elbow. "Where is my maid, the woman named Bridie? Is she well, is she all right—"

"Lie back, rest, m'lady. Your maid is fine; she rides on the other ship."

"Alone—on a pirate ship?" Lady Eleanor was distressed, but then added a wry, "Dear God! I can't believe I just asked that when I am on a *Scottish* ship."

"Only partially Scottish," Margot told her. "In truth, it's a Norse ship."

"Of course. Of course, yes, Norse. But as to Bridie—"

"She is confined, nothing more."

"Can you be so certain?" There was deep anxiety in her tone. Margot found herself eager to assure her, but as to just what promises she could make, she wasn't at all sure.

"She is fine; you are separated because you are not trusted, and that is all."

"Trusted? I should be trusted?" she inquired, her eyes narrowing.

Margot smiled suddenly. She'd heard a great deal about this woman; she was legendary, having been the rallying banner herself for a host of soldiers convinced that she was all but touched by God. She had been part of the English victory at Falkirk. She didn't look much like a warrior now. Indeed, if anything, she resembled a fragile sea nymph with a wealth of deep golden hair, tangled about the fine bone structure of her face. Her eyes, bluish gray like the storm at sea, seemed large in her face. At the moment, despite the defiance in her voice, she was stripped of all warlike qualities. She was vulnerable.

"I will leave you, since there is little — " Margot began. But the girl caught her hand, the gray eyes suddenly clearer, naked, and even betraying a little bit of fear.

"Wait!" she said softly. "Please."

"There are no promises I can make you," Margot said.

She shook her head. "No. Who are you? Why are you aboard this ship? You are the Norseman's wife?"

Margot hesitated, and shook her head. "Not his wife. He is the grandson of a jarl."

"But . . ."

"Am I with him? Yes."

"I see," she murmured, eyes downcast. Then she looked up at Margot. "Does he have — a wife as well?"

"No. Not as yet, Lady Eleanor."

"Then — "

"Thus far, he has refused to wed."

"He loves you," Lady Eleanor said.

Margot flushed at the Englishwoman's words. They were familiar, assumptive, and — Margot believed — true.

The beautiful English noblewoman seemed determined to

make Margot comfortable. She smiled and continued, "If he were to wed . . . well, marriage is a contract, and little more, so it seems. He will surely love you still, even if he is forced to marry. God knows, he could be contracted to a witch of a woman, a horrible shrew!"

Their prisoner was not at all looking down her nose at her, but trying to make her feel better about the situation. "What of Count de Lacville?" Margot asked.

Lady Eleanor drew in her breath sharply.

"Is he . . . cruel? Do you even know him?" Margot asked her.

"Alain? I do know him; he was an old and dear friend to my father. No, he is not cruel, he is one of the most gentle men I have ever met."

"Then you will be happy."

"Happy?" she repeated, musing the word. "At least . . ."

"What, my lady?"

"I will not be miserable, beaten, or abandoned," she murmured, eyes once again downcast.

Margot rose, suddenly feeling as if she, the commoner, were far more lucky. She didn't have legal rights, but what she did have was far greater.

"Wait!"

Margot paused. "I must go and—"

"Please, what's going on now? Is Wallace aboard this ship? Do we travel on to France? What . . . is going to be done with me?"

"That is up to the men, my lady. But you're wrong if you think that they are monsters."

Eleanor at last seemed to withdraw from her. She turned her face toward the cabin door. "I've seen what they do—"

"You've seen nothing—unless you've seen what Edward of England is capable of doing, m'lady," Margot told her.

The captive did not respond.

"I must go," Margot said. But she couldn't leave quite so easily. "I'll bring you something to eat, soon. Please . . . don't be afraid," she added.

"I am *Santa Lenora,* courage itself! I'm not afraid," Eleanor said quickly, but she was lying, and Margot knew it. The lady mocked herself.

Margot decided to leave her with the lie.

"I'll be back," she promised again, and left the cabin.

William's ship had come alongside the *Wasp* soon after the storm. Wallace had come aboard, and they sat then at the bow of the ship, drinking ale from Norse horns.

Apprenticed to his cousin, Arryn, as a young man, Brendan had come to know Wallace through his elder kinsman. He had never met a man he more admired, a greater warrior — nor a more intelligent man. Wallace was often underestimated by his enemies. He was a commoner, but his education had been excellent. He was muscled, tall, honed to perfection — but his victories had been earned more with careful strategy than with the force which had as yet served him well. In victory, and in defeat, he never faltered. He would die for Scotland, and Brendan was aware that in riding with Wallace, he made the commitment to do so as well. If necessary. But like Wallace, he prayed for life.

Tonight, the winds were calm. The moon touched the water. Where sea and horizon met could not be seen, and they might have been adrift anywhere in eternity.

"I like the pirate. De Longueville," William told Brendan. "There's an honesty in the fellow."

"He's been plundering ships at sea for years."

"Aye, and he honestly admits it," William agreed, a twinkle in his eyes. Born to his role as leader and warrior, he was striking in his very appearance of power. His voice had a power; his words an eloquence that could move men. And had.

But those close to him knew as well that he was a man, not a monster, and a simple man in his way, familiar with pain, but eager for moments in which to smile.

"So a wrong is right — if one admits it?" Brendan inquired. "Then in God's name, somewhere, there must be forgiveness for King Edward, since he admits to wanting to seize all Scotland and destroy all Scotsmen."

"I would rather an honest enemy than a dishonest ally," William told him gravely.

"Ah, now there's the truth of it," Brendan muttered, drinking deeply once again. He shook his head, keeping silent. But he couldn't help but think how very right William was — it had been said, and said again, that Falkirk might have been won, had John Comyn the Red not turned away from the battle with his cavalry. Comyn was cousin to the deposed King John, in whose name William continued to fight for Scotland. Robert Bruce, contender to be king along with John Comyn, had as yet never fought with Wallace. He had, at times, fought with King Edward. After the battle, however, Bruce and Comyn had held Scotland together in an uneasy, unholy alliance. But Robert Bruce had soon resigned his guardianship, and this time when they set sail from Scotland, there was rumor that he would soon sign a peace with Edward. He was a man with much to lose.

"Out with it, Brendan!" William said to him.

"It is merely something I think — now and then."

"Aye, let me hear it!"

He glanced at the man he followed. "All right. You have never faltered. You have fought for Scotland. Not for gain. Edward has tried to bribe you. King Haakon of Norway would gladly welcome you and give you lands — and a title. Philip is aware of your journey to France now, and in his travels our good friend the Archbishop of Lamberton has spoken highly of you at every opportunity. We've been to France before; feted at the French court. We've been to Italy, to Rome and back, and we seek to keep Philip now from a pact with England that can only hurt Scotland. No matter what, though, you'd be welcome in France. Philip is always eager to welcome you to his country, give you command of troops, and reward you handsomely. But you, sir — you stubborn ass, if you'll give pardon — you will continue to fight. Our nobles — bless their blackened souls — backed away when we were winning victories! They cry for Scotland, then squabble among one another. Who will be king? I won't fight if I won't be king. Sorry. But I admit, by God, I do wonder at times — just what we are doing, how can we ever fight Edward when we so endlessly fight ourselves?''

Brendan wondered if he had evoked Wallace's anger, but the man was grinning. Then he started to laugh, and gave Brendan a huge clap on the back.

''An ass, am I, sir?''

''Only at times — sir.''

''Aye, well there it is. If Robert Bruce rides with me, he loses everything. He holds too much that lies in the king's power. He wishes to marry an English heiress, and word had it that he was in love, deeply infatuated with the beauty, and there, ah, yes, there, many a man has lost himself, his soul, or even his country, for love.''

He was quiet a moment, and Brendan did not urge him on. The woman Wallace had once loved had been murdered by the English under bitter circumstances, and many said that her death was one of the reasons he fought with such vengeance.

Wallace lifted a hand in the air. ''Robert Bruce is still a friend to Scotland; you mark my words. Aye, he seeks a crown. That has been the single-minded obsession of his family for decades. God knows, maybe he is the right man to wear the crown. But just the same, John Comyn hopes to be king. They are both powerful men. I don't believe that John Comyn deserted us with intent at Falkirk; it is my belief that the horses broke and ran, and there was no rallying he could force.''

''You are looking at the man with a kindly eye. Some say he was eager for you to lose at Falkirk, that he doesn't want Balliol restored to the crown, though they are close kin, since, of course, he, too, wants the crown for himself.''

''Those in line for the crown do want it. Therein does lie the problem!'' Wallace murmured. ''Their weaknesses, and my strength. I don't want the crown. I want freedom.''

''But the army is broken.''

''Aye, that it is. And without the nobles, I can sway common men, but not enough to follow me in suicide against Edward again—not for now. Now, we must look to diplomacy, and whatever aid we can gain from foreigners.''

Brendan stared broodingly out on the water.

''And what now, young friend?''

Brendan shook his head with rueful disgust. ''When you resigned as guardian, and the barons met at Peebles, it was a member of my kin to suggest that your lands be taken as forfeit for you leaving the country without permission of the assembly? Sir David Graham!''

Again, William seemed amused. ''My brother Malcolm was there to stop any such foolishness.''

''But that he should—''

''Grahams have covered the countryside, Brendan. I do not hold you responsible for all who bear the name. And I know, as well, that David Graham has his own allegiances. He is loyal to Comyn, and is not to be blamed for that. My brother is a supporter of Robert Bruce; he cast his loyalty to the Bruce long ago. He tells me that we might forget our King Toom Tabard, and look to Bruce. He is the one who must one day save Scotland from the English, and then rule her. Ah, Brendan! It is difficult to see, in the midst of the blood that we have shed. Bruce and Comyn both sit back at times, praying for King Edward's death! He is aging, and his son prefers games, pastimes and the friendship of his favorites over battle. Perhaps waiting is the greatest weapon against Edward. He cannot live forever."

"Excuse me, but it appears he is living far too long."

"Well, we are on our way to see another king, a French king. One, who, as you say, will welcome us and be pleased with the penitent pirate we bring him." He was silent for a moment, studying Brendan. "A pirate . . . and an heiress. Interesting collections for the journey, eh? Though I have heard that the Lady Eleanor is still very ill."

Brendan let out a sound of irritation. "She is much better. Margot says she will live, and Margot is seldom wrong. If Lady Eleanor is ill, it is her own fault. She insisted on a swim."

Wallace laughed and slapped his knee. "Against all odds! Ah, well, a woman of my own heart."

"I don't think so. She sees you as we see Edward. I believe, in fact, that she thinks you have a tail and horns upon your head, and were spewed from the earth by the devil himself."

"Many an Englishman does. I am supposed to have ridden into battle wearing the skin of my enemies. I paint myself like a heathen. Well, I am guilty of many things, but not until such crimes were perpetrated on me, or on Scotland, did I retaliate in kind. I know about this woman. She led troops at Falkirk. Because men, claiming to be under my leadership, burned a village. So be it. I have burned many an English village. I have plundered and raped the English countryside where I could. I did not, however, murder innocents, but fighting men. Tell her to remember Berwick, where the king's men cut down even pregnant woman as they ran in the streets."

"Tell her?" Brendan queired. "We are in a precarious diplomatic position. She is a good pawn to hold in our hands. I had thought that you—''

''You fished her from the sea. She is your concern.''

''We are on a most important mission. Perhaps you should *not* trust her to me.''

Wallace stared at him curiously. ''And why is that?''

Brendan lifted his drinking horn. ''We have met before.''

''Aye?''

''At Falkirk.''

''Oh?''

''She very nearly killed me.''

Wallace stared at Brendan a long time, then laughed, slamming him on the back once again with his big hand. ''You? I've seen few men more proficient with a sword, nor more determined to use one.''

''We are all vulnerable.''

''But you? Ah, yes, of course. She cast off her armor, and found your Achilles' heel. Well, they do say, revenge is sweet, and before God, I must admit, there have been times when I have killed men and the pleasure in seeing them die has been great!'' His face darkened. ''So much pleasure, indeed, that I fear I myself will rot in hell for a hatred that deep.'' He sighed, looking back, and Brendan wondered whether he thought of killing the men who had murdered his father, or the woman he had loved. Or both. If vengeance didn't just become a part of life.

''Ay, yes, revenge can be sweet!'' He stared at Brendan again. The anger left his voice, replaced again by a touch of amusement. ''I wasn't, however, suggesting that you should kill the lass. All men must draw a line, you know.''

''I wasn't intending on an execution.''

''Aye, then. 'Tis up to you.''

''She was traveling to a French fiancé.''

"Then remember her value. And that we are always in need of funds. And greater diplomacy. And that many in the world see us as beasts."

"Are you saying that I must treat her as a valued guest?"

"The choice is yours, my friend. And bear in mind—I didn't say that it was at all a bad thing that the world sees us as beasts!" He rose, stretching his great length. "I'm for sleep. Eric stays awake by darkness; his woman is with him. I've been offered the comfort of his bed. I accepted—before I had heard you were displaced."

"The men sleep below in close quarters as they have on many a battlefield; I can curl up anywhere and rest. Last night, I slept in a chair. I can do the same again. I have been taught well," he said with a grin.

"Still—"

"Sir, you've not had near enough peace in your life. You are welcome to the cabin," Brendan assured him.

Wallace paused a minute. "Don't be downhearted, and certainly not for me, Brendan. Don't you remember Stirling?" He clenched a fist. "The feel of freedom, the taste of it! We lost at Falkirk, but not so greatly as you might imagine. Aye, we lost good men. But the whole of the country tasted that freedom. They saw the possibilities of what could be. That's why I fight. Even if I die, our people have the taste in their mouths, and that is something that Edward will never be able to take away. It is for Scotland. All for Scotland."

"Aye, for Scotland!" Brendan said, and he remembered his own battlefield vows. For Scotland, and for freedom. Goals worth fighting for, in whatever form the battle might take. Goals worth dying for.

With a nod, William left him.

* * *

She had dozed on and off, but she woke with a strange, uncanny fear. She bolted up, then realized the source of her unease.

He was back.

A candle burned on the desk. It was a dim light, but bright enough to show the man who stood just inside the doorway, watching her. She had no concept of how long he had stood there, just an acute unease.

"So you're alive," he said softly. The words seemed to carry no emotion, as if it made no difference to him whether she survived or perished.

She didn't reply; the answer was evident. She watched him, and he waited for a moment, then ignored her, unwinding the woolen tartan from his shoulders, and hanging it upon a hook by the door. He walked to the desk, picked up the candle, then came toward her. Despite herself, she edged back against the bunk, gritting her teeth. The candle was all but in her face.

"What are you doing?" she asked sharply at last, completely unnerved. The fever had left her, like the storm, it had raged and gone. But she still felt weak. Like a kitten with no strength.

"They say you are worth a great deal. I'm just trying to see why."

Impatiently, she reached out, thrusting away his hand with which he held the candle. Then she was afraid of her own action; she might have knocked the candle from his hand and caused a fire.

But she didn't knock the candle aside, and he didn't seem angered or bothered by her action. He returned to the desk, setting the candle down. Then he took the chair at the desk, leaned back, and stared at her.

"What are you doing, and why are you here?"

"This is my place aboard this ship."

"Indeed. Then why am I here?"

"It's a large and excellently crafted ship, but even aboard

the *Wasp,* Lady, there are only so many places where ... a guest might be kept. Especially an unwilling one who might enjoy a cold swim in the middle of the night.''

"Guest? I am a prisoner.''

"Prisoner—guest. Sometimes there is little difference.''

"Pirates, murderers—Scotsmen. Sometimes there is little difference.''

She couldn't see him well in the candlelight, but she was sure his features tightened. He shrugged. "The same, and far worse, could be said of the English.''

The depth of his tone assured her she wanted to go no further in that direction, and yet it seemed she had no choice but to meet his gaze, and converse with him. She shook her head, still weary, and angry that she should feel so weak when she wanted so badly to have all her wits about her to fight.

"Have you come just to torment me?'' she demanded.

He arched his brows. "Am I tormenting you?''

She didn't reply. She wished that she had. He stood and walked to her side, sitting on the bunk next to her, his eyes very intent. "Am I tormenting you?'' he repeated.

"Aye, that you are!''

"Well, good. I didn't think it would be so easy.''

"You're very cruel—''

"You nearly killed me. When I had given you mercy.''

"We were on a battlefield.''

"And I might have been buried there.''

"That is long ago now—''

"And you are the lady to the manor born, flying across the seas into the arms of the rich and noble lord who would be her husband!''

"Yes.''

"Alas! There's a small fly in the ointment. Flies. Pirates, murderers—and Scotsmen.''

"Would you please—''

"Aye?"

"Leave me be."

"Ah. Show you mercy?"

"Yes, if—"

"I showed you mercy once before."

"Indeed!" she flared suddenly. "So take care—I am crafty and cunning and enormously talented with a sword, and you can easily be buried at sea!"

A slow, rueful smile was curling his lips. He leaned toward her. "You don't look so dangerous now!" he said softly.

"You are a wretched creature, even for a Scot!" she told him. "I've been ill . . ."

"Very ill," he agreed.

"Go away."

"Nay, I think not."

She lay back, closing her eyes. "What is it, then? My value does not appear so great. I have been very ill, burning with fever. I must be pathetic, hardly appealing—"

"Not in the least," he assured her pleasantly.

Her eyes flew open again. He was still wearing a small, subtle smile. His eyes widened and his face lowered toward hers. "Maybe I feel that tormenting you . . . in any way . . . is my sacred duty!"

His face was close, very close. She should be longing to strike him. And she did, naturally. But she also held her breath, closing her eyes again, strange rivulets of fire tearing through her while she rued the wild tangles in her hair, the certain pallor of her cheeks.

She opened her eyes. He was still there. Unnerved, she cried out in anger, attempting to strike him. "Leave me—"

"Nay, lady, nay!" He caught her flying hand. His eyes never left hers. She trembled, gritting her teeth despite herself. "It's my place aboard this vessel. I intend to sleep here."

She sucked in her breath. "But—"

"I slept here last night as well."

"What? Oh, you are wretched. So it's your duty to torment me? Then go ahead. Be aware, of course, that a tarnished heiress is not worth nearly so much as a pure piece of property, that you risk the anger of the French king—"

"The anger of the French king? Are you that valuable?" he marveled, and she knew that he was mocking her.

"Aye," she informed him icily.

"Imagine that, lass!" His eyes skimmed down her length. "Who would have thought . . ." His tone was light, but then his blue shadowed gaze met hers once again. "And what of the English king, m'lady. Do we risk his anger?"

"That goes without saying," she informed him, fighting for calm and control.

"Good," he said, dropping her hand, rising. "I may be forced to greater lengths than I had thought!"

She lay silent, wishing she had a sword at the moment— and two strong English soldiers to hold him down while she cut him up, since she wasn't quite so confident in her own abilities.

He walked to the desk, found the carafe upon it, and poured himself water. He drank it reflectively, then took the chair once again, propping his feet up on the wood and leaning back. "I'm sure you'll improve as the illness passes," he mused.

She wanted to throw something at him. She realized that she had just been told she wasn't appealing enough to be ravaged.

Thank God, you idiot! Shut up and keep it that way! she implored herself.

But she couldn't seem to do so. "Dear God!" she exclaimed. "Surely, the illness has wasted me tragically, since I've heard that your people are exceedingly fond of even sheep!"

He had closed his eyes; he opened one, eyeing her casually. "The sheep usually look a lot better," he told her.

"I do then," she whispered, "most heartily thank the Lord for good-looking sheep!"

She managed to turn on her side, staring into the wall of the cabin, stunned that she could have gotten into such a discussion with this, of all men.

A second later she nearly screamed, and almost leaped from her skin. No sound had warned her of his presence, not the slightest whisper of air.

But he was there, by her side, whispering into her ear.

"Alas, my lady, maybe you'll improve before we reach France."

"I should rather die!" she informed him.

"Alas, so would I! But duty calls . . ."

Her shoulders couldn't have been stiffer; the soft, barely concealed laughter she heard made it all the worse as he walked away from her again, and this time, for good.

And yet . . .

His fingers had lingered just a moment too long in the strands of her hair.

Chapter 4

Corbin Clarin had just sat down to a breakfast of delicious baked fish and fresh bread when the storm swept back into his life.

Petite, dark-haired, sharp-featured, Isobel *was* attractive—as a deadly viper might be. She preferred London to Clarin, or even the great castle at York, perhaps because the Scots had been known to venture so far, or perhaps because she simply enjoyed the amusements to be had in London far more than the monotony of the north country.

Corbin loved London himself, but he despised his wife, and he dreaded waking each morning among the king's court to wonder with just which courtier she had spent the previous night. He had long ago learned to find his own quest for love—or the pretense of affection—elsewhere.

She walked into the great hall unannounced, drawing her gloves from her hands as she did so. "Miles!" I have come miles, and there is no one to greet me!'' she said, striding across the room to him.

Corbin leaned back, but didn't rise. He folded his arms over his chest.

''Had we but known, my dear, we could have thrown flowers before your feet! Alas, you sent no word of your arrival.'' Flowers? Had he known, he would surely have found some business to be about elsewhere. God knew, Edward nominally held Scotland now, but the whole of the country lay in Scottish hands, few of the southern castles were even under his control, and the unruly barons were always attacking somewhere, begging the king's pardon, running back with their tails between their legs, and failing to support one another in their fear that they should support the wrong man to take the crown — if Edward should ever tire of his subjugation.

Ah, yes! There were always Scots to fight somewhere!

She tossed her gloves on the table and stared at him with sharp dark eyes. ''I should like some wine after my long journey. I am parched.''

He rose, bowing to her with mockery, and approached the sideboard to supply her with a silvered glass of the requested beverage. He mused over the wine service as he poured. Venetian glass, beautiful. She had brought it to Clarin, part of her dowry.

He handed her the wine. She nodded her head in acknowledgment, her fingers brushing his in a way that was oddly suggestive for Isobel. They had married at a time when Clarin had still been great, when his uncle Leo still lived, and when the lands were not just vast, but rich. He and Alfred had expected to reap the rewards of titles stripped from defeated rebels and lands generously bestowed upon them by the uncle who had raised them, a just and giving man. She had brought wealth; he had brought valor. They should have been a beautiful couple.

The Scots had changed all that.

He poured himself wine and lifted his cup to his wife.

"To Wallace," he said with dry humor.

"One day that monster will justly burn!" she said. "He will suffer the greatest penalty that the law will allow, and when that day comes—"

"You will be there, watching, enjoying every bloodthirsty moment!"

She arched a brow, then pouted slightly. "You would call me bloodthirsty, when your beloved little cousin led more men into battle than you did yourself?"

"Not by choice."

Isobel turned away from him, looking about the room. "Fine tapestries."

"A gift from the Flemish villagers."

"Ah, for *Santa Lenora!*"

"Isobel, is there a point to this conversation?"

"Just that saints are better off dead."

"So are rabid bitches," he remarked smoothly.

She didn't take offense. "Where is Alfred?" she inquired, looking about. "Poor, dear, long-suffering Alfred. Riding expanses of land that will never be his!"

He stared at her without replying.

"Well, where is he?"

"Riding expanses of land that will never be his," Corbin answered.

She smiled. "And Eleanor has been packed off to France, there to meet her aged betrothed!"

"Aye," he murmured carefully.

"Well, then I shall stay awhile."

He arched a brow sharply. "Whatever for?"

"To spend time with my husband, of course."

"Why?" he demanded flatly.

"Eleanor is crossing the Irish Sea . . . my lord, you fool! Have you no idea of the dangers? The king has offered large sums to any seaman who brings in rebel Scots seeking aid in other countries, and dozens of pirates and misfits, murderers and thieves have joined in the quest!'' Isobel took a seat at the table, loosening the tie of her taveling cloak. ''Poor dear, she may not come back. And then, of course, should she reach France, she will wed Alain, is that correct? And there, I've no doubt, go her chances of creating the required male heir for the property.''

Corbin walked over to her, planting his hands on the table before her. ''You'd best pray that she does reach Alain; his fortune is necessary if we are ever to regain the riches of Castle Clarin, and turn the land back into a productive region. And though Alain may be old and doddering, many an old man has fathered a child.''

''I don't believe he is capable; his first wife had children by a previous marriage. She was still very young when they wed. No, I have studied this situation carefully.'' She drew a finger idly over the flesh of his hand before her. ''Doesn't it ever irritate you that Eleanor is a countess, and that you are Sir Corbin Clarin, and no more? Have you no ambition?''

''Aye, once, Isobel, I thought to conquer the world and make my own way within it. Then life happened. Ah, yes, and you are a part of that life!''

''Yes, I am.''

''My dear, I've yet to understand your point.''

''We can inherit.''

''Isobel, Eleanor is the lady of this manor, and if she were not, I have an older brother, one who actually works hard, and is deserving.''

''Ah, yes, but he has no wife, no prospects before him, and . . .''

''Isobel, I am still confused. Nothing has changed.''

''Ah, but things have changed!'' She rose, placing a hand on his chest. She had her talents. She chewed mint constantly, and her breath was as sweet as the morning dew. Her perfume was delicate and arousing. Her exploits were humiliating to a husband, but they had taught her keen talents in bed as well. She was charming, sharp, shrewd, and had earned a place at the king's court. He hesitated, wishing to put her away from him, but intrigued as well.

"What has changed? Have you decided upon some foul play for my richer relations?" he inquired harshly.

"No!" she protested with deep innocence, and her fingers played down the length of his chest, and lower still, and he grit his teeth, staring at her. "No, dear, how could you suggest such a thing? I've merely thought that the time has come when someone produce an heir for the property, and with Eleanor at sea, where there are Scots, thieves, pirates, and opportunists all about, that leaves . . . us."

"Alfred could marry."

"Alfred has shown no inclination to do so yet. Alfred is called to battle far too frequently."

"I, too, remain at the king's command."

"That is true. More and more so every day."

"I see. So you've decided to come see me, and hope that we can conveniently and quickly conceive an heir — the quicker the better, because marital relations with one's husband can be so boring, and because that same husband might be so rude as to die upon the battlefield in the king's command?"

She smiled, spinning from him, pulling pins from her hair, dropping them on her path to the staircase. She paused, turning back. "Are *relations* with your wife such a ghastly thing to contemplate, Corbin? Dear husband, just what is it that I'm asking of you? Nothing more than your marital duty — and a chance for your son to inherit all."

He started toward the staircase, pausing, looking up at her. "And what, my dear, if we are not so magnificently fertile? We have been married some time, and God knows, my lady, as does all of England, that you've not been exactly devoted and faithful.''

''But intelligent and able, my love. We've not borne fruit, because I've chosen thus far that we should not. Really, Corbin, I'd not have you—or the king or the nobility—question the paternity of my child! The time has come!''

''But if it hasn't, Isobel, what then?''

''Then, husband, I will have entertained and enraptured you, and none shall feel pain.'' She frowned, reaching down, gently touching his face and suddenly looking very small and very beautiful. ''We have led separate lives. What I ask is not so much, is it?'' Her voice had grown husky, and indeed, she asked nothing but, for a change, to be his wife. His lover. He so seldom trusted her. But they were here, in his family home. And the length of him burned with a fire of long submerged desire unique to this woman. ''Most men would be attacking me where we stand, on the stairs!'' she reminded him with a whisper that seemed to stroke the length of him, inside and out. Amazing what a voice could do, a look, a touch.

''Aye, that they would,'' he agreed. He threw up his hands. ''As you wish! Dear God, my aim is to please.'' And he swept her into his arms and carried her quickly up to his room.

The stairs wouldn't do at all. His brother would return, and he didn't intend to be interrupted for hours and hours to come. Such opportunities did not come frequently in his life.

They were still at sea. In the two nights since their encounter after the storm, Eleanor had seen little of the man with whom she shared the cabin. He came, she knew, because there were traces of him. Once, the length of tartan, left on the hook. Once, a horn of ale left on the desk. Then a book, left lying open. And once . . . just an *impression* of him. A feeling that he had stood near her, looking down at her while she slept.

She was ready to crawl up the cabin walls. The only person she really saw was the Norse woman, Margot, with her snow-blond hair, powder-light eyes, and soft-spoken comings and goings. She would have stayed again, Eleanor thought. She would have talked; she would have helped to keep her sane, except that the tall, snow-blond, muscle-bound Norse man would appear too often, and call her name sharply. And she would follow him out, as if he were the sun and moon, all in one.

There were books in the cabin. They had helped. Wonderful books, beautifully scripted, many of them copied in Irish monasteries, signed by the monks. There were Greek and Roman histories, legends, Irish fairy tales, even passionate dissertations about Viking raids on the British Isles and beyond. Some were in French, some in Latin, and a few, she surmised, were in Norse. She knew nothing of the language, which was frustrating, because often, the few phrases of conversation she could overhear were spoken in that tongue. She had not been surprised to discover how many of the Scots were familiar with Latin and French; the church taught the former, and most young men, with any hope of moving up in the world, were familiar with the language most frequently spoken at the courts in both Paris and London. Being so near even lowland Scotland, she had learned Gaelic as a child — her father's determination. But Norse . . . Viking raids had ended long ago. Only heathen northerners, highlanders, might have occasion for the use of such a language. She had thought so often of her enemies as being barbaric, so much less civilized than Englishmen. She had never imagined them to have a greater education than she, the daughter of a scholar as well as a warrior, with the blood of nobility in her veins.

But even the books could entertain her only so long. She had ceased to be afraid moment to moment; if they had meant to slice her to pieces, she was fairly certain they would have done so by now. And if they were on a mission to the French king, it was unlikely that they would do well to arrive with the blood of a French nobleman's fiancée on their hands. She was not suffering; she had never minded sailing, though she did despise being locked up and confined. She was well fed: Margot brought her fresh dishes, wine, water, and ale. She was even brought water with which to bathe, and once the fever had broken, she had felt better, stronger, almost immediately. Her trunk of belongings was in the cabin with her, and nothing had been taken. She bathed and changed with unease, never sure when the door to her prison might open, but the other occupant of the cabin seemed only to come at night. Margot brought her meals at regular intervals. She was never disturbed.

She thought that it was the fourth night she had been aboard when she woke suddenly in the near darkness with the feeling that someone had just left the cabin. She opened her eyes carefully, afraid that person might still be with her, but the cabin was empty. Something, however, was wrong, different. She puzzled over the situation for several moments, then realized that she had not heard the bolt slide shut.

She sat up, sliding her feet carefully to the floor. Clad in a long linen nightdress, she scurried across the floor and tested the door, barely cracking it.

The door lay open.

Still, she stood within the cabin, dismayed to realize that the open door seemed to do her little good. She remained on a ship at sea. She was no longer certain if they were in the Irish Sea, or if they had reached the English Channel; they seemed to be taking a circuitous route. If she escaped the cabin, what then? Another dive into the sea? No. Reason had returned. She didn't want to die. She leaned against the cabin wall, a deep desolation settling over her. The door was open, yet she remained trapped. Maybe he knew that, and so bolting the door was no longer necessary.

But still . . .

Perhaps she could slip out unseen, and at the least, listen in on a conversation that might give her a clearer indication of what would happen when they reached France. She slipped outside the cabin, and in the shadows, tried to get her bearings. There was a corridor ahead, and a third deck below, and topside, of course, were the helm, the masts, the sails.

She crept up the stairs first, cautiously peeking above the deck level. It all seemed quiet, though there were men manning the ship by the darkness of the night. She came back below, then dived behind the covering of a storage wedge as two sailors walked by. As she held her breath, waiting for them to pass, she heard conversation. She realized that there was a center cabin above her, on the main deck, and she sped toward the stairs again, and up them, then along the rigging to reach the upper, central cabin. There were windows fore and aft, port and starboard, and she realized it was where leaders might meet on the ship, and yet be aware of any activity at sea — all around them. Now, ducking down by the starboard window, she could see that a lantern burned on a table, and that the pirate, de Longueville, sat there with the tall Norse captain and another man who seemed quite large as well, brown-haired and bearded, muscled and strong. She gritted her teeth; tremors raking her as a single word tore through her.

Wallace!

For a moment, she was tempted to throw life itself to the wind. She had no weapon — foolish, but she hadn't come out to attack anyone. She wanted nothing more than to fly into the cabin, assault the man, and tear him to pieces with her teeth, hands, and nails alone. Idiocy, of course. She might as well attack a stone wall. She inhaled deeply, forcing herself to stillness, forcing herself to listen. "You see," Wallace was saying, "it is not so much an official voyage that I'm taking. Other men, trained as diplomats, men of the Church, have come to Philip, have pleaded with the pope. I've come now with the hope that my reputation and my abilities to persuade can give some good to the Scottish cause. The pope, I've heard, has recognized Scotland as a sovereign state, and said that our allegiance is to Rome as a Christian nation.''

"The French king is always seeking mercenaries, God knows, half the battles waged by nations are fought by paid foreigners," the blond captain, Eric, said ruefully.

"But mercenaries . . . a pirate?" de Longueville inquired.

"I've heard that the king would readily give pardon to a pirate who has plied his craft upon English ships," Wallace said. "It is certain that he will not seize you as a member of our party — even if he has entered into a new agreement with Edward.''

"Aye, now that's true," Eric offered. "I've known the king in his business dealings; no matter what his agreements with the English, he is ready to do anything possible behind Edward's back.''

"Maybe it is a sad thing, in a way," Wallace offered, "to be a king who has fostered so very many enemies. The Welsh are forced to serve him, but hate him. France is forever before him. And we, the Scots. By God, no matter what the cost in blood, we will not go the way of our distant cousins, the Welsh.''

"What if, however, we were to be attacked?" de Longueville queired. "Perhaps by English ships, joined by Frenchmen, ready to take the head of a pirate — or a savage outlaw?''

"We have the woman. A Frenchman's English fiancée. They will take care," Wallace said.

She sucked in her breath. So she was going to be a pawn. A pawn to be used to avoid justice! She had to get back to the cabin, pretend sleep, lull them into leaving the cabin door open at all times. Then she could escape when the neared the French shore, swim in, and leave her captors in sorry shape indeed!

She rose in a spin, ready to fly back to the prison of her cabin as quickly as she could. But she gasped as she spun right into the body of the man how had evidently stood silently behind her, watching her, waiting, as she had watched the others.

"Lady Eleanor, good evening, how very good of you to join us!"

His hands fell upon her shoulders. The hardness of his features decried the lightness of his tone.

She stared at him in silence.

"You've nothing to say for yourself?"

"I owe you no explanations."

"Come then. Come in and meet Sir William Wallace."

She had little choice, being turned and prodded, and when she did not move quickly enough, it seemed that she was off her feet until they reached the entry to the cabin, where the three men quickly moved, rising, hands ready to reach for swords or knives. Even upon their own vessel, it appeared they were ever ready for violence to be offered.

"We've a visitor," Brendan said briefly.

"Ah, the lady of Clarin," William Wallace said, and he studied her oddly. His voice contained a certain gentle amusement, which she couldn't begin to understand. He had been bitterly defeated at Falkirk. She certainly hadn't caused that defeat, but she had been there, and she had been hailed as a rallying point for the men of the smaller towns and villages north of York.

"How do you do, my lady. I am William Wallace, of Scotland."

"Every child in England knows who you are," she told him.

"A monster, no doubt."

"Men in my village were herded into a barn and burned like cattle, at your command," she told him.

"I didn't ride against Clarin, my lady, I gave no order there that men were to be put to death by fire. But that is no matter. Many men have died at my hands, and at my command, but the death toll I have wreaked does not begin to compare with the murder done by Edward of England. I bear you no ill will, however, for choosing loyalty to your people over the comprehension of your king's desire to conquer a people.''

She was still for a moment, realizing the way that the four men stared at her. Wallace spoke French beautifully, with a quiet eloquence she had never expected. Strange, in a way, for the four men in the cabin were all of an exceeding height and broad in the shoulders. At the moment, their manners were excellent, but the Scotsmen wore their tartans about their shoulders in a wild, barbaric manner. The Norseman had a mantle of fur, and only the pirate seemed to be dressed in the manner of a gentleman. They were a strange company by whom to be surrounded, and she, in nothing but white linen, hardly armor between herself and these enemies. She had thought Wallace to be the worst monster on earth; they did use his name to terrify children in the countryside, to keep them close to home. Yet at the moment, she was most aware of the man at her side; he seemed far more the greater danger to her person.

''Edward was invited to Scotland when the line of secession was in question,'' Eleanor said at last.

''He was invited as an adviser, not as a conqueror,'' Wallace said sharply.

''Are you suggesting that I should forgive and forget what was done to my home, and allow you to use me in your game with a king?'' she inquired.

She stared at him. The pirate suddenly made a strange sound and turned away from her.

''I would like it if you would cease to hunger for my blood on a personal level. Aye, yes, and maybe understand,'' Wallace said. His voice was low.

Brendan's was not so pleasant when he spoke next. ''M'lady,

I have taken great pain to forgive and forget quite a bit, for the duration of this voyage.''

She turned on him uneasily, suddenly aware of the candle-light in the room, of the way it filtered over them all, and seemed to make the linen of her nightdress transparent. If she should decide to spy again on a ship in the midst of the night, she mocked herself, she must take care to dress with greater thought for the occasion.

''We met on a battlefield,'' she told Brendan.

''Aye. And we learned who granted mercy — and who did not.''

She looked back at Wallace. ''How are you in danger from me, sir? I carry no weapons.''

''Any man — or woman — can acquire a weapon,'' he reminded her with humor.

''I've offered no harm to anyone as yet,'' she told him.

Once again, the pirate, de Longueville, sniffed. Eric Graham laughed out loud. At her side, and just slightly behind her — where she was unable to see his face — Brendan remained silent.

''I've heard you've quite a talent with a sword,'' Wallace said.

''Not really. Simple defensives are known by most sensible men or women living on property in the borderlands between Scotland and England; I am scarcely of the caliber of your warriors with their tremendous prowess at battle.''

''Men and women have different talents, on and off the battlefield,'' Wallace murmured. ''Who is to say who holds the greater prowess? Battles are not a simple matter of power; they are in the mind, the strategy, and mostly, they are in the hearts and souls of those who wage them. We fight for our lives, Lady Eleanor. We fight for our freedom, our land, and for our hearts. Edward fights to gain greater glory, to prove himself the conqueror of all that he sees.''

''My people fought because northern barbarians swept down

and ravaged their fields, and attempted to take the fortress that is my home,'' she said evenly.

"She will never see the truth of the situation,'' Brendan said with sudden impatience.

"Perhaps,'' Wallace said, sitting on the edge of the table in the center of the cabin, watching her, a gentle amusement still in his eyes. "But were she to promise not to put a knife in my back, I would believe her.''

"Um, she would opt for a sword instead!'' Brendan muttered.

Wallace's smile deepened. "I would like to offer you greater freedom about the ship, my lady.''

"How kind — since I have been detained from my own vessel.''

"Mon Dieu! Someone should tell her the truth!'' de Longueville said irritably.

"How can we — we don't know the truth,'' Wallace said, his eyes never leaving her.

"What are you talking about?'' she demanded.

"It's none of your affair,'' Eric said.

"Surely, it is,'' she said, staring at him.

"You talk, you Scotsmen, talk, talk!'' the Frenchman exclaimed. "Were she my prisoner still — ''

"But she is not,'' Brendan said firmly.

"Perhaps it is time for Lady Eleanor to retire for the evening,'' Wallace said sharply.

"Wait, I — ''

But Wallace took her hand. With smooth charm that startled her so that she didn't think to wrench away, he kissed it in a gallant manner. "Good evening, m'lady. We'll speak again.''

"Good evening, my lady!'' de Longuevile mocked. "The savage Wallace is so courteous. Had you left her in my care, she would not be questioning commands. What a waste! Think of what King Edward has done to the Scots. Aye, breed them out, seize their wives! Ah, but we'll be so polite. This would not be so difficult if she were my prisoner—''

"But she is not. We have come to an agreement, and in her state as hostage, she belongs to Sir Brendan," Wallace said firmly, and she was startled to feel the blood race to her cheeks. "If he choses courtesy, it is what we will offer. No matter what the rumors—or those things we are capable of in battle!—we are not *monsters*. Not even so much as the English. Lady, I seriously suggest you retire.''

"But there is something happening here that I don't know about. You've told me nothing—''

"M'lady, there are many things you don't know about! Ah, and it's been such a pleasure having this . . . converse here. All of us. But it is time to go," Brendan said firmly.

She felt the fall of his hands on her shoulders and gritted her teeth. "I don't wish to retire, I want to know—''

"Perhaps the fever is returning!" Brendan said with mock concern. "William, I shall see that she makes it back to the cabin, and return.''

"Aye, then.''

"No, I'll not—'' she began, but to her consternation, she was simply plucked up in his arms, and he strode from the cabin with her. She shoved furiously against his chest, then tugged at her gown, afraid that his hands upon her might have tugged up the hem much farther than was comfortable. Or safe.

"Let me down!" she cried, then she dropped her voice, aware that there were seamen on deck, and aware that they were stopping to watch her forced progress along the ship. "Dammit, let me down, I—''

"In another minute, you fool, the Frenchman would have been at his bit, raping you then and there on the table.''

She fell silent for a moment, shocked. She struggled for a comeback, realizing he still carried her toward the stairs to the lower deck.

"Better a Frenchman than a Scot!"

"Shall I bring you back and give you over to him?"

He came to a dead halt. She dropped her head low against his chest.

"My lady, the choice is yours! You will say something!"

She swallowed very hard. And still, he waited. And she didn't know if he would, or wouldn't, turn her over to the pirate. Something inside her mocked that if she hated the Scots as she swore she did, violence at the hands of de Longueville would be better than uncertainty with this enemy.

But she gave her answer at last. "No!"

"Pardon, my lady, I want to be certain that I heard you correctly?"

"No."

"No . . . no . . . no what?"

She flung her head up, angrily meeting his eyes. "No, don't turn me over to the pirate."

He smiled, smug, pleased. "Thank the Lord! Some sign of intelligence and reason does lurk in the recesses of your mind."

"You're the ones who are in alliance with a pirate!"

"He's not a bad fellow."

"Oh! He attacks ships, kills men, robs, thieves, plunders and rapes. But he's not a bad fellow."

"You honor your king. It's true that he has raped a country and ordered the cruel use of hundreds, perhaps thousands, of young brides. De Longueville, at least, has no intention of killing you."

"No? Then why is it that he sneers and coughs and snickers, and makes insinuations about things that I don't know?"

They had reached the stairs. "You may put me down. I can walk."

"But I can manage."

He did. For his size, he was exceptionally lithe and agile, maneuvering through the narrow spaces with expertise, but leaving her clinging to him so that she didn't fall — or find her head crashed into the ship. They reached the cabin; he opened the door. And it was only once they were inside that he let her slowly stand, sliding down the length of his body to do so. Her eyes remained upon his, her cheeks flamed again, and she tugged at her nightdress, aware that it rode up her thighs, that her legs were bared, and frantic to remedy the situation.

"Well, I am duly returned to the cabin," she murmured.

"Aye, so you are."

"You are due back."

"Aye, that I am."

"Your duty to Sir Wallace awaits you. To the man who claims he had no part in the slaughter at Clarin."

"If he claims that it is so, it is so."

"Then you must serve him, at all costs."

"Um. And you must serve your masters as well."

"I have no masters. Only memories."

"Such pride! Yet here you are . . . seized first by pirates, then hostage to a defeated, but never broken enemy."

She stood very still, keenly aware of the dark blue intensity of his eyes as he stared down at her.

"Thank God," she murmured, "that I am the hostage of a man who hates me."

"Hates you?" he repeated. "Nay, lady. You hate us. I don't hate you."

"I . . . I cried for mercy, remember? And then —"

"I don't hate you. Did I want vengeance? Definitely! But hate you . . . not at all. You taught me an incredible lesson, my lady. Never, ever, be swayed by an image of innocence or beauty. Therein lies the most deadly of all danger! Mercy, ah . . . would I be so foolish as to offer it again? Most unlikely. And mercy, to you, my lady? Never!" he voiced very softly. His fingers just stroked the length of her hair. For a moment, his eyes made the most idle journey over her face, her throat, her breasts. He offered her a grim smile. "Wallace, you see, is a man of his word, not a monster at all. As to the rest of us . . . we have learned from our tormentors. But you will excuse me, of course? Duty does call."

He turned then and left her.

And that time, when the door closed, the bolt slid as well.

And when it did, she realized that she had just stood there, still as a frozen doe, as he had mocked her, touched her. She trembled, and not from the cold.

She raced to the bunk, and curled there in the depths of the blankets. She waited, her heart hammering.

He was angry. He had been taunted. She was his prisoner. He would come back.

Hours passed.

He did not come back.

And as she had every night aboard the ship, at last, she slept.

And lay undisturbed.

Chapter 5

Eric had taken the helm himself; Brendan sat with de Longueville and Wallace, listening again to the pirate's story.

"You know nothing of the man who approached you?" Brendan persisted once again, sipping the Fremchman's wine from a slender glass. It was excellent — deep, rich, red — yet he had to admit to a preference for clear, cool ale. But the pirate was, interestingly enough, a man of refined tastes, and he was eager that they share what he considered his finest cache of wine — taken from an English ship whose noble passenger had just made the purchase of the wine in Bordeaux.

"I did not take the request too seriously at first," de Longueville told him. "We slipped into the port — under a false flag, of course, but it is a poor place to berth, and filled with cutthroats and thieves — a place, I'm certain, King Edward would demolish, if he ever had the time or energy left over from his battles in Scotland and abroad! As it is, his barons refuse him service, and he must rage in silence and twist what he says, or else bring down a bloodbath upon his own country. But why do I go on? We are in agreement here that the English king is swine!'' He made a clicking sound with his tongue. ''There are those who know I dare the port so close to mortal enemies when I am in need of water. They are aware of the talents of my crew with their knives, and aware as well that I reward my men richly who turn their gaze aside when I am present. There is a tavern there, and a whore I know well; she introduced a drunkard to me as I was imbibing a fair share of ale myself. This drunkard set down a purse before me and said that there would be an English ship leaving the following day — from a more reputable port, naturally — and that it would carry Lady Eleanor, Countess of Clarin, and that she was a worthy morsel, a rich prize in her simple being, and should be plucked from the sea. There would be a hearty ransom for her, reward in itself, yet a richer ransom could be gained back at the same port — if she were just to disappear. I thought little of the fellow's words, but when he was gone, I opened the purse, and I had been left a modest sum. Prepayment, I assumed, for what might be acquired if the lady were to be stopped.''

''She was to be murdered?'' Brendan said, frowning, and casting his gaze toward Wallace.

''That wasn't specified. The word used was 'disappear.' There are many ways for a woman to disappear, monsieur.''

''So there are.''

''To the south, below our Christian countries, there is a slave trade that seeks just such treasures.''

Brendan leaned back, wondering how he could feel so enraged on his hostage's behalf. ''And you would have sold her so?'' he inquired.

The Frenchman shrugged. ''Not so easily, I assure you. With interest, I inquired about the woman. Indeed, she was a countess, and indeed, scheduled to sail out to meet with Count Alain de

Lacville in Paris, where they were to be married. The lady herself, is not so rich—landed, and with a pedigree near to kings, but alas, enwrapped in poverty, due to the war-torn devastation of her hereditary lands. The arrangements for her marriage were made by a cousin who guards the property in her stead. I found the assignment to waylay her rather curious, despite the fact that her death would give the property over to other kin. The property is in desperate need of new income, and the marriage is necessary for Count de Lacville's wealth to restore the property to any hope for the future."

"Very curious," Wallace murmured. He looked at Brendan. "The English sell one another right and left; cunning and greed and espionage are all about, while we are fixed on one goal and one obsession. Our goal remains so distant because we battle among ourselves in Scotland as well. It is amazing that any man lives out a decent life on his own land, tending his family, or loving his wife."

The sound of Wallace's bitterness was startling to Brendan; he faced the knowledge that the barons did not truly accept him in victory, much less defeat, yet he still looked to the future for his country. He sounded weary now.

The Frenchman shrugged his shoulders. "You will not be monsters! That is your choice; for me, I am glad of the peace I will make. For now. In the end, I will sail back to Scotland with you, I think."

"Really?" Brendan queried, amused by the man who had a strange sense of scruples—and indignation.

"I will lift my sword for the nobility of a higher cause—and for land, should that cause ever be won," he added. He looked at Wallace and grinned. "I will earn a place to live out a better life, to tend a family. And love a wife. For the moment . . . I would not be so noble. She is sent out to wed for the glory of French wealth! Yet someone would see her dead. My wicked ways would surely be more kind than what her family has intended, and the lady is a rich morsel in herself, as I was told."

"Take care, pirate—" Brendan warned softly.

Again, the Frenchman threw up his hands. "Aye, she is in your command. A pity. She has more than youth and great beauty; she has life, spirit—"

"And quite a tongue on her as well. She would lead a husband on a merry chase," Wallace said, drinking more wine. He had a palate for the wine and seemed to appreciate it well enough.

"We wage war against the English, and that is our pursuit in France, and in life," Brendan said suddenly. "She is a part of England, so much so that she donned armor and rode to war."

"Shall I sell her to an Arab emir then?" the Frenchman inquired. "She would fetch a pretty, pretty price!"

"Despite the things said about me, I've yet to make war on women," Wallace said.

"She took arms against you," de Longueville reminded them, amused by the situation.

Brendan rose, amazed at the way his teeth clenched and his fists balled at his sides. "We are not on the battlefield now. The quest is far greater than the fate of any woman. We have her, and Philip will want her. She is in our custody, but we need the French king's help. We will bring her to the French court."

"The emirs would keep her alive, and treasure her at that!" de Longueville muttered.

"De Longueville," Wallace said quietly, "not even you can imagine the blood I have on my hands, and the things I have seen to want vengeance to such an extent. Brendan knows the truth of it; Lady Eleanor must be turned over to the French king. It is the only diplomatic possibility. Her marriage has been arranged; there is nothing cruel or unusual in such matters—"

"Aye, heiresses are bought and sold in marriage each day.

But someone wanted this heiress to disappear,'' de Longueville reminded them.

"I have met this man to whom she is promised," Brendan said. "He ordered no murders, and he will protect her. I will, in fact, suggest that he keep her in France for a time, and watch for those around him.''

He left the cabin, aware that both the pirate and Wallace were watching him, each with his own thoughts.

He returned then to the cabin. She slept. Yet it appeared that it had taken her some time to do so. Usually, the bedcovers were pulled to her ears, as if she would disappear within the ship's bunk. Tonight the covers were all about. She was curled to a side, as if she'd tossed and turned. The length of her hair fell in a gossamer of gold about her face. He held a candle near her. A mistake. The light fell upon the thin linen of her gown, and delved beneath it. The shape and form of the lady were delineated. Not that he wasn't aware of the graceful curve and supple beauty of his hostage. He was. Had been. But memory could be exalted. Could be. He had taken no liberties with his mind's eye. So few years ago . . . he had been betrayed at her hands. He had sworn justice — not justice, but revenge. He had been duped, taken, humiliated, nearly killed, but he had survived. Survivors thirsted for vengeance. They lived for it. Here was the moment. But his enemy was completely vulnerable, and a far more worthy opponent than he had ever imagined. Unable to resist, he set the candle on the ledge of Norse pine at the head of the bed, and reached out to smooth tendrils of hair from her face.

This lady did not need enemies. She gave her heart, soul, and loyalty to a family willing to sell her to the highest bidder.

Her skin was achingly soft to his touch. And with what the candlclight did to hcr body . . .

He turned away from her, blowing out the candle.

He stood in the darkness, muscles taut, pained, rigid from

head to toe. She was his prisoner. His. Whatever should befall her was well deserved.

There was a greater goal! He reminded himself.

Hard to remember such lofty — and often hopeless — ideals, when the flesh seemed to burn, the body to quake. Yet, equally, he had never allowed the slaughter of innocents. Never attacked a man from behind, even in the insanity of the battlefield with blades flying all around him.

They were men. Seeking a dream, a people, a nation, freedom. They were not monsters.

The darkness settled. He listened to her breathe.

At last he walked away.

Eleanor awoke to the sound of splashing water. Opening her eyes cautiously, she saw that he was across the cabin from her. She could see his back as he bent over a washbowl on the stand against the opposite wall; his back bare. She looked downward, her view half-hidden by the desk between them. Bare . . . how far? Why was she looking? Knowledge, simple knowledge, of course. He was broad in the shoulders, flesh sleek. Muscles taut and tense. His waist was narrow and trim. And below that . . .

He turned suddenly, drying his face. She closed her eyes, pretending to sleep.

There was no movement, no sound, nothing.

She opened her eyes. She gasped. He was almost on top of her, standing by the bunk, studying her face with rich amusement. "Sleeping, my lady? Resting well?"

"I was — "

"And Wallace claims that there is virtue in your honesty!" he exclaimed.

"I was sleeping — "

"You're a liar!"

"Obviously, sir, now I am awake."

"Ah." He had a linen towel in his hand. He was still drying his neck and shoulders. He stepped back. She closed her eyes. Almost completely. But he wasn't naked. He had stripped his leggings, but he was wearing the tartan wrapped around his lower half, and only his calves and bare feet were visible.

She started, giving away the fact that she was watching, when he took a step toward her. "Well? Were you enjoying the seascape?"

"The seascape?"

"The view, m'lady. You were watching me."

"I wasn't watching — "

"But you were."

"Perhaps I was certain that you were hiding horns and a tail, as a good beast or devil would do."

"Such a liar!" he exclaimed, tossing the towel toward the washbowl and taking a seat by the side of the bunk. She quickly eased herself up, her back against the wall of the bunk, as she watched him with a breathlessness more alarming to her sanity than any simple fear.

"I try to be alert any time you are in the room," she said coolly.

"Then you fail miserably. You sleep with an irritating ease, most of the time."

"Oh? Do you stare at me through the hours of each night to know such a thing?"

He grinned. "M'lady, I do not need to. I come in, and you are as still as an angel at rest. You scarcely stir. This morning, however, you lay awake. And watched."

"As I said, I expected a tail."

"Alas, you were disappointed."

"Oh, no. I do believe it is there. Along with the horns. Somewhere."

His grin deepened for a moment. For once his eyes danced

with rich, cobalt amusement. "Be truthful, Lady Eleanor. You lay awake. Watching."

"It was amazement—that a Scot should bathe."

"Ah, a cruel slur. Extremely cruel. What else?"

She caught her breath for a moment, her eyes wedded to his. "What else? It is evident you practice your craft of dealing death very well. You have fashioned your arms into weapons and your flesh is covered with scars."

"That it is," he said after a moment. She nearly shrieked when he reached out for her hand, but she swallowed back the scream she would have released as he forced her to touch a thin white line on his shoulder. "That, *Santa Lenora,* was the first I was to receive. From an Englishman who assaulted the home of the kinsman where I lived. His pregnant wife was butchered, among other atrocities practiced that day. And this . . . defending a border castle . . ." He laid her hand flat against his chest. She felt the deep thunder of his heart, and the rigor of muscle tissue as he moved. "This—the battle of Stirling Bridge. And here . . . well, this one . . ." He drew her hand inexorably toward the top of his head, "this one, you can't really see, unless you part the hair. It's the one I received at Falkirk. But you, lass, ah, you walked away without a scratch!"

She jerked her hand back. "Oh? How can you be so sure of that?"

"M'lady, I am sure of everything about you."

"And how is that?" Her eyes narrowed sharply and her heart seemed to skip a beat. "You watched as I bathed?"

"You admit to watching me?" he queried.

"No—but you, you—"

"I was there, m'lady, when you were near to perishing of a fever, brought on by a plunge into an ocean, followed by a night in soaking cold clothing. I helped strip you, bathe you, dry you, and get you into bed."

"Oh!" she gasped, fists clenched at her side, a fever seeming to race through her. She was so angry she slammed her knotted fists against his bare chest, and was barely aware when he captured them both. "How could you, you — bastard! You and your Wallace sit here and talk about courtesy and the fact that you're not monsters, but you — you — "

"Pardon me! When your death seemed imminent, I was not considering my manners."

"Death would have saved me . . . this!" she exploded.

"Forgive me. I hardly think that you are so suicidal, nor is there honor in throwing away life. And what is the . . . *this* that you suffer so drastically?"

"Being . . . here."

He folded her hands before her and sat back. "I don't think you're suffering."

She stared back at him, then tried to slide by him. "If you won't leave, I will."

"Nay, lady. You'll not."

His hands were on her again, pushing her back. Her head fell upon the linen-covered feather pillow. His hands remained upon her shoulders, holding her down. When he spoke, he leaned low, his face very close to hers.

"Do you want to know, my lady, what I think?"

"No. But I believe you'll tell me anyway!"

"Aye, I will. I think that your family is selling you into the arms of an ancient old rock."

"Alain de Lacville is a very fine man — "

"Yet scarcely breathing."

"You don't know — "

"Oh, I do know. I met the old gentleman years ago, right after the battle of Falkirk. Aye, you're right. He has a good mind, and a courteous manner. But he is very, very old. And rich. Maybe you'll even be allowed to marry where you choose when he does depart. But then, my lady, perhaps he will simply rot slowly away, and you will be the honorably chaste and loyal wife until you've no youth left yourself. You've not much ahead for you in the way of excitement. Therefore, you were watching me.''

She stared at him, blinked, and then exploded.

''Oh, my God! You are outrageous. You don't know how ridiculous that is. By God! Sir, your ego is as inflated as your sword arm. You know nothing of Alain; rotted, ancient, as you claim, he is still one of the finest men I have ever met, you know nothing—''

''I know that you don't want to marry him.''

She broke off, staring at him, wondering how he could know so much about her situation, or her feelings.

''Marriage is a contract,'' she said flatly, her tone hard. ''Marriage is an honorable contract between houses and families.''

''Your duty, eh?''

''Yes!''

''You'll never have a family.''

''Oh, really? Perhaps I will have dozens of children.''

''That's most unlikely. You're being sold. To a very old man.''

''If so, it is because your people destroyed my home and family, and left a village of innocent farmers and craftsmen to starve.''

''There is scorched earth all over the borderlands. It is a travail for everyone, but while Edward persists, the sorry situation will remain.'' He was serious for the moment, his eyes cold, hard, and passionless. ''Aye, and there it is. When Scotland wins her true freedom, England may lie at peace.''

''Well, sir, for the time being, would you be so kind as to leave *me* to lie in peace?''

''Aye, lady. As you wish it.''

He rose and walked away from her, collecting his clothing from the arm of a chair near the wash water. His back to her,

he donned leggings and a clean linen shirt, then looped the tartan over his shoulder, pinning it there with a silver brooch. He started out, then at the door, he looked back. "Lady Eleanor, *Santa Lenora!* You do, for now, remain my hostage. So feel free, when so inclined, to watch where you will."

"I always keep my eyes on my enemies."

He smiled. "So do I, my lady. So do I."

Chapter 6

Later that afternoon, the sails came down, the ship made fast.

Hearing the men's shouts, Eleanor tested the door again and was pleased to find it unbolted. The Norseman's ship, most probably followed by the pirate's ship and the other two vessels in the Scottish company, dropped anchor. Listening to the seamen, despite the Norse so many of them were speaking, Eleanor ascertained that they were anchored outside Calais. The name of the port meant little to her. In her father's house, she'd had tutors to teach her language, geography, history, and of course, religion, but she'd never been outside the country before. But the French were certainly civilized, despite the fact that the French and English kings were constantly at one another's throats. Alain was immensely wealthy and powerful, and his name was surely known throughout France; if she could reach a safe harbor and ask for help, she could reach him without becoming a pawn in the Scotsmen's quest for foreign aid in their continued rebellion against the English.

She kept to herself, listening with great attention. Wallace remained aboard this ship. He was closeted in the central cabin with his companions, where they formed their plans for landing, sending word to the French king that they were in his country, and seeking an audience. She didn't dare let any of the Norse or Scottish men know her intent; they would send out an alarm in seconds. But if she didn't act quickly, she would find herself surrounded by the enemy. Escape would then be impossible.

She dressed in her lightest clothing, careful to place her gold and silver coins in the inner pockets of her gown, and to carry, as carefully, an unusual Celtic pendant of her mother's, studded with rubies and emeralds. One lesson life itself taught was that men could be bribed, and safety, and passage, purchased. She was wary, of course, that she burden herself too heavily. She couldn't possibly steal a boat. Slipping over the side of the vessel and swimming to shore was her only hope.

Laden with enough for survival, she paused to pray — then turned to flee.

She escaped the cabin quite easily enough. On deck, she smiled at the various seamen, or nodded gravely, whichever seemed most appropriate with the individual men, some of whom smiled and whistled and sang easily themselves, and some of whom seemed to be dour upon all occasions. When every one of them seemed exceptionally busy, she made a pretense of returning to the cabin, but when their backs were turned, she slipped over the side.

The distance from the deck to the water seemed great. Again, the water was fiercely cold. She plunged endlessly before gaining enough control in the deep, dark frigid water to stop her descent and crawl her way back to the surface. She broke it, gasping desperately for air. She breathed in raggedly, goose bumps rising on her flesh as the chill breeze struck her. She was instantly afraid that her flight had been noted, and she looked to the ship with fear. But there were no men shouting an alarm, and no one was coming after her.

So he watched his enemies, did he! she thought, and not without a certain sense of smugness. He had underestimated this enemy.

Now, as he had once before.

She shivered so that she almost put a tooth right through her lip; she hadn't meant, that day long ago at Falkirk, to murder. She'd seen enough blood that day to put the fear of injury and death into any man. Aye, he'd paused for her, and there was his downfall. Her escape today did him no harm. He should know what it was to demand freedom.

She turned her back on the ship and swam.

The distance to shore was far greater than she had imagined, and seemed even more so, weighed down as she was with her money and jewels, in the severe cold. And the activity on the immediate docks gave her pause. Despite her freezing state and exhaustion, she forced herself to swim further southward, so that she would not need to arise where her reception might not be one offered with warmth and dignity.

Having come this far, she meant to succeed, and to reach the French king without the company of her enemies.

She also meant to survive whatever strangers she might encounter.

When she reached a spit of beach, she crawled onto it and fell flat, gasping and gulping air, so exhausted that she couldn't even curl into herself for warmth. She closed her eyes, fearful at first that she had killed herself—her heart was beating so rapidly it seemed ready to burst from her chest. She tried to breathe deeply, and as she did so, she felt the frantic pounding of her heart begin to slow.

But just when she thought she had gained control of her life, she froze, feeling the touch of a blade at her throat.

Her eyes flew open. Stunned, she looked up, then scrambled away from the point of the blade.

It was wielded by a strange cutthroat — a man with a sweeping, fur-trimmed cape over a tunic, fine leggings and soft leather boots. She could see little more of him, for his face was largely covered by the brim of a drooping, feathered hat, and a patch covered his one eye and a mask most of his face.

As if he were a leper.

She inhaled so sharply she nearly choked on her own breath. She started to cough — then backed away and scrambled to her feet, the point of the sword following her throat all the while. When she stood, he still hadn't spoken, and she began to defend herself with words. "I've done you no harm, why are you accosting me?" This was France, and he must surely be a Frenchman. He must understand her; as was customary among English aristocracy, she had learned the Norman French of the royal house of Plantagenet before the native English of her home, and the Gaelic Scots of her too close neighbors to the north.

He pulled the sword away, still without speaking, and walked around her. She turned, afraid to have him at her back. But as she followed his movement, she saw that he was not alone; two other men had come upon the rocky shore. They surrounded her.

"All right, listen," she said slowly, her hands gripped into fists at her sides as she tried for a firm, authoritative, regal tone, and a bravado she was far from feeling. Courage was not easy when she stood there freezing and shaking, the taste of the ocean still on her lips, her clothing crusting to her with each frigid gust of the wind. "I am here to meet one of the most important men in all the realm of the king of France! If anything happens to me, he will hunt you down and hack you to pieces, bit by bit. Do you understand?"

For long, unnerving moments, no one spoke. Then the masked swordbearer stepped forward again.

"I have money. I can pay you to leave me alone!" she shouted.

To her relief, the man sheathed his sword.

"You must help me. If you do, you will be rewarded. If you don't, you will be chopped up into little pieces."

He understood, she thought. He was probably a thief and the worst cutthroat in Calais. But he understood money.

"You understand?" she said.

Apparently, he didn't.

He reached for her. She cried out, stiffening, ready to fight, but his grip was firm; she was forced to him, her back to his chest, pinned there by the strength of his one arm. She shrieked along and began to struggle in earnest as she felt his hands on her clothing. She kicked, and squirmed, and was sure she did some harm, because she heard him grunt. But the way that he held her, like a constricting snake, she could scarcely breathe, she couldn't begin to use her arms. Indeed, it was as if he were crushing her, asphyxiating her . . .

But his own left hand was free, foraging through her clothing.

He found the pockets where she carried her money and her jewels.

His men were coming forward. One, a short, slim little fellow dressed in a fine, fur-trimmed tunic, stood in front of her, grinning. "I think our friend has decided that he doesn't need you to give him money — not when he can take it."

She still could barely move. The other two men, dressed in stolen finery, no doubt, came closer, helping her attacker to steal from the deep pockets of her clothing. She twisted and squirmed and kicked, all to no avail. Her feet were caught, wrapped in someone's belt, she was borne back down upon the sand, and her sodden clothing all but torn from her body. The masked wretch who might well have been sealing her doom with disease if she were to survive the attack suddenly straddled her prone form. She fought with such desperation that she nearly knocked the mask from his face, but he caught her hands, and bound her wrists with a strip of fabric torn from the hem of her dress. She cried out with ever-greater panic, but one of the thieves came forward with a fur blanket; it was thrown over her face. She next found herself being hoisted up, and minutes later, thrown over the haunches of a horse. A man mounted the animal as well.

He gave the horse a kick and it burst into a gallop. Not a bad gait for a large horse, if one were actually riding the animal! But she was flopped about, crashing into the moving, muscled shoulder of the horse, and then into the knee of the man, and into the horse again. It seemed they rode far. They must come to civilization! She thought. And refusing to accept her own most likely doom, she made plans to scream her loudest the second she heard activity around them. Someone would help her. Someone would understand when she said that she had come to meet Count Alain de Lacville. They would realize the jeopardy in which they had cast themselves!

In her heart, of course, she knew that Alain himself could never dash forward to her rescue; he was far too frail. But he would send dozens of men to avenge her, and these thieves now accosting her would hang from the highest post in France, if they were not cut down by the flashing steel of Alain's knights.

Yet, when at last they came to a halt, she heard no commotion around them. And when the rider dismounted and reached for her in the smothering folds of the fur blanket, she was shaking, and unable to stand, much less find the breath to scream. Her knees refused to straighten; she would have fallen. The leper picked her up; she shrank within the blanket, as if she could inch away from the touch of the man who held her. She was lightheaded; it was so difficult just to breathe that she prayed at that moment only to have the blanket removed from her face so that she might draw a clear cool breath freely from the air once again.

In a few moments, her prayer was answered. They entered a

building; she heard the clump of boots against wooden flooring. There were stairs, she knew, because they were rising. Then she was tossed down on something decently soft; rope bedding with a feather mattress, she thought fleetingly. Then she tore at the fur covering on her face, ripping it away.

Tousled and sodden and trembling still, she looked into the masked face of her oppressor, and could see nothing, not even the color of his eyes, for the brim of the hat he wore covered them. Fear singed through her like lightning bolts, for she had no idea of where she was, other than a barren room with wooden flooring and walls, somewhere near Calais, France. He stood at the foot of the bed, staring down at her. Her clothing was wet, torn, and plastered to her, and she gasped for breath with even greater desperation as she realized the extent of her peril. Death was one thing. But these men could make death a long and excruciating process. How many of them were there? Just what might they do to her? And even if Alain avenged all this, what good would it do her, abused, broken, lying in her coffin?

She wet her lips. "Please . . . this is a situation that you cannot win. If you hurt me . . . kill me, Alain will kill you . . . have you killed. You will die. He will hunt you down through all of France. Torture you. Help me. Help me get to him. He will reward you — "

She broke off because her captor was turning away, ready to leave the room. Relief filled her. He didn't intend to ravage her. Relief flew from her heart as quickly as it had come. He didn't intend her harm *at that moment*.

But he would come back.

"Wait, you don't understand. You really don't understand. You will die. Painfully. Horribly. Of course — "

She broke off. If he was suffering from leprosy, as his mask suggested, he might be ready to face the swift death of a sword. And if he was suffering from leprosy, perhaps it would be best if she were to suffer a swift death now herself . . .

The door opened and closed. Her captor had left.

She flew from the bed to the door, then hesitated, waiting. She was certain then that he stood right outside, waiting for her to try the door.

She waited. She was right. A few seconds later, she heard a bolt slide quietly into place. She backed away from the door. This was a room, just a room. Plain, simple. There was the rope bed on its frame, covered by the thick mattress and linen sheets.

The sheets appeared clean enough, and the wooden floors were swept. There was a plain wooden chest with a pitcher of water. That was all.

But there was a window in the room. Shivering, the fur cast aside, she hurried to the window. To her delight, the shutters opened at her touch. She looked out and her heart sank. She had hoped for an alleyway, for a street with nearby buildings. She looked out on a field. This house they had come to was apparently on a little hill, far enough from the town of Calais to be surrounded by land. Still . . .

She looked down. She seemed very far from the ground. But if she could escape the room, there were no walls that she could see surrounding the place. If she could escape, she could run. She was certain that they were on a rise, and that the busy town must lie just below.

As she looked out the window, she started, her heart slamming, as she heard the bolt sliding again and the door start to open. She jerked back into the room, closing the shutters, moving away from the window.

Her visitor was a woman. She was perhaps thirty, maybe she had been very pretty at one time in her life, but she had a lean and wary look about her now that gave a pinch to her features and a jaded appearance to her eyes. Those eyes and her hair were a rich, matching shade of sable brown; she wore her hair free, with no headdress of any kind, so it fell down her back in thick, dark waves. She assessed Eleanor, hard eyes running over the length of her with a surprising malice.

"You will come," she told her with a sniff.

Eleanor straightened. "I will come where?" she demanded.

"To have a bath."

She stood her ground, miserable again in cold, clammy, salty clothing, but still loath to part with it — especially among this company.

"I will stay here, I think."

"You wish to remain wet and cold?" the woman inquired.

"I wish to hear that I am to be brought to my fiancé, or that he is on his way to find me. I will wait until then."

The woman's smile deepened with mockery. "You will wait then until you are old and gray."

"I will wait, nonetheless."

"You will not wait. You will come with me."

Eleanor estimated that she was at least the same size as the woman, and though she did not have a sword, she was capable of a good fight.

But the woman had no intention of tackling her. "You will come with me, or other arrangements will be made."

That made her uneasy. And she was more uneasy when a second woman came behind the first. This one was a bit taller and broader. Actually, she was nearly a giant, blonde and blue-eyed, she might have been a Nordic goddess from Valhalla. She was a striking woman, and surely an equal in size — and power — to most men.

"There is difficulty?" she inquired, looking from the brown-haired woman to Eleanor.

"She does not wish to shed her wet clothing."

Now the blonde assessed her.

"You must."

She felt the thunder in her heart as she looked at the two accosting her. The blonde as well wore her hair free. They were both clad in linen, not rich clothing, but neither were they clad as the poor or beggars. There was something unusual about the clothing worn by the pair, and she reminded herself that she was in France now. But it still didn't seem quite right.

"Listen, please," she said, trying for control and reason, "I truly don't think you understand who I am—"

"Oh, we know precisely who you are!" the brunette said.

"I am worth a great deal of money!" she insisted.

The two looked her over and started laughing.

"Look—"

"Please, come now. We are busy."

Eleanor stiffened her back then walked toward them, thinking that she might step past the pair, make a mad dash for the stairs, out the door, and into the countryside. The idea was mad, indeed, but it seemed she had very little to lose.

And so she inched her head up and started past the two. She came to a wood-paneled hall, and saw the stairs. But the brunette had forseen the reason for her compliance, and before she could start to flee, the woman was at her side, grabbing for her hair.

"Stop!" Eleanor shrieked, grasping her hair, spinning, kicking out since she couldn't inflict a blow with her hands. The brunette screamed, hopping on one foot. The blonde stepped forward, capturing Eleanor with a grip to the arm that threatened to dislocate her shoulder.

At that point, the small Frenchman in finery came running up the stairs, the leper behind him. "What's going on here?" the Frenchman demanded.

"She doesn't want a bath!" the brunette said sourly.

The leper in the mask pushed irritably past the dapper Frenchman, and Eleanor started backing away in sheer panic. "No, no, I will—"

Too late. He plucked her up by the waist, half hauling her, half dragging her, down the hallway to a room where a wooden tub filled with steaming water awaited. She was dropped and spun, and as she desperately tried to catch her breath, she heard the fabric of her tunic begin to tear. She tried to turn, but the strength of his arms pressed her back into place. She cried out, swore, and turned again, arms flailing. And still, though a grunt assured her she had gotten a blow in, she was really only aiding the destruction of the fabric about her. Torn and wet already, her shift and tunic fell despite the way she grasped at cloth and flailed at her attacker. And when it was gone, she screamed again as his hands . . . his bare hands . . . fell upon her waist, lifting her, then dropping her into the tub. The heat startled her for a moment; she threw her arms around her knees, drawing them to her chest.

He was gone. Her clothing lay in tatters, but he was gone. Relief filled her.

But then the two women stepped into the room. The blonde approached her, laughing, dipping a deep curtsy. ''Soap—m'lady.''

''A cloth, Countess!'' said the brunette, tossing a linen cloth into the steaming water. Eleanor stared at them with a deep and rising hatred that kept her from bursting into tears of frustration.

''And here, for your hair,'' the blonde said, producing a little vial. ''Sit back, and I will tend to it for you.''

''Don't touch me!'' she grated out.

The blonde looked at the brunette and started to laugh. She ran her tongue over her lips. ''La! Anne-Marie! The countess is afraid of me!''

Anne-Marie doubled over in laughter, approaching the tub, fingering a lock of Eleanor's hair. Eleanor flinched away, adding to her amusement. ''Ah, chérie! You have no need to fear us—neither Hélène nor I have a preference for women, eh, Hélène?''

''Not unless the price is high—very, very high!'' Hélène agreed.

Staring at the two, she realized at last that she had been

brought to some wayside inn, a place indeed occupied by cut-throats — and prostitutes.

Her stunned amazement, her eyes wide on them, brought the pair to gales of laughter once again. But then, oddly enough, something in her sudden silence must have brought about a hint of sympathy, in Hélène, at least.

"We're not going to hurt you," she said, her voice low, without a hint of mockery. "You would have caught your death in that icy clothing. Indeed, what were you doing, in the midst of winter, tempting the icy water? Especially after — "

"Hélène!" Anne-Marie said sharply.

There was a stool near the tub. Hélène set the vial upon it. "For your hair," she said again. "We will leave you, but we are just outside. Do you understand?"

"Perfectly," Eleanor said.

The two looked at one another, then stepped out. The door closed behind them.

Eleanor lowered her head, trembling, and felt the heat of the water warm her stiff and frigid limbs. She leaned back, trying not to shake, praying for a bolt of lightning to bring the saving grace of a *plan* to her mind. She couldn't understand this; these people were rogues, whores, thieves — they must need the income she could provide! And yet they laughed at her offers of reward and ignored her threats.

They had really left her alone, she thought after a moment. And the water had warmed her, and the soap was clean-smelling and sweet, and it was good not to be cold, and to feel clean again.

Yet, to what purpose?

She started to shake again, thinking of the leper who had seized her, the man in the mask. The man with the sword, who spoke not at all, but seemed to be the leader of these wretches. Did any of it matter? If he was indeed diseased . . .

She sat up suddenly in the tub, remembering his hands. *His hands.* Bare of the gloves he had worn earlier. Touching her. She had glanced down at them, even in her fight, even in panic.

They had been healthy hands, the flesh unblemished, unbroken. So he was not a leper; he hid his face for another reason. Was he horribly scarred, or an outlaw wanted by the crown of France with such ardor that he dared not show his features anywhere?

As she reflected on the possibilities, the door opened. She hugged her knees to her chest once again, looking around, instantly defensive. It was the blonde, Hélène. "You have finished, m'lady? Ah, you haven't started on your hair. I'll help."

"No. I will do my own hair."

"As you wish."

Anne-Marie entered, coming to Hélène, whispering. Eleanor could make out almost nothing, but then she heard, ". . . bargain for her."

Hélène turned back to her. "There is a towel, there, beyond the stool. And clothing. Not what you are accustomed to . . . but, better than what you had, eh, m'lady?"

Hélène left the room. Anne-Marie started after her, but paused, bending down to the tub to whipser at the back of her neck, "Do your hair well, m'lady. *He* likes the sweet smell of clean hair and perfumed flesh!"

Eleanor gripped the tub. "I do not care in the least what *he* likes."

"But you should. Because if you don't . . . well, we'll have to see that you do. Do you understand, *English?*"

Anne-Marie left the room without awaiting her reply. Eleanor braced herself, wishing for the power to slap Anne-Marie silly. But aware that the woman would return — and hopeful that someone was indeed out there bargaining for her, she sank into the water, washed her hair, and forced herself to enjoy the warmth.

But then, suddenly, the tub seemed as cold as her future. She glanced to the door, afraid it would open. It did not. She jumped up, found the towel, and dried quickly. She had been left an unbleached linen shift, and a pale blue woolen tunic to slip over it. She dressed, glad of the clothing — even if it did belong to the despicable Anne-Marie. She had barely smoothed the fabric when the door did open, and the woman in question came for her.

"You must return to your room. Quickly. You have a visitor."

"Who?" she asked, swallowing hard. She tried to control her shaking, hoping that they didn't mean the "he" who liked his women with clean hair.

"Move!" Anne-Marie said.

On simple principle, she stood her ground.

Anne-Marie cocked her head to the side. "Shall I call for help?"

"Move to where?" she asked.

"Back to the room."

"I will do so," she said regally, preceding Anne-Marie from the room, aware that the woman was right behind her. She glanced longingly for the stairs, but she didn't want to chance another encounter with the French cutthroat who had brought her here, not when she was being returned to the room with the window that just might promise freedom, and not when the overheard words "bargain for her" kept hope flowing in her heart.

She stepped into the room. The door slammed shut behind her. She hurried to the window, opening the shutters, looking out again. The hope she had felt began to wane. There were no trees near the window. The ground was a sheer drop that seemed very far away. How far would she get if she leaped out — and broke a leg?

She heard the bolt sliding and once again closed the shutters and spun around, stepping away from the window.

The door flew open.

She gasped, stunned.

It was Brendan who had come. A mile high, filling the doorway, his tartan around his waist and cast over his shoulder. He was very much the Scotsman in this land of the French, and in all her life, she had never even begun to imagine that she might be glad of a Scotsman.

"Brendan!" she whispered his name, and without thought, went flying across the room, throwing her arms around him. Startled, he caught her, lowering her slowly against him, lifting her chin, meeting her eyes. "You don't know!" she told him. "Thank God, you've come. You don't know how bad these people are!"

"Worse than Scots?" he inquired, appalled.

She stepped back, aware of his mockery, her cheeks flaming as she realized the way in which she had greeted him. "Brendan, have you come to get me out of here? I loathe your murdering countrymen, yes, and I was convinced life was far worse when you first came upon the pirate's vessel, but . . . Alain will reward you if you have come to help me. Surely, you have . . . ?"

He stepped completely into the room, closing the door behind him. "This is a very grave situation, grave indeed. We are not Frenchmen, we are not an army, we are rather at the mercy of the thieves here."

"But, surely, there is some kind of law, and you can send to Paris, and—"

"Ah, yes, well, we can send to Paris, but that will take time. And I'm sure you've realized just what kind of place this is for wayfaring . . . sailors. And travelers."

"You mean murderers and thieves!"

"Well, yes."

"But, Brendan, you've come—"

"I came as soon as I could, knowing you were here," he assured her. "I was stunned, of course. What happened? When you were so close to reaching your beloved fiancé and the French king? Did you fall overboard?" he asked, and she didn't know if he was concerned, or mocking her.

The latter, she was certain. "Yes, I fell overboard!"

He nodded and turned toward the door again.

"Brendan!"

"What?" He turned back.

"What are you doing? You can't just leave me here, you can't!"

"My lady, *you* have brought about this situation."

Fear and anger filled her. "Oh? Did I attack my own ship?"

He arched a brow. "Nay, lady. But neither was I the first to do so. Our intent was to deliver you to the French court. Now . . ."

"Brendan, don't you dare leave me here."

"I will do my best to negotiate your release." He hesitated. "We, are, of course, nothing more than poor outlaws ourselves. I'm afraid I need your permission to seek compensation among your belongings on the ship."

She exhaled, staring at him. "I . . . I was wearing what I had on my person!" she whispered.

"Ah . . . when you *fell* overboard."

Again, he started to turn. She went to him, placing a hand on his arm. The turned back to her, staring at her hand. She drew it back quickly. "There must be something you can do."

"Oh, my lady. I will try. I will try everything in my power. God knows, we wouldn't want you left in the clutches of a crazed, mute cutthroat, would we? The fellow is probably more than half mad, a leper—"

"He isn't a leper."

"Oh?" He arched a brow, staring at her intently.

"I saw his hands. When he wore no gloves. Perhaps he is scarred."

"Ah, yes. Maybe his face was slashed severely in the battle that lost him his tongue."

"Brendan, you must do something!" she whispered.

"Naturally, of course, I will do so."

"You wouldn't leave me here — for vengeance, would you?"

He paused, leaning against the door, assessing her with a slow smile. "Vengeance? Against the rare beauty who asked me for mercy just seconds before a complete betrayal?"

"We were on a battlefield!" she reminded him.

He didn't reply. She lowered her head, then could bear it no longer. She crossed the two feet between them, placing her hands on his chest, looking into his eyes. "Please, for the love of God, Brendan, please . . . I am begging you, help me. If ever . . ."

"If ever what?" he demanded sharply.

"If ever I could help you again, I swear I would!"

He stared down into her eyes for a long moment. He took her hands in his. She was startled when he placed a light kiss on each, his eyes meeting hers all the while.

"My lady, I will do my best."

He turned.

"Don't go! Don't leave me!"

"I must."

He removed himself from her, firmly setting her from him. He left the room. She heard the bolt slide. Then she heard voices.

The sounds faded. She sat at the foot of the bed, unable to stop shivering. She threaded her fingers through her still damp hair, trying to loosen the tangles. Time passed. No one came.

Perhaps an hour went by. Then another. Then the bolt slid. She leaped to her feet, anxious, hopeful.

It was Anne-Marie who entered; she brought a tray bearing

food and a wooden tankard. She set it on the one piece of furniture there was. "Bread, cheese, fish, wine. Ah. And a brush," she said, her back to Eleanor. Then she turned, her smile smug. *"He* likes his women with smooth, flowing hair."

Eleanor's eyes narrowed. "I have told you that I don't care in the least what *he* likes."

"Shall I stay then?" Anne-Marie inquired, her tone falsely sweet.

"I will not be here long," she said.

"Oh? Because of the Scotsman? *He* has sent the Scotsman away."

"What?" Despite herself, Eleanor asked the question quickly and sharply.

Her panic provided Anne-Marie tremendous pleasure. "The Scotsman had nothing to offer, not on him. He knew that to fight would be to die. Jacques told him that no *Englishwoman* was worth dying for, and to that, he had to agree. You will see Jacques yourself. Later, of course. Now, do I stay and do your hair—*my lady?"*

"No."

But Anne-Marie didn't move. Desperate to be alone again, Eleanor picked up the brush and nearly ripped out what felt like half her hair in her attempt to make it smooth and tangle free so that she could rid herself of the Frenchwoman.

At last, Anne-Marie turned and left the room. The bolt slid into place.

Eleanor raced back to the window and threw open the shutters. Night had come. She was dimly aware that she hadn't eaten at all, and that the fish smelled wonderful, but her desire for escape was stronger than even her hunger. Opening the shutters still provided no real answer. She looked back to the bed.

The fur blanket that had nearly smothered her earlier remained. And there was more. The rope bed had been covered in linen sheets. If she ripped them off . . .

She did so. Even tying together what she had, her makeshift rope wouldn't quite reach the ground. But if she could come within a few feet of the ground . . .

She set to work. Carefully, silently she moved the bed inch by inch to the window; it was all that she had to secure her linen rope. She ripped the material with her teeth to best tie it together, and secure it to the foot of the bed. She worked quickly, aware of the darkness, aware that any minute the bolt might slide — and the door open again.

At last, she was done. She crawled over the rough wooden windowsill. And slipped down, down, down . . . into the night.

She reached the end of her linen escape line. The ground was just below her . . . a small drop.

She swallowed hard, prayed . . .

And dropped.

Yet even as she let go, a scream began to form in her throat. The night had suddenly come alive.

And she fell . . . fell . . .

Not to the earth, but into the arms of the scarred French rogue who had seized her.

Chapter 7

Naturally, she fought. She fought like a wild thing.

She kicked, writhed, screamed, bit, and scratched. All to no avail. He wore a coat of light chain mail beneath his tunic and cloak. His hands were gloved again. The leather mask protected his face. She was like an eel, twisting and turning, but still, she did him no harm, and as he made his way around the house and to the front door, the others were there, laughing at her, shaking their heads, amused by her desperation.

The slim little Frenchman was in the main room when she was brought back in. He shook his head as she was set down to stand before the fire. She wanted to attack them all, but she refrained, standing dead still, staring at them with all the regal fury in her soul. "You idiots! You cannot begin to know how you will pay for this!"

Still, they laughed. The slim little man, and the two male companions who had been there with him on the beach. Anne-

Marie and Hélène were there as well, though Hélène was quickly sent up the stairs to retrieve the bedding she had cast from the window.

The man in the mask stood before the fire then, his back to her. Jacques. That was his name, wasn't it? That's what Brendan had said — before the great brave Scot had deserted her!

She whirled on him, talking to his back. ''Jacques! I can get you a pardon from the king. I can reward you richly. What I carried in my clothing was nothing, nothing at all! Don't you need money?''

He spun on her, and stared at her.

It was the little Frenchman who spoke for him. ''My lady, there is a lesson you must learn. Not everything in life can be bought. Many things are far greater than riches.''

''But . . .''

''You must go back upstairs.''

''Why?'' she whispered.

''He will come to you. You will understand.''

''No, you don't understand — '' she began, but he was coming toward her, and she backed away. ''I am an heiress in my own right! You can't do this!''

Jacques remained with his back to her. The slim man was coming toward her; the other two were also hemming her in. But before they could reach her, Jacques suddenly turned away from the fire, his cloak flying in the firelight. He stepped past the other men and caught her hand, pulling her to him. ''No!'' she shrieked, trying to free her hand from his hold. ''No!''

But she couldn't free herself, and when she fought his hold too wildly, he merely picked her up, his arms like bars, and no matter what her fight and fury, he traveled up the stairs, came to her room, and threw her down upon the rope bed that was now barren of sheets. She gasped for breath, ready to fight again, to scream . . .

But he turned away, leaving her. The door slammed. The bolt slid.

She lay still — exhausted and desperate. She breathed for long moments, staring dismally into the shadows of the room. Then she rose and paced.

The bed had been pushed back in place. The tray remained. She poured wine and drank it thirstily. She poured more and noted the knife that had been left to cut the bread, fish, and cheese. She stared at it, then clutched it in her hands. She'd kill him! It was a very dull knife. She'd do little more than bruise him with it!

She lowered her head, then turned back to the door. The knife was dull, but long. She stared at it, then flew to the door. She slid it through the opening, holding her breath. It went . . . she pushed deeper and hit the long wooden bolt.

She fell to her knees, lowering the knife, bringing it up again. This time, she hit the bottom of the wooden bolt. It was heavy. Wedged into place.

She would never move it.

She had to, and she had to do so quickly.

Sweat broke out on her brow as she tried again and again, winding both hands around the handle of the knife, working slowly, up, up. Her wrists ached, her fingers felt as if they'd break. She kept at it.

She almost had it . . .

Her grip slipped; the bolt fell back with a thud. She sat back, terrified, listening, her heart thundering.

Nothing. They hadn't heard below.

She waited, then started again. She forced herself to concentrate; she ignored her aching fingers, burning wrists, and the pains that seemed to shoot through her arms and straight to her torso. Slowly, slowly, slowly . . .

The bolt raised . . .

She kept her fingers on the knife handle and used her shoulder to shove the door.

It creaked open.

Despite the agony in her hands and arms, she forced herself to let the bolt fall slowly, slowly . . . and then it was down, against the door frame. She stood, shaking. Barely able to believe her good fortune and determined not to be caught again, she moved silently and oh, so, carefully into the upstairs hall.

They were all below, she thought, for she could hear voices coming from the room with the long table and the hearth and fire.

"Well, my fine sir!" Anne-Marie was saying. "You certainly owe me! She kicked me! You should see my shin!"

Hélène laughed then, delightedly. "You should have seen her face when she thought Anne-Marie and I might have at her! Ah, but then we told her we were neither one fond of other women—"

"Unless the price was right!" Anne-Marie laughed.

"Indeed, she surely thought herself in the gravest danger!" Hélène said.

"But we could have been hurt, you know! She fights like a tigress!" Anne-Marie sighed.

"She is a wild thing, all right," the skinny little Frenchman added.

Eleanor crept along the stairway, looking down, concentrating on moving in complete silence. The room was off the entryway; if she could keep from being heard, she could creep very, very low — and make the front door and freedom.

Someone turned from the fire and took a seat at the table. The masked man. Jacques. But his gloves were gone again, and he had taken off the mask. She couldn't see his face. His back was to her. One booted foot rested upon the table; he idly played with a wooden trencher on the table with his left hand.

The Frenchman was shaking his head. "She could have killed herself, crawling out a window like that!"

"That is the point," came a different voice.

There was another man in the room. She nearly gasped aloud when she saw who it was, but she caught herself, clamping her hand over her mouth. *Eric!* The big Norseman was unmistakable as he spoke and took a seat at the table across from Jacques.

"Ah, the point!" the slim Frenchman said. "She kills herself, and what have you — nothing! I admit to feeling a certain degree of guilt. I have never come across a young woman so vibrantly determined on her freedom!"

"She will never have her freedom," the supposed *mute* Jacques said then. "She is an heiress, bartered, bought, and sold, but since she has a penchant for death-defying swims and dangerous leaps, she deserves a lesson in the real horrors that might happen upon such a lady. She hates Scotsmen too much to trust us to see her to safety? Then she must see what else the world has to offer."

She was close, so close to the door, but at the sound of *Jacques'* voice, she went dead still, the fury inside her like a living fire. In all her life, she had never been so angry.

Brendan!

She should have known, oh, God, she should have known! No wonder they were laughing at her so. They had done this to her on purpose, left her to ponder in terror and anguish. *He* had done this to her, made her think that they had left her, that she was at the mercy of a common murderer and a den of thieves.

She wanted to throttle him. She was so angry that she thought she might be able to do so, but she forced herself to stay still, to think. It would be a far greater vengeance, she knew, to really escape him than to try to get in one good blow against him. So she swallowed her anger, kept moving, and listened as they all laughed over a question Eric had asked about some part of the charade.

She reached the bottom of the stairs. She was ready to move to the door when Hélène, sitting by Eric, suddenly looked up. She stared straight at Eleanor.

Eleanor stared back.

"Mon Dieu!" Hélène gasped.

Eleanor ran.

She sped for the door, jerking it open. She was nearly outside, into the night, into the yard before the house where a half dozen horses grazed, where real freedom awaited.

But a hand clamped on her arm.

Crazed, desperate, she tried to bite. She was jerked around, picked up. Her hair blinded her. She didn't realize that it was Brendan again who had come to retrieve her until he stood her before the fire, and she tossed back her hair and met his eyes. How had she been so fooled? How had she failed to see the blue of those eyes, even beneath the mask? How had she missed the blue-black sheen of his hair, the size of him, the height . . .

His hands!

"All right, so we tricked you. You deserved it—" he began.

But he didn't see just how thoroughly she had been tricked, or how angry she was.

"You *bastard!* You, you . . . *Scot!*" she raged. They had been eating. A knife lay next to a slab of beef. She seized it, wielding it at him. "You want to be a tongueless mute? Well, sir, that can most certainly be arranged!"

"Eleanor, put the knife down."

"Eleanor, put the knife down?" she repeated incredulously. "Are you out of your mind? I will slice you into tiny little ribbons! You want a scarred face? That as well can be arranged!"

"Eleanor, stop!"

She wished that she could stop. There was quite an audience around them. Both women, their faces somewhat ashen now.

The little Frenchman, the two others, Eric. All silent—and staring.

But she felt as if she were a strung bow, taut to the breaking point. A cry tore from her lips, and she hurled herself against him to attack. She was no match. He caught her wrist before she could offer him the slightest danger; she dropped the knife when it seemed her hand was about to shatter. He brought his arm around her, holding her tight to his chest.

"All right, can I let you go now?" he whispered against her ear.

She nodded. He released her.

She turned on him, her fists flying in raw fury. She caught him with a good blow to the jaw, but she hurt her knuckles when she pummeled his chest; he was clad in light mail. Still, she would have continued, except that he caught her up again, crushing her against him while he turned to the others. "You will excuse us, please; I believe this is a matter we're going to have to discuss in private."

"There is no matter to discuss; you will die for this, hang from the highest rafter—"

She broke off when he picked her up and threw her over his shoulder so that the air expelled from her in a whoosh of sound and she was left gasping. He took the steps two at a time despite her weight, and made it into the bedroom of her incarceration before she could draw enough breath to berate him once again. Darkness had come, but a candle burned upon the chest, and a fire sent flames that glowed and illuminated the room, bringing warmth to the winter day.

She was heedless of both the light and the fire, set for her comfort. She knew, at that moment, only rage and humiliation. "How could you, how could you—" she demanded, thundering against his back, heedless of the damage done her hands, until he leaned over the bed, dropping her upon it. She was up on her knees in an instant. "Oh, you are heinous, beyond—"

"And you *fell* off the ship!" he told her, leaning toward her so that she fell back again. "We seized a ship, and saved you from a pirate. Not an ill deed was done to you, but you dived into icy water and risked killing yourself twice to escape us. All this while our intent was only to see you back into the loving, tender arms of your fiancé!"

His return attack was so vehement that she actually fell silent for a moment, staring at him.

"A pawn!" she cried then. "I was to be used as your pawn!"

"Was that so terrible that you would risk rape and death?"

"What you did was horrible, so horrible — "

"Why? Because I had come to know you well enough to suspect you might try to swim ashore? I had men watching you all the time, my fair, *gentle,* English beauty! Aye, I waited on shore with a few friends. And we tricked you, lady, that we did. Something you well deserved!"

She shook her head. "I am *not* your pawn. I wanted my freedom — "

"Freedom! Well, that, dear girl, is something that we have fought for, bled for, and died for, these many, many years now!"

His passion left her in silence, needing breath again, moistening lips that had gone very dry. He suddenly pushed away from her, striding to the window from which earlier — eons ago, now — she had tried to make her escape.

She moved up to a sitting position on the bed. She stared down at her own hands for a minute. God, they were shaking! She looked up at his broad back, at the rich darkness of his hair. And suddenly, she was on her feet again, flying to him. He ducked in anticipation of her attack. He caught her arms as her knotted fists flew upon his chest again. "You bastard, I was so scared, so scared, so scared . . ."

The pressure of his arms increased; she was crushed against his chest, and her palms and cheek lay against him there. She could hear the beating of his heart. Then his thumb and fore-finger were on her chin, and he lifted her face, meeting her eyes. "Why now? Isn't one monster quite the same as another? Wouldn't a French monster be better than a Scottish monster?"

She shook her head slowly, watching him.

"I thought that he . . . you . . . Jacques . . . the monster . . . would . . . would come. Would come to me at night, and . . ."

She shook her head again, studying his eyes, the fine, strong, sculpture of his face. "And I would have died, you wretched man, because . . . because I wanted . . ."

"You wanted what?" he demanded heatedly.

"I—I—you!" She said, the last word a whisper. It was something she had never meant to say. Something she hadn't admitted, even to herself, until that moment.

But that moment had come. And she couldn't take back the words, and she wasn't sure that she wanted to. She felt as if she flushed from head to foot in the deepest shade of crimson, as if the ocean roared in her ears. He stared at her, stunned, his cobalt eyes darkening, his hands seeming to tremble as he held her. She lowered her head, no longer able to face him.

She hadn't said this. She couldn't mean this. She did.

"What?" he queried, his voice a whisper as well.

She shook her head, unable to speak, hardly able to breathe. But he gripped her shoulders, giving her a firm shake, causing her head to fall back again, her eyes to meet his.

"Tell me again, explain what you just said," he persisted.

She couldn't. She had given away far too much, made herself far too vulnerable. And Alain! He did not deserve this. She would not dishonor him. But still . . .

"Speak to me, damn you!" he cried.

"I will do what is expected of me," she told him haltingly. "And I have been betrothed to a good man, a very fine man. And I will . . . I will try to be a good wife, to make him happy. But . . . he is a man nearly three times my age, and . . ."

It was his turn to lower his head, for his eyes to stray from hers. "So," he said, with a rueful tone, self-mocking. "I would be an experiment, my lady, a memory? Then you will marry the ancient lord de Lacville as you've been told to; you will live with what you think is honor, and try to make him happy."

"You will ride off and die for Scotland," she told him. "A false dream."

His hands tightened upon her. "It is not a false dream."

"Neither is what I offer Alain a false honor."

"So just exactly what is it that you offer me?" he asked tensely.

She searched his eyes again, surprised by the intensity and passion within them. "It isn't what I offer," she said softly. "It's what I ask."

He released her, turning away. He strode across the room, his back to her. His back remained to her as he said, "After what I have done, here . . . you would be with me?"

She was silent so long that he turned to her. She tried to keep her eyes level with his. They fell.

"Yes," she said simply.

He came back to her.

He lifted her chin, brushed her cheeks with his knuckles, studying her eyes. Then he turned his palm, and stroked her cheek with his fingertips. "It is what you *ask?*" he said. "Then surely, my lady, I must oblige."

"Don't mock me!" she whispered.

"If I mock anyone at all, my lady, it is myself, and myself alone."

He lowered his hand, and captured her lips, his fingers still lingering with the lightest touch upon her cheek and chin. His mouth came gently upon hers for but a moment, then seemed to fuse there, his lips and tongue parting hers, a sweet, desperate, wet heat arising there. She had never imagined what just such a kiss could do, had not expected the searing fire that seemed to sweep from her lips to her abdomen, engulfing all between and around. Her knees threatened to give; she trembled with hot and with cold, flames seeming to sear her flesh, her blood, her soul within. Passion — hard, swift, demanding, rose to dominate his touch. His tongue swept into her mouth, tasting, filling, arousing. She held his shoulders, clung to them, yet then, suddenly, she was no longer on her feet, but swept into his arms. His lips parted from hers, and his eyes seemed to pinion her then with their blue fire and he spoke in a ragged whisper. "You are sure, you are sure that this is what you want? For what you ask of me, I give most willingly, yet I will not accept a look of regret in your eyes, or words of reproach or of anger."

She moistened her lips, amazed that they could have gone so dry so quickly, and startled that they seemed so swollen, so eager, so ready for his slightest touch again . . .

"I am sure of what I want!" she promised.

He carried her across the room, to where the fur still lay atop the mattress, and he laid her there, finding her mouth again, kissing her with a thorough passion that left her breathless and quivering. He rose slightly, his fingers upon the ties of her woolen tunic, and then on the linen of her shift. She felt the brush of his hands on the bare flesh of her midriff as he maneuvered the clothing from her.

"The light!" she whispered. "The candle, it is light—"

"Aye, 'tis light, and I would have it so."

"Aye, 'tis light, and I would not!"

"Would you hide in shadow, Eleanor? What from, me, yourself? No shadows, no darkness, and no pretense."

But he smiled, stretched above her on the strength of his arms, and kissed her lips before moving again. She felt awkward, half-clad, the warm red light of the fire on her nearly naked flesh, the candle glow too telling. But his lips touched hers briefly, harder, and with a searching, a questing, until she felt evermore breathless, and he pushed away from her, rising to cast aside his own clothing. He tossed off the tunic he wore, then struggled with the leather buckles that held the coat of armor in place. She found herself rising; her fingers upon the straps as she aided him. The mail fell to the floor, far heavier than it had appeared on his body. He shed the shirt he wore beneath it, then his boots, and leggings, as she waited on the bed on her knees, eyes lowered, awkward again, uncertain, wishing again for shadow.

She was aware again that the fire cast dancing waves of red and gold upon him. Beautiful, enchanting tongues of fire seemed to cascade over the length and breadth of him. The dance of heat and light caused muscle to ripple and gleam, flesh to glow. He reached for her face, gentle fingers brushed her cheeks, until her eyes came to his. She reached out, a hand upon his chest, tracing the shadow dance cast there by the flicker of flame. She felt the quick contraction of muscle, the sharp intake of his breath. A strange wonder filled her, along with elation and fear. Desire, a sense of excitement within her flesh, body, and soul, took flight; she hesitated, but his hand covered hers, so much larger, darker, massive, it seemed, holding the delicate length of her fingers against him. And she was still so uncertain, wishing she weren't so awkward, a sense of shame still part of the wonder. Yet she knew as well that she had, indeed, wanted this fantasy, that it was magic, and that even the flames rising against the stone of the hearth were aware of the magic, and one with it. She scarcely moved, feeling the rapid pulse of her own heartbeat, fluttering in her chest like the wings of a bird. And she could not help but think, *Whatever was to come, she would have this!*

He cupped her head, cradling it with his free hand. Again, his kiss evoked a liquid fire, not unlike the dancing flames that rose in the hearth, as molten as the flow of a smith's silver. With that kiss, he leaned her back until they were once more stretched upon the fur on the mattress on the rope bed. There, that kiss took flight, like the rays of the sun, spreading out upon her. She felt the liquid silver of his tongue upon her shoulders, her midriff, her breast. Silver became gold, like the apex of a summer's day, the heat touching her flesh, permeating it, bringing the dance of the flames to each of a million points of life. She shivered, trembled, writhed, and when she would cast her head aside, flaming with a moment's remembrance of the modesty she had so fleetly cast aside, she would see his eyes, and something within them made her feel cherished as well. His arms were around her, his hands were upon her flesh, and she felt she belonged there, as she had never belonged anywhere before. He paused a moment, poised above her, when all of her flesh felt part of that fire, when his kiss had traversed the length of her, and she reached out, shivering, for she had been fire, and where he had left her now, she was cold. But still, she touched his face with fascination, the planes of it, and met his eyes, and saw in him his youth, strength, and valor, and she wondered how she could have thought anything other than that he was completely magnificent. He caught her fingers upon his cheek, held them, kissed them, and told her simply, "I could die in you."

She smiled slowly, wonder in her eyes. And then that which had been gentle and soft gave way to passion; the cold was gone, for again, he touched her, hands upon the length of her, tongue upon her breasts, creating wild sweet patterns. She felt the fullness of his sculpted body, the hardness of his aroused sex against her. His hand slid between her thighs, and she waited, on fire, anticipating, but he slid further down the length of her, again laving her belly with the hot wetness of his kiss, lower to her thighs, higher again, directly between her limbs, and it seemed that she all but leaped from her own flesh, for the sensation was so vivid, so shatteringly sweet, outrageously intimate, and compelling that her gasps were those of astonishment. It was as if he had found the very source of the sun, the center, the place from where all dancing flame began, and there, the world began to burn. She instinctively writhed at first to escape such an intimacy to cause such a shocking sensation; then she writhed because she could do nothing else, because the sun was about to explode in the sky . . .

It did so, and a rain of shimmering gold seemed to burst forth from within her, then cascade down upon her, so startling that she was scarcely aware of the fur beneath her, the touch of fur at her back, the world itself. Yet before she could drift from that moment of shimmering light, she felt the sleekness of his flesh against her own, and she gasped anew with sensation as she felt the fullness of his body as he moved into her. There were seconds, perhaps, no more, of a startling, blinding pain, yet he whispered words of assurance, moved with supple finesse, touched her, and the pain fell away, faded into the warmth of the sun, and there was nothing again but a dance of fire, and a mindless desire to be with him, to touch the ripple of muscle, to taste, move, and be one with him, to be held as she was and give what it was that she received.

The moment came; tension gripped him. She felt the great power in the length of him, and again felt a shattering explosion of fire, of the sun, of a golden radiance. The heat of his body seemed to melt into hers, to hold her on a cloud of quivering steel and then fade slowly, slowly, slowly. The fur beneath her tickled her flesh. She had been burning, now she cooled. Candlelight glowed and danced around her, and yet the room was different, as she was different now, and would never be the same. He did not release her easily for though her muscles ached and a haunting inner burning remained deep within her, she was loath for him to leave her by the slightest fraction of distance. His flesh was sleek and damp, touched still by the candlelight and fire, and in his eyes, the dance of the flame continued while he studied her face, her eyes. And she thought that with him as well, something had changed, was different, and he could never go back.

She thought that when he spoke it would be gently; words perhaps of the amazement he had felt. But at last he brushed her cheek with his knuckles and a slow, soft smile curved his lips. "Interesting ending to the evening, my lady."

She caught her breath, heart hammering. "*Interesting*. Well, sir, thank you," she murmured.

His smile deepened. "Interesting, amazing. Astounding."

She knew that she trembled. She did not want to say many of the words that might have fallen from her lips. She had said that she wanted this. She had, with all her heart. She had claimed that she would have no regrets.

Yet she might.

For in all her life, she might not ever have anything so sweet again . . .

"Ah, well, then," she tried to murmur lightly, still far too aware of the naked man atop her, and the intimacy between them, "I thank you again."

He sobered, yet his smile remained, wistful, gentle, as he said, "I thank you, my lady. For I will remember this night until the day I die."

"Before you die," she murmured, "there will surely be scores of lasses, Scots, French, *English,* and one day, the woman you will call wife. I doubt then that you will remember me, the enemy who succumbed far too easily."

"Never too easily, and the enemy by birth and circumstance," he told her.

"You longed for vengeance."

"You nearly killed me."

"In this," she said softly. "Perhaps you have found your greatest vengeance."

She never knew his answer, for there came a hard pounding

on the door. "Brendan! Are you alive? Or has the lady managed to do you in at last?" It was Eric.

"I'm well!" Brendan called back quickly. He stared into her eyes. "She has not skewered me." With a rueful glance, he rose. His back to her, he found his clothing, leaving his mail in a corner of the room. She started to rise. "Nay, if you would sleep, if you would rest, you will not be disturbed." Fully clothed, the warrior again, he told her, "You have not been the prisoner you thought yourself for some time, my lady. And though the fellows who set upon you are friends, and friends of the Scottish cause, there are those about who are in truth lethal between this place and Paris." He swept her a bow. "You are in our company, and we would not allow it otherwise, but I pray that you accept the hospitality here as well."

She clutched the fur to her chest, rising in the bed. "The hospitality here, sir? I am not a prisoner, yet I am not to leave?"

"Ah, well, think of yourself as a ward of the Scottish people, held for your safety, and cherished indeed."

"I remain a prisoner."

"You remain cherished and that is all."

He departed, the door closed, and she was left with no choice but to ponder his words . . .

And tremble at the time gone by.

Chapter 8

"Sire, the Scots have arrived at Calais."

Seated at a table in his great bedchamber, still in his night apparel and enjoying a meal of pheasant and cheese, the king acknowledged the news brought to him by his messenger, Count René Breslieu.

"Ah." It was a different matter, now, the Scots arriving. He had known that Wallace had set sail for France. News carried amazingly fast across the Channel.

Breslieu, a young nobleman endowed with personal charm, agility, a strong sword arm and a very able horse, often served as his messenger, especially in cases such as this. His ears were nearly as sharp as his sword.

"It's all very dramatic, Sire," Breslieu continued, standing at some distance from the table. "Apparently, Eleanor of Clarin was upon the high seas, on her way to meet our own Count

de Lacville, when her ship was seized by the pirate de Longueville.''

Philip almost choked upon a juicy morsel of pheasant. He
nearly rose.

''But a young knight on Wallace's lead ship caught the
pirate; everyone went to arms, and there was a pact signed
between them—''

''What of the Englishmen aboard the ship?'' Philip asked.

''Spared—those who survived the pirate, that being most of
the men. De Longueville has far more often been after human
goods than human lives. The English crew were sent in small
boats back to the coast of England. Wallace will plead a pardon
from you for the pirate, in lieu of his good behavior toward
the lady promised to our own Count de Lacville.''

''Hm,'' the king said, and leaned back, observing his messenger, while he considered the news.

Philip of France was an intelligent man and a fair ruler with
the constant thought that first and foremost in life, he was a
king.

He was also a handsome man, a capable king, and a warrior,
as befitted the times in which he ruled. Comparatively tall, and
blond, he knew that many of his subjects spoke of him as Philip
the Fair, and he liked the description. The term, of course,
referred to his appearance, but he liked to believe that it was
also an assessment of his judgment. He was a careful king, but
he also believed in his heart that he had God-given rights, as
well as responsibilities, and he was deeply religious, though
frequently at odds with the pope. He was a moral man, and
through his wife, Jeanne, he was king of Navarre as well as
France. France was indisputably his domain, and having reigned
now for over sixteen years, he had both confidence in right,
and in his right to determine what that might be.

Despite his attributes, he was aware himself that in many
ways, he did not compare with Edward I of England. Few men

did. Longshanks, as the English monarch was known, was taller than most men, could wield a sword with the finest, and backed down from no man. When he decided to decimate an enemy, he did so with a determination so fierce, little could ever stand in his way. Philip admired him and despised him.

Recently, he had become his brother-in-law.

The game of kings was never an easy one.

Throughout the years, he had fought the English and made pacts with the Scots. He had, in fact, been at war with the English since 1294. Through all the fighting, though, at times, he had made treaties with the enemy.

War was expensive. He was a king known for promoting royal power and containing feudal power, but he was also a king known for alleviating taxation.

The French and the English had fought bitterly over Gascony; so many people had died, so much of the countryside had been ravaged. His men had fought with the Scots; the Scots had fought with his men, including William Wallace and many of the men now in his retinue.

Philip acknowledged Edward for all that he was, but he admired Wallace with a far greater wonder, because the man was a complete enigma. Kings fought for their domains, for their personal aggrandizement. Knights rode off on crusade for the glory of God — and for whatever personal riches they could claim. Barons, earls, counts and dukes fought for power, to hold what was there. Wallace fought simply for a land, and for his people. Defeated in battle at Falkirk, he had come soon after to Paris, and while pleading his case with Philip, had had proved his worth by taking up arms while the fighting in Gascony was still going on fiercely. Wallace and his men were willing to risk their lives in any cause for Scotland.

Sometimes it seemed an incredible waste of valor.

Philip now held Gascony. He had regained it when he gave his sister, Margaret, to Edward for his second wife. The English king, it was said even among his enemies, had adored his first wife, Eleanor of Castile, but having been such a loving husband, and still a king, he had seen fit to wed again. Philip, of course, had weighed all angles. Edward was old — and reckless to a fault. He had lived hard. His new wife would not bear him the heir to the throne, nor could she reign as a dowager queen. She might not be queen of England for long at all. Also, negotiations had begun regarding Philip's own daughter, Isabelle; she would wed Edward's eldest son and heir, and there would be the needed link for the future. Philip's grandchildren would rule England, as they would rule France.

And so, the king of France hadn't given the English king his most beautiful and desirable sister, but rather the younger Margaret. She was sixteen, sweet, charming, and with an admirable integrity for such a young woman. Edward was . . . well, much, much, older. That was one pleasure Philip could take in life; Edward of England might be tall, but he, Philip, was young.

To look at the world was intriguing. Bitter wars fought long and hard could be ended with the stroke of a pen — and a marriage. Indeed, there was no contract so important and strategic as that of a marriage.

For his sister, he had obtained Gascony once again. And signed another treaty.

That was the way of the world.

And still . . .

He would be delighted to entertain Wallace — his brother-in-law's most hated enemy — at his court. No matter what papers he had signed, he hadn't forgotten the man, Wallace, or his service. Besides, *he,* Philip, ruled France, remained King of France.

And this was France.

"Well, sire, what news shall I carry to Calais?"

"De Longueville spent his pirating days attacking Englishmen, I have heard," Philip said.

Breslieu cleared his throat. "Aye, Sire. I believe he took a number of Spaniards as well, but did seem to hold regard for those vessels bearing flags of his own nationality."

"I assume then, that a pardon might be arranged."

"And as to the Scots?"

Philip pushed back from the table and rose. "They are welcome at my court. Indeed, we must assure Count de Lacville that his bride will soon arrive safely to our care. And . . ." He hesitated. "The abdicated king of the Scots, John Balliol, resides so near. We must make him welcome, also." There was contempt in his voice. When Edward of England had first begun setting a vise around Scotland, most learned men of the day had agreed that John Balliol should rightly inherit the Scottish throne. The claimants to the throne had come down to the descendants of the sisters of King David, and he was the descendant of the eldest sister. But a poorer choice among the nobility could not be found. Balliol was not a bad man, just a weak one. His first attempt at power had been ruthlessly crushed by Edward. He had abdicated and been banished to Rome, under papal care. Now, he was living in France, and doing so happily. Men fought in his name, but Balliol was far happier an outcast in France than a king in Scotland. He hadn't the stomach for the job. He hadn't the valor and integrity of a Wallace — or the cunning of a Bruce.

"We will be delighted to see our good friend William Wallace, we will pardon the pirate when the petition is made, and we will reward the young hothead follower of Wallace who rescued the betrothed bride of our good servant Alain de Lacville, and see that all are reunited."

Breslieu bowed low to him. "Sire, as you command."

Philip seated himself again as Breslieu departed. He smiled slowly and reached for the wine. A good wine, though a young wine—a very young wine—from the estate granted to the exiled king of Scots.

He hoped that Edward heard of this meeting. He'd be angry, of course. But what was a king to do? Philip thought mockingly. After all, the Scots were returning an English noblewoman to him, to the arms of her rightful French betrothed. All kings negotiated upon necessity. Edward must understand.

Yes, he must understand.

And still, he'd be furious.

Philip started to laugh out loud. Aye, Edward would be angry. He might just have an apoplexy.

Eleanor's captors, whom she had assumed to be the worst manner of thieves, harlots, and brigands, were not.

The following morning, the statuesque Hélène tapped gently at Eleanor's door. "Countess, you are awake?"

She was only halfway so. She shrank beneath the fur, but Hélène did not enter the room. "M'lady, we must watch out for your safety, of course, but I thought you might like to see some of Calais."

"Pardon?"

Hélène laughed. "Word has gone out to the king of your arrival; we believe an escort will be sent. We, cannot trust you alone—there are too many cutthroats about—but with an escort, I thought you might enjoy a walk."

"Aye, yes, yes! But I need to wash and dress—"

"Of course. I'll bring fresh water. And your trunks will be brought as well."

She heard Hélène's footsteps receding, and she lay back for a long moment, thinking about what she had done. It had seemed . . . something she desperately wanted. And rightfully so, because she knew what her life would be: She meant to be a good wife to Alain, and bring prosperity to Clarin, and be the young woman of compassion and integrity her father's child should be. Her life was preordained. She, of course, loathed the Scots who had slaughtered so many people in their vengeance! But still . . .

Something in her ached terribly this morning. Ached and reveled. She could remember his every touch, the sound of his voice, his whisper, the feel of his lips, his flesh . . . aye, his flesh, taut, smooth, the feel of muscle beneath, the heat, the stunning heat . . .

She had wanted to know, and she had wanted a memory, and she had wanted, just for a brief moment, *him*. But what she had done was to create a lifetime of torture for herself, for aye, she had a memory, and it would haunt her, and she would never forget.

"Water!" Hélène called as the door opened, and she brought in a large ewer and bowl. "I'll give you time," she said pleasantly. She smiled at Eleanor. "Your trunks arrive behind me."

Eleanor sank deeper within the fur as youths she had not seen before lugged in her heavy trunks, then departed with Hélène. The door closed behind them softly as they left.

Eleanor rose quickly, shivering as cool air touched her naked flesh. She trembled as she washed and dressed, for it seemed he somehow remained with her, and as she splashed her face with cool water, she realized that she wanted him now with a great urgency; there was an agony in her soul unlike anything she had ever imagined. With a greater fervor, she washed herself, and reminded herself of the brutal truth. He was an outlaw without a real home, an enemy of her king, one of them — the hated Scots. He would spend his silly life following after Wallace — and having his head removed with his hero as well, most probably! She was a woman with great responsibilities, and that was the brutal truth in life. And a greater truth was that they had nothing in common, despised one another's loyalties, and were not just nations apart, but worlds apart. She really didn't like him at all; he had played a terrible trick on her, and they had all laughed at her, and she . . .

Had thrown herself at him.

She straightened. Pride, she assured herself, must somehow come to her salvation. This was not a casual game she played. Word had gone out to Philip — a king. She was betrothed to a French nobleman. Lives could be at stake.

There was a tap at her door again. "Lady Eleanor?"

"I am ready."

As ready as she could be. She had chosen a simple blue tunic, a soft gray underdress, and warm hose. She eschewed any of her fur trimmed cloaks for a simple Flemish wool. She was glad, when Hélène opened the door, to see that her escort was dressed similarly. "Come then, we're to the baker and the market."

Anne-Marie was waiting at the foot of the stairs. She seemed friendly and rueful, though not apologetic as they left the house.

"The ruse was not my idea, of course," she assured Lady Eleanor promptly. "But, la, Brendan was angry that you would have so little faith in the Scots getting you to Paris!"

"One has to look out for oneself in this wretched world," Hélène said. "Lady Eleanor was right to seek her own freedom."

Anne-Marie gasped as if Hélène had said something horrible. But Hélène defended herself. "Look at the many terrible things which have happened to women in the wars with *Edward!*" She spat out the name. She looked at Eleanor. "Wallace's woman was murdered in her own home for refusing to tell what she did not know. And he has never been the same since."

"Aye, he's wreaked vengeance everywhere," Eleanor murmured.

"They have all become bitter and cruel," Hélène agreed. The house seemed some distance from the town, but she moved quickly, and Eleanor found that she was hard-pressed to keep up with her. Anne-Marie was accustomed to the pace, and she continued Hélène's explanation.

"Which is why Brendan was so angry with you. He said that you had foolishly risked your life time and time again against men who meant to get you where you wished to go."

"So what is right?" Hélène persisted. "How was Lady Eleanor to be certain?"

"Diving from a ship to the docks of Calais could have landed you in the hands of stupid men who would not know your worth, and who might have killed you for the gold in your skirts alone," Anne-Marie said. "And if you had been left to de Longueville alone . . ."

"Anne-Marie!" Hélène said. "We were told—"

"Aye, look to the harbor. "A cold day, but a beautiful one. Look at the sun shining on the masts—"

Eleanor came to a halt, causing the other women to do so as well.

"What about de Longueville?" Eleanor demanded. "He is a pirate; he seized ships, but I believe now that he is no cold-blooded murderer, but a man to ask ransom for those he captures."

"Usually, of course," Hélène said. "Come along; we'll not have the best choice at the fish market. It is a beautiful city, our Calais. A big city, but you'll not see so much from here—we are near the docks, the outskirts, but look! We go down the slope, and it will not be easy to see, but the city is a lively place! So many goods hawked along the streets," Anne-Marie told her.

"If we get going," Hélène said impatiently. She started off briskly. They had reached an alley fringed by shuttered houses. Eleanor followed, determined that eventually she'd have her answers. But the other two women were moving very quickly, and for the moment, it was fascinating to be in the narrow streets. It was a large city, houses abutting one another, some very old, some new. Children played, kicking stones in an alley. Housewives threw open their shutters, shouting, ''Attendez! L'eau!'' She backed against a wall as a stout woman cast out the morning's wash water—and the morning's waste—with a haphazard throw.

''Watch! Watch! They are quick and careless along here!'' she cried.

A baker passed, his goods balanced in a straw basket on his head. A donkey cart carried a tinker with his various needles and scissors and sewing goods. The street was busy, and dirty, and boisterous, but it felt good to be out, and to see the town, and all that went on with such industry.

On a street corner, a vendor peddled what he hawked as ''bonjour vin.'' He saw them approaching and advised, ''Ah, ladies, gentle, light, and sweet, a taste of the grape to just quench and soothe the palate!''

Anne-Marie decided that she must have a taste, and they stopped, drinking from wooden cups. ''Be she the countess?'' Eleanor heard the little man whisper to Anne-Marie.

''Aye, so she be, and watch your tongue!'' Anne-Marie advised.

''You're taking the lady to be Alain de Lacville's wife to the fish market, and I should watch my tongue!'' the fellow demanded with laughter.

''You should watch it, else Wallace should slit it!'' Hélène warned.

The fellow backed away, but a moment later, as they left him, she heard tones strummed on a lute, and the soft sounds of a ballad.

Seized by a pirate, to be a fine prize, upon the Arab plain,
Seized by a Scot, to be a fine prize, against an English king,
But a Frenchman is to be the saint,
The one to end the ring,

Ah, the beautiful lady of Clarin, alas,
Shall face but the pain of betrayal again.

Eleanor stopped walking and stared at both of the other women.

"Come, come, my lady," Hélène said. "The little jackanapes is right—we shouldn't really have brought you out. You're a countess, far superior to such a jaunt as this—"

"What is it that everyone knows and no one tells me!" she demanded.

"Nothing!" Anne-Marie denied quickly.

"Nothing that we can see," Hélène amended, seeing Eleanor's eyes. "You must ask Brendan, or Wallace. Or de Longueville himself."

She turned, and Eleanor knew that was the end of it for the moment, but the joy had gone out of the morning. They purchased bread, fish and even flowers, all to be brought to the house, and they returned, Hélène and Anne-Marie still speaking lightly. "Am I allowed to ask this," Eleanor said as they approached the wild and overgrown expanse leading to the house, "How have you come to know the Scots, and isn't it dangerous, perhaps, with the French king's sister now wed to the English king?"

Hélène laughed. "Well, for one, I am not French at all."

"Scottish?" Eleanor asked.

"A little. Mostly Norse."

"And I," Anne-Marie said, "have a French mother, and a Scottish father."

"And even Jacques!" Hélène said. "His father is a Frenchman, and his mother kin to Douglas of Scotland."

"A fine warrior," Anne-Marie commented.

"Aye, and that's true," Hélène said.

"So . . ."

"The French may have signed a treaty with England, but

believe me, the alliances with Scotland over the years have been deep and binding.''

''And here, in Calais . . . what do you do?'' Eleanor asked, surprised to feel her face flushing.

''She thinks that we are really . . .'' Anne-Marie began.

''Prostitutes!'' Hélène said.

They both went into gales of laughter.

''It would be the appearance you have given!'' Eleanor said tartly.

''But, of course!'' Anne-Marie said. ''We are not prostitutes. We are . . . messengers. We stay on the coast, we watch the comings and goings of others, we keep our ears open.''

''You are spies?'' she inquired.

''Messengers,'' Anne-Marie repeated firmly.

''And more, perhaps,'' Hélène said quietly. ''We are all interwoven, you see. Friends and relatives—who do not care for Edward I, the tryant of England. He has his right to be king—of England. He destroyed the Welsh, obliterating his enemies. It is what he intends to do to the Scots. While he also reneges on the French. We are all loyal to a man who fights for simple freedom. Our place at the moment is here, and that is all.''

''Are you related to Eric?'' Eleanor asked her.

She smiled. ''Eric is Brendan's cousin. The Graham family and the Norse have had ties for many, many years. And yes, I am related to Eric, though not to Brendan. Eric has long been an adventurer, yet loyal to Brendan's cause, and Brendan has said that no man in the world has the integrity of William Wallace, and no matter what battles are lost, the English will not have the wild northern and western isles that remain either heavily Norse, or under Viking domain. And aye, simply in the lands that once belonged to Picts, or those that were ruled by Moray before his death soon after the Battle of Stirling, freedom is not forgotten.''

"Freedom," Eleanor told her, "is often only a word—"

"Aye. Because you're not at all free, are you?"

"I was seized by a pirate and handed over to men who are my enemies—"

"I don't mean that at all, and you know it," Hélène told her. She sighed. "Forgive me; you are a countess, and about to marry a man admired here in France, a man known for his valor and integrity as well. But you are not free. You are not free of your family, and you are not free of your king, and you will do as you must and live out your life in your English prison, no matter how great the power of your king. Again, my lady, I beg your forgiveness."

For a moment, she just stared at Hélène, wanting to argue, knowing she had all the right words and protestations, but unable to find them. "It is not that I am not free," she said at last. "I am responsible to the country of my birth, and to people of my small part of that country. They have suffered heavily in this war we have waged with the Scots, and most of them are innocent of any wrongdoing against anyone. They seek livelihoods, a way to feed their children, to live, and so much has been decimated—"

"And you will marry the Count de Lacville, and your people will live happily ever after," Hélène murmured.

"I have chosen to marry the count," she said quietly.

Anne-Marie let out a loud sniff at last. "Ah, yes! In lieu of a monster, so it is said!"

"You really don't begin to understand—" Eleanor protested again.

"We understand perfectly," Hélène said. "You are very noble, and very rich, and if you don't make such an advantageous match, then Longshanks will step in and take the matter from the hands of your family—such as they are!"

"There you go, hinting again!" Eleanor said. "Tell me—"

"Countess! I am freezing!" Anne-Marie interrupted. "We must get back in the house."

"You must tell me—"

"You must ask Brendan."

"Look, please! I don't understand—"

Hélène interrupted with a deep sigh. "You must ask Brendan."

"I shall."

She hurried on into the house ahead of them, walking straight to her room.

He should have stayed away. Brendan knew it. The king's messenger, Count Breslieu, was arriving soon with a welcome and an escort from Philip. They had all known that news of their arrival would reach Paris quickly; today Wallace had sent a personal message to the king. All was in good order: despite the current "peace" the French were enjoying with the English, Philip would prove his independence at any given chance. He was not Edward's lackey.

He should have stayed away.

He could not change the situation.

Nor could he stay away.

When he arrived, Anne-Maried advised him that Eleanor was in her room. He walked up the stairs, saw the closed door, and considered knocking. He tapped lightly in warning, but did not wait for her to bid him to enter. He opened the door, closing it behind him.

She stood by the window, magnificant in soft blue. She had worn no wimples, veils, or headdress of any kind since her arrival, and she did not do so now. The sun in the rectangle of the window cast a glow upon her and the bound length of her hair down her back seemed in glory. Her features were defined, regal, beautiful. His breath caught in his throat; for all the strength in his muscles, they trembled. What had one night done, he wondered bleakly, to a warrior, an outlaw, and a commoner?

She knew he was there. She did not turn to him. He walked to where she stood by the window.

He didn't touch her.

"I warned you: no regrets," he said, and the words were far more harsh than he had intended.

She lookcd at him at last, her eyes grave. "I have none."

"The king is aware — "

"I know."

"So you are safe; you will soon be where you meant to be when you started out across the sea."

"Yes, I know."

"Thank God. I had thought you were contemplating the possibilities of flying out the window."

A small smile touched her lips. "No." Then she turned to face him squarely. "No regrets. But I am weary of whatever it is that your people whisper about behind my back."

He stepped away from her, walking to the hearth with a pretense of warming his hands at the blaze.

"If you don't wish to talk to me, sir, you are welcome to depart."

His back, to her, stiffened. Ah, yes, there she was — the countess. The noble lady, the tone of voice, the absolute expectation.

He turned back to her.

"My lady, don't use such a tone with me."

"I have suffered much at your hands. My tone is of little consequence."

"You've suffered?" he inquired.

She had the grace to blush, but she did not look away.

"I have every intention of talking to you. And to Count de Lacville."

"What?" she said sharply, and he was certain that the breath was caught in her lungs, that a certain fear crossed her eyes.

"De Longueville was paid in Liverpool to go after your ship. Specifically."

"I beg your pardon?"

"I held such information from you when I deemed that it might be exaggerated, or even a lie. But since you will marry de Lacville and return to Clarin, you must be aware of the dangers you face."

"Sir—"

"You have enemies, my lady."

"You are saying that someone paid de Longueville to come after me? To what end?"

"Your disappearance."

"That is a bald-faced lie!"

"De Longueville had no reason to lie."

"If I have enemies, sir, they are the Scots. The people who slaughtered innocents on hereditary estates, and those against whom I took up arms."

"De Longueville had no reason to lie."

"De Longueville is a rogue and a pirate—"

"Out for gain, my lady, not murder."

"Oh? And did he intend to murder me?" she inquired scathingly.

"No. He probably wasn't sure of his intent. Being a pirate—and a businessman—he would have considered his situation and realized that he would make much more by delivering you to Alain de Lacville and receiving payment from both ends. Then again, a good pirate knows how to sail many seas. You might have spent your days in the company of Moslem infidels. A woman with such coloring as yours is a prized treasure among many a good harem."

She stared at him incredulously, then walked to the door, opening it. "Go, Sir Brendan."

He leaned against the hearth, crossing his arms over his chest. "You asked for the truth. I have given it to you. You are in danger from your own people."

She shook her head. "No. You don't understand. While I remained at home, *unwed,* I was the least threat to anyone in my family! If I die childless, the property reverts—"

"We both know that when the situation came to the king's attention, he would have found a husband for you. Again, a countess with hereditary lands ... still young, in her child-bearing years, not just retaining all her teeth but an ethereal beauty as well ... Edward is no fool. He would have pondered long and hard and chosen for you, had he not approved a marriage to the very rich Frenchman de Lacville!"

She still stood staring at him, fiercely angry. "My cousins are not just good men, strong knights for the king's service, but they are men of honor and integrity as well."

"Is this argument for me, or yourself?" he inquired.

"It is no argument. I state fact."

"As I have done."

"Will you please get out?"

He walked from the hearth to her at last. Closer. He could breathe her in. He was almost touching her. Not quite. She flattened against the wall. The door remained open.

Staring down at her, listening to the ragged intake of her breath and all but certain that he could hear the pounding of her heart, he closed the door.

She stared into his eyes.

"I will warn Count Alain de Lacville, of course."

"He will laugh at you."

"Will he?"

"He knows my family."

"He is an intelligent man."

"You have mocked him for being old."

"He is old—but intelligent."

She lowered her lashes, then her head. He caught her chin with his forefinger, drawing her eyes back to his.

"We haven't much time."

"You are a liar. A liar, a trickster, a monster—a Scot."

"The last, most definitely."

"You are the most horrid and despicable man I have ever met."

Her breath was coming faster.

"I do apologize for that," he said. "We are what we are, and none of what I am could I change, would I change."

"I—you . . ."

"And none of what you are would I change in any way, my lady, for you are a simple taste of beauty, and perfection."

"I still hate you. Absolutely. Completely. You are a monster. A Scot."

"You have made the words synonymous."

"And so they are."

"Such might be, and has been, said of the English."

"I loathe you."

"Shall I really leave?"

"No."

"Because it is my turn, you see. I want tonight. I want you. I will remain a Scot. An outlaw. A monster. But Paris is close. Too close. So tonight . . ."

He lowered his head. Found her lips. They were sweet, tasting of soft mint. Warm, wet, seductive. He was a fool. No matter. Might as well burn in hell for this as well as his other sins. He cradled her chin, tasting her lips first, savoring the breath of sweetness, then ravaging her mouth with the evocative weapon of his tongue, hungering to the depths of his soul. He could not drink enough of her to fill himself. He was intoxicated by the scent, the feel, the taste. His fingers feathered over her neck; his lips followed them there. Her clothing seemed the greatest barrier, a bastion like a stone wall, and he fumbled with the multitude of ties that held her tunic at her side. The gown she wore beneath was laced at the back and he swore inwardly, praying that he didn't push too hard as he twirled her about, fumbling again with linen ties that seemed hopelessly entangled in the length of her hair. Seconds seemed like eons, but the ties were freed, and she was again in his arms, and she rose on her toes to meet him this time, the length of her pressed hard against him, the fullness of her breasts and anguish of seduction against his chest, her hips against his groin, creating an eruption of hunger, raw longing, anticipation. His fingers stroked the sleek nakedness of her back, entangled into the unbound web of her hair. His kiss seared her lips again, her throat, the hollow there, fixed upon the firmness of her breast, focusing upon the hardened peak of her nipple, drawing, sucking, tasting, until she cast her head back, crying out.

He lifted her then; set her upon the bed, his eyes never leaving hers. He would not forget this. For she stared up at him with no inhibition, leaned up as he caught each of her fine shoes and cast them aside, then looked away at last, showing her ankles, her calves, and then the soft inner flesh of her thighs as he drew away the finely knitted hose she wore. He looked at her then, and her eyes met his, and her heart seemed to flutter like a bird's. He pressed his advantage, parting her thighs, burying himself within her intimately, with strokes of the tongue that teased and seduced, drawing her forth, giving no quarter and no mercy, until she called his name. His name. He rose atop her, barely able to deal with the closures of his own apparel, and not at all able to pull it all from himself and cast it aside. He was within her, moving with a speed he fought to control, obsessed, desperate, longing to be forever where he was, gloved within the woman, yet all too aware that his own seduction of her had sent him spiraling toward a fierce and violent climax. He struggled; he fought. To have more, to give more. But she came with him. Flew where he flew. Touched the raw earth, sweated, panted, writhed. And again . . . cried out.

He gritted his teeth, jackknifed his body. Erupted. The relief that filled his body was blinding, the warmth engulfing. He'd known his share of women—such was a warrior's fate, and perhaps his reward. And sometimes, his death. He'd known women. None like this. Men would rut where men would rut, so was the philosophy, often, of those on the run. Like food, sustenance, breathing. All were alike in the dark.

But not her. Not this woman he would return to, a moral, ethical, noble, and ancient noble at that, but one he admired, and worse. Liked.

He fell by her side, but not away from her. Never away, when the time ticked so quickly by. She breathed deeply, breasts rising and falling quickly, flesh damp and glimmering in the glow of firelight. She turned into him, burrowing against his chest. "Perhaps I don't hate you. Just who you are, and what you stand for."

He stroked her hair. "You can hate a man for standing for freedom?" he asked her quietly.

"Why do you think that the king's men are not free? Why don't you do as many a Scotsman has done; swear allegiance to Edward, serve him, receive his benefits as Englishmen do—"

His hand froze, then his fingers threaded into her hair, forcing her face upward, that he might meet her eyes. "Because I am not an Englishman."

"But half of your country—"

"My country is afraid."

"I'm so afraid that you will die!" she whispered, and he lost the spiral of anger that had been building within him, and he realized he held her hair too tightly.

"So shall we all," he said.

"But—"

"How can you have seen what you have in these days gone by, talked with Wallace, a man willing to risk far more than death, *for nothing but freedom,* and not understand?"

"As you have said, one man's freedom is not another's. I saw what was done to my people. I smelled the horrid, pathetic scent of human flesh — roasting. What, sir, have you to say to that?"

"I was not there. Nor was Wallace. To condemn any people for the cruelty wrought in a war of defense — "

"You would do so!"

He clenched his teeth, aware that she rose over him, stared down at him, eyes luminous, hair a fan over her breasts that was far more a tease than a shield.

"I would have peace for the moment."

"But — "

"Even France and England have called a truce!" He rolled her over suddenly. "Are you capable of peace?"

"Of course. But — "

"Are you capable of quiet?" he demanded.

Before she could answer, he halted her comments with the fierce pressure of his lips, the assault of his tongue. Soft, muffled sounds escaped her. He lifted himself from her.

"Well, not exactly quiet!" she told him.

"Your mouth — "

"Can be occupied in other ways!" she assured him.

And then she showed him.

Oh . . .

She showed him.

The soft flick of her tongue was a liquid aphrodisiac, saturating his flesh, rendering his muscle to tar, then to steel. She moved over him, moved ever so slightly hesitant, then bolder, and bolder. She teased with her lips and tongue, her touch, the stroke of her hair. Here, there . . . still, teasing, until the blood in him threatened to boil. She teased. He prayed. She settled down lower; her sudden aggression rang a hoarse cry from his lips. He thanked God for the simple moments in life. He forgot there was a God.

Then he lost what control he had, reaching her, lifting her, bringing her down upon him . . .

Thundering into the night. There was no thought then. Not until later, much later. And then his thought was, *God, I cannot bear this*. But the reply could not change. *God, I must*.

And curled against him, later still, she whispered, ''You know that I do not hate you, nor do I even hate Wallace. But you are still my enemy.''

Enemy, monster, outlaw, Scot.

He rolled her back to him. ''Not tonight, my lady. Not tonight.''

She opened her mouth.

But for once . . .

She did not argue.

Chapter 9

With Hélène supervising, the servants had created a veritable feast. Though it was winter, there were preserved vegetables. There were many kinds of fish, dried meats, wines. Theirs was a simple house on the outskirts of the city by the docks, but when they chose, they could create a meal to vie with that of the greatest manor.

Eleanor had not yet come down. Brendan sat at the table between William and Eric, unaware that he had been brooding until Eric elbowed him roughly. "Brendan. More wine?"

"Aye, that I will," he responded, smiling at Hélène who had been waiting for his reply. More wine was poured into his cup. Then he realized that William was watching him, and had probably been doing so for some time.

"The escort comes tomorrow," William said.

"I am aware of that."

"Are you? Do you remember that we are outlaws?"

Brendan tried not to scowl. "I am aware of that as well."

"Are you?"

"Indisputably."

Wallace watched him still. "We face swords and arrows and therein great danger, but that is to the flesh. I would not see you hurt, lost within your soul."

"Hurt?" he inquired, staring hard at Wallace in return. He shook his head. "I am aware that I am a commoner, knighted on the field of battle, but a commoner still. An outlaw in the eyes of the English king. And I never forget the cause, William."

"Really?" William said, smiling slightly. "I do at times. I think of how I would love a home, land to till, children to watch, scold, train, raise into manhood. Sometimes . . . sometimes I want life more than any quest."

"You could have all those things. You are welcome here; Philip would gladly give you land and a house. The Norse king would just as gladly welcome you there and give you land—"

"But they could not give me a home, for their land is not my land," William said. "And the children I would raise would not have the father I would wish to be."

"You said—"

"I said that I am human. I have lost a woman I loved with all my heart, but there are still times now when I see a certain face, hear the softness of a woman's voice, and think of what might have been. The moments come—and the moments pass. That's not to say a man should not accept anything from life. Or that I will not marry again. But you, young friend, have strayed into dangerous territory."

Brendan lifted his wine, and leaned close to Wallace. "It is you who said that the prisoner was mine."

"Aye. But then, she is no longer our prisoner, is she?"

"I am aware of that."

"By tomorrow, perhaps, we will ride for Paris."

"And that is tomorrow, isn't it?"

Wallace studied him gravely, then agreed with a shrug. "Aye. That is tomorrow."

Eleanor chose that moment to come down. She was elegant in soft ochre and gold, a gown with long flowing sleeves. She moved with grace and fluidity, but despite her noble bearing, there was an easy smile on her lips when Hélène greeted her at the foot of the stairs, and when she entered the hall, he was surprised to see that she even had a pleasant nod for Wallace as he rose to greet her.

"My lady," he said, bowing to her.

"Sir William," she returned, politely inclining her head as well. He moved his hand with a flourish, inviting her to sit.

"You're aware that an escort is coming, and that we'll be traveling to Paris."

"I am."

"Then you'll be pleased to realize that you need make no more deadly attempts to escape our company."

"Aye."

"The accommodations may not have been what you are accustomed to, but this house is our best offering."

She smiled. "Sir William, are you afraid of what I might say to the king?"

"My lady, I'm afraid of the day that I may be torn limb from limb, and meet my maker. But as to what you choose to say . . . that is entirely your own concern."

Her smile deepened. "You mean that, don't you?"

"Indeed."

She raised the cup before her. "To you, sir. I shall be sorry on that day when they do tear you limb from limb."

Wallace laughed, seeming to feel it was his turn. "You mean that, don't you?" he inquired.

"Indeed, Sir William, I do."

At that moment, composed, serene, so regal, she slipped. Her eyes moved down the table, and touched Brendan's. He was startled by the sudden depth of pain in them. And the innocence, the loss, the vulnerability.

What you perceive as such! he reminded himself.

Yet he smiled, slowly, returning her gaze. Wallace's words haunted him. *Hurt to the soul.* He did wish to give up his prisoner.

"My lady!" Margot, who had been seated at the side of Eric, rose, smiling with pleasure to see Eleanor again. Eleanor rose again as well. The two left the table to come together, meeting with an embrace.

"So you are part of this treachery!" Eleanor scolded.

"Only in that I feared you intended to jump from the ship, and gave warning," Margot told her. "When I knew that you were safe in our keeping. And all is well, is it not? Aye, Brendan decided on something of a trick, but . . . you could have gotten yourself into grave danger!"

"That from a woman who sails with the worst of the brigands!" Jacques said cheerfully.

"Margot, Lady Eleanor, I beg you, don't forget the meal!" Hélène chided. "My lady, you must sample the fish. Onward to Paris, mind you! You'll taste eels, fish, and birds, but they'll taste no finer than what we serve here. And our wine is the sweetest!"

"Of that, I've no doubt," Eleanor murmured, as she smiled ruefully to Margot, and sat back down. She graciously thanked Hélène as the tall blond woman served her.

There was talk about the food, which they all admired, and Wallace said that he wished he had Hélène along on many a lonely trek. But then the tone grew serious as Jacques cleared his throat.

"There has been further talk that Robert Bruce will indeed

sign himself to King Edward.'' He sat at the far end of the table and spoke unhappily.

''It's been expected,'' Wallace said.

''It remains a blow,'' Eric stated.

''Too often his behavior becomes a blow,'' Brendan said. ''I don't think there will be any surprises. Still, there will surely be more information when we reach Paris.''

''John Balliol will come to court, William,'' Jacques stated.

''That, too, is to be expected,'' William said.

''How long do we fight for a man with no stomach to manage his own throne? We don't even ask him to seize it! It's our necks we risk,'' Eric demanded.

''It's his own he risks if he returns,'' Wallace said.

''So we fight for a figurehead,'' Brendan murmured. ''And freedom—of course.''

''The nobles will one day rise. I know it,'' Wallace assured them. ''I swear it; the day will come. But I hadn't imagined to engage in such conversation this evening. We mustn't allow the countess to leave us believing that we are true savages, nothing on our minds but war. Jacques have you the lute?''

''Aye, that I do.''

''Play us a tune.''

Jacques rose, found the instrument, and handled it tenderly. A moment later, he strummed a melody, and the sounds of it were soft and sweet and poignant. Jacques had a fine voice, and he sang the ballad to go with it. It was an ancient ballad, about a maiden left behind, and a dying warrior, his blood enriching the earth and the legend and the myth of the land, and all that was to come. It was very beautiful, but when Jacques had ended, he looked up, and they were all still.

Brendan leaned foward. ''Mon ami, that is beautiful. Too beautiful, perhaps, for the moment. Do you know something . . .''

''More cheerful,'' Eric burst in.

He rose from the table, grabbing Margot's hand. "A dance, my fair beauty?"

"Indeed, my fine sir!" Margot agreed, laughing.

The two rose to the floor. The tune was fast, wild, light. Eric and Margot followed a very courtly manner of dancing for perhaps two minutes, but then they were spinning and laughing.

"A pity we've no pipes!" Wallace said, then he turned to Eleanor. "My lady, dare I make the suggestion that . . ."

Eleanor rose. "Only, sir, if you can teach me that step."

"It's from a May Day dance in our wild highlands, my lady, where they still believe in the spirits of the earth, and I shall do my very best to show you."

Brendan watched them, sipping his wine, still somewhat amazed. Enemies. They were still enemies. No matter what had gone on between them, she had made that clear. Yet she danced now with *Wallace*. He shook his head, wishing he were not so obsessed with watching her, the way she laughed, the way her hair fell, the sparkle of amusement in her eyes.

"Sir Brendan?"

Hélène held a hand out to him. He joined her. And on the floor, they danced, yet, when Jacques started up again, Brendan found that they had changed partners, and that Eleanor's hands were in his, and he was meeting her eyes himself. They moved around the floor, and she seemed to know the steps exactly, and she told him at one point, "It is a lovely dance."

"From a lovely country. You can't imagine the colors of the highlands, the cairns, the mountains, the rises, falls, lochs, the beauty."

"No, perhaps I cannot, for I've never seen it."

"The islands in the west are glorious, rugged, with the sea spray wild against them, and the water itself blue and gray and ever changing."

"And red," she said softly.

"Red?"

"Drenched in the blood of outlaws," she murmured, and pulled away from him, returning to the table, apparently for more wine.

The evening wore on. He wasn't sure exactly when she slipped away, or when Eric and Margot departed, and the others seemed to slip quietly from the hall. He remained alone with Wallace, and they watched the embers in the dying fire, and Wallace reminded him, "The escort comes tomorrow."

"Aye."

"Would you waste what time you have?"

And so he rose, walked up the stairs, and came to her room.

There, he paused, and braced both hands against the door. He was a madman.

Would you waste what time you have? Wallace had asked.

And he wondered, would she be awaiting him?

The night was so still. The fire did not even crackle. The flames waved and danced, red and gold, but made not the slightest sound.

And so she could hear her heart, beating within her chest, pounding. Each rise of her breath seemed like a gust of chill winter wind, and she prayed for the blaze to warm her. She didn't want to leave. The room had become a haven, because *he* came to it, and as long as she lived, she would not forget the way this fire burned, the colors it cast upon the wall, upon him, the sheen it created of crimson upon his flesh, and the contours of his body.

She waited.

She had laughed, she had learned the dance, she had whirled to the music of the lute. Wallace had spoken of the pipes, and she had yearned to hear the music. And in her heart, she thought, she was a traitor, for these people had brought death and destruction; yet she had come to realize that they too had died, and bled, and that they bled for a cause in which they believed, against a king she had believed she had honored, did honor, would honor. She closed her eyes and tried to remember the horror at Clarin when the Scots had come, but against her lids she saw only the dance of the flame, and remembered only the glow and warmth, and her heart beat harder.

She waited . . .

And at last, the door opened, and in the darkness of the night and the dance of the flame, he was there. She sat up, letting the covers fall, and saw only the silhouette of the man, there in the door. She knew his height, his stance, and breadth of his shoulders. He stayed a moment, and she thought that he watched her, against the dance of the flame, and seeing her, he would know that she waited, for she wore nothing but the drape of her hair over her breasts, and even at his distance, he must hear the pounding of her heart. Aye, he would know that she waited . . .

Would he know that she had prayed?

At last he left the door, and it closed in his wake. And she would have risen to meet him, except that too quickly, he was with her.

She was in his arms.

And she prayed that the flame could dance forever.

He woke to the first faint streaks of light in the eastern sky. She slept still.

Embers burned softly in the hearth, but the morning had come. And yet he lingered. She lay entangled with him, limbs entwined, hair soft, warm, and sweet against his chest. He barely moved, but savored the haunting scent of her hair and flesh, the feel of her, the sleekness of her form. There was the faintest tap upon the door; it opened a bare crack. " 'Tis dawn," came a deep, softly spoken voice, and he realized that Eric had kept vigil for him.

She would marry her count; she had never wavered from that vow. And he was sworn to a cause he had no right to threaten, yet if he were willing to cast all ethics and morals aside along with the dream, he would avail himself nothing, for she was sworn to her course, and had no intent to alter from it. Yet in the dawn he was tempted to seize her, demand that she give up her count and her land, and swear that it was nothing, that she must cast it all aside, and run with him, and fight with him, aye, fight . . .

The English. Her people.

His fingers trembled. He touched her hair and pressed his lips against her shoulder. He held there, simply breathing. Touching her. Each muscle within him knotted and groaned; he gritted his teeth as if he were cut by steel. And still he held. Breathing. As if he could breathe her in, and hold her somehow within him . . .

But he could not.

Then he rose, and dressed, and paused just one more moment, pulling linen sheets and fur around her. Once again, he touched the softness of her hair, and thought that she needed no cast of flame to make it burn with a golden splendor.

He turned then, and forced himself not to look back.

He left the room, closing the door behind him, and feeling the soft sound as if it were the whir of a headsman's axe.

In the hall, Eric waited.

"We ride to greet the escort," he said.

He nodded. "So we do."

Count Breslieu was a pleasant sort, gallant as he greeted Eleanor, charming, but not flirtatious. He was eger to hear about her well-being, yet concerned that they should depart. He was traveling with two of the king's knights, and two ladies to serve her should she need any assistance.

She informed him she was quite well, and that she had no desire to ride in a conveyance, but would much prefer her own horse, as she was eager to see the countryside. That could be arranged.

They left Calais with a fairly large party: the French escort party of five; Wallace, riding with a group of six of his men, Brendan and Eric among them; the pirate, le Longueville, Margot, and Hélène. There were also the five servants to see to the baggage wagons. Her maid, Bridie — whom, God forgive her, she had almost forgotten — would be awaiting her in Paris. She was grateful, of course, but she wondered if Bridie would know her still, she had changed so much in so little time. Or had she? No, the changes were on the inside. But today . . .

He had left her simply that morning; not a word, not a good-bye, not a prayer for the future. He rode ahead at first, conversing intently with Wallace and Breslieu. Margot and Hélène flanked her, staying at her side. Hélène pointed out many of the beauties of the countryside as they rode.

They stopped for the night at St. Omer, where they were warmly welcomed by the brothers at the seventh-century monastery.

The following day dawned bright and clear and, after morning prayers and a light repast, saw them to Arras. Eleanor, with Margot and Hélène at her side, paid a visit to the local weavers, where she couldn't help but purchase a beautiful *milles fleurs,* a fitting gift for Alain.

After a restful night at a local inn, they continued to Amiens. Before they left the city the next morning, Breslieu said that they should stop at the cathedral of Notre Dame, and pray for a continued safe journey, and for the futures of Scotland and France.

It was a beautiful place, still under construction, yet the nave and altar were fine, with great arches and ceilings that might have touched the sky. A priest was awakened for mass, and when she knelt at the altar, she realized that Brendan was beside her. She dipped her head low over her hands, trying to remember that she was in God's house.

"Praying that you will be a good and loyal wife?"

She looked to her side, expecting humor and mockery, but Brendan's eyes were grave.

"Perhaps. I should be. And you, sir? Are you praying that you might smite all Englishmen and win freedom for Scotland?"

"No, my lady," he said simply. "I am praying to forget you."

He rose, and left the altar, and she was left to bow her head again, fighting the sudden sting of tears that came to her eyes. She remained kneeling there, unaware of the passage of time until she felt a hand on her shoulder.

Breslieu.

"Forgive me, my lady. The king would greatly admire your piety, but it is time to ride. We will ride without careless haste, yet with a moderate rate, and will bring you safely to Paris and Count de Lacville by the morrow."

She rose as bidden. Her head still bowed, she followed him from the church, and allowed him to help her to mount.

The countryside was beautiful. She tried to see it, to enjoy it, to respond when Hélène or Breslieu made a point of showing her the landscape, bare as it might be, with winter still upon them.

Brendan did not keep any special distance. At times, he rode with Breslieu; at times it seemed he was in deep conversation with Wallace.

At times, he was behind her.

They reached Beauvais with the darkness, and Eleanor discovered that their accommodations had been planned.

She was given the finest room at the manor of the Count

Clavant, at court himself at present, and yet, glad to be the absent host for their party. A meal had been prepared ahead of time, but at this table, she was the only woman present; Margot, Hélène, and the other two women sent from court to serve her would eat elsewhere. Only Breslieu, Wallace, Eric, and Brendan were at the table with her, and it was only after several glasses of wine that Breslieu himself, though previously cordial and charming, seemed to let down a bit of his guard. Each time he spoke of affairs, however, he apologized to Eleanor.

"Sir William, you do have your balls, sir! Oh, do forgive me, my lady. To come upon the French shore — with a French pirate. I tell you, the king's hatred of old Edward — do forgive me, my lady — assures his safety, and of course, your previous service to our king, assures your own, as always. Why, he'd be delighted to give you a spit of land and set you at the head of his armies — "

"And I am delighted to have such a great king's confidence," Wallace interrupted.

"Well, with warriors such as yours . . . ah, Brendan! Remember, we rode in Gascony together, when you followed William here, soon after Falkirk. Sweet Jesu, but I don't remember such a fighter elsewhere! You hacked your way through a score of English knights that day, my fine fellow!"

"It was a fierce battle," Brendan said tightly.

"Oh, I am sorry, my lady!" Breslieu exclaimed to Eleanor. "With your beauty, I keep thinking of you as French!"

"A strange compliment, count, but I thank you," she murmured.

Breslieu looked at Eleanor, assessing what he saw, then asking with a sudden hint of anger. "The pirate did not harm you in any way?"

She smiled pleasantly, lifting her glass. "We barely spoke. I was not harmed."

"Ah, and then you had these lusty fellows seizing the pirate! There's rumor, though, that you didn't trust a Scot, my lady. Did you really dive overboard — in winter?"

"Twice," Brendan answered for her.

She didn't look his way. "Where I come from, sir, it is easy to mistrust the Scots."

"Ah . . . well, you're among Frenchmen now, eh?"

"Aye, among Frenchmen," she murmured.

"So, my lady," he teased, "did you find the Scotsmen to be evil?"

"Only when they plucked me from the sea," she returned lightly.

"Twice!" Breslieu said, and laughed, shaking his head. "My lady, of course, rumor precedes you, but you do supersede it admirably."

"Again, thank you."

"Though not all men are glad for such a willful bride."

"Would they rather a senseless twit without the reason or intelligence to fight back?" Brendan demanded suddenly.

Breslieu looked quickly to him. "Not I! But then, how good this is to see. For my lady, you led troops at the battle of Falkirk, I heard, when so many Scots were so bitterly defeated."

"I did not lead troops; I was among them."

"A sign of God's beauty, grace, and justice!" Breslieu said.

She did not reply. The table was silent. Breslieu cleared his throat.

"Well, here you are, you see it, a truce among enemies."

She looked up at last, eager to see Brendan's eyes. He was watching her, as she had expected. She lifted her glass. "A truce."

"I admit, my lady, to a trace of envy," Breslieu said. "My friend Alain, Count de Lacville, is a very lucky man."

"Aye, that he is," Wallace said firmly.

She felt the strangest chill around her heart.

*   *   *

The French ladies, Mademoiselles Genot and Braille, were sent to attend her as she prepared for bed; she waited for them to leave, despite the fact that she was no longer in the care of the Scots. She was among Frenchmen, as Breslieu had told her. Brendan would not come to her in this manor. And yet she prayed that he would. He mustn't, she thought; it would be suicide. Yet, tomorrow, they would arrive in Paris, and God knew what awaited them there. If they were found out, Breslieu must, for French honor, challenge him, and Wallace would defend Brendan, and there could be a fight, would be a fight, and the ideals of a people, of a nation, would be compromised. No, she must pray that he did not come.

The ladies cared for her clothing, brushed her hair, readied the room. They chatted a bit, but were careful as well, not spreading gossip, lest she repeat it. She was an unknown to them, as they were to her.

She could barely sit as her hair was brushed.

And yet, when they were done, she remained at the table, staring at her reflection, and wondering bleakly what she had done to them both.

He would not come. Could not come.

Yet moments later, she was startled by a sound at the windows, and going there, she discovered that there was a balcony.

Brendan had just grasped the long nose of a protective griffin, using the stonework to crawl over the ornamented stone wall. She threw open the mullioned windows just as he appeared. He was kilted this evening, nothing but a linen shirt beneath, with the wool plaid fastened over his shoulder. He leaned against the corner of the stone balcony wall.

"I decided against the stairs," he told her.

"Most certainly, a wise choice," she told him gravely. "And a foolish choice."

"We've not yet reached Paris."

They stood in the moonlight still. That, too, was foolish.

"No, we've not yet reached Paris," she agreed. He lifted his hand; she took it, and quickly retreated into the room.

She did not sleep that night. The hours were far too precious. She lay beside him, running a finger down his chest. "Remember a time, aboard the ship, when you said that I was pathetic at best?"

"Ah, well, you were very ill then. I did say you might improve."

"And now you've risked a balcony for a night—"

"You did improve."

"I am worth a risk."

"A thousand risks. Yet I must take care. You always knew your own value."

"It is not so great."

"You underestimate yourself."

"I believe you thought once that I far overestimated my own value."

"Ah, well. We Scots are known for taking risks."

"For Scotland."

"We have no choice."

"Neither do I," she said softly. "Neither do I. And once I marry—"

"You will be a good wife."

"Yes. I have no choice."

"But you do, you know. You could run with a Scottish outlaw."

"Run with you?" she said softly.

"The accommodations are sparce. Sometimes the shelter of an oak. In wind, in rain, in snow. There are the occasional castles; the north country holds hard to old ways, and Edward does not venture so far."

"And the warring barons change their minds with the wind,

signing treaties one day, taking up arms the next. And you fight for a puppet king — ''

''For Scotland — ''

''You could go to Edward and beg his forgiveness. It is said that the only man to whom he will not offer life for loyalty is Wallace.''

''I have been with Wallace far too long ever to accept the English king's promise of justice. And I am not a man to change his loyalty with the wind.''

''But . . .''

''If I swear my loyalty, my lady, it is for life.''

She traced the fine strong features of his face, wondering for a moment if there wasn't a way that she could run . . . with an outlaw. She wondered if he meant his invitation, but he could not. For they were in France, and she was sworn to a famed, if aging, French knight. He would risk everything they had come to achieve.

''I will never, ever, forget you, Brendan.''

Perhaps he did not mock her then, for he touched her cheeks and found them damp. ''I will never let you forget me,'' he said. And he took her into his arms, and they used what was left of the night. When morning's first light arrived, she begged him to hurry. She watched him turn the length of his plaid into a cloak, preparing to descend into what remained of the darkness. Then she held fast to him once again.

''Brendan . . .''

He went down upon a knee, taking her hand. ''My lady, know that I do swear my loyalty to you, that if you are in danger, I will come to you.''

''Brendan,'' she murmured breathlessly, drawing him up, ''you mustn't say such things. I will go to England. To ever come to me would be such a risk — ''

''We are fond of risks.''

''For Scotland, we have both agreed.''

"Scotland is worth a risk. And so, my lady, are you."

She clung to him once again, then lowered her head, shaking. "I will marry Alain. I must, and I will."

He lifted her chin, studied her eyes, kissed her lips. Long, carefully, lingeringly. She closed her eyes, and prayed the world would stand still.

It did not.

When she opened her eyes, he was gone.

Chapter 10

The ride to Paris had seemed long and cold. Brendan spent the day with Eric and Wallace; Margot and Hélène were by Eleanor's side, and from time to time, Breslieu rode back to her place in the party, inquired as to her welfare, and seemed to watch her suspiciously.

She was exhausted, and miserable, and she hoped it would be better when they reached the city — when they were parted, when she no longer had to watch him ride, and *know* that they would be parted.

Still, at long last, when they reached the outskirts of the city and then the bridge leading to the Île de la Cité, she had to admit that Paris was beautiful, and that there was a grandeur to the island in the middle of the Seine. There were buildings, fine and stalwart. The Cathedral of Notre Dame de Paris rose from the mist upon the water in noble magnificence.

Then, slowly, she became aware that Brendan had been riding

behind her, and he edged his horse up to ride by her side. "I remember being so overawed when I came here. This magnificence, set so in the water . . . I hadn't traveled far until then. Not that I don't believe in our own beauty. We have ancient abbeys, too, with cathedrals, castles . . . and of course, a great deal of rough, wild landscape as well."

"The cathedral is magnificent," she told him smiling. "But . . . it is no finer than our Westminster Abbey."

"Southwark does not compare to this," he told her.

"You've seen Southwark?"

"Aye." He gazed at her, smiling. "But you've not seen such great places close to your own home. In the borders, you'll find the greatest treasures. We've the abbeys of Jedburgh, Kelso, Melrose, and Dryburgh. They rise with incredible grace from a countryside filled with soft fields, high hills, wild, desolate moors, with the North Sea to the side, and the sky above. They are grand, my lady, as fine as any, and no warfare or ruin can take from them the beauty of what they are. I've seen your England. Aye, great places such as the castle at York, the tower in London."

"Well, there, sir, you'll see my point. The great tower in London is spectacular. And King Edward has ordered very handsome castles — "

"Strong castles — to keep the Welsh from ever reclaiming Wales, to reinforce the troops he sends out to all corners of the island to subdue a land that does not belong to him, to enslave a people who do not owe him homage."

She couldn't help but feel a surge of loyalty, a determination to defend her homeland. But when she looked at him, she saw that his eyes carried a gray cast to match the darkness of his mood. She lost the desire to argue. Especially when he offered her a wry, weary smile, and said, "England and Scotland are both quite beautiful. Admit that is a grand cathedral, striking and beautiful, as fine as we—either of us—have seen," he said softly, his gaze touching on her.

She smiled. "It is a grand cathedral," she said. "As fine as either of us has ever seen."

"You'll probably be married there, my lady," he said, spurring his horse, and moving on.

Before they reached King Philip's palace, another escort arrived to meet them. Eleanor was startled when she realized that Alain de Lacville was among the men riding to bring them to the palace. Their party came to a halt. He rode forward.

Alain rode well. For all his years, he sat straight in the saddle, tall and proud. His features, though deeply grooved, were fine and lean. His eyes were deep set, dark brown, and he had a full head of wavy silver hair. He was dressed in his heraldic colors, and a squire rode behind him, carrying his banner. He met Breslieu, Wallace, Brendan, and Eric, at the lead of the party, and she saw that he smiled, and welcomed all of them warmly, listening to something Wallace said, then looking at Brendan, and embracing him once again, before taking his hand in a firm clasp. Then he moved on, coming to her horse. He gallantly bowed to her, and took her hands, searching her face, as if he feared for her health.

"My dear, sweet Eleanor! Welcome, my lady, you fall under my most devoted protection here. I pray that you are well."

"Exceedingly," she said softly. Her heart seemed to catch in her throat. He would marry her to rescue her. She had spoken of the time when they reached Paris; but she had been betraying him all along. And yet . . .

She ached. She loved Alain. A good, dear friend.

She was in love with Brendan, and that love would haunt her all her life.

"It's been a long journey for you. A very long journey. Come. There will be warmth and sustenance at the palace, where you will stay, until our wedding."

And so the party rode again, to the palace. Grooms and servants were everywhere to assist them.

"You'll have time in your quarters, my dear, and then you'll meet the king," Alain told her, escorting her.

She turned back, looking for Brendan. She couldn't see him in the bustle of activity in the yard.

"Eleanor? Is there something you need, someone . . ."

"No, no. I'm fine."

The ladies trailed behind him as he led her into the palace. It was magnificent as well. High arches, gleaming stone entries, tapestries of embroidered Sicilian silk. As they moved through a long hall and up a single flight of steps, Eleanor realized the importance Alain must hold with the French king. They reached a grand set of double doors, and Alain pushed them open. The chamber was spacious. A large bed was set on a dais covered in silk. The hearth extended half the length of the wall. There was an elegant mirror above a chest, a curtained antechamber, and windows that looked out on an inner courtyard.

"Rest, my dear," Alain told her. He lifted her chin, studying her eyes. "My poor child. Your father . . . well, he had different plans for you. I was so sorry to hear of his death. And you! The chances you have taken, dear, dear, child. Please remember, I am your friend, have been your friend. I would not hurt you for the world."

She touched his face. "I would not hurt you, sir." *She had already done so!* she thought. *Even if he never knew.* But God, he could not know how in hurting him, she had scarred her own soul.

"My lady, oh, my lady, Eleanor!"

Bridie suddenly came bursting in from the antechamber. With no ceremony, she threw her arms around Eleanor.

"Bridie!" Eleanor said, and hugged her in return.

"Oh, I was so afraid for you, so very, very afraid! But then, I must say, upon the ship where they kept me, the Scotsmen were the kindest of captors, polite, and courteous, to a maid such as myself! And I tell you, of course, I did give them all a piece of my mind, as soon as I ceased to be terrified for my life. Why even that rogue pirate was a decent fellow, and I had thought . . . oh, I had thought all manner of things . . .''

''Which might have occurred, if it hadn't been for young Graham,'' Alain said, interrupting Bridie. ''Such dangers at sea . . . and I had feared only rough waters. Ah, well, you're here now, and that is what matters.''

''That is what matters,'' Eleanor repeated.

''Oh, my lady—'' Bridie began again.

''I will leave you to rest and refresh, and return in a few hours time to bring you to the king,'' Alain said, interrupting quickly.

He kissed her forehead, and departed.

The door closed. ''Oh! Eleanor, to have you in my sight again,'' Bridie went on. ''Will you forgive me if I admit that even Wallace was a decent man? You cannot imagine the languages he knows, and how charming he can be—oh, forgive me, but he did quiz me about Clarin, and he told me that such actions were not his. Oh, not that he did not admit to brutality! But he claims never to have ravaged a town in a manner to slaughter women and children and innocents, and oh! He did lock men in a barn to burn, but they were soldiers sent to trap him, but he was warned of the trap . . . and oh, dear, you look exhausted; we'll summon a bath, a very hot bath, with steaming water to ease your sore bones . . .''

''That will be lovely, Bridie.''

''You are well? The scoundrels didn't hurt you?''

''I am amazingly well.''

''Oh, my lady, I have to tell you. There was a seaman, a young fellow named Lars. He's a Douglas, though, Norse mother, Scottish father, and he . . . well, he took my breath quite away. I was almost sorry to come to Paris, to part . . . do you think he is here now, that he rode in with Wallace?''

''Perhaps, there were a few in the party I did not know well. Yes, I think one might have been Lars,'' Eleanor said, amused, and loving Bridie, and grateful to see her, but so very exhausted and heart-weary.

''I shall send for the bath.''

''Please.''

''The water will soothe you.''

Nothing will ever soothe me! she thought.

King Philip, for all his beliefs in his God-given rights, did not make them wait. Brendan had thought they would adjourn to their quarters, but the king was ready to see them straight upon their arrival, so he and Eric joined Wallace as they entered the king's private council chamber. They were all clad in their highland garb, no mail worn beneath tunics or tabards, just their swords at their sides and their knives at their calves. They approached Philip with the courtesy due a king, but he quickly bade them rise, and greeted them in an affectionate manner, immediately calling for wine and sustenance, and sitting with them at a table before the great fire that burned in the room. He was a striking man, tall, with an appearance of being slender, yet there was substance to him, and he knew the art of warfare. He was interested in events in Scotland, and listened as Wallace spoke, assuring Philip that the Scottish spirit never broke, despite the fact that his army had been decimated at Falkirk.

Philip, in turn, explained his current position, his latest treaty with Edward. Naturally, under such circumstances, he couldn't offer troops. They were, of course, always welcome at his court, he'd naturally arranged a meeting with John Balliol, or ''King John,'' as the guardians of Scotland continued to refer to him, and if he could offer supplies or comfort in any way, he was pleased to do so. Brendan watched as Philip spoke, and thought again that all the world played the game in the most expedient way; Philip spoke in excellent terms, but gave them nothing. He thought that this voyage had been in vain, that they had been better off waging their forest wars against the supply wagons of the English in Scotland. In the midst of winter, most of the roads to the north were all but impassable, and whatever English goods passed through the lowlands were usually ripe for the taking.

"You've done me great service, as usual," Philip told them. "It is to my greatest sorrow that I cannot do more. Now, as to the pirate Thomas de Longueville . . ."

Despite whatever disappointments Wallace must be feeling, he leaned forward as he spoke in defense of the pirate. "De Longueville is a French loyalist at heart, your Grace. He has spent his years upon the sea in pursuit of your enemies. He wearies, however, of the status of a thief of the sea, and humbly asks your pardon."

"I'm assuming he is ready to share his largesse with his liege?" Philip inquired.

"Indubitably," Wallace assured him.

"And what of the greatest prize aboard the pirate ship?" Philip demanded. "As you are aware, Count Alain de Lacville is one of my most trusted advisers, and a knight without whom many a past campaign would have failed."

"He never would have brought harm to the lass," Wallace assured the king. At that, Brendan lowered his head, remembering all that de Longueville had told them. Would he have realized the importance of Count De Lacville and sought a greater reward from him? Or might Eleanor have disappeared?

Philip stared straight at him then. "You are the man who seized the pirate ship?"

"Aye."

"What is your assessment of de Longueville?"

"An interesting fellow."

"Would he have harmed the Lady Eleanor?"

Brendan weighed his answer. "He has taken down many an English ship. One does not do so without a measure of violence. I saw his manner of battle, and he would kill in a fight, aye, but I'm sure he had no intention of taking a sword to the lady."

"That's not what I meant."

"I believe that his desire to most humbly beg your pardon is sincere. As to what a man might have done . . . Sire, I am in no position to say."

"Thank God, then, that you took the lady into your care."

"Aye, thank God," Eric murmured solemnly, but his irony was not lost on Brendan.

"He has taken and hidden many great prizes throughout the years, and he is willing to give these all to your greater glory," Wallace said.

"And to my coffers, emptied by warfare?" Philip inquired wryly.

"Precisely," Brendan said.

Wallace lifted his hands. "We all know that war is costly."

"I will take the matter of de Longueville into deep thought, but he seems a worthy man to receive forgiveness from his king. You must be weary. Take your leisure for the night. Tomorrow evening, we will celebrate the betrothal of de Lacville and his lady. You will, of course, attend?"

"Naturally," Wallace said.

"Your Grace," Brendan said, leaning forward quickly before they were dismissed, "I would have a word with Count de Lacville, if I may."

"He is eternally grateful, owing a debt of gratitude to the lady's father, as well, I believe," the king said. "He intends to thank you—"

"It isn't his thanks I seek—"

"I'm sure he intends a magnificent reward—"

"Nor a reward—"

"We will take a reward," Wallace interrupted sternly.

"Warfare is expensive," Eric reminded politely.

"I simply crave a word with him."

"You'll find him in the knights' hall, the blue chamber," Philip advised, "for whatever matter lies between you."

"Aye," Wallace said, eyeing him sternly, grinding his teeth.

"Do you care to divulge what affair this is?"

"I fear for the lady, that is all, your Grace," Brendan said. He thought that Wallace audibly sighed, and he wondered if his mentor hadn't been afraid that he had gone entirely mad, and meant to bare his heart and soul to the lady's would-be husband. "The pirate swears he was paid in the port of Liverpool to find the lady, and see that she did not reach France, nor return to England."

"The English! Ever devious," Philip said, relishing the evil of his enemies. "But do you think it's true?"

"If so, I fear the danger."

"I ask again, would the pirate have harmed her?" Philip demanded.

"Your Grace, the pirate is a businessman. I believe he willingly pocketed the money paid him, with the full intent to simply ask de Lacville for an even greater ransom."

"Good business is not a sin," Philip murmured, "while the English . . . Go, and tell my friend de Lacville of this, and warn him he must guard his lady most carefully."

"*That* is, indeed, my intent," Brendan said.

Alain de Lacville was a man Brendan both liked and admired. They had first met on the field of battle, when he had arrived with Wallace, following the loss at Falkirk. William, despite his passionate belief that one day the people *and* the nobles of Scotland would rise in union against the English, was a realist.

Realizing his army was lost, he had immediately turned to ancient allies for support. In France, there had been no better way to cultivate the good will of the French king than to take up arms with him against the English.

De Lacville had been leading French troops as they stormed a fortification. Brendan had seen a weakness in a wall, and the French count had been more than willing to listen to the plans of others. Brendan had led a surge against the weak point, and they had prevailed. He and de Lacville had gained an instant recognition of one another at that time. He felt a fondness for the old knight, injured a dozen times over, loyal, courteous, pious, and never lacking in courage. His quest to warn de Lacville of the danger Eleanor did not accept as very real was important to him, yet as well, he was earnest to see the man.

To assure himself that de Lacville's age and injuries would keep him from being a husband as well? he queried himself as he traversed the halls of the palace. Aye, that as well. He had been a fool. He had known from the beginning the ultimate end of this relationship. The burning he felt now was an anguish he had brought upon himself. There was no other way for this to finish. If he were to attempt to abduct the lady, he'd be quickly arrested and most probably beheaded. He would destroy his own people, destroy Wallace, everything they had fought for, died for. He had vowed himself that he would never cease to fight — until Scotland was free.

Nor did he have the right, for Eleanor's own cause was determined. She meant to marry de Lacville; she was a countess, and strongly passionate for her own land. He had no right to interfere with her desire to uphold her betrothal, and live the life of a noblewoman in her home — ravaged by his people.

De Lacville was stepping from his room as Brendan arrived, but the old man was quick to greet him with an embrace and words of gratitude.

"I am in your debt, and of course, sir, plan to make what

earthly compensation I can!'' de Lacville told him, encouraging him to enter, and join him for wine from his own estates. Brendan did so politely, sipping the wine, but he was beginning to get a headache; he longed for a long swallow of cool ale from his homeland.

''What compensation you would make, sir, is not necessary, but I have been informed by my fellow outlawed and impoverished Scots that on behalf of my country, I am to accept it.''

''It will be given in the best spirit,'' de Lacville assured him.

The count's apartment at the palace was rich. Tapestried, warm, with a great hearth of stone and marble, and a long window, covered now, but which must look out on the great cathedral of Notre Dame de Paris. The coverings on the bed were fine, embroidered with infinite detail. He looked away.

''I didn't come here for reward, sir — ''

''You would not do so.''

''Thank you for that assessment of my character, sir, but apparently, we are all willing to accept a price for our goals. But I have come because I think you should speak with the pirate, Thomas de Longueville, after he has made his peace with King Philip.''

''Oh?'' The sharpness of his tone suggested that he was suspicious of the pirate — and ready to do battle with the rogue if he had harmed Eleanor.

''No, Alain, it is nothing evil he has done. But he came to us with a story about being accosted in Liverpool before he sailed.''

''Thomas de Longueville was in Liverpool?''

''Sir, Longshanks might be a king with a wicked sword against his enemies, but no ruler is so great as to wipe out the bands of sea-raiders. There are many places at such a port where a man pays his way, and no questions are asked. Aye, it's easy enough for any pirate with means to find a good tavern in Liverpool.''

"Go on."

"He was approached by someone who paid him to seek out Lady Eleanor's ship, to abduct her, and see that she didn't return to England."

"He's certain?"

"So he says."

De Lacville shook his head. "The man to benefit from her disappearance would be her cousin, Alfred of Clarin. But he is the man who first approached me, since he had sworn to my lady's father to see her safely wed." He cleared his throat. "I would not have been my own first choice for Eleanor—I was an old man when I first held her upon my lap when she was a babe. But I know her, and the situation, and in honor of her father, I am delighted to give whatever aid, shelter, and strength I can offer to the lady."

"She is a beautiful woman, sir, loyal to you," Brendan heard himself say. She was loyal, and fierce in de Lacville's defense.

"You have done us both a great service," de Lacville said.

Brendan lowered his head, not quite able to meet the man's eyes.

"If I am ever of service to you, it is I who am grateful," he said, managing to look up.

"I promise you that I will return to England with the lady, and I will use all my resources to discover what evil may be afoot."

"Then I will rest assured that she is safe in your care, sir."

"Naturally."

Eleanor met only briefly with the king of France that day, and she well understood the description "Philip the Fair." He was a handsome man. She met him in family chambers with his wife, Jeanne, and his children, and she was introduced to the young Isabelle, who was betrothed to the king of England's son and would one day be queen of England. Also present were Louis, who would be king after his father, and young Philip and Charles, his brothers.

Queen Jeanne was kind, making Eleanor welcome, and telling her what esteem Count de Lacville received from them all. She was also intrigued to hear about the high seas adventures, curious about Thomas de Longueville, and concerned, because, apparently someone had informed the king about the pirate's story that someone had paid for her capture.

"Apparently Brendan . . . Sir Brendan . . . believes that my family must be guilty. He is mistaken. They were eager for my marriage and my happiness. I'm afraid that what they fail to realize is that I'm considered something of a pariah to their people—I was at Falkirk. A figurehead, imagined to be far more than I am. But there is a hatred that runs deep between the two peoples, and I think it not unlikely that a Scotsman with means—perhaps the relative of a fallen hero at Falkirk— would gladly see my demise."

"That's possible, of course," Jeanne mused.

"It is the only answer."

"Yet, Scots rescued you from the sea."

Eleanor hesitated. "Wars create faceless enemies. We hate a people we don't know. Then, of course, we discover that men and women are universal, and that it is easy to hate a faceless name, and not so easy to despise individuals. It's true as well that the Scots were happy to rescue me, for the ransom de Longueville would have demanded became a reward the Scots could claim."

"Such is the world, my dear," the queen told her. "But all is happy now. You are here, Count de Lacville is here, and the marriage will take place quickly, so that none can doubt that you stand with a wealthy and powerful baron, and cannot be taken lightly."

"Of course."

She spent that evening dining alone with Alain. He had ordered a meal in her rooms at the palace. She tried to be casual, to speak about France, her enjoyment of the country, the kindness of the people.

He seemed quiet, watching her.

"You are eager for this marriage, my dear?" he asked her. Her heart skipped a beat. "Yes."

"I had a visitor today."

"Oh?"

"Brendan."

"Ah, yes."

"He is a fine young man."

"Yes, so it seems. For an enemy."

"He remains your enemy?"

"He is a Scotsman. Clarin was ravaged. Men were burned to death."

"At his command?"

"No."

"Do you know what the English have done as well? At Berwick, where the king himself was present, he only stopped the slaughter when a woman bore a child as she was being slain."

She set down her fork, no longer having an appetite. Alain seemed not to notice. He was watching her.

"He has a great fondness for you," he said.

"He has a great fondness for Scotland."

"Aye, that's true. But what of you, my dear?"

She feared the telltale rush of blood to her features, and wondered for a moment what Brendan might have said to him. But then, she knew that Brendan would have said nothing, made no admissions; the choice to make a confession would be her own.

"He is a Scot."

"It's all that simple?" Alain queried gently.

"Yes."

He sat back in his own chair, watching her. "I am very old, you know."

"I believe you are the same age as King Edward, who has recently taken a sixteen-year-old bride, sister to the king of France."

He smiled. "I am the same age. But not, I'm afraid, in as sound a condition."

"Please don't say that."

"I am only warning you, my lady, that I am not such a . . . prize."

"To me, you are. You are kind, intelligent, giving . . ."

He leaned forward. "Not so giving as you might expect."

She fell silent, uneasy, but then he smiled. "In a few hours, we'll say our vows. When that occurs, I will accept nothing less than your complete loyalty."

She nodded, and reached for her chalice, needing a sip of wine. "I intend to give nothing less."

"My lady, you will never have a real bridegroom."

"I don't . . ."

"Understand? No, of course not. I am not just old, Eleanor, but ravished by poxes. I bear up well in public, and this, of course, is a secret you will take to your grave. I am incapable of being a true husband."

He paused for a moment, watching her. She was appalled by the joy she felt in her own heart. She had meant to be the best wife to him she could be, but she had abhorred the idea of being with him. Not because it was he, she realized. She simply wanted to be with no one else other than . . .

Her enemy.

"At best," Alain continued, "I will have a few years to give you. But I hope in that time I will give you what you need; the means to rebuild your Clarin, to take control, to choose, at a later date, the husband you will take in the future."

She sat very still, and shook her head. "You're telling me . . ."

"I haven't long to live. My doctors have assured me."

She shook her head. "You mustn't die. You are far too dear a man."

"You mean that, don't you?"

"With all my heart."

He rose and came around to her. She protested as he cracked his way down to one knee, but he would do so at her side. "I will cherish every minute of having you as my wife."

"I swear, sir . . ."

"You needn't swear to me. I believe that you are in love with him."

She was amazed at the tears that sprang to her eyes. "I . . . no, I . . . couldn't — "

"No. You couldn't, and mustn't. Not now. He will ride with Wallace, and God knows, eventually, he might well have his fool head removed from those broad young shoulders. But I do not begrudge what you might have shared, my dear. Despite my infirmities, I am a proud man, and I will not be made a fool or a cuckold, but until you say your vows, my lady, you are guilty of no sin against me. Do you understand?"

She touched his silver hair. "I would never hurt you."

"I know that you would not. Neither, lady, would I cause you any pain I could avoid for you. But for the time . . ."

"Sir, everything I do, I do with my eyes wide open, with all intentions of being your wife, your countess, and lady of Clarin."

"I know, Eleanor. I know that. Now, help an old man back to his feet. I'm for my own bedroom, my lady."

When he was gone, Bridie came in, chattering away. She talked about how noble and wonderful the count was, and how glad she was that Eleanor had reached Paris safely. She was so talkative, she didn't notice that Eleanor had little to say in reply.

"And to think!" Bridie said, crossing her slender chest. "I had thought we were dead upon the high seas!"

She laid out Eleanor's nightclothes, and brushed her hair.

"Is there anything else, my lady?"

"I'm fine, Bridie. Tired."

"Then, I'll leave you, of course."

Bridie slipped away, closing the door to the antechamber. Eleanor stretched out on the soft bed and fine sheets.

She lay awake.

A few minutes later, she thought she heard the soft opening and closing of a door.

Her heart quickened. She sat up. It had not been her door to open. She realized that Bridie had opened the door from the antechamber to the hall.

Bridie . . .

Bridie was slipping out to meet the lover she had met aboard the pirate ship.

Eleanor lay back down.

In the elegance and splendor of the palace, she lay awake.

And alone.

Chapter 11

They were housed in a building just beyond the palace, and it was there that John Balliol came to see Wallace.

Wallace gravely gave Balliol an account of what was happening in Scotland.

"All was lost with Falkirk," Balliol told them. He was a slim man, his face not old, but showing the strain the years had taken.

"All was not lost at Falkirk!" Wallace said angrily.

Brendan gritted his teeth, wishing that Wallace could see more clearly that they fought a losing battle here, one far more fatal than Falkirk.

He stood, striding to stand between Wallace and Balliol. "Sire, you do not see the spirit that lies behind the people —"

"I see the greed and corruption of the clans, and the lowlanders who are more English than Scottish, ready to bend their knees to Edward," Balliol said. "I see Comyn and Bruce, ready to claim the throne, ready to kill to achieve it. I see those who ride for the Scots one minute, then take flight in the same battle to fight on the other side, eager for Edward's rewards!''

"Jesus, Mary, and Joseph!" Wallace swore, "no great prize is won without a fight!''

"Perhaps, once . . ." Balliol said. "Sir William, you had the people. But they were decimated at Falkirk. The barons refuse to follow you—''

"But there are men, aye, nobles among them, who do fight the English, who set against them from Scottish castles, who rob them blind. The dream remains, John. You must have the stomach to achieve it!''

Balliol lowered his head. "I subjugated myself to Edward. I have abdicated the throne. I have kept my head upon my shoulders.''

Wallace gripped the arms of Balliol's chair, staring into his face. "I remain willing to set mine upon the block. Come back to Scotland.''

Balliol was silent. Brendan noted the fine cut of his clothing, the style of his boots. Balliol had been humiliated before his people, he had been paraded through the streets. But when exiled in Italy, he had been shown courtesy. Here, he was living in great comfort.

He was not coming back to Scotland.

"I cannot come back now," Balliol said at last. Brendan gripped Wallace's shoulders, holding him as Balliol rose. "Secure freedom, sir, and I will gladly rule. What good a king would I be, headless?''

Eric, who had sat by the fire and had not moved, answered that question. "A martyr, sire. And the people would rise in your name!''

Balliol stared furiously at Eric, then spun around. He left the room. Wallace's hands were knotted into fists.

"If I die, turn to Bruce," he said.

"I heard yesterday that Bruce has married, and signed his peace with Edward."

"It is a peace that will not last."

"Bruce is a turnabout!" Brendan reminded him.

"Aye. But he isn't a shrinking, sniveling coward!" Wallace said angrily, and he walked away, leaving their chambers.

Brendan watched him go, thinking he should follow. But Eric had risen at last. "Let him go. He's right."

"Who is right? Balliol? Or Wallace?" Brendan demanded bitterly.

"They're both right. But John Balliol is a weakling, and a coward. And Bruce is a turnabout, but by God, he has courage."

"Something has died within this room," Brendan said, clenching his teeth.

Eric shook his head. "Balliol—as far as Wallace is concerned. But not the dream, Brendan. The dream stays alive."

"Aye, the dream, the cause, Scotland!" Brendan was startled by the bitterness in his own voice.

"Think of the men who have died for it."

He closed his eyes, summoning to his mind the battle of Falkirk, the screams of the dying, the carnage, the blood. John Graham, dying, reminding him . . .

They had to fight. They had to fight until freedom was won. And if they did not, then all their loved ones had died in vain.

"Aye, we'll keep fighting," he said. "No matter what the cost." He followed Wallace out. The city of Paris teemed around him. Workers with wagons of materials headed for the site of the cathedral, still creating that masterpiece of white stone that glinted in the sun.

He closed his eyes. The winter air was good. It didn't smell of human waste today, but of fresh baking bread. Children laughed in the street.

He needed to leave Paris. The dream was fading here.

Each time now that he remembered Falkirk, he remembered the pain, the anguish, the sounds, the screams.

Yet . . .

He saw her face as well.

Aye, they needed to leave Paris.

The king had ordered a magnificent banquet.

The hall was beautifully furnished, the servings were as rich as Hélène had told Eleanor they would be at court.

A full boar with an apple in its mouth, and festoons upon its tusks, was in the center of the head table. Pheasants appeared ready to take flight. Wine was served in ornamented carafes resembling birds and animals.

Jugglers performed in the center of the hall, hounds barked now and then, wagging their great tails as a scrap was thrown their way. The king and queen sat at the head table, surrounded by the greater nobility, followed by the lesser nobility, followed by the king's knights, the poets, the court physicians, and the scholars and artists. Music played throughout the meal, jesters amused, acrobats twisted their bodies in impossible ways.

Eleanor didn't know if the food was good as well as beautifully served; she could only push morsels around on her plate, aware that Brendan sat with the Scots farther down from the center of importance, where she sat with Alain. She pretended to eat, she drank wine, she clapped at the entertainment, chatted with those around her.

When the floor was cleared, the king stepped out with the queen, and danced to the music of his fine players. He beckoned others to follow, and Breslieu, on the other side of Eleanor, asked Alain's permission to lead her to the floor. The dance sent partners changing, meeting, changing. She was so startled to meet Brendan in the middle that her breath caught in her throat, and she did not realize she was not breathing until instinct caused her to gulp in a rush of air. Their hands met; he bowed gravely. "My lady."

Then he was gone, until the music brought them back together again.

"All is well?" he inquired.

"Very well. And you, sir?"

"I am eager to return home."

"As am I."

"I had thought you would be concerned for your nuptials."

"Yes, that as well."

He was grave that night, and strikingly handsome, hair black in the glow of the flambeaux set in the walls, eyes seeming as dark as well. He was freshly shaven and wore a fine tunic with his Graham colors woven into the ochre garment. He moved very well, as she had learned. His touch, and his eyes, lingered on her. Then he bowed, and moved on to the next partner, some nobleman's younger daughter, dark-haired, vivacious, lovely. He smiled, laughed, moved with her, and Eleanor hated herself for the stab of raw jealousy that swept through her. She would marry; he was a free man, of a different nation, a different belief, and he would end tragically, and by God, she would have forgotten him by then.

Yet they came together again. "You look lovely, my lady," he told her.

"So do you."

He arched a brow. "I'm lovely? I must tell Wallace so."

She blushed.

"Will you leave soon?" she asked him.

He nodded.

"Back to the fight."

"Aye."

"I will pray for you," she said primly.

His lips curled in a smile. "Aye, then, you must. Tell me, do you think God listens to your words?"

"I will confess all my sins to Him, and be absolved, and aye, then, I believe He will listen to me," she said.

"I will pray for you as well," he told her. "God believes in men who know how to fight."

The music changed, and partners changed, and she found herself dancing with the king. "Your Grace," she murmured.

"A handsome, stalwart fellow, your rescuer, eh, my lady?"

"Aye, I believe so," she murmured uncomfortably.

"I like him very much; such a mind and sword arm are not always easy to find."

"I'm glad, your Grace."

"I'd hate to see him . . . well, you know, Lady Eleanor, there is nothing more important in life than duty."

"I am aware of that."

"You will marry Alain, as you have sworn."

"As I have sworn."

"Thank God, child, that you have no foolish dreams in your mind."

"Sire?"

The king smiled. "Well, duty would compel me to hunt you down and destroy you both. Wallace would be devastated, Clarin would fall to the mercy of your kin . . . and Edward would be glad of the head of a Scottish rebel on his table but angry for the loss of yours. How messy . . . wars, treaties, alliances . . ."

"I am pledged to Alain. I love him already, for he is an old and dear friend."

"Bless you, my child." He kissed her forehead then moved on.

She was surprised to find that Alain had come to the floor. "The king is very fond of you," he said, his breath a wheeze as they moved to the music.

"I'm glad."

"He will send one of his own confessors to you, before the wedding."

"That is kind of him." She saw with distress how uneven his breathing was. "Alain, I grow weary. May we sit?"

His eyes touched hers with gratitude. "Aye, we may." They returned to the table. The music seemed to grow louder. Her head seemed to pound.

"Alain, may we . . ."

He was watching the king. But at that moment, his king lifted his hand, listened to something the queen was saying, and bid the company good night.

"Aye, we may leave."

Brendan had returned alone to their assigned quarters when a servant announced that a messenger had come for him.

He found a tall priest in the dress of his order, a harsh wool cloak and cowl, gravely awaiting him.

"Aye?" he said to the fellow.

"Sir Brendan Graham?"

"Aye."

"You are blessed, sir. I have a message for you from the king. Our great sovereign Philip of France and Navarre finds you to be a gallant man. Foolish, and unlikely to live long, but possessing both courage and strength. He wishes you were a Frenchman."

"That's a great compliment."

"Aye, indeed. He considers marriage a sacred commitment."

"So do I, Father."

The man smiled. "A contract, once made before God, is not to be broken."

"I would not break such a contract."

"Or allow it to be broken in others."

He hesitated, knowing what was being said. Or, at the least, thinking that he did.

"I would never dishonor such a promise by another."

"That is what the king thought that you would say. And that is why he sent me."

Her head was pounding. Eleanor wished that she could escape her own skin.

When Alain left her in the room, Bridie was waiting. She chattered, giving hints that Eleanor was welcome to question her.

Eleanor wished that she had the heart to do so.

Bridie helped Eleanor with her elegant apparel, and offered her a nightdress, the sight of which at last drew her from her self-reflection. "What is this?" It was a stunning gown, but not hers. White silk, with embroidery, it was fine and cool and sensual to the touch.

"A gift from the queen."

"For my wedding—"

"No, no." Bridie's eyes rolled. "Wait until you see the one she sent for the wedding! This is just one of the many gifts she has sent."

"How very kind. I must thank her first thing tomorrow."

"Kind . . . and a waste," Bridie muttered.

"What?"

"Oh, Eleanor! My heart just breaks for you because I know now . . . well, I did mention Lars to you . . . such a man! I know, well, oh, my God, Lady Eleanor!" She crossed herself "We have . . ." As her voice trailed, her face turned crimson. "God forgive me, we've *been* together, and I can't help but be so sorry . . . you're so young, and so lovely, and Count Alain is so . . ."

"Old?"

"Forgive me."

"I am grateful for Alain."

"Of course. I should never have told you—"

"Bridie, I would never judge you—"

"If you did, if you whipped me, if you threw me out, why, took my head! It would be worth it. Oh, my lady, you don't know . . ."

"Bridie, I'm sure you'll tell me. But, please, not to-night . . ."

"Dear Eleanor, you look so tired. Aye, I'll leave you. I, well I . . ."

"If you're meeting Lars, please, go with my blessing."

"Oh, my lady!" She rushed to Eleanor, throwing her arms around her.

"Bridie, go!"

Eleanor sat on the bed, her heart thundering. What if she were to give it all up and run, a compromised woman, to ride with an outlaw in the forest?

He would be slain.

She could never allow it.

There was a tap on the door.

"Aye?" she said, walking to it and pausing.

"I'm your confessor, my lady," she heard in a muffled voice.

She opened the door, and a man, very tall, in the heavy, encompassing robes of his vocation entered.

"I'd thought to come to the chapel—" she began, but he pointed a finger to the floor, curtly indicating that she should kneel.

What could she possibly confess to this man? Yet a confession was sacred to a priest; before God, he could not repeat a word she said.

Still . . .

"My lady?" Gruffly, he indicated the floor again.

She was about to confess to carnal sin, and she was ironically gowned for such a confession, in her gift from the queen, the nightdress of pure white silk.

She immediately went to her knees and folded her hands in prayer.

"Bless me, father, for I have sinned.

"And you will do so again," came a deep voice, rich in amusement.

She looked up. He had cast back his cowl. Brendan stood before her. She leaped to her feet, backing away from him, then striding at him, ready to slap him. He caught her hand, pulling her into his arms.

"It would be a sin not to take the night," he told her.

She struggled against his hold. "You're not just a fool, you're an idiot. If you're caught here, they'll have your head—"

"I won't be caught."

"If you are, they will kill you—"

"I will die happy."

"You have to get out of here!"

"What will you do if I don't leave, call out for the guards?"

"You'll die—"

"I'll die a happy man."

"Brendan—"

He swept her up into his arms, tossed her upon the bed, and landed beside her. She started to protest anew but he caught her wrists, pressed them to the carved headboard, and found her lips, his own so forceful and passionate that if she could have, she would not have protested. His mouth was almost brutal with longing, the sweep of his tongue a flame. His lips did not part from hers until there was no breath within her, until she trembled, her limbs too molten to refuse him, her mind too numbed. He released her long enough to cast aside the coarse wool robe, to rise, and untangle himself from the kilt and plaid he wore. Then his nakedness was against the sheer barrier of the silk, and the heat of him seemed to burn through it, and she could feel the force of his sex against her thighs. She reached out, touching him.

"This is madness!"

"Aye!" But his hands were upon her, cradling her flesh beneath the sex, and it did not seem a barrier to him for he caressed her through the fabric, and the wet heat of his mouth covered her, his tongue laving her breast over the silk, wetting it as well, creating a friction that aroused her unbearably. She tugged at his hair, but he ignored the summons, moving against her, his touch frenzied, almost violent in his hunger. His hands slipped beneath the gown, his mouth continued to move atop, his tongue pressed the material to her erotically and intimately and she was afraid then that she would cry out, and gasped and bit down and the silk was gone and his liquid touch was against her and she writhed into him, as if she would die herself if she didn't reach the pinnacle now promised to her. She throbbed, burned, and gripped his shoulders then, gasping and biting her lip when the climax seized her, shaking when the silk was torn away, and he was within her, and the desire began to build again with each swift movement of his hips.

When he fell away, she was the one incensed, burrowing first to the sleek dampness of his chest, hands upon each ripple of muscle, lips moving down the length of him, the magnificent length of him, honed and scarred and muscled and taut as a strung bow. She took him into her hands, into her mouth, heard the grate of his teeth, the groan that escaped him, and felt his power as he reached for her, dragging her down beneath him, burying himself again in the anguish and ecstasy of desperate longing. The world seemed to cease around them, except for their thunder, the wind that swept them, the gasp of each breath, the drum of each heartbeat. He shuddered and tautened and broke; she felt the wave that filled her, warmed her as no other essence in life, and then they were still, he beside her, limbs entwined, apart, and yet, as one.

"You will marry soon," he said.

"Aye," she told him. And there was silence. "They will kill you if I do not."

"What if I were willing to die?"

"I am not willing that it should be."

He rose then, suddenly, abruptly. There were so many more things she wanted to say. She longed to talk.

"Brendan . . ."

But he was apt and able with his dress. He was wound in his plaid, clad in his cloak.

"Brendan, please . . ."

"My lady, God bless your marriage," he said briefly.

And he was gone.

The king of France was ready to be generous — especially since he had acquired a good-sized revenue from the pirate, Thomas de Longueville. In the large courtyard separating the complex of buildings at the palace, they counted crates of arms and armor, barrels of wine, and foodstuffs.

Food was indeed a boon, with so much of the borderland laid waste. The food was a generous gift; it remained winter in France, and they were receiving goods from Philip's own store.

Eric hefted a sack of grain on a wagon; Collum counted it off on the official document sent to them by Philip. Brendan had gone for another of the sacks piled by the wagons when he heard the bells of the great cathedral begin to ring.

He paused. Eric came, and stood before him, hands on his hips. "We've not finished."

"Why are the bells ringing now?"

Eric stared at him, grabbed another bag of grain and walked to the wagon. Brendan followed him. Margot, who had been counting the barrels of wine, looked up with a sigh. "Why not tell him? He knows that the wedding is taking place."

Eric stared at Margot. "You've just told him!"

She shrugged, and turned back to her work.

Brendan picked up a sack and threw it on the wagon. Wallace was at the front, giving instructions to the driver.

He walked around to Wallace, followed by Eric and Margot.

"The wedding is today?" he demanded.

"Aye, Lady Eleanor is to wed Count de Lacville today, at the grand cathedral of Notre Dame de Paris," Wallace said flatly, staring at him.

"You've known, of course. And you didn't mention it."

"We were asked to attend," Wallace said. He sighed. "I did not think you would want to go."

"Oh, on the contrary. I must be there!" Brendan exclaimed. For a moment, he fought the inevitable. He had not believed that she would do it! How could she? His fury with her was great. He wanted to cry out. How could she do this? The strumpet, harlot, whore, fool . . . *English!* Ah, yes, she could be bought. For a pile of stones and a patch of land, she would wed an old man, she would betray . . .

Betray what? Him? A man with nothing but the sword he wielded, and the gain gotten of his wits, a gain he would desert at any time to ride for . . .

A dream.

She had never lied. She knew her duty. She would marry de Lacville. Reign supreme in Clarin South of Scotland, far south from Scotland.

And she would pray for him, of course.

What did he have to offer her? Nothing. What had he ever had? Nothing, nothing at all. He could offer her hardship, fear, and possibly death. Nothing more. He had known that she must do this, and he had known that his empty, unformed desires could not be fulfilled. To stop the wedding, he would have to betray Wallace, his men, his family, his country. Could he have done it?

"I need to attend the ceremony," he said.

"And what then? What will you do?"

"Protest in the name of decency?" Margot whispered.

"Margot!" Both Wallace and Eric stared at her, harshly stating her name.

She turned and walked away.

"I need—to see it. And end it," he said.

Wallace stared at him, then threw up his hands. "Collum!" he called. "See to the end of the packing!"

"Aye, William!" Collum returned, questioning nothing.

"We'll go," William said.

He started for the horses.

"We are ill-dressed for a wedding," Eric noted. He was in leather pants, boots, and a long woolen tunic. Wallace and Brendan were in their plaids.

"We are dressed as what we are," Wallace said, and continued.

Brendan was already on his horse.

The cathedral was beautiful and solemn. Last night, she had come here to see the priest, her confessor, and it had seemed immense and hallowed. It hadn't been in the confessional though, that she had felt she'd made her peace; it had been while alone in the great arched nave and looking at the splendor that God had allowed man to create. She had Alain's forgiveness, she knew, and however wrong she might have been, she felt that she had God's understanding. She hadn't realized what she was doing when she had begun; there was a certain price she would pay for the rest of her life. But now, she was doing what she must, and she needed no penitence to suffer, if what she had done had indeed been a sin in God's eyes. She was ready.

But as she walked down the aisle, to be given to Alain by the king, the peace she had found deserted her. She was swept by seconds of panic, wishing that she could break from the royal arm, and flee.

Marriage was not to be entered into lightly. She would make promises she must keep.

The cathedral itself seemed alive. Incense hovered like a fog. Monks chanted in beautiful song, and the Latin prayers seemed to close around her heart.

As she walked, she had a moment of mad hope, thinking that *he* would come, that he would storm down the aisle on a white charger, purer than the day. He would sweep her up and they would ride . . .

But there was nowhere to ride, and the vision faded, and she prayed as she walked, not for her marriage, but that he would not come, for if he did protest, he might be killed, and if he didn't protest, and she knew that he was there, her voice would falter, and he would see . . .

But Alain had told her that the Scots were probably on the road back to Calais, and their ships, and they would sail back to Scotland.

Thank God. He was on his way back to the wretched dirt and rock he called Scotland, to his insistence on bleeding into the ground he had so hallowed . . .

She nearly tripped; she was steadied. She walked forward, blinded by the incense, and the great sacredness of the cathedral, and moisture that blurred her eyes.

If he was there . . . one word, one look. She would not go through with this charade.

Aye, but that was truly an empty dream.

*   *   *

They arrived when the ceremony was well under way.

He saw her walking, reaching the altar, on the arm of the king. Saw her given over to the man who awaited her.

Surely, she could not do this!

She could not . . .

If she turned once . . .

Just saw his face . . .

But she did not turn. The priest began speaking the Latin words he had heard before, intoned, rising, falling.

The great cathedral was filled with the scent of incense. The bride and groom knelt; once again, monks sang in rich, deep, voices, and the great nave seemed filled with the sanctity of ritual and promise.

At the altar of the cathedral, she bowed her head along with her aging count.

The priest began to speak the words that would join them as man and wife. He seemed to speak on and on, caught in a haze, a vision that did not end. And at last he made demands of the couple before him.

He heard her words. Soft, muted. But sure, unfaltering.

The priest held a golden band. He touched it to the bride's fingers, the first, the second, the third. "In the name of the Father, the Son, and the Holy Ghost."

And it was then that he left.

He walked out of the cathedral, Eric silently at his heels.

He came to his horse, mounted, and rode.

And he did not look back.

Chapter 12

It was six weeks before Eleanor returned to Clarin with Alain.

News of her homecoming had been sent ahead when they docked, and moved far more swiftly than she did with Alain. He could not ride for long periods of time, and even the rocking motion of a wagon disturbed him. Still, she was surprised and touched by the greeting her cousins had prepared. The road to the castle was lined with the tenants and craftsmen who lived and worked in the village and environs; they were ready with flowers, greetings, and cries of welcome. When they neared the castle, the household servants were outside as well, Alfred on the step, Corbin beside him. Even Corbin's wife, Isobel, petite and dainty and beautiful, had appeared for the occasion.

She wondered how Corbin was managing.

But King Edward, having so recently wed the French king's sister and beginning negotiations to wed his heir to the French king's daughter, was feeling benign toward the French. The king himself might have ordered Isobel to Clarin to greet such a well-regarded Frenchman as Alain de Lacville.

Eleanor was proud of the appearance given by her home. She waved happily to those she passed, and when they came to the entry of the castle, she leaped down, hugging Alfred, and then Corbin, and even Isobel, who seemed to expect such a show of affection. Alfred and Corbin were both acquainted with Alain, since he had been a close friend to her father throughout the years, even when war had broken out between their two countries.

Isobel was quick to greet Alain, making him feel at home as they walked up the steps to what was actually the second level of the castle, and the great hall. "My dear Count de Lacville! It is such a pleasure to have so noble a man for a cousin-in-law, yet it is difficult to understand why you two have chosen to come here! I have been told your estates in France are truly magnificent."

"I am blessed, indeed, madam, but as my eldest son does well enough by what will be his inheritance, it seemed expedient to come here, to my wife's property."

"Which, of course, Alfred handles admirably!" Eleanor said, rising on tiptoe to kiss Alfred's cheek, and bringing a blush to his face.

"The meal is set, of course," Isobel informed them. "We may dine at any time. If you require some time to rest . . ."

"We are exceedingly well," Eleanor assured her, "but perhaps you'd all be willing to wait until we've had some time to repair somewhat from the ride?"

"Of course!" Isobel said. "I've taken the liberty, Eleanor, of moving your belongings to your father's suite. There are the two rooms there . . ."

"Thank you so much," she murmured.

"Count de Lacville, I do hope you'll find our north country

hospitality worthy, when you are accustomed to the grandeur of Paris,'' Isobel continued sweetly.

''I'm sure I shall be very comfortable.'' He smiled. ''I have felt welcomed in this home many times before, and I've always been comfortable. And now, of course, wherever Eleanor chooses to be is where I am happiest.''

''I can well imagine,'' Isobel said sweetly.

''I hope you're comfortable,'' Eleanor told her, ''when you're accustomed to the grandeur of London.''

Isobel was silent for a moment, then her smile deepened. ''Wherever Corbin is, of course, is where I am the happiest.''

''Really?'' she inquired.

''Of course!''

Eleanor looked at Corbin, who shrugged. She thought that Isobel stepped on his toe then, but she couldn't be certain.

''I'll show you—'' Isobel began.

''I know where *my* father's chambers are, Isobel. Thank you so very much.''

Eleanor kept a firm hold on Alain's arm as they walked up the steps to the third level. Clarin was probably cold and drafty compared to the beauty of his estates, and she was sorry to make sad comparisons of her own home. She felt guilty. She loved her home, and though the lands had been ravaged, they were slowly coming back. This winter was hard, exceptionally hard, but they would make their way through it, and all would be well.

There were two rooms, and a large dressing chamber to the suite, and even indoor ''necessary'' closets, due to her father's love for all things Roman. Though there were two doors to the hall, she made a show of walking together through the first, certain that Isobel was watching her every move. When they were inside, Alain staggered a little.

''I do believe I need to lie down.''

''Aye, Alain, you must rest,'' she said, helping him to the

bed. He had traveled with his servant, Jean, and she knew she should call him, but she could help him from his outer winter garments, and bring him water, and get him settled first.

He caught her hand when she adjusted the covers around him.

"You are a good wife," he told her gently, dark eyes warm and kind.

"Don't talk of dying or of leaving me, do you hear?" she demanded. "You'll leave me to that monster!"

"The petite little dark-haired beauty?"

"Aye, that monster!"

Alain laughed. He touched her hair. "I'd never leave you, if it were in my power."

"Don't even talk of it."

She began to fold the clothing she had taken, and smooth the sheets around him.

"Do you think of him often?" he asked softly.

She rose. "No," she lied. "He has gone back to Scotland. I am here, with you."

"That's not the same, is it?"

"Alain—"

"Please, I hold no fault with you."

"And I pray that you live long, and stay with me for years and years."

He smiled and closed his eyes. "I would dearly love some water."

She brought him water. He seemed to want to sleep. She slipped into the smaller of the two chambers that had been her father's. The lady's room was lovelier, she thought. The furniture was old, finely carved—with Gaelic designs. Once upon a time, there had been an era of peace at the borders. Some of the tapestries in here had come from the Flemish living in the Scottish borders. The books had been finely crafted by monks at Melrose Abbey.

She didn't want to think about that. Fresh water and a pitcher and bowl had been left for her; she cooled her face, and quietly left the room, leaving Alain to rest.

She found Corbin alone in the great hall. "Ah, cousin! My poor dear! So you have gone off, married Father Time, and returned." He poured himself a glass of spirits. "You bested a pirate and the Scots once again. Foolish me — I worried sick when I heard of your adventure. I should have worried for poor Wallace!"

He teased her, yet she thought there was self-ridicule in his words.

"I didn't best the pirate or the Scots. The pirate intended to sell me off to the Arabs for a fair price; the Scots knew I'd be worth more to Alain."

He walked over to her, taking her into a gentle hug, and holding her. "Eleanor, I missed you. I was worried sick. The news, as we received it, came first from vague reports by other travelers, then officially from London, as Philip sent word to Edward."

"I'm sorry you were so worried. But you've had company here."

"Isobel. Ah, yes, the arms of my loving wife."

"She's been here since I've gone?"

"Amazingly so."

"You're not pleased."

"I'm still puzzled. Aren't you?"

She had to laugh; he did seem bemused. "Maybe she has changed her ways."

"She wishes to bear an heir — being quite certain you won't do so, and my good brother is too busy actually working and obeying each of King Edward's summons to arms."

"Have you been called to serve with him in another campaign?" she asked worriedly.

"When isn't there a campaign?" he replied vaguely. "I am

tempted to send back messages that we have served, that you were on the briny sea, giving the Scots hell once again. You did give them hell, didn't you?''

"Oh, yes.''

He shook his head. "Poor cousin . . . I do hurt for you.''

"Why?''

"Alain is a fine man, but . . . ah, well, when am I proper, or discreet, to you, at any rate? To be bluntly honest? You should enjoy your youth, your beauty . . .'' Despite his words, he hesitated. "The one thing I will say for Isobel, she does enjoy her sport. She is an absolute witch, but . . . very good at what she does. I wish that I could send her away. I can't quite manage to do it. But there is the point. We are young, and there are benefits to marriage, and you should . . . well, you can't, I mean, I can't imagine . . . I mean, he is *old.*''

"Corbin, thank you for worrying about my earthly pleasures.''

"He may die, you know.''

"We'll all die, one day.''

"You do seem . . . not happy, but resigned.''

"I am — resigned. Tell me, what news of the Scots?''

"Wallace is back in Scotland. He has lost his army, but there are still strong factions of renegades about, and they've attacked English outposts, supply wagons, and made a few punitive raids, but not far across the border. The Comyn faction continues to fight, though Robert Bruce, you know, is to be married to an English heiress, and is in Edward's hands at the moment. Tell me about Wallace. Was he painted like an ancient tribal Pict? Does he have horns, and is he seven feet tall?''

"He wasn't painted the times we met, and yes, he is tall, no he is not seven feet, but well over six. He had no horns, but his teeth are in fine shape.''

"He bit you?''

"No!" she said, smiling. "No. He was human. And he denied being part of any force that came here."

"He would."

"Why would he need to? I was his prisoner at the time."

"They are all renegades, that is the problem. Outlaws, and thieves."

"They have been attacked and killed, as well. More so," she said, and was amazed that she could be standing here, defending the Scots.

"We burn, slaughter, ravage, and pillage them, and they do the same to us. Ah, well," Corbin said. "It hasn't been forever, you know. Before King Alexander died, and the Maid of Norway after him, we were at peace for years with our northern neighbors. But the Scots cannot be at peace with themselves; if ever they were, they'd be a formidable enemy indeed."

"The Scots," Isobel said, sweeping into the room, "are waiting for King Edward to die. Alas, I believe he will refuse to do so, and that wretched man who seized you from the sea will die a terrible death himself, most assuredly."

"Wallace didn't seize me — a pirate did. And he had the most fantastic story, Isobel. He said that he was paid to accost my ship."

"What?" Isobel responded with unfeigned surprise. "Ah — and there you go defending the Scots! Some wealthy baron who decried your position at Falkirk surely must be guilty — if there is a guilty party. Pirates are liars, you know."

"I'm afraid I can't generalize about pirates, Isobel. I have only met the one pirate leader myself."

Isobel laughed. "Dear Eleanor! What does it matter, you are back safe and sound."

"To the delight of finding you here."

Isobel helped herself to wine, paused in the pouring, added more to the glass. "It helps, in the north country."

"If you despise the place so, why do you stay?"

"Alfred was consumed with arms and training and the slightest command spoken by the king; you have now married a rich ancient. Corbin and I are all but obliged to create an heir for the future safety of Clarin."

"How noble. Maybe the ancient and I will yet create an heir," Eleanor informed her, then felt uneasy that she should have spoken so, even to put Isobel in her place. Why fight with her? She was here, for once, with Corbin. And though he truly seemed to have no real love for her, she was his wife, and he was apparently enjoying her sudden maternal urge.

"Of course, Eleanor, I do wish you all the best in that regard. But just in case . . . well, the family must live on."

"Incredibly noble, Isobel."

"Well, thanks to Count de Lacville and your marriage, Clarin will rise to substance again. We must all look to the future."

Alfred entered the hall then. "I have been over the ledgers, and must set accounts straight tomorrow with you and the count, Eleanor. The north wall is nearly complete, but there has been a call to arms again—"

"The king is waging another battle?" she asked, dismayed by the alarm in her voice.

"The king is always waging another battle. But the Duke of York has sent out summonses, and those we must obey as well. Naturally, from Clarin, we are expected to provide men and arms. We are accustomed to the fight; you must not worry needlessly, nor will we ever allow you to ride again."

"Indeed, even marriage turns into danger when the Lady Eleanor is involved!" Isobel said sweetly. "But, of course, in a few months time, Alfred and Corbin must go, since your poor count cannot!"

"Ah, but dear Isobel! How will you bear your husband being torn from your side?"

"We all must suffer in such times," Isobel said sweetly. "I

will suffer my husband's absence, and you will suffer the presence of yours!''

"I do not suffer, Isobel. You cannot imagine what age teaches a man," Eleanor told her. "If you'll excuse me, I'll see if he is ready to dine."

She smiled, and left the room, with all of them watching after her.

They were still within the forest; long days and nights of strike-and-run raids made them as wary as any wolf in the woods.

Brendan heard the slightest rustle in the trees, and stepped back, waiting.

Thomas de Longueville, pirate, had changed his ways — just barely. Having received a full pardon from the French king, he had decided that life in Paris would not be to his liking. He had chosen to cast his fate with the Scots, and was proving to be as wily and agile on land as he had been at sea. He was small and slim, capable of great speed, and of climbing a tree with the same expertise he had used on a ship's rigging. He reached Brendan with little more than that slight rustle, but he was somewhat out of breath.

'' 'Tis the wagon coming, just as we were told." He paused, hands on his knees, taking in a deep breath. "There's ale, great barrels of ale, and more trunks than you can imagine. They might well contain the armor Lord Hebert ordered for the men at the fortress they're building on the river. Freshly fashioned by some of the finest masters in Germany! And there might well be some silks as well, ordered by the Lord's lady — what a waste, for they say she is uglier than a mastiff"

"And how do you know all this?"

De Longueville grinned. "One of Lord Hebert's dairy maids. A plump and garrulous little lass, with a tart tongue in many ways. A lovely lass, though, with a fine affinity for all things French.''

''Aye, and there he goes, bragging of his prowess again!'' Liam MacAllister moaned.

''The Scots are good; the French are better,'' de Longueville replied, unoffended.

''How far are the wagons?'' Brendan demanded.

''No more than five minutes,'' de Longueville replied.

''How defended?''

''Four guards in the lead, two at the sides, four in the rear.''

''In armor?''

''Mail and helms.''

''Eric, we'll take the lead?'' Brendan said, and his cousin nodded. ''They've one chance to surrender; Liam, you and Collum will await their reply, then go for the men riding at the side, and Thomas, you'll take the rear with Ian, Edgar, and Garth, get up in the tree with me; string one of your sharpest arrows.''

''Aye!'' came the agreement.

They parted, and melted into the trees, Brendan taking an oak branch that stretched out over the road. In less than a minute, they heard the hoofbeats on the road, and the heavy roll of the wagons.

Brendan waited until he saw the lead riders appearing, then dropped from the tree to the center of the road.

''Whoa, there, my friends, where are you headed?'' he called out.

The rider in the lead paused, a look of contempt on his face. ''Out of the way, Scotsman. Or we'll slaughter you like a pig.''

''And roast him up and send him to the king!'' said the fellow at his side.

He surveyed the riders quickly, assessing that he knew none of the men. They wore the colors of Lord Hebert, a man truly despised in the region for his autocratic rule of the lowland lea he had been commanded to hold by King Edward. He had forced farmers into hard labor at the rebuilding of the old Roman ruins he meant to turn into a mighty fortification, working some of the older men to death — and preying upon their wives and daughters.

"Ah, and what king would that be?"

"Why, King Edward, you daft savage!" the first man said.

"But Edward is no king in Scotland. Ah, my fine sirs — didn't you notice when you rode this way? This is Scotland — not England."

"Slay the rascal, and let's be going on!" the second man said impatiently.

"Slay me? Why, I was about to offer you your lives," Brendan informed him.

"Offer us our lives!" the first burst into laughter, causing his visor to fall. He quickly adjusted it, angered that he might have looked a fool.

He nudged his horse toward Brendan.

"Ah, sir! You might want to take note of my friend, atop that branch. Indeed, you're clad in fine mail beneath the colors of a murdering, usurping fiend, but at this close range . . . ah! See, my friend is smiling. For a filthy savage, he has learned a quite incredibly accurate aim. I believe he can strike your face . . . perhaps your throat, or even pierce that mail right in the vicinity of your heart."

The man gave pause, looking up. Garth smiled, but didn't move a muscle. His bow was strung; the arrow was aimed.

"Throw down that weapon, man, what, are you a fool?" the man demanded. "We've a party of twelve well-armed fighting men — kill me, and they'll pick you apart like carrion!"

"Surrender the wagons," Brendan commanded quietly.

"Idiots!" the man swore.

"We will let you leave with your lives."

"We will butcher you like the wild hogs you are!"

He nudged his mount forward. Garth let the arrow fly. The knight grasped his throat, and then the shaft of the arrow. Brendan, sword drawn, went for the second rider, drawing him from his horse and finding the point of weakness at his neck nearly as fast as the arrow had flown.

The other riders were moving up, but Brendan was on to a second combatant, and Garth had strung another arrow. Collum and the others let out cries and emerged from the woods, and minutes later, they had the five English survivors sitting awkwardly together in the center of the road.

Brendan quickly ordered de Longueville and Collum to see that the wagons were brought on ahead, the goods to be dispersed. He and his remaining men surveyed their prisoners.

"Do we let them go?" Brendan asked Eric.

"They did refuse to surrender."

"Norwood refused to surrender, not I!" cried one of the men.

"They do say we're savage beasts," Eric reminded Brendan.

"Ah, now, they're not so hard on you. Too much Norse in your blood, cousin."

"I resent that! Is there such a thing as too much Norse in the blood?"

"No offense intended, cousin, I'm merely pointing out that you might, perhaps, not be quite so much a savage as a full-blooded Scot—"

"Brendan, there's probably not a full-blooded Scot among you, the Norse have been here so long—"

"Teaching us to fight like berserkers, chop our enemies into little pieces?" He turned toward the English, his sword in hand.

One of the men rose, "Wait, please. We rode in the rear, and had no chance to accept your offer of surrender."

Brendan studied the speaker. He was young; he'd barely grown a few whiskers. He stood tall, though, not flinching. He awaited his judgment with a vein pulsing hard at his neck, but with stoic dignity as well.

"We need their mail," Eric said.

"I'd just as soon not have mine all bloodied," Liam stated.

"They've really fine swords there," Eric reminded him.

"Well, we've already taken their swords," Brendan pointed out. "But then, I agree, 'tis much easier, having help removing those coats of armor from live bodies rather than trying to struggle with corpses."

The Englishmen were quick to rise at that—and fumble awkwardly to remove the mail.

"Ah, well, that's one now!" Eric said cheerfully. "But I've a mind to burn those wretched tunics that herald such a man as Hebert!"

"In the bodies—or out?" Brendan inquired.

"I'm not sure that much matters—"

"Ma's e do thoil e!" The young man who had risen to speak said suddenly.

Startled, both Eric and Brendan turned to the young man who stared straight in Brendan's eyes, and repeated *please* in Gaelic. *"Ma's e do thoil e!"*

Brendan looked at Eric. "He's a fine accent."

"Scottish mother," the fellow said quietly.

"You're fluent?" Brendan inquired.

"Aye." He looked at Eric. "And in Norse, as well. My mother is from Iona."

"And you're wearing the tunic of an English butcher?" Eric demanded.

"English father," the young man explained.

"A waste, a pity," Eric said.

"Aye, you'd be faring better with us in the woods."

"Let me live; and I swear, I will serve you better in the woods," he vowed.

"What's your name, lad?" Brendan demanded.

"Gregory, sir."

"Gregory . . . well, we will let these fellows live. We did not intend to do murder. They are, however, hated tunics. You'll leave them. And the capes."

"We've bare linen shirt and hose —" one of the men protested.

"Nice hose," Eric said.

"Aye, I've a use for those," Liam said with a sigh.

"You heard him!" Brendan said.

"You'd leave us with nothing —" the protester said, astonished.

"Naked Englishmen, alone in the woods!" Liam said, tsk-tsking.

"Imagine all those English tallywhackers, a-blowin in the breeze, all shriveled with the cold. Why, 'tis downright dangerous. An angry fishwife could come along with her gutting knife, and leave the fellow a limb short!" Eric commented, shaking his head.

"Well, they'll not be attacking our farmsteads so," Brendan mused.

"Sir," Gregory interrupted. "Begging your pardon, but the coming of spring is not so warm in Scotland. If you'd leave men to freeze, might as well cut their throats."

Eric looked at Brendan. Brendan shrugged.

"I suppose I can do without new hose a while longer," Liam said, sighing.

"Go!" Brendan told the Englishmen. "Go!"

They started to move, uncertain, unsure. They came toward the Scotsmen.

"Not that way!" Brendan barked. "Southward — back to England."

They quickly turned. Walking at first, they looked back, and then started to run.

All except Gregory. He stood still, waiting.

"Go, son," Brendan told him.

But Gregory stood still, watching as the others ran now, getting farther away.

"Go!" Brendan persisted. "Would you walk back to England alone?"

"I could be of use in the woods," Gregory told him quietly.

"Ye canna trust an Englishman!" Liam warned Brendan.

"I'd not betray you," Gregory said.

"You just betrayed your own," Brendan reminded him.

Gregory shook his head. "I was allowed to leave for service in York, but then taken to serve with troops under Lord Hebert. By his order, I was taken out to a field to learn to use a sword, and then commanded to come to Scotland. It was a service I did not seek." He hesitated. "Lord Hebert would have butchered every man of you, had the situation been reversed."

"Don't underestimate us," Eric warned. "We have been known to slay a few men."

"That I know. I see the bodies beyond you. But it's wrong. Wrong that a king should claim a land that is not his, and wrong that we kill our neighbors time and time again so that Edward may grasp for all in sight."

Eric turned his back on the young man. "You canna trust an Englishman!"

"I say we give him a chance," Brendan said after a moment.

" 'Tis your funeral, if you choose," Eric told him.

Gregory came walking toward him, and lowered to a knee. "I never gave oath of fealty before. I swear now, my honor, to you, sir."

"Get up, lad," Brendan said. "We've seen it often enough — words and vows do not prove fealty. Actions do. We shall see how yours stand up. Gather the swords and mail!" He said to the others. "We'll move from the road before one of the treacherous bastards doubles back — and makes it to Hebert."

That night, they dared a campfire deep in the woods. They

were protected by the river to their one side, and the protection of a steep hillside to the other. They always had an escape route planned, wherever they took shelter.

The goods from the wagon had already been divided; most of the weapons were on their way to Wallace who was meeting with John Comyn, the Red, a fierce fighter with an eye on the crown himself, though he was kin to Balliol. Comyn had never catered to the English, and he was a warrior, if perhaps, he did not have the diplomatic or tactical skills of Robert the Bruce.

Thomas de Longueville had found some beautiful silks; he meant to give some of them to the lovely little dairy maid who had been so talkative in bed.

"La!" de Longueville said happily, modeling the silk. "My round petite will be lovely in this."

There had been a barrel of apples among the goods, only slightly damaged and aged. They sat around, enjoying the sweetness of the fruit in the coldness of the night, watching de Longueville's antics.

"Ah, lovely—and dead—if she's caught wearing it by the mastiff, Lady Hebert!" Eric told de Longueville.

"Perhaps it will not be so healthy for her to remain where she is after today!" de Longueville mused. "We'll move her north, eh, Brendan? There are many cows in the highlands!"

Brendan nodded. "Aye, she needs to slip away by night."

Gregory spoke up. "Where I came from—" He broke off suddenly.

"Where you came from what?" Brendan demanded sharply.

"Well, they've suffered greatly from the Scots; the village was razed . . . and many were burned to death. Alive. That's why, when the Duke of York called out for more men, it did not seem such an evil thing to be taken for training, though it was not what I would have desired."

"A call for more men!" Liam spat. "When Edward has

much in his hands, now, with his truce being made with Robert the Bruce!''

"Did the man have a choice?" Eric inquired quietly.

"Ah, Eric!" Liam said with disgust.

"Aye, now, wait," Brendan said, putting up a hand. "I've considered him the worst of turncoats myself, and, aye, he seeks the crown! But you can see the way the man was thinking; John Balliol, freed from Rome, across the channel in France. That was a fear to King Edward, and surely to Bruce as well, for if Balliol had returned — ever does return — he is the king. There was the matter of Bruce falling in love with Elizabeth de Burgh — whose father is Earl of Ulster, and one of King Edward's most staunch and loyal supporters. And then — " he said, putting a hand up again to stop the protests about to begin, "there was the matter of his family. A large family, brothers and sisters, far too close to the English king for comfort."

"He did put a fine fight for a few years; his army at Carrick was strong," Eric said. "A threat to the English before — a boon to them now. Mark my words, though, he is a Scotsman. He'll weary of his subservience to Edward in time."

"Aye, but if he rises, will the people rise with him?" Liam demanded.

"He'll have a lot to prove," Brendan agreed. "If he wearies of his subservience. For the moment, the English position is good."

They were all silent then, staring at the fire. Eric cleared his throat. "Where is it exactly, young master Gregory, that you come from?"

"A small but fine place, just north of York. Clarin. 'Tis a beautiful land, a valley, rich with streams — "

"Where?" Brendan demanded, tensing.

"Clarin. There's a fine stone castle, begun soon after the arrival of William of Normandy — who did not so trust the Scots himself. There's a fine mixture of people there, English, of course, but many of Scottish descent, and some who have married Flemings, and of course, some with Norse and Danish blood—''

''Clarin,'' Brendan said.

''Aye. You know of it?''

''We know the lady there,'' Eric said.

''Aye, then! You're the men who took my lady at sea—''

''Aye,'' Brendan interrupted roughly, and again, the group fell silent.

After a moment, Brendan said, ''How fared the lady of Clarin, when last you saw her?''

''Ah, well, she is well! Though I fear the count sickens.''

''Sickens?'' Eric inquired, and added, ''You mean he ages?''

''No, he is ill, very ill. A sickness in the stomach, and the bowels. It's sad. The lady does set such store by him.''

''How do you know this?'' Brendan asked sharply.

''Because Lady Eleanor is frequently about, seeing to repairs on the walls, visiting with her tenants, the craftsmen, and all. Clarin isn't London, you know. Or even York. Yet I believe she is a far greater lady than most; she talks to her people, she visits them when they're sick, brings gifts when a child is born. You can see her eyes, though, how troubled she is, when one asks about the count.''

''She is such a great lady,'' Brendan said, his voice still too harsh, ''but she sent you off to fight for the English—when it was not your choice?''

''The Duke of York sent out a call for men,'' Gregory explained simply. ''To learn the use of arms ... it seemed a way to perhaps better my position in life.''

''Aye, well, you've bettered it!'' Collum said with a laugh. ''Now you are an outlaw.''

''If you win your freedom, I will have bettered my life,'' Gregory said.

"If," Eric murmured.

"When," Brendan said firmly.

Gregory proved to be as valuable an asset as Thomas de Longueville. Well versed in many languages, he could listen in on any conversation spoken, and with his youth, agility, and speed, he was able to slip in and out of many places — and appear innocent all the while.

On a day about three weeks after he had first come to ride with Brendan's company, he came back with news about Hebert's castle. The following Friday, the main body of Hebert's men would be moving out — ready to attack Wallace and Comyn north of the forest. The still not complete fortress would be vulnerable.

And Wallace and Comyn could be warned of the attack.

Brendan listened gravely to all he had to say, then dismissed him, musing over the conversation.

"How do you know we can trust him?" Eric asked. "How do we know it's not a trick to draw us into the fortress?"

"We watch before we leap," Brendan said simply. "We send warning right away to William and John, and then we prepare ourselves to move in once we're certain that the English have moved out."

"We could be dead men, trusting this lad."

"We could be dead men any day."

Eric shrugged. "Who wants to live forever?" he muttered.

Chapter 13

Eleanor loved Clarin. It was good to be home.

The castle was drafty, and not nearly as fine as Alain's estates just outside Paris, but there was a heritage, she thought, that was unique to their north country. Old customs with the serfs and tenants remained; ancient wiccan holidays had combined with Catholic holy days. Certain days were given to feasts, and certain days were given to rest.

Interceding when the village had been under attack had given Eleanor a relationship with the people that she cherished. She was welcomed in every home, and she was glad to visit the sick, the elderly, and those in need of help.

She had known that she would never forget Brendan, but she hadn't realized that she would be haunted by memories, day after day, and in her dreams. Riding around the estate with Alfred was something she enjoyed; looking into the lives of her people gave her pleasure. If she could not find a real happiness herself, she could at least provide it for others, giving permission for marriages, and visiting newborn babes. Life went on, and with it death, and it was sad to attend burials as well, but important, and she was very glad to keep as busy as possible.

The days were bearable.

The nights, when she lay alone, haunted her. Awake, she would pray for the dawn, sometimes see to Alain, who seemed to toss so restlessly in the adjoining room, then lie awake again.

Day. Aye, day was better.

Night was memory, a haunting that seemed to grow more grave with time.

She kept so busy when she first returned that she didn't notice how Bridie moped about. One afternoon, when she had spoken to her several times and her maid had not answered, she walked to the window where she stood, looking out at the grounds. They were alone; Alain was in the great hall with Alfred and Corbin, giving instructions to the builders and brick-layers who continued to strengthen the fortification. They were in Alain's section of the chamber; Eleanor had brought in a bouquet of the first spring flowers and set them in a vase, hoping they would cheer him, since he had not felt well since they had arrived.

''Bridie!'' she said sharply.

And when her maid turned to her, her eyes betraying a wretchedness similar to that of what she was feeling, she instantly regretted her tone.

She walked to her, putting an arm around Bridie's slender shoulders.

''What is it?''

''Oh, my lady, what will I do?'' Bridie wailed.

And she realized, in her own anguish, she had forgotten the nights that Bridie had slipped away, and how she had talked about her Lars.

Eleanor hesitated. She loved Bridie. They had been together forever.

"Perhaps . . . perhaps you could go to Scotland," she said.

Hope leaped into Bridie's eyes, then faded. "From your kindness, yes. But my lady, I don't know his feelings."

"But . . ."

"He has no home. They live in the forest when they are in Scotland. He told me what a great difference it was—being given such kingly treatment in Norway, France . . . even Italy. But in Scotland, they keep the fight for freedom alive, and do so by harrying the border."

"Bridie, don't give up hope. Perhaps in time . . ."

"I don't have time," Bridie said. She stared at Eleanor. "And neither do you."

"I . . . don't know what you mean," Eleanor said.

"My lady, I beg your pardon. But I believe you do."

Aye, she did. And she had yet to talk to Alain, but . . .

She was deeply grateful for the life growing within her. Relieved, even, to know that the child couldn't possibly be Alain's, and therefore, was a part of Brendan she could hold and keep forever. The babe would be her father's grandchild; Clarin would be his.

"Aye, I'm having a child," she murmured. "Bridie, I'll find a solution. I'll write—"

"How? And to whom?" Bridie asked softly.

Eleanor took her into her arms. "There are always means of communication. Even to enemy outlaws, fighting in the woods. But no one will take you from me, and no one will judge you, or ever send you from this house. I swear it."

"How can you bear this, my lady? How can you?"

"I must. This is my home, and . . ."

"And?"

"I sincerely doubt that I'd really be welcomed by—by the Scots myself."

"He loves you; I saw it in his eyes, any time he was near you. Just as I saw the way you looked at him."

"Let's pray that others did not have such keen eyesight," Eleanor told her.

"You could run, you know. Go to him."

Eleanor shook her head. "Not now. Even if I could . . . leave everything else, I could not leave Alain. He isn't well. He needs me."

"But the child is Sir Brendan's," Bridie said flatly.

Eleanor was about to answer when she thought she heard movement from the adjoining room. She brought her finger to her lips, and tiptoed quickly across the room. She paused at the door that joined the two; then threw it open.

The room was empty. But she thought she heard a clicking sound, as if the door to the hall had opened and closed. She hurried to it and opened the door, looking out.

There was no one in sight.

She closed the door. A strange foreboding closed around her heart.

That night at dinner, Isobel was talkative. She asked Eleanor about one of the farmers, who had been ailing.

"Old Timothy is not very well, I'm afraid," she said sadly. "He cannot walk without hunching over, and his wife is ill now as well."

"So they live in that fine little cottage, and will produce little," Isobel said.

"He worked all his life on this land," Eleanor said. "He has given a great deal."

"Ah, Eleanor! You will defend all the peasants! Yet, once you have a score of such fellows, Clarin will fall to waste!"

"Clarin will not fall to waste. Timothy has two grown sons who do more than a fair share of work."

"Fine, strapping lads!" Isobel agreed. "They'll be called to service against the loathsome Scots! Then, what will we do? Perhaps old Timothy and his ailing wife could be moved to a small place, and their good cottage given to a younger man, with fine young sons of his own, to till a better field. I'd never suggest that we don't care for the aged, of course . . . Alfred! Corbin! Wouldn't my idea be of greater sense — and value?"

"We are doing well enough," Alfred said with a shrug.

"But we could do better."

"If we lack anything this season," Alain put in firmly, "we will bring in supplies from France."

"But Alain, your children in France surely work their hardest to improve your holding there. Clarin should not be a drain."

"Isobel," Eleanor said, maintaining her temper the best she could, "perhaps you'll be so kind as to remember that Clarin is held in my name, and now the count's, through *my* father."

"But it will revert to Alfred, should you not have a son. Oh, Eleanor! You've not got a happy announcement for us, do you?"

Eleanor was afraid that blood was rushing to her features. She fought to maintain a calm. "Isobel, no, I've no announcement for you."

Isobel smiled. "There, you see? It is for Alfred, and Corbin, and the heir I might one day bear myself, that I cannot help but feel concern."

Eleanor rose. "They say that London grows beautiful at this time of year, Isobel."

"Do they? It's still cold here. And colder still, in Scotland, I'll warrant."

"And what is your concern with Scotland?"

"Only that our men will go and fight there again, of course," Isobel said sweetly. "I shall pray that weather improves before they are called to leave.

* * *

The next morning, Eleanor sat her horse in the field, watching Corbin and Alfred drill young men.

It was a bad time for exercises such as this. It was time for the spring planting.

But it was good for all the men to be trained; too few had known how to wield weapons when they had been so horribly set upon by renegades. She still feared for her people. Wallace had admitted to a multitude of raids and attacks, and he did feel himself entirely justified in his war against the borders. He had only denied burning those innocent of waging war against him. There were no promises from anyone that war would not come here again, or that it would not be brutal. It was necessary to train all the young men possible.

As she watched the men spear scarecrows and battle straw-stuffed dummies, she was surprised to see that Isobel was riding that day as well. Her cousin-in-law approached her, waving. "Good morning, Eleanor."

"Isobel," she murmured.

"Does it make you want to bear armor again, and go rushing to the defense of your country?" Isobel inquired.

"No. It makes me sad to think of the horror and death that follows any battle."

"Ah, Eleanor! You are a true paragon. Of virtue, that is. Aren't you?"

"Isobel, please, if you have something to say to me — say it. And if you find yourself too miserable here, I'm sure that it would be far more comfortable to await this latest campaign in London. You can bear a child there as well as any place, and no matter where the child is born, if I don't provide the heir and Alfred doesn't marry, well . . . you can return when the time is right!"

Isobel didn't answer for a moment. Eleanor thought that for

all her determination and zestful effort, Isobel had yet to conceive the child she was so ardently — and openly — planning.

"Corbin remains here for the time. So will I. By your good grace, kindness, and benevolence, of course."

"The property remains his home, and Alfred's, as my father wished. You are Corbin's wife."

"Aye, we are kin. That's why I've come to warn you."

"Warn me?"

Isobel appeared very grave. "There's rumor afloat."

"Oh? And how have you heard this rumor?"

"Your husband came here with men and servants of his own."

"And his men come to you — with rumor?"

"I have befriended a few."

"Um."

"Enough to know that Alain has sent men to Liverpool in search of the truth."

"What?" she said sharply.

"Your husband is a dear and noble man! He listened, of course, to the pirate's story that he was paid to seek out your ship on the Irish Sea! He has sent them to make inquiries."

Eleanor said nothing, not wanting her to know that Alain had not discussed his fears, and his determination to find the truth, with her.

"Apparently, certain rogues in Liverpool mentioned the fact that if you were not quite safe from the brigands before, you are now. Clarin will never be attacked by the Scots."

"I was Wallace's prisoner. His forces were decimated at Falkirk, but his words still carry great authority."

"Yes, so it's said. And there's another outlaw, a pupil of his, so they say, who had made astonishing raids, and cut deeply into the English efforts to rule the savage ruffians in the south of Scotland. His word carries great weight as well."

"Really."

"They say you became his mistress. Poor dear, it might have been to save your life —"

"The Scots did not threaten my life," she said. "And whatever words come from the streets of Liverpool do not interest me."

"But you see . . . the Frenchmen talk as well."

Eleanor clenched her teeth, then took in a deep breath. She looked to the troops, and heard Alfred's sharp commands. She turned back to Isobel. "How is it, Isobel, that you draw such conversations from these men? Do you visit them at night? Do you fear my cousin will not prove himself fertile enough? Would you foist another man off as my cousin's in order to secure Clarin — should I fail to produce the heir?"

Isobel didn't even rise to anger; she smiled. "What of you, Eleanor of Virtue? Would you foist the bastard of a Scottish rebel and outlaw upon your husband?"

"Isobel, as I said, I have no announcement to make at this time."

"Alas, neither have I," Isobel murmured. "Eleanor, don't be cross with me. In truth, I merely came to warn you about what was being said."

"How very kind of you. But you'll excuse me, I have no time for rumor. I believe I can give some assistance to Alfred."

She spurred her horse and started across the field.

Alfred was stunned when she insisted on helping to give instructions on the proper use of a sword.

She took his heavy weapon, hiked up her skirts, and gave a solid lesson indeed to a youth who was just learning to handle his own steel.

She practiced till dusk, exhausting herself.

And even then, her soul remained alive with fury.

And unease.

* * *

Brendan drew up his plans to attack Hebert's holding, his diagrams drawn in the dirt with a stick, his men at his side, giving grave heed. The night before the attack, they all knew where their meager forces would be, and when, and where, they would move.

As arranged, they came as close as they dared to the fortress before dawn on Friday. They watched, they waited.

Dawn came. Nothing. Eric's eyes conveyed his lack of trust in their newfound friend.

But then, the courtyard became filled with activity. The stronghold was manned by about fifty men; horse soldiers all. Within an hour, thirty had ridden from the fortress.

Heading northwest.

When the last of them had gone, Brendan sent Gregory back to the gates in a tinker's wagon; Garth, able to perfect a north country accent, drove. Once they were in, Garth drew attention, pretending to be a vendor of needles.

Gregory slipped to the gates. Brendan counted his time, knowing that there were a few moments that could still prove Gregory's news to be a trap — and they could fall in. But as they surged across the fields for the walls, the gate — his job to lower — fell open, and the Scots were able to rush the fortress.

Within two hours, the structure was secure. The remaining defenders were locked into the dungeon. Hebert was not among them.

Brendan had to agree that Lady Hebert looked like a mastiff. She might well bite like one, too. They didn't give her such a chance, sending her instantly packing toward the north where she could be held for ransom.

Eric doubted that anyone would pay to have her returned.

They set up their guards and sentinels and waited again.

When the English troops returned, weary and despondent at the quarry which had given fair battle and disappeared into the mists, they were allowed in — only to find themselves surrounded and trapped.

Lord Hebert was among them. He found himself on equal footing with his men in the dungeon.

That night, they celebrated in Lord Hebert's newly built great hall. The supplies were plentiful. They drank, roasted beef and lamb and all manner of fowl. There was wine and good ale. Brendan sat in the lord's chair by the roaring fire and watched the festivities. A number of men had been killed that day, but a number of Scottish citizens had lost their bondage to the enemy as well.

If they could hold the fort, he knew.

He met de Longueville's milkmaid, who was far more voluptuous than round, and the envy of many a man. Those not on guard feasted and ate too much and drank too much, but such a fine victory as this, so easily won, did not come often.

Eric pressed his shoulder. "Eat! Drink! Be merry. Find a lass; bed her."

He looked at Eric. "Someone must stay sober."

"Aye. You were almost so. Until the young Englishman mentioned Clarin."

Brendan didn't respond.

He had spent the months after leaving France eating, drinking, fighting, and winning — being merry. He'd found many a lass. He'd learned that the bitterness in his heart could not be so easily expunged; and this evening, he was content enough to watch the cavorting of his fellows.

"Brendan, if the old fellow dies, you have to realize, she will always be a million miles away. She is raising troops to ride against us, even now. And if she were not — "

"I am still wanted dead or alive — preferably alive, to die a slow and agonizing death. I am aware of all that," Brendan said.

"Then start to live again."

Brendan stared at him and leaned forward. "I am very much alive, though by our day to day lives, we probably share as great a percentage as de Lacville in the odds against dying tomorrow."

Eric lifted his hand. "You know the saying, Brendan. Who wants to live forever? That's why you must live for today."

Brendan pointed to Margot, across the hall, laughing at one of Liam's antics. "Perhaps you should live for today, since there is no assurance for tomorrow."

"And what does that mean?"

"It means you should marry her."

"You know that it's not possible. My father—"

"Your father is in Shetland; you are here, she is here. You risk your life, but not your father's wrath?"

"I'm afraid of no man—" Eric began, then laughed. "All right, so I fear his . . . disappointment."

"Were I you," Brendan warned him. "I would be more afraid of losing her."

"Well, cousin, you are not me. You are brooding over the enemy, a woman you can never have."

"Go to Margot," Brendan said quietly. "Leave me to brood alone."

"When you are done brooding, tell me. I'll find you a woman."

"When I'm done brooding, I'll find my own."

Eric laughed, clapped him on the shoulder, and went to join Margot. He slipped his arms around her. Margot leaned back into them, looked up at him, and smiled.

Brendan eased back in his chair, watching them. At the moment, he was tired.

Just tired.

* * *

The following day, Wallace arrived with John Comyn, and they set about putting a Scotsman in charge of the castle, manning the fortification, and guarding it.

They meant to hold it.

While he and his group prepared to move out, Gregory came up to him.

"I'd like your blessing, sir, to leave for a few weeks."

Ready to mount, Brendan paused, looking at him. "Why?"

"I need to go home."

"Why?" His question was one of surprise rather than anger.

"There's someone I left behind. I'd like to bring her here."

"If you're taken by the English, and any man recognizes you as a man gone to the enemy, you'll be arrested, face a mock trial, and probably a brutal death," he warned.

Gregory shrugged. "The men with me were not from Clarin; nor did they know I changed my allegiance. They were too busy running when you said the word to realize I'd been left behind. At any rate, sir, I don't intend to hand myself over at the castle. Just slip home, and then away."

"Who are you going back for?" Brendan asked cautiously. Margot was the only woman who had ever traveled in their company. She was indisputably with Eric, who was a frightening prospect for any man, and she was careful in helping when hiding in the woods preparing food — and living under the most extreme circumstances.

Gregory smiled. "Not a woman, sir. Well, yes, a woman. My sister; she is two years older, and all I have in the world. If I am ever recognized or discovered, as you warned, they may seize her, harm her . . ."

"Of course. You have my permission. Take the sorrel mare over there; she is a Scottish pony, and can't be recognized as any mount from an Englishman we might have captured or killed.''

"Aye, sir, thank you. I'll be back soon enough.''

Brendan nodded, watching as Gregory took the horse, waved, and started off.

Eric came to stand by him. "Where's he off to?''

"England.''

"Had enough of the woods, eh?''

"No. He's going home for his sister.''

Eric shook his head. "His sister?''

"Aye.''

"He'll not be back.''

"I warrant, he will.''

"Um. He'll come back with an army of Englishmen, ready to ride into the forest, and furrow us all out.''

Brendan shook his head. "He'll be back. I know it.''

"Aye? Do you know it?'' Eric demanded. "Or do you think he'll bring back some word of the countess.''

"Both,'' Brendan said curtly, and mounting his horse, he began to ride.

Eleanor ceased to worry about Isobel as Alain began to fail.

She didn't understand what was ailing him. He tired easily; he had since their marriage. But he had never suffered so wretchedly as he seemed to do now. His stomach emptied on him time and again; there were days when he could barely get out of bed.

They talked frequently in those days; he told her that yes, he had sent men to Liverpool, but he had discovered nothing. She told him what Isobel had said, yet held back the information that she was indeed carrying a child. Brendan's child. It seemed too soon. She would tell him in time. And she prayed that he would believe that she had never betrayed him after the marriage, as she had vowed that she would not.

Then, the days when he was well enough to talk began to come few and far between.

She spent hours with him, soothing his brow with cool water, just sitting by his side. She sent for the village doctor, who bled him and leeched him — and seemed to make him worse. On a day when the doctor had come and Alain had cried out throughout the treatments, she threw the doctor out angrily, swearing that he would kill her husband, rather than cure him.

He seemed to rally; then, three days later, he was sicker. Isobel came to the room, asking after him, sweetly, solicitously.

When she left, Alain said dryly, "She's looking to see if I'm dead yet."

"Alain! Please . . ."

"Perhaps she doesn't realize you can re-marry."

She shook her head. "I will never re-marry."

"Then you'll allow her to produce a two-headed monster to steal your father's heritage."

Eleanor bowed her head, trembling. She knelt by the side of the bed, holding his hands. She shook her head. "Alain, it's time that I tell. She frightens me, because what she says is true. Her offspring — two-headed or other — will not have Clarin. I'm expecting a child." Tears stung her eyes. 'I am quite certain now, but I swear to you, once our marriage vows were spoken, I did not betray you. It was before — "

His hand shook, but he touched her head. "Eleanor, I know."

"I did not see him again — "

"Eleanor, I know, my dear. He was at the church. I saw him there. I saw him walk away."

"What?" she said, startled.

"Aye, Brendan came to the service. He did not wait for it to end, but left the church, and the Scots rode to Calais that day."

She laid her head against his shoulder, shaking. "I would never have hurt you in any way — "

"Eleanor, a child is a blessing."

"But the world is so dangerous! And I must ask you . . . if you'll allow me . . ." she whispered.

"Eleanor—"

"With your permission only, I'll let the world believe—"

"I will be proud if you let the world believe the child is mine. Does anyone know?"

Eleanor nodded. "Bridie, but no one else. I wanted to wait. Until I could be certain that . . . that I was expecting, and that I . . . could carry the child."

"You won't be able to keep it a secret much longer."

"Alain, Bridie is . . ."

"Ah, yes, of course, she fell in love with one of the fellows as well."

"She does love him. I have tried to think of a way—"

"The fellow must know. And if she wishes to go to Scotland, he'll be a groom."

"Alain—"

"I will see to it."

She smiled. He meant it. He would do it.

"As for me, Alain, I will tell no one else—yet. Isobel may talk all that she wants. I want you to get well, first."

"Aye, my lady, I would like nothing better than to announce this together." He was quiet a moment. "You can never let Brendan know that the child is his. He would move the earth— and lose his fool head—to claim it."

"Why? He may have . . ."

"Scattered dozens of children in a dozen places?" Alain asked, and she blushed. "Nay, lady, I think not. He is fiercely proud, and comes from a race that takes great store in a family name, and in their heritage. I feared, indeed, that he would come for you in the midst of the wedding."

"But he did not."

"You had told him you wanted it."

"And I did."

Alain smoothed her hair. "You wanted to do what was right. I hope it was right, my dear."

"I hope that it was right as well. I hope that I have not hurt you. England has made you ill, and you're suffering so."

"I have never suffered to be near you. And you have made me very proud, pretending always that I remain a robust and virile knight, a husband in truth."

"Alain."

"Aye, Eleanor."

"You are a husband in every important way."

"You are too kind."

"Nay, my lord, you are too kind. And I do love you."

She heard his soft sigh. "As you loved your father."

"Alain—"

"It is enough."

"And don't worry. I will see to the fate of your maid."

But he could not do so.

Three days later, he had a violent setback.

In the middle of the night, he awoke. She heard him choking and came rushing into the room. To her horror, he had staggered up. He clutched the headboard; blood trailed from his lips.

"Alain!" she shrieked, and came running to him. She helped him back to the bed, caught a cloth and water, and wiped his face. He was stark white; he heaved. He tried to speak.

"I'll call the doctor!" she assured him.

The doctor! For all the good that he had done! But she was helpless now herself, and she burst out into the hall, shouting for help.

Alfred burst from his chamber, obviously from a deep sleep.

Corbin and Isobel emerged as well.

It was equally obvious they had not been sleeping.

"Alfred, please, someone must go for the doctor; it's Alain, he's taken a terrible turn . . ."

Alfred steadied her. "Go back to him. I'll get the doctor."

She rushed back into the room. Alain was up again, doubled over, biting into his lip to keep from crying out with the pain.

She held him, staying close, trying to stop his ragged shaking as the attacks seemed to seize him over and over again; it was as if he would be sick to his stomach — yet the insides of his stomach already seemed to be out. She tried cool cloths, and a sip of water, but the water came back, and he groaned with the pain seizing him.

The doctor arrived. He recommended cures that made no sense to Eleanor; there was nothing in him, but the doctor meant to purge him.

As they spoke, Alain began to toss on the bed.

He cried out suddenly.

"It is as if I'm poisoned, poisoned!"

They both stared at him. Isobel, in the corner of the room, leaped to her feet. "Oh, my God! Oh, my God!"

"He is not poisoned!" Eleanor said contemptuously. "Doctor, please — "

"Eleanor, Eleanor, where's Eleanor?" Alain called out.

She rushed to him. "I'm here, I'm here!" she said, holding him, the dear white head to her breast.

"Eleanor, the pain . . ."

"Oh, Alain . . ."

"Poison!" he said, and started to toss and turn. "As if I'm poisoned . . ."

"Alain, Alain, my poor Alain!" she whispered. She stared at the doctor. "You can do nothing to cause him more pain! You must help him!"

But even as she spoke, Alain began to thrash with such a violence that she was thrown from him. He screamed, winding into a tight fetal position on the bed.

And then, he went still.

She rushed back to him, taking him into her arms. He rolled slightly, staring up at her, his mouth working.

"Eleanor . . ." he whispered.

And then he died.

She felt it as the life went out of him, felt the change as his spirit left him, as death claimed him. In her arms, his hand still upon her own, a trickle of blood on his chin once again, his wise brown eyes still open on hers.

A sob escaped her, and she bit into her lip. Tears slipped silently from beneath her lashes.

She brought her fingers to his eyelids, closing them.

"Rest well, dear friend!" she whispered.

She cradled his form to her, holding him close, needing the warmth that would too quickly escape from his body.

"Eleanor—" Alfred began. "He is gone."

"I know."

"Come away," Corbin said, walking to stand behind her, placing a gentle hand upon her shoulder.

"Please . . . I need a few moments with him alone."

They were all silent. No one had moved. She didn't even realize it at first, she was so lost in the pain of seeing him suffer so . . . and losing him.

But then the silence wore on, and she looked up, and even Alfred was staring at her strangely.

The doctor was the one who spoke, walking forward suddenly.

"Poison!" he said. "We shall see."

Chapter 14

"How dare you!" she cried out with such fury in her voice that they all backed away. She was shaking; hands clenched into fists at her side. "How dare you even think . . . get out! Get out, all of you!"

She started forward with such a fury that the doctor disappeared with an astonishing speed. The others followed him.

Isobel the last.

She closed the door behind her as she left.

The silence in the room settled over Eleanor. She stood still for several long minutes, then the anger drained from her, and all she felt again was the pain, the deep anguish, that such a fine and noble man should die in such excruciating pain.

She went back to the bed, where he lay. The warmth was fading from him; his body began to stiffen. She held him to her again for a long time, her tears falling upon him. She rocked him, just holding him.

Then slowly, she began to wonder if he had been poisoned. He had suffered such violent spasms. She had seen rats die so, when they had set out poisons in the barn . . .

"My God, how I have wronged you, how I have wronged you!" she whispered.

She didn't know how much time passed then; she felt numb. At last, she stretched him out on the bed. She cleaned his face, and knelt by the side of the bed, and she tried to pray, but her mind seemed as cold and numb as the body of the man before her.

And still, she stayed there.

Sometime in the night, she fell asleep upon her knees. She awoke at the touch of gentle hands on her shoulders.

"My lady, you must come away. He must be prepared for burial."

She looked up. Bridie, slim and grave and looking old beyond her years, stood behind her.

"No one will touch him, Bridie. No one but you, and his own manservant."

"No one, my lady. Come. You must have some rest."

She allowed Bridie to help her to her feet. "Bridie, the doctor said that he was poisoned. And even Alain cried out the word."

"He was old, my lady. He was ill. Everyone knew it."

"I wronged him so."

"My lady, you did not poison him."

"My God, I would never have done so!"

"Shush, shush. It's all right. He adored you."

"I hurt him."

"You gave him his last happiness."

"I love him . . . but never loved him."

"You gave him what he needed. Believe me, Eleanor, you gave him pride, and a tremendous joy."

"He died because he came here."

"My lady, you must get some rest. You will injure the child."

That sobering thought gave Eleanor pause at last. Bridie pulled her away, toward the adjoining room, and her own bed. Eleanor stopped once, going back, tenderly kissing his cold forehead, smoothing back the white hair, touching the fine structure of his face.

"Come now."

Eleanor obeyed. Bridie led her to her own room, and gave her a goblet.

"What — ?"

"Mulled wine. It will help you sleep."

She drank the wine. She lay back, and lay awake. Bridie sat at her side.

"You're skin and bones, you know," she told her maid.

Bridie smiled. "I'm afraid so."

"The babe will show soon."

"Aye."

"Alain meant to help you; to get you to Scotland. I had not forgotten you."

"My poor dear, I know that you would never. Eleanor, you mustn't be distraught. Allow the wine to work, your soul to rest."

She closed her eyes. The numbness was still with her. Bridie pulled the warm wool blankets around her.

"We . . . I will still find a way for you."

"You must find a way for yourself, my lady," Bridie said. She kept talking, soothingly. Eleanor drifted. Exhaustion, and the strong heated wine took their toll.

She drifted into sleep with Bridie at her side.

For the next two days, she gave little heed to anyone. She chose clothing for Alain, and sent for Richard Egans, the finest carpenter in the village. He set to making a splendid coffin for the count.

Alain was laid out in the great hall.

The villagers came in deep sorrow, all to pay their respects. They prayed. They left new spring flowers at his side.

He would be buried from the small village church. Father Gillean, the rotund little priest who had led the souls of Clarin for nearly fifty years, spoke with Eleanor, allowing her to choose certain passages to be read for the funeral. The fourth morning after his death, Count Alain de Lacville and Clarin was borne upon the shoulders of six young men of Clarin, and carried to the altar of the ancient stone church. The service was read. Eleanor stood with her family, Alfred at one side, Corbin at the other.

Isobel at Corbin's side, crying daintily.

Yet when the service had been read, and the body would have been carried to the grave site, someone from the far rear of the church cleared his throat.

Eleanor heard the footsteps as they moved down the aisle, but she remained oblivious until she saw the man in the colors of the Duke of York standing before her.

He was not a man she knew, but obviously a man of some importance. His family emblem was emblazoned on his tunic as well.

She had not expected him, but apparently Alfred had. He looked at her gravely as the man approached. "Eleanor, Countess of Clarin and de Lacville?"

"Of course," she murmured.

"My lady, you will return to the castle with me."

She stared at Alfred.

He looked miserably to the floor, then into her eyes.

"Word of the count's manner of death has created a stir, Eleanor. This is Sir Miles Fitzgerald. He has been sent by the Duke of York to look into the . . . circumstances."

She stared again at the man who had come.

"My husband is not yet even in the ground—"

"My lady, he will not be set into the ground until my physicians have conferred with your doctor, and the body is examined."

"Why didn't you tell me about this?" she asked Alfred.

"You were so upset. I didn't want you to be further disturbed."

The numbness which had seemed to surround her for days departed then, cleanly, clearly. "I am being accused of murder, and you didn't want to upset me?"

"My lady, at the moment, we are merely seeing to the count. Your husband was a very important man. With the rumor about, the French will be demanding answers. Alain was a personal friend of King Philip, you are aware."

"Of course, I am aware," she said. "Well, Sir Miles, you wish to speak with me? Then indeed, let's return to the castle."

She left the church in the lead, aware that Fitzgerald followed her closely. Outside the church, she saw that he had been attended on his ride here by a number of knights. They had not gone so far as to clad themselves in armor, but they were well armed, and appeared a stalwart group.

Ready to use force to take one lone woman?

Or to use force, if necessary, if anyone should protest their decision?

They sat in the great hall. Corbin brought her wine; she refused it.

Fitzgerald sat at the head of her table. The place where Alain had taken his meals, when they had first arrived.

"There is talk of poison. Your husband cried the word before he died," Fitzgerald said gravely, watching her. Neither Corbin nor Alfred sat. They stood behind her, as if they would leap to her defense.

She was glad of them.

She was not glad of Isobel, seated away from the table, near the fire.

Watching. Avidly.

"My husband had been ill since he came to England," Eleanor said. She leaned forward. "He died in agony."

"There are those who believe you killed him."

"Why? Why would I have killed him?"

"You are a young and beautiful woman. Married to a much older man."

"I chose to marry him!"

"There are those who say you chose an old man, knowing you must marry, before the king stepped in to make provisions for you."

"I knew I must marry, yes. And I chose Alain."

"So that he would bring prosperity back to Clarin—and die soon, leaving you a young widow with—perhaps—the right to choose a second husband entirely on your own."

"This is ridiculous!" she protested. "I did love Alain; aye, he was older! He was my friend as well as my husband, a very best friend—"

"But not a lover?" Fitzgerald queried softly.

She felt an icy grip, as if around her throat.

"Look," Corbin protested. "You do not know Eleanor, Sir Miles. She is loved deeply in this village for her kindness, and for her efforts to save lives. You never saw the tenderness she showed to her husband."

Fitzgerald sighed. "Believe me, this is a very sorry occasion for me, but I am sheriff for this region, responsible not just to the Duke of York, but to the king of England as well. Such an unhappy matter! But in England, we have laws. And we honor our laws. My lady, we must continue."

"Please do so," she said curtly.

"You were taken at sea by the Scots?" he inquired.

"I was seized by a pirate, then the ship was taken by the

Scots who happened upon it. I was then brought to Paris, and handed over to Alain and King Philip."

"And what of the Scots?"

"What of them, sir?"

"You came to . . . respect your captors."

"They did not mistreat me. I told you, I was taken to Paris—"

"By the king's greatest enemy."

She gritted her teeth, breathed slowly, then answered. "Perhaps you did not hear about incidents that occurred here, sir. A number of my people were horribly burned to death in a raid. Clarin was nearly destroyed. I rode—a *woman*—at the battle of Falkirk. I assure you, sir, I did not seek out the Scots."

"Nevertheless, they became your captors."

"Aye."

"You came to know them . . . intimately."

She stood. "Sir Miles, I did not kill my husband. I loved him. I swear by the Holy Trinity, I did not kill my husband. Are we finished?"

Fitzgerald stood as well. "Madame, it is believed that you formed more than a friendship with the heinous outlaw, Sir Brendan Graham, and that you grew intimate with the greatest enemies of your king, Edward of England, Wales, Ireland, France—and overlord of Scotland."

"I never betrayed the king in any way. And I did not kill my husband. Are we finished?"

"Madame, you will not leave your room until we have finished . . ." Here even he looked uncomfortable. "With the body. Are we understood."

"Perfectly."

She whirled around, leaving the hall. She felt as if eyes bored into her back as she walked. She turned.

Indeed.

Isobel was watching her . . .

And trying very hard not to smile.

Brendan's men were careful to choose their military targets with deep thought as to their worth — against the risks that must be taken.

He was alone with his band in the borderland at the time; Bruce holdings were now loyal to the king of England, Red Comyn's men were still improving Hebert's fortification, and Wallace had traveled to Edinburgh to confer with the Archbishop of Lamberton, a rare breed of military holy man who was doing his best to walk a fine line with the English presence — and keep the fight for freedom alive.

The men knew how to infiltrate through the countryside, and most importantly, how to eavesdrop, question the people — and even English guards at various points — to know what was happening where, and when, along the borders.

But on a Monday morning in early May, Brendan was taken by surprise when Eric, who had been scouting with Thomas and Collum, burst into the secluded copse where they had camped — and where he now shaved carefully at a stream — to tell him that a group of armed and armored knights was crossing through the forest.

"Who are they?"

"I believe they've come from the motte and bailey castle just due north," Eric said. "They wear the king's colors, as if they were conscripted for his special command."

"The king — "

"The king is definitely not with them," Eric said, shrugging with disdain. "He's not an old fool; if he were ever to arrive in Scotland with so small a group, every man, woman, and child in this country would risk death just to scratch his face!"

"Which way do they ride?"

"South."

"South!"

"Aye, 'tis a curious group. Armed heavily, prepared for battle — yet moving away from us. Maybe civil war has erupted. Perhaps we should let them go. We don't know what they're doing."

"We can't let them go, for precisely that reason."

"They are wearing more than just mail; these are mounted knights, protected by plate as well."

"Then we will have to bring them down hard," Brendan said.

Eric understood Brendan's meaning perfectly.

"Aye, we'll set traps in the road, but we must hurry then."

"Aye."

But Eric paused, a glimmer of amusement in his eyes. "You missed a spot. Aye, nay, that's just an ugly chin you've got. Not enough Norse blood in you, me lad!"

"The ugly spot remains; there is plenty of good Scot's blood."

"Idiot blood; we've but a handful of men against at least twenty well-armed, well-trained men."

Their swords rested by an oak with branches that dipped over the stream. Brendan reached for Eric's, and tossed it to him.

"Who wants to live forever?" he queried.

"I, at least, shall go to Valhalla. You will have to do penance for years in Purgatory," Eric informed him, deftly catching the heavy weapon.

"You lie; you are baptized a Christian. And they will let you rot with the sinners far longer than I."

Eric grinned. "Maybe we shouldn't die."

"Indeed. Let's not!"

*   *   *

The day stretched out endlessly.

Once, she attempted to leave her room. One of the men, a goodly fellow over six feet and appearing to weigh near a ton, greeted her at the door.

"I would like my maid," she said.

"I'm afraid that is impossible, my lady."

"Why?"

"You stand accused—"

"Accused. Not condemned," she said.

"My lady, I'm sorry. Another woman—"

She slammed the door before he could finish.

Later, however, she heard a tap at the door. She answered it, and was surprised to find Corbin. He appeared ill, his handsome face ashen.

"May I come in, Eleanor?"

"Of course."

He entered the room. He paced, then sat in a chair before the fire. She sat before him.

"Eleanor . . ." He lifted his hand in a futile gesture, then shook his head miserably, and leaned forward. "My God, Eleanor, I'm so sorry for all of this! I know that you are not guilty, but they will not listen to me. And we can do nothing . . . for these are the king's men. To stop them . . . well, Clarin could not withstand the king's army."

"I know that, Corbin," she said. "But how have these men come here? Why?"

"We knew that the Duke of York had ordered Fitzgerald here . . . but I had thought it was just to clarify the count's death."

"Oh, he has come to clarify!"

"We didn't know he'd come to accuse!" Corbin said.

"How?" Eleanor said. "How then . . ."

"The doctor."

"What?"

"Our good doctor went to them. When he left here that night, I thought little of it. But he was angry with you, Eleanor. He said that he was curing the count, but that you kept getting infuriated with his medical methods, and threw him out."

"Alain had no blood left—and he kept taking more and more!"

"Eleanor, I'm just telling you what happened. Again, he complained as he left here, but we thought nothing of it, we were all ... at a loss. I didn't know that he had left the village ... of course, he has not shown his face again."

"I kept the little bastard from killing Alain, and here I stand accused of poison!"

Corbin took in a deep breath, staring at her. "Eleanor, I have hovered about the best I could. They have taken the count's body and inspect it still and ..."

"Aye?"

"There are signs of poison. A blackness beneath the nails ... certain tinges to the flesh ... there's not much I know about such matters, but the experts can find traces that ... he might have been killed."

"Corbin, I didn't kill him! My God, if I'd wanted to re-marry, I didn't have long to wait anyway! He was old and in poor health from the moment we said our vows."

"Eleanor, you didn't, certainly ... but who else? Who else would benefit from his death? Not Alfred or I—his death only allowed your re-marriage while you were young—and very fertile."

Eleanor moistened her lips. "Isobel?"

Corbin shook his head, frowning—and dismissing the thought completely. "My wife is a shrew, mean as a rabid wolf, but she is always open in her contrivances. She wants a child—but she wanted you with Alain as long as possible. The longer he lived, the older you became, the less chance that you would bear a child.''

Eleanor sat back. *Unless Isobel had heard her conversation with Bridie, and knew that she was already with child*. Then, she needed to die along with Alain. What better way to kill her than have her executed for Alain's murder?

Still, now, she was especially afraid to share the fact that she was with child with anyone. The fact might put her — and the child — even more at risk.

"I didn't kill Alain. And I don't trust your wife.''

"Eleanor, I swear to you, I will do everything in my power to prove your innocence.''

"Thank you.'' She hesitated, afraid for herself — and for others in her household. "Corbin, do you know where Bridie is?''

"She is safe enough — for the moment. Since she was with you when you were attacked at sea, then with the Scots, and in Paris with Alain, they believe that she must be extensively questioned. She is being held in solitude in her room, just above you.''

"Thank you. Don't let them hurt her, Corbin.''

"I won't.''

"Do you need anything, want anything?''

"No.''

"They have brought a woman with them to attend you.''

"I don't wish to have an attendant.''

He rose, and kissed her forehead. "I'm going to go back and demand to know more about what is happening.''

She nodded, looking down at her hands.

He lifted her chin. "I know you, Eleanor. And God will prevail.''

"He must,'' she said, smiled, and let him go.

* * *

When night fell, there was a tap at the door again. Expecting Corbin, she ran to the door and opened it.

A woman stood there; as tall and slender as Bridie, but as dour as Bridie was pleasant. She was austerely dressed in stiff linen; her lips were primly compressed, and her hands were folded before her.

"If you need any assistance, Lady Eleanor, I am here."

"Ah. Well, I don't need any assistance."

"My lady, a tub and water are being brought now. I will see that they arrive, and assist you."

"Truly, I need no assistance." She wanted to slam the door, but controlled the impulse.

She hadn't asked for a bath to be brought. She hadn't seen anyone to ask. Curiosity plagued her, and she didn't want to antagonize these strangers in her house any more than necessary.

"I thank you, and if I do need any assistance whatsoever, I will, of course, ask that you be called."

She closed the door quietly.

A moment later, there was another tap. She opened the door. Two of the young villagers had arrived with a tub. One was Tyler, the son of old Timothy, a handsome lad of about sixteen with a thick thatch of dark hair. The other was Gregory, whose parents had died one after the other, just a few years ago. He had lived with his sister until called to train for service in the king's army. She hadn't seen him now for a very long time.

"Tyler, Gregory, my deepest thanks," she said, welcoming them as they brought the tub. She was about to ask Gregory what he was doing back, but a strange glance from him warned her to keep her silence.

"Ah, my lady, here, before the fire?"

"Fine."

"The water comes behind us."

Two more of the village youth appeared bearing buckets of water; they were emptied into the tub but for one.

"That goes to the kettle, to be warmed above the fire again," Gregory instructed the other man. "My lady would have the water very warm. Here, I'll take care of it."

He took the water bucket. She thanked the lads, and they left, along with Tyler; Gregory made a pretense of putting the water into a kettle to set over the fire. When the others had gone, the door remained ajar. She looked at it, then at Gregory, who shook his head and mouthed the words. "Don't close it, m'lady. They will think it suspicious."

She walked over to him, hunching down as if to stoke the fire. "Gregory, what are you doing here? Suspicious of what?"

"Me. I shouldn't be here."

"I know that. Why are you here?"

"I came for Molly."

"Your sister?"

"Aye."

"Gregory, she is not in the castle," she advised him softly.

He offered her a quick grin. "I know that. She is already on the road north."

"North?"

"I am riding with the Scots now."

"The Scots!"

She almost spoke too loudly. He brought a finger back to his lips.

"With Sir Brendan Graham."

She almost gasped aloud again, but quickly covered her mouth.

"Gregory, that's madness — "

"The man spared my life — and the lives of others. A generosity from an enemy I don't suppose comes often."

"But, you remain—"

"Nay, my lady," he said, shaking his head. "I ride with the Scots."

"You'll wind up killed, Gregory," she said sadly.

He smiled. "No more so than riding for Edward."

She had lowered her head, trying not to speak of Brendan, but she had to ask.

"How is he?"

"Clever and wily as a fox. He takes a nick in the flesh here and there, surely, but fares remarkably well."

"He'll still get himself killed."

"My lady, you are the one in danger now."

"I didn't kill my husband."

"No one who knows you would believe you could do such a thing."

"They will not prove me guilty."

"My lady, they have already determined that you are."

"I must stand trial—"

"Aye, you'll stand trial. And there's no proof that you did not. The doctors have determined that Count de Lacville did die from poisoning, slowly administered, and when he did not die quickly enough, you fed him a lethal dose."

She stood, fury sweeping through her. "I didn't kill him—but if they are right, and he was poisoned, then someone is guilty. And I swear—"

"My lady, you are in grave and serious trouble. Tomorrow Fitzgerald will listen to the final diagnoses of the doctors . . . and then you will face trial. They'll take you to London. And you may well face a death penalty. Edward may decide that you must lose your head—to appease Philip of France."

"How do you know all this?" she asked with dismay.

"I listen well—though these are not facts kept secret here in the castle. Due to the love borne you by the people here,

Fitzgerald may send for more men before trying to escort you to London for the trial.''

She touched his hand briefly. ''Thank you, dearly, for this information. But you must follow your sister, quickly, and leave the north of England. If anyone knows that you have changed your allegiance, you will be executed, and quickly, with a rope from the nearest branch.''

''My lady, I will come back—''

''You will not! You will not risk your life for mine. Do you understand?''

''My lady, when I find Sir Brendan—''

''By the time you find him, I pray that I will be long gone. Or that I will have discovered my own method of escape. Now, please, you must go, and quickly. I would not have any harm come to you.''

He looked to the door, then kissed her hand quickly. ''My lady—''

''If it were possible without costing the lives of everyone here, my cousins would have made a move by now. I won't have scores of men dying on my behalf.''

''Not even for justice? For the count?''

''I won't have a war on this property again, women and children ridden down, village and people ravaged.''

''But my lady—''

''I am not without some talent for escape,'' she told him, smoothing back her hair and smiling. ''And thank you—you have already taken a terrible risk.''

He nodded bleakly, ready to leave. She caught his arm. ''Is he really well?''

''Sir Brendan?''

''Aye.''

''I swear it, my lady.''

She released his arm. ''I'm glad. I . . . pray for him. Go now; go quickly.''

"The water."

"What?"

"The water has boiled. I should pour it."

"Yes, yes, of course."

Just as he was pouring the water, the oversized guard peeked in. "Come along, lad," he told Gregory.

"Aye, sir."

Carrying the last empty bucket, eyes downcast, Gregory left the room.

Eleanor closed the door behind him. She stared at the water, and decided on a bath. Leaning back into it, she pondered his words, closing her eyes as the steam wound around her.

She might face a trial; but she had already been judged guilty. Someone had killed Alain. Mercilessly. Isobel. It could only be. There was no way to exonerate herself, and prove the truth. For all appearances, Isobel would have nothing to gain by Alain's death.

While she . . .

Isobel would have seen to it by now that the "rumor" about her Scottish lover was well circulated. Edward would be the final judge in this matter, as Alain was a beloved subject of his new brother-in-law. Edward would be incensed that any loyal Englishwoman would willingly fall to a savage, heathen, rogue of a rebel outlaw — a man in the service of the loathed Wallace.

She was condemned, without being tried.

For a moment, her heart beat too quickly. Gregory had seen Brendan. He was alive and well. Still fighting with his ragtag band. His head would remain on his shoulders no longer than hers.

He would come for her, she thought whimsically.

No. She was not worth Scotland to him. Nothing was. Her own family, in command of guards and sizable troops, dared not help her lest they all be cut down. He mustn't come for her . . .

She prayed then that she would be long gone before he ever appeared. Not even he could stop what was to be, though he had stopped her often enough . . .

That thought caused her to look to the window. She gazed back to her bed, and wondered if she couldn't rig a rope of bedding once again, and make it to the courtyard. If she could do so . . .

And reach the crypts and dungeons, there were sewage laden tunnels that followed the water to springs beyond the walls.

If she was to escape, she must manage on her own. She had some time at least . . . a day and a night.

She looked uneasily to the window.

She could well kill herself, trying to slip out.

Yet they *would* kill her if she did not!

Chapter 15

Brendan lay in wait so long that it seemed the branch of the oak would give way with his weight. But they had set the trap; whatever time it took, they were in position, and there was nothing to do but stay silent, and let the time pass.

At last, when twilight was nearly gone, he heard the approaching horses. From across the road, Eric signaled to him. He returned the signal. A whisper went through the branches.

They might well be abetted in this scheme by the deplorable state of the road. The Romans had long ago carved it, on their few prods into Scotland, before they decided that the riches to be gained were not worth harrying the warlike people of the north. Since Alexander's days of peace, wars and lack of funds had let the roads worsen from what the weather itself was likely to effect. Deep grooves marred the road; it had rained, so the terrain was slippery and dangerous.

He listened; felt the oak vibrate. They were not coming

quickly, but the horses were heavily laden with the riders in the armor. He wished they would opt for a little more speed, but with night coming on, they would not do so.

The horses came closer and closer.

They paused; Brendan swore, listening. Someone asked if they shouldn't stop for the night, but the lead rider replied tersely. "Nay, we'll not bed in this forest!"

"We are armed men against a handful of outlaws—"

"We'll not stop until we've cleared the forest!"

The horses came on again. Brendan's heart began to beat faster. He could see faces in the trees, all tense. They waited. The horses moved with a greater speed.

They reached the trees—and the all but invisible ropes stretched between them. Three horses in the lead; they immediately went down, screaming and shrieking in panic. One of the great animals backed into the others, causing another group to bolt. They, too, were caught in the web set to trip them in the road.

Screams and shouts went out; more horses floundered; men, in a panic, were caught beneath them. The others scattered, seeking the danger that only then leaped down upon them.

Indeed, they were like prey, caught in a tangle, and the Scots were like spiders, falling upon them, catching them in their webs.

"What, ho!" Someone shouted.

"Rally, rally!"

"Rise!"

"My leg is broken."

"Roger's skull is crushed."

"Rally, gather, form ranks!"

It was not to be; the felled Englishmen were left to flounder; those still horsed were dragged from their bolting mounts. They were heavy in their armor, awkward in the confines of the woods. Though they outnumbered the Scots, and gave good battle, they were caught, as if in quicksand. Men were trampled as many of the horses managed to bolt; others were slain as they gave fight. And when it at last appeared that they had the advantage, Brendan shouted out, "Surrender! Your lives will be spared."

"Nay, you heathens will cut our throats!" Cried one man. "Men! Cowards, wretched dogs, stand tall against these ragged outlaws, fight!" He rushed Eric, who sidestepped him, and indeed, neatly slit his throat before he could turn and take Eric down with his sword.

"Surrender!" Cried one of the survivors.

This time, there were ten.

"Who will speak for you?" Brendan demanded.

One man stepped forward.

"And you are?" Brendan inquired.

"Lord Gilly. Lord James Gilly," the man said.

"Gilly, *Lord Gilly.*"

"You promised our lives," Gilly reminded him.

"A promise I intend to keep — unless one of your men raises a sword to me."

He stared at Gilly.

"Drop your weapons," Gilly commanded.

Steel clattered to the earth, thunking and clanking. Brendan looked around the circle of his men, now surrounding the English.

In a body, they lowered their weapons. "We're curious, Lord Gilly. Why is such an esteemed body of men moving southward?"

Gilly was silent.

Brendan smiled, pointing northward. "More rebels do lie in that direction."

"We're called on an English matter. Not to fight the Scots."

Brendan leaned on his own sword. "Lord Gilly, I beg to

differ. Scotland lies yonder, so if you are not headed to fight us, that was surely your previous activity."

Gilly stood silent.

"Be so good as to inform us regarding this English matter you are riding off to handle."

"We are to see that a prisoner is taken from her home without trouble, nothing more."

"Her?" Brendan arched a brow to Eric. "A troop of armed and armored men is sent to take one woman?"

"A murderess," Gilly explained. "We are taking her to trial."

"How like the English. She is labeled a murderess, but has yet to go to trial."

"The evidence is clear, I'm afraid."

"So all you men are sent?"

"It is an English affair—"

"But you are Scottish prisoners, and I am curious."

Gilly shrugged beneath the weight of his armor. "The lady is loved in her land. She must be taken, for the king's justice."

"A noblewoman?"

"Countess Eleanor of Clarin and de Lacville. It is her husband, an old, renowned French nobleman, who was poisoned."

He nearly fell from his sword.

"When is she to be taken?"

"The day after tomorrow."

"Where?" he asked brusquely.

"To London, and there to stand trial, and meet her judgment."

"And death?" he said harshly.

"As I have said—"

But he had heard enough. "We'll have your armor, gentlemen, and your clothing. A few of these fine, stalwart fellows will see you north; no man who holds the peace will be harmed. Your families will be notified, and we will gladly see that you are ransomed home. Lord Gilly, I will have another word with you, and quickly!''

He took the man down the lane while Eric ordered the knights to help one another off with their mail. The few squires in the company came forward, and the clanking of the steel seemed very loud in the night.

''I need to know everything you know about this situation,'' Brendan told Gilly. ''The count is definitely dead? Why is the lady accused? How many men are at Clarin, and beneath whose authority have they come?''

''The Duke of York sent out the sheriff, Sir Miles Fitzgerald. He has, if I understand correctly, ten men beneath him. Apparently, at the count's death, the symptoms of his illness suggested poison, and an examination of the body was demanded.'' Gilly stared at him a long while. ''It was a sad duty, but one to which we were called to obey. I knew the lady's father well; a fine man. I remember the countess as a child, sitting upon his lap while he read stories from around the world. It is a tragedy that she should come to such an end.''

''A tragedy, indeed. Clarin is not so small that she does not offer her own troops.''

''It is feared that her own people would refuse to obey the order to bring her to trial.''

''So there are about ten of the sheriff's men?''

''Aye; we would have brought the number to fifty.'' He cleared his throat. ''We were a trained fighting force.'' He sounded confused, as if he still weren't sure himself how they had managed to fall to a small number of outlaws in the forest.

''This is news I am deeply grateful to have,'' Brendan told him. ''I'll see that you are ransomed quickly, and that you and your men are detained in the best comfort we have means to offer.''

Gilly bowed to him in acceptance. Brendan moved back to the body of his men. Eric had the armor gathered, the men's tunics taken, and the situation well in hand. "Off to the north you go, good fellows," he told the Englishmen, striding for one of the horses. Liam was assembling the men to move back along the trail, the way they had come.

Eric walked to Brendan, halting him.

"You can't go riding off to Clarin."

"I must."

"You'll pull the noose right around her throat."

"They have her condemned already."

"Brendan, damn you, you must come up with a plan. We must come up with a plan. It is sure death—"

"I'll ride alone. I'll have no man's death upon my shoulders."

"Brendan! Has your fear made you daft!"

Brendan paused, breathing deeply. "Aye!" he muttered. Then he sighed. "I'll take care. I'll ride like no madman. I will come up with a plan."

"We'll come up with a plan."

Brendan leaned low to him "We may not live forever, but I know that you'd like to see a few more years."

Eric grinned. "Liam will not let you ride alone. Nor will Collum. And a number of others."

"We need an escort to take the English north."

"Aye. We'll split."

"We cannot leave them short—"

"Brendan, note the road."

He did. It was littered with the men who had fallen. Hagar, a huge Scotsman, kneeled sadly by the head of one of the horses brought down. The animal had broken its leg. Hagar was much fonder of animals than people—especially Englishmen. With tears in his eyes, he took the horse's head, smoothed its nose, and in an instant, broke the animal's neck, ending its pain.

Brendan looked back to Eric.

"We'll bring Hagar," he said quietly.

"Now there's a plan," Eric agreed. "At least the seed of one."

"May we ride south as we take it further?"

"Aye."

"And we'll bring the arms—and the colors of these fellows."

"You have a plan?"

"Not yet. But we'll be prepared."

Thomas de Longueville strode to him. "We ride south?" he inquired cheerfully.

"Aye, if you'd join me."

"I'd not stay away. You know, a pirate and a good fight."

"A deadly fight."

"I've beat the gallows once. God rides with me."

"Let's pray He does."

The following morning, Eleanor was working with the sheets she had gathered when a firm rap came at her door. Composed, she cast the sheets on the bed, covered the knots with a pillow, and walked to the door.

Miles Fitzgerald stood just outside. "My lady, I am heartily sorry, but an escort will arrive in a day's time. It is my duty to bring you to London. I have no choice but to bring you to justice for the murder of your husband."

"I didn't kill him, sir," she said quietly. "I am innocent."

"My lady, I wish that were so. With all my heart. But I must do my duty."

"Indeed, you must."

"Make yourself ready for the journey to London. You will have the day and night to pack and prepare."

"As you say. I will defend myself; I am innocent."

"I will send a priest, that you may cleanse your soul."

''You may send your priest; my soul is amazingly pure.''

''God help us all,'' Fitzgerald said softly.

''I know He will help me,'' she said simply.

''Good day, my lady. I do pray for you.''

''And I do forgive you your duty,'' she told him. He turned, and she closed the door. For a moment, far more anxious than she would ever let on, she paced the room. She forced herself to get back to her work.

She was running out of time. Tonight. It must be tonight.

She knotted, twisted, used the weight of the bed to test her work. At each sound of a movement in the hall, she hid it all again beneath a pillow, waited, and started up again.

An old crone brought her meals. She did not see her family. She was offered water for washing, but not another bath.

She prayed that Gregory had made it safely away.

And she thanked God that he could not reach Brendan. God knew, the Scots were rash. He could come . . .

The very idea raised incredible hope in her heart. Hope she quickly dashed. She would not kill him as well.

At times, the very real threat of facing an execution came to her, and the panic she felt was paralyzing.

The day passed; twilight came.

Soon after, there was another rap at the door. She was amazed that her keepers at least kept up such a show of courtesy. But she was, of course, even as an accused murderess, a noble one.

She hid her sheets, plumping the pillows above them.

''You may enter,'' she called.

The door opened.

The light in the hall beyond her room was dim. She squinted for a moment.

There, a silhouette in the night, stood a man. Tall . . . filling the doorway. He was cloaked in encompassing brown wool.

A cowl covered his head, and most of his face.

She stared at him blankly, then rose, remembering.

Paris, the palace on the Île de la Cité, and the night that *he* had come to her so.

I have sinned! She had told him.

And you will sin again! He had replied.

Her heart took flight.

She could not help but feel a ray of ecstatic hope — but then her hope was mingled with dire dread. He had come for her! The fool.

He would die for her.

Aye, for the duke's men were everywhere. Brendan would be killed as well. She had to get him to leave, quickly. And still . . . she was shaking. She couldn't stand.

She grabbed his hands, so weak that she fell to her knees. "You have come!" she cried out.

The man cast back the cowl that had covered his face. It was not Brendan. It was a tall, gaunt-faced priest with the eyes of a fanatic.

"Of course, I have come. The Church will hear all confessions. You will forfeit your mortal life, but it is my duty to see that your soul goes to Christ! Confess, my lady, and the king will make every effort to see that you may keep your head upon your shoulders, though Philip of France will scream long and hard, demanding your blood. Count de Lacville's heir will demand that your life be sacrificed after the cruel treachery you practiced upon so noble a man!"

In horror, she stood.

"I did not kill my husband," she said icily.

"If you confess — "

"I will not confess to what I did not do!"

"God, and the king, are kinder to those who admit their deeds."

"Again, I tell you, I did not kill my husband. And you are not my confessor. If I need advice or counsel, I will call my own priest."

"You no longer have such a privilege."

"Then I will speak with God directly. Leave me alone. I have nothing to say to you."

"You put your immortal soul in peril."

"I do not; God knows my innocence."

He pointed a long finger at her. "Being a man of God, I will give you another chance."

At last, he left. She followed him to the door and leaned against it, trembling.

Brendan rode long and hard, Eric, Thomas de Longueville, Hagar, Liam, and Collum with him all the while.

They stopped only briefly to rest the horses, and to discuss what manner of approach they might take. They could not storm the castle, not with six men.

"We have the colors taken from Lord Gilly's men. We can ride in as the English escort," Eric mused.

"If Hagar keeps his mouth shut," de Longueville said. "His French has a heavy Scottish burr."

Hagar frowned.

"They will be expecting a much larger contingent of men," Brendan said thoughtfully. Then he lifted his hands. "I have no better idea. We can say that Lord Gilly was taken ill. I will be Sir Humphry Sayers, taking his place. There would have been many more in our party, but the Scottish raids have become more virulent in the last week. We've lost men, we are in danger of losing English fortifications."

"Who knows you at Clarin?" Liam asked him.

Brendan shrugged. "Eleanor, of course. And her maid . . ." he began hopefully, then shook his head. "Count de Lacville traveled with some of his retainers. They will know me."

"We wear the armor beneath the tunics, and keep our visors down," Liam suggested.

"All we have to do is get a distance from the castle, and then attack the sheriff, and his men," Eric said slowly. He smiled suddenly. "It might well work. Most English don't believe that we savages are capable of so many languages."

"I don't believe that Hagar is," Thomas said, grinning.

Hagar gave Thomas another frown. "It's a language for pretty boys — and English," Hagar drawled.

"Why you — " Thomas began.

Eric cleared his throat. "Gaelic, French, they are both languages for pretty boys. Norse, my friends, is a man's language."

They both turned on him, and saw that Eric was laughing.

"You're all far too amused," Liam said glumly. "We are about to ride to the devil."

Eric rose, ready to mount again. "It's all a ride, my friend. We should laugh to the bitter end. Come."

They were barely back on the road before Brendan raised a hand, hearing the sound of a horse coming their way. With a gesture, he warned the others.

They melted off the roadside. Brendan dismounted, keeping a hand on his horse's nostrils to keep the animal from shaking his head, and giving away his position.

A lone horse trotted along. The rider suddenly became aware of danger, and paused. Brendan frowned, waiting.

The horse took another step; the rider realized his danger. He started back.

Not wanting anyone to ride ahead and give warning that there were riders coming, Brendan quickly leaped on his horse, and started after the lone horse. It was a harsh ride; his quarry knew he was coming.

But as he drew alongside the mount, he saw two things. The rider was not alone atop the horse. A young woman rode with a man.

And the man was Gregory.

Gregory recognized him at the same time. They reined in.

"Brendan, Sir Brendan, oh, my God, thank God!" Gregory exclaimed. "I thought you were the English, the Scottish! A cutthroat out to kill us. I can't believe that I've reached you; we meant to ride night and day, praying! Brendan, you don't know what has happened—"

"Aye, but I do, lad."

"They're going to kill her! The Lady Eleanor. Execute her for supposedly poisoning her husband!"

"Aye, lad."

"There has to be something to do. There has to be."

"Aye, Gregory—"

"I saw her, and she said that I mustn't come to you, that you would die, too, and—" He broke off. "You know?"

"Aye. We came upon a group of men who were summoned to be the escort to bring her south."

Coming up behind them, Eric said, "Perhaps we should draw off the road here, and hear what else Gregory can tell us."

They did so, sitting in a circle, sharing the food Molly, Gregory's pretty young sister, had brought. Brendan hadn't thought about food. Not until the bread hit his stomach. He thanked Molly.

"She is indignant, of course. She is kept in her room, and they aren't letting her family see her at the moment. I kept my head low, and worked about the castle."

"And no one recognized you?"

"Of course. But I have many friends at Clarin."

"Tell me," Brendan said, "the English were called in force because the sheriff thought there would be trouble taking her."

"Aye, there could be."

"What of her family?"

"Alfred and Corbin seem distraught; Alfred is withdrawn and worried. Corbin is passionate, saying they must do something."

"What about the Frenchmen who accompanied de Lacville?" Eric asked.

"They seem to disbelieve what they are being told. They were with her at the count's estates in France, and in Clarin."

"So . . . if there is a fight, it will be with the sheriff's men," Brendan mused.

"The guard at Clarin will be obliged to a pretense of fight, naturally. And there are many trained men there."

"It will be best if we slip in, and slip out, as we have said," Eric advised.

"Actually, we don the English apparel, and ride to the gates."

"Keeps us from the fear of being caught immediately," de Longueville commented.

"Aye. Hagar, you will do no talking," Brendan said. "Not that I don't, personally, enjoy your French. We just don't wish to be caught."

"You will be the brawn," de Longueville said. He tapped his head. "We'll do the thinking."

"What about me?" Gregory asked.

"You will take Molly on north," Brendan said.

Gregory shook his head. "You need me."

"And why do we need you, lad?" Eric asked.

"Because I know the castle. I even know the sewage system, should we be forced to use it. There's a maze of channels beneath the place. Say we ride in, and ride out — as planned. I know who people are. I can warn you."

"You've your sister."

"I can wait in the woods," Molly said. "I'm not afraid. You do need Gregory. He knows the layout of the castle. In fact, you'll need to speak with Eleanor, to warn her, lest she try something on her own to put everyone in danger."

Brendan was silent for a moment. "Our plans sound good, but we could be caught with a single word or deed; we could be given away by someone we don't expect to know us — Gregory is right; we need him."

"Aye!" Gregory said happily. He looked at Eric. "Do you trust me now, then?"

Eric looked him over and shrugged. "More than less. If you should ever betray us, though, I'll have Hagar break your neck before we're cut down."

"I'll not betray you," Gregory said steadily. He gave Brendan his attention. "The lady must be warned. She is not a woman to sit idly about, waiting for a headsman's axe."

"That's true," Eric murmured.

"Well, Gregory, my fine friend, have you any ideas?"

Gregory grinned. "I think I do."

Chapter 16

She was ready.

She remembered the ship, and the house in Paris, and gave herself courage by realizing that she would have gotten away then . . . if not for Brendan.

Sir Miles Fitzgerald was not Brendan. He didn't know her, and wouldn't expect her to risk a broken limb — or a broken neck — in her determination to flee their mockery of justice.

She moved to the door of her room, leaning against it. She heard nothing outside.

From the bed, she gathered her long cord of bed sheets, and hurried to the window. Looking out, she saw that no guard had been posted on the inner castle parapets below. Her breath came fast.

She had a chance.

She fixed the cord strongly to the heavy wood bedpost. As she did so, she kept an eye on the door — praying she wouldn't hear a tapping. She tightened the linen cord, tightened it again, and watched the door. Then she moved to the window, tossing the cord outside. As she watched it fall against the stone, desperately hoping she had given it enough length, she heard a sound in the room.

She spun around.

The door had opened and closed without a tap.

And the wretched priest was back again. There was no way to hide her means of escape. She moved quickly to grasp the sheet.

''No!'' The word emitted harshly from him. Or had she spoken herself?

The man was across the room before she could get her form out the window. His hold was brutally strong.

''Man of God!'' she cried. ''You wretched, self-righteous, bastard.'' She squirmed and kicked.

''Wildcat!'' he exploded, pulling her away from the open window. He did so with such impetus that they fell to the floor together. She was angered, fighting wildly against him, scratching, clawing . . . managing a kick that caught him unaware. He groaned; releasing his hold for a minute. She took the advantage, flying to the window again, but he was right behind her. Again, he caught her. She spun, striking out. The arms of the man were like shackles.

''Shush!'' he commanded

''Let go—''

''You little fool! Stop it!'' He swung her again, arms about her, bringing her down. She squirmed madly on the floor, but no matter what she tried, he caught her, and in seconds his weight stilled her legs, his fingers clamped around her wrist, and she could barely breathe.

She was thoroughly caught, vised, and all but stilled. She nearly cried out with the sheer frustration of being so beaten. His hand then fell over her mouth. Stunned, she realized there was a soft burr in the voice, a voice she knew well. The cowl fell back, and she saw his face. She lay still, stunned. His hand moved from her lips. Her gasp escaped.

This time, the ''priest'' *was* Brendan.

''Brendan!''

''You should have known!'' he grated. ''It's not as if I have not worn this guise before. Madam, you have injured me grievously. The future of my line in Scotland might have perished here.''

''I didn't know—''

''Again, it is not a guise I have not used before.''

''A priest—a real priest, not my own, came before. I thought then that it was you—''

''Oh? You *assumed* I'd risk the entire English nation and come for you?''

''No! It was the robes!'' she protested. They still lay entangled. She could not believe he was there. His face, so close. Eyes sharp on her, flesh warm, vibrant. She clenched her teeth, trying not to tremble. This was madness.

''You shouldn't have come for me,'' she said. ''I was doing quite well on my own.''

''I don't think so. Your escape line wasn't long enough.''

''It was! I worked long and hard. And it was a plan,'' she lied suddenly. ''Only if I thought it necessary.''

''Only if you thought it necessary! When else would it be so!''

''Ease up, I beg you!''

He did so, rising, pulling her to her feet. She lowered her head, longing to throw herself into his arms, determined that she must not do so now. She turned away from him, walking to the window. The sheet hung to the stone floor below.

He was right. It had not been long enough. She might well have fallen to the stones, and broken her neck.

She kept her back to him, feeling a greater sense of fear with each moment that passed. *He was here, with the sheriff's armed men, Englishmen. There would be no fighting his way from this threat of death!*

"You'll note the cord by which you would have escaped, lady."

She had done so. She turned to him.

"I'm good at jumping."

"And crawling down more walls with a broken leg?"

"I remain in the castle now, and I might have been on my way through the water tunnels We're not out of here yet, are we?" she demanded. She was shaking. He was there; he had come for her. She should have been on her knees in gratitude. At the least, she should have been in his arms . . . one last time. Touching his face. Remembering.

He was mad.

She looked quickly to the outer door. They could burst in at any time.

"Where is the real priest?" she asked.

"Gone to converse with his maker."

"You killed a priest?" she demanded.

"He's trussed like a hog in the crypts below the church. There's another fellow there much more friendly to our cause. Of course, he instructed me to tie him up as well—he has a fondness for the food of the women of Clarin—and for his own head as well."

Her heart skipped a beat. "He helped you?"

"Aye, he did."

"How did you . . . manage?"

"My lady, we can play such games of question later. I dare not stay long; you are not penitent. and you are a shrew."

"I am not penitent for what I did not do—"

"Eleanor, I am not accusing you! I am telling you the situation. I have but a minute here. Tomorrow, you'll see me as part of your escort."

''What?'' she demanded, astounded. ''This is truly madness—unless I begged pardon of King Edward and came to the English side?''

''Now, that would be madness!'' he said.

''Sir, you are the outlaw with a price on his head then—in England.''

''And you've barely got a head left, my lady, so pay me heed! When you see me tomorrow, do not recognize me, do you understand? Eric is with me; de Longueville as well. You must pretend that you've never seen any of us.''

She stared at him, trembling still, unable to believe he was there, so overwhelmed by the sight and scent of him that she could barely concentrate on his words.

He had turned to the window and was hastily drawing in the sheets.

She set a hand on his arm.

''What of Fitzgerald's men?'' she asked.

He shook his head. ''What would you have me do, my lady? If they put up a fight . . .''

''He is only doing his duty.''

''Then I pray that he'll have the good sense to surrender.''

She was silent, hoping that he was right—and that Fitzgerald would be the one needing mercy.

She lowered her head. ''I didn't want more men to die for this!'' she said with anguish There is still a way out. I am accused, not condemned.''

He was very still, studying her. ''I won't leave you here. Because you're mistaken. They will see to it that you die.''

She looked up at him. ''As you noticed, I did not intend to stay. But perhaps it would be best if I did. Surely, they will have to give me a trial. I have been known as *Santa Lenora*. Legends travel. No one has offered me any harm; it is not unusual that I should be taken to London for a trial. I can defend myself in court, and that way, no man risks his life—''

"Our lives are risked being here!" he told her.

"But there will be greater danger! You and your men should go. Tonight! Before there is a chance you'll be discovered. And I won't have my people killed either. I must be able to clear myself. If he was poisoned, then someone else is guilty. If I run, it will appear that I did do the deed. And before God, I didn't. Someone will speak on my behalf. I do believe in God, Brendan. And he will intercede. I didn't do it. I'd have never killed Alain, never—"

"God *has* interceded, my lady. We are here," he said angrily.

She backed away from him, shaking her head. "You cannot get away with this!" she said softly. "You take too many risks; you've grown too desperate—"

"We've grown *able!*" He stepped forward, catching her by the shoulders. His jaw was clenched as he stared down at her. "Listen to yourself!" he said harshly.

"There are laws in England, good laws—"

"And justice can be miscarried."

"Brendan, I am grateful. Good God, I am grateful. Don't you see? Grateful enough not to let you die for me!"

"We won't die!"

"I—won't go along with your plan. You must get out of here, leave Clarin now. I'll betray you in the morning."

"No, my lady. You will not. You're arguing this, because you want to believe that in the end, your precious England will save you. You know it's a lie. Otherwise, you'd not have been halfway out the window."

"I've had time to think it clearly through. My cousins will not let me go alone. One of them will come to London. I will be defended—"

He let out an oath of frustration. "What?" He demanded harshly. "Damn you! You will not stay behind! You'll not risk your fool neck to the block. Why would you, lady? For a pile of stones; this land, dirt, your dead husband's riches?"

"For my good name!" she cried out.

"It's far easier to clear a name, lady, alive than dead!"

"Brendan—"

"I have to go. They know that you will not confess. Don't dare think to betray me in the morning, if you truly want this to end without bloodshed. You don't recognize me, or any of the men."

"Don't you see? It's impossible. Some of Alain's people will know you—"

"Not as I appear tomorrow."

"Brendan, I'm begging you, warning you, this is a fool's plan—"

The door suddenly opened before she could speak again. The guard looked in. "Father, is there trouble?"

With one last grim and warning stare into her eyes, Brendan lowered his head so that the cowl hid his face.

"Alas, trouble in Hell, with this one, there will be!" he muttered.

Head bowed, he walked out of the room.

Her knees would hold her no more. She sank to the floor, quivering.

She had dared dream that he would come!

And now he was here.

And she was terrified.

Brendan left Eleanor's room simply; outside her door, he told the guard to watch her well.

Going out the main door, he was relieved to see that although the sheriff had set a guard at her door, and his men stood sentinel at the entry and the gates, the family was alone in the great hall. He'd received descriptions of the people and the place from Gregory. There was Alfred of Clarin, a tall, stern, proud man, pious and moral, carrying a great weight of responsibility on his shoulders. Corbin, his younger brother, handsome and charming, with more of a sardonic look at life, and an acceptance of being the second son, landless other than the family's holdings, and those his by the good graces of first his uncle — and then his cousin. Eleanor.

Then there was Isobel, Corbin's wife.

Petite, elegant, a rare beauty. She sat before the fire as he passed the hall slowly. His first thought had been to leave as soon as possible.

His second thought was to listen.

"You cannot go with her to London!" Isobel was protesting, taking his hands. She appeared the true and loving wife. Her words were earnest.

"Alfred manages the estates with far greater talent than I," Corbin returned, drawing his hands back. "Someone must go."

"You can neither go!" she said, rising. "The king has sent out his call; you will be required to fight, to lead northern troops, when he is ready for his next assault. Corbin, you can't go to London! You'll be arrested yourself for failing the king's command. Alfred, tell him that he cannot go."

Alfred looked at her. "One of us must go."

"That is madness!" she said furiously, stamping a foot. She walked back to the chair where Corbin sat, brooding as he stared into the fire. "You risk everything! Corbin, she isn't innocent! I'm telling you, she was eager to get rid of her husband."

"Isobel, she *cared* for him. Don't you understand that?" Corbin said.

"The doctors know that he was poisoned. Don't you understand that?" Isobel replied. "Precious Eleanor! She would do this, she would do that! Are you both blind, are you deaf?"

"Isobel — "

"What other explanation is there?" she demanded.

"A contamination in the food supply — " Corbin began, but Isobel had already swung around to attack Alfred.

"Did you kill him?" she demanded.

"Good Lord, no, woman!" Alfred exclaimed, outraged at the very suggestion.

"Eleanor would gain from the count's natural death," Isobel said. "You, alone, Alfred, would gain from Eleanor's death."

Alfred strode across the room, slamming his hand on the table as he replied to Isobel. "I'll not take kindly to such words again, madam. I do my fighting in the field. Poison is a woman's work, slow—and vicious."

Isobel was silent for a moment, then she said softly. "There you have it, Alfred."

"Eleanor would never do such a thing."

"Even if she was desperate?" Isobel queried.

"And how would she be so desperate? She took great care with Count Alain. He saw the world rise and set in her every move."

"But I believe she was desperate," Isobel said softly. "You see, I think she is expecting a child."

"A child would have been gloriously welcomed by them both, Isobel," Corbin said, rising at last from his seat before the fire.

"Not if it was not the count's!" Isobel said softly.

There was silence for a moment.

"Isobel, what are you implying?" Corbin demanded.

"You both love your cousin," Isobel said, "and I understand that you don't wish to see that evil can exist, even in such a great heart! The French murmur of it; rumor abounds. Eleanor was seized surely, but then gave way to her captors. She formed an alliance with Wallace, and with Graham—the man to seize the ship from the pirate, the wolf in the forest who preys upon any party attempting the old Roman road north. Perhaps she was forced at first . . . but it is said that even the French king saw what was happening, and gave her warning."

"Isobel, this is a pack of lies. Rumor," Alfred said angrily.

Isobel shook her head. "She didn't sleep with her husband. They kept separate rooms."

"The majority of the noble and wealthy in the known world keep separate rooms," Corbin said.

"And separate beds."

"For years, my dear, we did the same," Corbin informed her. "Were that a crime, we'd have both lost our heads long ago."

Isobel was not satisfied. "He was — incapable."

"Oh?" Corbin inquired, pouring himself a large draft of ale from a pitcher on the great wood table centered in the room. "Did you discuss this with the count?"

"A woman knows."

He threw up his hands. "My cousin would not kill the knight she chose to marry because he was . . . incapable."

"He would find out about the child."

"Isobel, what makes you so certain she is expecting a child?"

Isobel was silent a moment, then smiled slyly and repeated, "A woman knows."

"I will ride with my cousin, Isobel, and that is that," Corbin said firmly. "She must have a voice to speak for her."

"As you will. But you will have your brother destroyed if you do."

Alfred had sunk into the chair at the head of the table. He pressed his head between his palms. "We will take that chance, Isobel," he said. He shook his head. "God, but this has made me ill as well!"

"Perhaps it is something you've been eating," Isobel suggested slyly.

He looked up at her. "Well, my cousin has been locked away now, so she could not be guilty, could she?"

"I heard the doctors. Alain was poisoned slowly," Isobel replied.

Brendan had heard enough. He decided to start out. As he crossed the hall, Isobel looked up, and saw him.

"Father!" she cried out, leaping to her feet.

For a moment, he contemplated the idea of pretending he had not heard her — and continuing on quickly out. But he did not want to arouse suspicion, and so he halted.

Isobel came to him, hands folded before her piously. "Father, has the lady confessed her sins to you?"

"No, madam. She protests her innocence. We will, of course, continue to pray for her soul as she journeys to London."

Corbin came over. "Perhaps she is innocent."

"God knows the truth, my son." He kept his head lowered.

"I will come with her; I will prove the truth."

Brendan hesitated, wondering if the man's desire to uphold his cousin's innocence — and her life — was sincere. He did not want her family on this supposed journey to London. Eleanor didn't want bloodshed on her behalf, but it was likely to occur. She would protest the slaying of her kin, he was certain.

"Perhaps it would be best, as your wife suggests, if you were to remain here."

"Even you, a man of God, stand against her!"

"This is England; she will be granted a fair trial — won't she?"

"The evidence stands against her," Alfred said wearily from the table. "Father, may we offer you wine, ale?" he added, as if remembering the hospitality of the castle.

Alfred did not look well. Brendan was tempted to test his role, but then decided against eating or drinking anything in this house. He also felt an inner fire; a startling anger against the very woman he had come to save. *Was any of this true? Not the poisoning; he refused to believe Eleanor a murderer. But as to a babe, and her relations with Alain . . .*

"No, sir, my sincere thanks. I must hurry back to the church, and pray. And I am weary."

''You are not the man who came earlier,'' Isobel said, frowning earlier.

''Aye. We thought that different men of God might find a change in the lady's story.''

''And was there such a change?'' Corbin asked.

''No, sir, there was not. If you will excuse me I will leave, and I will pray for you.'' He gravely made the sign of the cross above Isobel's head. ''The Lord watch over you, madam.''

''Amen,'' she murmured.

''And keep you from his place of Purgatory for women, where the sinners who have spoken too much, and too quickly, where the wicked iron of a scold's bridle to silence their wagging tongues until the dawn of eternity has long gone on.''

He left before Isobel could respond.

He returned to the rectory where his men had dared to cast off the heavy armor, and enjoy the round Father Gillean's fine supply of food.

Father Gillean had warned them that he must be left muddied, dirtied, apparently beaten, and tied like a hog for slaughter, along with the fellow churchman, the sheriff's far more aggressive priest, before they departed in the morning.

But apparently, though he had been frightened, and determined to be trussed when they first arrived, he was now at a small table in the rear of the room, playing chess with Hagar, who had an uncanny talent for the game. He was drinking wine, and softly swearing here and there.

Thomas de Longueville had done the cooking, with Gregory, who had first approached the church, and given him the idea of entering the castle as the lady's confessor. Now, de Longueville served the meal, and was telling them all they were a group of unkempt wild men, living on berries and raw butchered meat so long that they knew not of the finer gifts of the earth God had granted to flavor their food.

Brendan didn't know what the surprisingly versatile Frenchman had found with which to cook, but the bowl of stew he sat down to was hot and appealing and he all but wolfed it down before he realized that Eric was staring at him, ready to hear what had occurred.

"You reached Eleanor with no difficulty?"

"I walked into the castle, up the stairs, and into her chamber."

"Aye?"

"And found her ready to fly out the window," he said, scowling.

"She knows then, that we have come?"

"Aye—and she told us to go home."

Eric laughed. "She meant to escape on her own."

"So it appeared—yet when I insisted she'd break her fool neck, she claimed to have a change of heart. She claims now that she wants to face her accusers, and that she will find justice."

Eric leaned forward. "She'd not betray us in the morning? I'm ready to risk my life—but not if the damsel is unwilling."

"She will not betray us," Brendan said angrily.

"Then what makes you so irritable?"

Brendan hesitated. "It is a matter between the lady, and myself," he said. Then he called across the room. "Father Gillean!"

"Aye, my son."

"Has she always been so stubborn."

"Aye, like a mule!" he replied.

They all laughed, and Gillean broke away from his chess game, coming to stand before Brendan.

"Aye, son, stubborn as a mule, loyal to a fault. She did not kill her count, and for that reason alone, I've given you what aid I can. I remain an Englishman, you know. And if you come around these parts again . . ."

"You'll thack and whack us!" Liam finished, laughing.

"I am English, bound to my king."

"Yet we are here," Brendan said quietly, watching him.

Gillean hesitated. "Aye. Yet you would be here with or without my agreement. The night is is better spent upon a chair, than laid out like carnage upon a cold stone floor. And in my vocation, sir, a man must answer first to God — and then his king. But thank the Lord, the two have always agreed before now. Now, if you'll excuse me, I'll get back to that great lumbering heathen fellow of yours — and my game."

Gillean walked away.

"We are ready for the morning?" Brendan said.

"We are ready." Eric told him. "Aye, we are ready."

Clad in their armor, visors covering their faces, Brendan and his men sat their horses, waiting. Miles Fitzgerald, as sheriff, served his duty, escorting Eleanor from the house. She was dressed in a warm, fur-trimmed cloak, a garment that seemed to state her position in life — but was also warm and fit enough to sustain a long journey. She walked with her head high, hair knotted in a braid, a simple band and veil covering it. She left the inner wall ahead of Fitzgerald. Brendan shook his head to see that Corbin had indeed meant to follow and defend his kinswoman.

She reached Fitzgerald's contingent, a group of twelve men mounted and armed, but not clad in armor. A group of villagers had gathered at the castle.

A tomato was thrown. It hit Fitzgerald in the face. He swore angrily, instantly reaching for his sword. His men followed suit.

Eric, at Brendan's side, cursed softly in Gaelic.

Eleanor placed a hand upon Fitzgerald's arm. "Please!" she said loudly, calling to the crowd. "Don't fear for me—I will find justice. These men but do their duty. I beg of you, for me, cause no trouble."

They watched from their small distance as Fitzgerald led Eleanor to a waiting horse. She didn't mount. She started a low conversation with him.

"What the hell is going on?" Eric asked.

"I don't know," Brendan said, watching.

The two kept talking, Eleanor insisting, stubbornly shaking her head.

"I shall have to see to this," Brendan muttered.

"You can't ride over there!" Liam protested.

"I must."

Brendan spurred his horse, trotting over to the group.

"What is the delay?" he asked curtly, steadying the English warhorse he had chosen.

"The lady is insisting we bring her maid."

He stared at Eleanor, his face hidden, except for his eyes.

"There are other maids, my lady."

"Bridie must come."

"Why don't we bring the fool woman and be done with this?" he demanded of Fitzgerald.

"She was asea with the Lady Eleanor, and in France with her. She could be an accomplice."

"She could be a witness in my defense," Eleanor said irritably. "And I am to receive a fair trial, am I not?"

"She could be dangerous," Fitzgerald muttered.

"She is skin and bones!" Eleanor protested. She stood very still, the wind just moving the soft fabric of her veil. "I will not leave without her."

Brendan looked at Fitzgerald. "Sir, there are battles to be fought in Scotland," he said gravely. 'We can waste no more time over a lady's maid. I beg you; bring the woman. I will be responsible for her.''

Fitzgerald stared up at him. "As you wish."

Brendan rode back to his armored men. Again, they waited. Bridie was brought out, her eyes wild with fear, Eleanor assuring her.

Eleanor declined Fitzgerald's offer of assistance, and mounted on her own.

The crowd was murmuring. Brendan rode back to Fitzgerald. "Sir, the time to ride is now."

"Aye!" He started forward, leading the party. Men surrounded Eleanor. Corbin, clad in a coat of mail, his tunic proudly bearing the colors of Clarin, rode behind her.

Brendan and his men flanked the others. They headed out the gates, and still the people followed them, rushing the soldiers' horses, trying to reach Eleanor.

"God go with you, lady!" cried a woman with a babe at her hip.

"God knows the truth!" came the vow of an aproned smith.

"Out of the way!" Fitzgerald shouted to an elderly man. "Out of the way; you'll be trampled."

"God bless you, and aye, keep me in your prayers!" Eleanor said. "I have put myself in God's hands, and I know He will prevail!"

The people fell back. Brendan had a brief glance at the torment in her face. Then he looked forward, riding ahead, flanking the other riders to take care with the men and women hounding them, human beings who appeared fragile next to the great size and weight of the chargers.

At last they cleared the fortifications at Clarin; Fitzgerald determined to gain a greater distance, and the horses broke into a lope.

Soon, the last gleaming of a stone turret was behind them, and they slowed the gait. The way to London was long. There would have to be stops overnight. But every hour of their ride brought them deeper into country held in the strong grip of the king of England.

As they had arranged, they did their best to maintain the rear. Brendan judged their distance; while they rode west-southwest, he didn't fear the distance they traveled. They had determined they would break when they reached the stream they must ford to reach the fork to the south, and London.

De Longueville seemed to delight in trying to draw the sheriff's men into conversation. However, his mockery of Hagar's accent had kept the great fellow maintaining his own level of talk — a grunt here or there when he was addressed by one of the others.

Eleanor rode quietly, exchanging a word only now and then with her cousin. Only her eyes betrayed her tension.

At length, Fitzgerald turned back. "We'll stop at the stream!" he commanded.

The order fit in well with Brendan's plan.

They came to the stream. Fitzgerald called the halt.

His men began dismounting; Brendan's men did the same, positioning themselves for the assault.

Yet even as he began to dismount from his own horse, Fitzgerald stopped him.

"There is no need, Sir Humphry, for your men to dismount."

He held still. "My men, and horses, are thirsty as well," he said.

"As you wish. But we will part company here."

"Your pardon, sir?"

"We are away from the rabble in the village. You are ready to continue the king's war against the savage forest rabble in Scotland. I am freeing you from this duty."

"You have claimed that you ride with a dangerous woman."

"We are away from those fools who would jump to her defense and be slaughtered."

"We dare not leave you," Brendan said.

"There is no more danger. If the lady flees, we will hunt her down, and she will forfeit her life on the spot."

"She is to be taken to trial!" Corbin exclaimed angrily.

"She will not flee," Fitzgerald said, still watching Brendan. "Sir Corbin of Clarin will be sliced to ribbons should she make such an attempt."

"That is not the king's justice!" Eleanor cried.

"Aye, lady, but it will keep you in your place."

Brendan dismounted, as if to lead his horse to drink. Eleanor had not dismounted. He prayed she would not do so. He approached Fitzgerald, aware that everyone watched as he did so.

"This is not the command I was given."

"I am in command now, and I am telling you — you are no longer needed."

He stared at Fitzgerald, buying time. "The way you speak, sir, I fear for the lady's chances of reaching London — and a trial to establish her innocence or guilt."

"It is not your affair."

"I say that it is."

"We will part company here!" Fitzgerald swore furiously.

"Aye, then," Brendan said. "As you wish; we will part company here."

By that time, Eric had come behind Fitzgerald. He didn't draw a sword, he had a knife at Fitzgerald's throat. The blade brushed along the man's vein.

The sheriff's men had gone for their weapons; however, they must have quickly seen their disadvantage. Only one made a move, and Fitzgerald was quick to shout out, "Hold, you fool! This fellow has my life in his hands!"

"A wise assessment," Brendan advised. "Drop your swords."

The sheriff's men stood hesitantly. Their eyes moved furtively to Fitzgerald's. There was something wrong with the entire situation, Brendan judged, but at the moment, he hadn't the time to ferret out the Englishman's motives.

"You are interfering with the king's justice!" Fitzgerald raged, his eyes rolling from side to side as he tried to see the man who so threatened his existence.

"Am I the one interfering?" Brendan inquired. "Or had you appointed yourself judge and jury, sir? Did you intend for the lady to reach London for trial?"

"Don't be a fool! I am allowing you to follow the king's orders."

"Well, you see, as it is, I don't follow the king's orders. Have your men drop their weapons. Now. Or you'll die before a fight can begin."

Eric pressed the blade closer. A thin trickle of blood appeared at Fitzgerald's throat.

"Drop your weapons!" Fitzgerald thundered.

Swords were slowly dropped.

"Ah, fellows! The knives as well," Brendan suggested.

Eric had yet to release Fitzgerald.

"Have your berserker lower the knife now, Humphry, or I swear, I'll see you hanging by the neck," Fitzgerald warned Brendan.

But Brendan took his time, as Eric knew he would.

"Hagar, have we a bit of rope for these fellows? Liam, they've some fine steel there, if you'd make a collection."

"You've gone beyond, Humphry!" Fitzgerald warned. "This is treason. Treason against the king's sworn officer—"

"I doubt the king is aware of any of this business, Fitzgerald," Brendan said. "But that is no matter. Collum, give a hand there, if you will—see that they are good strong knots in the rope—we don't want our friends leaving the peace and the serenity of the stream too soon. Gregory, seize up a few of the swords if you will."

"For treason, sir," Fitzgerald grated, "they hang you first, rack you, wait until you're half dead, bring you back to life, castrate you, and rip your guts out, and then, only then, do they end the pain by axing off your head.''

''Aye, I'm aware of the method,'' Brendan said. ''Perhaps you could tighten that knife, Eric, he seems to have too much room to wag his tongue.''

''Aye, tighten, eh? A pleasure,'' Eric responded amiably.

Fitzgerald fell silent.

His men, still bewildered, and under the bulging fury of his eyes, made no comment, still and silent as their hands were tied.

''See here,'' Corbin protested at last. He had been seated on his mount, silent, and bewildered throughout the proceedings. ''I believe in Eleanor's innocence, but Sir Humphry, you will face the king's wrath—''

''What do we do with him?'' Liam demanded.

''Leave him,'' Collum suggested bluntly. ''Sir, you'll dismount—''

''No!'' Eleanor cried suddenly. She didn't understand Fitzgerald's motives any more than he, but she seemed to realize that she wouldn't have made it to London in his care. ''You can't leave Corbin with these men.''

''He's one of us!'' Fitzgerald said fiercely. ''Whomever you may—be.'' He squeaked the last as Eric once again put pressure on the knife.

''You cannot leave him!'' Eleanor repeated, her blue-gray eyes fiercely upon Brendan's.

She was right.

''Ach, man! '' Liam protested. ''We're already riding with a woman—begging your pardon, Lady Eleanor—and her skinny maid—''

''Why, you surly beast! I can ride better than many a man!'' Bridie interrupted indignantly.

But Liam ignored her. "Now we'd be riding with an Englishman as well?"

"Scots!" Fitzgerald hissed suddenly.

"Dear Lord! Blest be the saints!" Collum muttered. "The man's observant."

"Aye, does that mean I can speak me 'burred' French now?" Hagar asked.

Brendan didn't reply. "Corbin of Clarin rides with us."

"I do not ride with Scots!" Corbin hissed.

"Aye, then, will you die to an English sword?" Brendan asked.

"Corbin, these men will kill you, don't you see?" Eleanor told him. "They didn't intend for us to get to London!"

"Why, 'tis all true then, isn't it?" Fitzgerald mocked. "The lady of Clarin, turned to the Scots, slays her husband for her forest dog of a lover!"

"I never killed my husband, sir," Eleanor said coolly, "And I believe that you're aware of that fact."

"Shall I slice his throat, my lady?" Eric asked politely.

"No," she said, swallowing hard. "There's been enough blood."

"Time to ride," Gregory suggested, collecting the last of the swords. The Englishmen stood by the water, unharmed other than the confiscation of the weapons, and each man with his hands tied at his back.

"You'd leave us so?" asked one of them.

"Someone will come upon you soon enough," Collum advised, mounting his horse. "We've left you with plenty of water," he said with a shrug.

"This path is not so well traveled—" protested another.

"Well enough," Brendan said.

"Do we tie the Englishman?" Liam asked Brendan.

Brendan shook his head, staring at Corbin. "He'll cause no trouble."

"I do not ride with Scots—" Corbin protested again.

"He'll cause no trouble," Brendan repeated, and the man fell silent. "That is nearly it, then." He strode by Liam's horse, collecting the last feet of rope with which to bind Fitzgerald's hand. "Sir? If you will be so kind."

"I will see you hanged."

"I thought you intended to see me disemboweled."

"I will ask for the executioner's job myself," Fitzgerald said.

"Hadn't you asked for it already?" Brendan suggested, his warning whisper at the man's nape. "You did intend to kill the Lady Eleanor."

Fitzgerald didn't reply.

"Your hands!" he repeated.

Again, Eric allowed the knife to bite.

Fitzgerald offered his hands behind his back. Brendan tied his wrists together securely, and too tightly. Eric, at last, moved his knife, walked to his horse, and mounted.

He stood in front of Fitzgerald. "You owe the lady," he said softly. "I know a treacherous snake when I see one, sir. I would have killed you."

"Indeed. I think it's a mistake not to kill you, but . . . she doesn't like bloodshed." Brendan stepped away, mounting his horse. "Eric, take the lead, please, and briskly, I think."

Eric did so. Brendan waited until the others had turned and moved out, carefully shielding Eleanor and Corbin in their midst.

"Coward!" Fitzgerald called out suddenly. "Scottish whelp. You don't even show your face, bastard!"

Brendan moved his horse closer and closer so that Fitzgerald was forced backward — until he fell on his backside into the stream.

"Your name isn't Humphry, bastard!" Fitzgerald hissed in fury, drenched, water falling into his eyes. "What is your name? I'd know it — for the day I gut you!"

Brendan allowed his mount to splash more water at Fitzgerald, the great hooves churning up mud as well.

"My name? Today, interestingly enough, it might as well be 'justice'."

He turned the great destrier, spurred him, and raced to catch up with the others.

Chapter 17

Brendan set a rapid pace. It was doubtful that the Englishmen would be found for some time, but if they were, there would be no place else the Scots were heading except north, and so it was necessary to get as far as possible as quickly as possible without killing the horses.

Corbin caused no trouble, but rode in a grim silence.

Despite the distance — and the fact that the English did have a strong hold on the lowlands — crossing the border sent them back into the terrain they knew so well, and where they were able to disappear from the road, melting into the trees like spring snow.

They stopped only once more to water the horses and they slowed the gait, but kept moving, until late in the night. Brendan was determined to reach the ruins of an old Roman fortification, rebuilt by Scots, abandoned, rebuilt again by the English, then abandoned in the days after Falkirk when the English had been so proud of their victory — and so unaware that the fight was still going on.

The walls hid horses and men from the road. There was cover from the elements, and even some old comforts left behind, blankets, rickety chairs, uneven tables, and even a keg or two of ale. They had carried food, taken along on one of the sheriff's destriers, a warhorse turned pack animal for the journey.

When they dismounted, it was agreed that they would take the night in two shifts, and leave again to travel further north by first light. Eric had suggested that they ride until they reach the fortification they had taken from the Englishman Hebert; it was under the control of their own men now, and manned and able to withstand a long assault or siege.

For that night, they would sleep in the ruin of stones in the woods.

"I'll head first shift," Eric told him.

"Aye."

The horses were first secured with their treasure of arms and weapons, then Eric chose Liam and de Longueville to take the first shift with him.

Brendan entered what was once the great hall of the ruin, and saw that Gregory was unpacking loaves of bread, cheese, and dried meat. Bridie helped him.

Eleanor was deep in conversation with Corbin.

Her conversation broke off when he entered.

Corbin saw him first, set his hands on Eleanor's shoulders, and passed her to stand before him. "It seems I must thank you first. It is difficult to believe, and I'm not sure that I do believe — a man of Fitzgerald's stature would have dared keep my cousin from the courts. He'd had to have slain me to do so, and explaining both of us dead would not be easy."

Brendan didn't answer him at first; he walked to the table, taking a skin of ale, and drinking until the road dust seemed at last to settle in his throat. He set down the skin, addressing Corbin.

"There would have been no difficulty. He would have said that Eleanor tried to run. In his story, he would have said that she garbled out some confession. Naturally, you, being her kin, would have come to her defense. They would have been deeply sorry, but you would have died as well."

"Did you know he meant to do this? Why?" Corbin demanded.

"I don't know," Brendan said. "Have you any idea?"

"None whatsoever."

"Did he know Alain?"

"No," Corbin said. "I have met him before, serving on the field, and in London. He never came to Clarin. A messenger arrived shortly before the funeral, telling us that word had reached York regarding the death of the new French count of Clarin, and that the duke's representative would be arriving to question the circumstances."

"Then he is not overcome with grief at the death," Brendan said wryly.

"No."

"But he was never at Clarin, so he did not do the deed himself," Brendan continued.

"No," Corbin said.

"Then it is curious indeed."

"That he would have dared my life is dubious as well. There is nothing to be gained by my death."

"No?"

"I don't inherit. My brother, good and trustworthy and hard-working, gains the property . . . if Eleanor does not leave a male heir. My death leaves nothing to anyone."

"I'm afraid you were just in the way. Indeed, I tried to dissuade you from riding last night; I was afraid of your reaction, while still assuming I rode with honest English soldiers, when we parted company.''

''I would have fought you, naturally.''

''And I would have tried hard not to kill you,'' Brendan said softly.

Eleanor, standing still and silent, watching them, seemed to pale. She was more than pale. She appeared drawn, he realized, almost fragile. Somewhere in the ride, she had lost the simple headdress. Even in the dim light of the few torches they had lit, her hair seemed to burn deeper than gold. It trailed down her back. She looked like a waif, delicately beautiful, ethereal.

Naturally, she'd be worn, and weary. Her husband had died, she'd been accused of murder, and now, had made an escape.

To the enemy.

And if Isobel wasn't a complete schemer and liar, she was expecting a child. His.

''Though grateful, sir, in the extreme,'' Corbin said, ''I am not one of your number. Am I to remain a prisoner?''

Brendan helped himself to a portion of bread and cheese, walking on, found a place by the wall, and sank down against it. He studied Corbin while wolfing down a bite of the bread. ''We desire your company, sir, until we reach a stronghold,'' he said at last. ''But if I were you, I'd take extreme care going back to England.''

''And why is that?'' Corbin asked, frowning.

''Well, we didn't kill Fitzgerald and his men, so they'll surely stand against you. You heard his conversation; you know that he tried to part from us when he still believed us to be his own countrymen. You might accuse him of attempting murder, or, at the least, tampering with the king's justice. Naturally, he'll be prepared for such a lie, assuring any who offer such an accusation that you, like your deadly cousin, were in league with the Scots.''

''But it's not true!''

"Nor are the accusations against Eleanor, as we both know. But that wouldn't have saved her from the headsman's axe — of Fitzgerald's sword." He finished with the bread and cheese, crossed his arms, and leaned back against the wall.

"This is all preposterous. I must return to England; Alfred will know that I am no turncoat, or traitor to my king."

"After we are secure, sir, you may do as you choose," Brendan told him. "I'll not hold you against your will." He closed his eyes, making it plain he wanted to rest.

"We must both return," Eleanor said suddenly. "The truth must be discovered—"

Brendan's eyes flew open. "You, madam, will not be returning anywhere."

"But there is law in England," she began to protest again. "And something is very wrong. Fitzgerald claimed to have authority all along; perhaps he did not. Perhaps there was a reason, and he was even responsible himself somehow for Alain's death. If we return, we will speak together. It will not be one voice against Fitzgerald, but both voices—"

"I'll speak with *you* tomorrow, my lady."

"Brendan, you must see—"

"I repeat, my lady, I'll speak with you tomorrow." He closed his eyes again.

"Brendan—"

"My lady!" he flared angrily. "*Both* voices. What good will your voice be? Your husband is dead. Poisoned. At the threat of removal to London, trial, and possible execution, you were saved by your— you were saved by the Scots. I don't think your word will mean much in support of your cousin's, madam."

"All Englishmen are not evil—"

"I did not suggest that they were," Brendan said impatiently.

"If you don't want to talk to me—" she began.

"Oh, indeed. I intend to talk to you. Not now. Tomorrow. I know you are familiar with the word."

Once again, he closed his eyes.

He knew that she stood there, staring at him. He knew, as well, when at last she walked away, surely longing to wake him with the bash of a wine skin over his head.

There was a lot he wanted to talk about.

But not surrounded by others.

Perhaps he should have cared more for her comfort that night; he was too angry. As yet, a 'thank you' hadn't slipped from her tongue. Nay, she was ready to gallop off again to a land where they were set to hang her, guilty or innocent.

Eric came to wake him in the middle of the night. Gregory and Collum were aroused to join him. They kept vigil at the walls until the dawn broke. Then they woke the others, and started riding again.

He rode beside Corbin for part of the day. The man seemed immersed in thought, and when he saw Brendan studying him, he explained, "I still can't fathom it. Fitzgerald suddenly decides that Eleanor, renowned to the point of being called *Santa Lenora,* should die rather than stand trial, and that I am expendable, to die with her. Alain was poisoned."

"Is Alfred concerned for the inheritance?" Brendan asked.

"My brother? Good God, no. He is responsible and pious to a fault; he believes deeply in God, and that God sees all, and that man will suffer for his sins on earth. I, on the other hand, believe a certain amount of sin on earth only makes a man more fit for the rewards beyond death."

"Ah. So did *you* murder the count?"

"What on earth for? No. As I've said, I'm sure I'm guilty of many sins. But murder is not among them. And even if the motive is sheer pleasure alone, there is motive for all my sins. There is nothing I gain by Alain's death."

"What about your wife?"

"Isobel?" he queried. "Isobel, God knows, is capable of much, but she wouldn't have wanted Alain dead. She had a sudden desire to reproduce after our many years of childless marriage. Eleanor's father has not been gone so long . . . and with Eleanor married to an old man, and Alfred keeping his romantic affairs to a shepherdess or milkmaid here or there, it did seem that a child of ours would inherit. That's just as well; without me, she'll not have that child, and not inherit the property.''

''What if she is already with child?''

''Isobel? If so, she would have announced it from the highest tower in the land. For other women it would be a natural occurrence; for Isobel, a personal achievement worthy of the world's acclaim.''

By dusk, they had reached the fortification.

In little time, it had changed greatly. Walls had been finished, heightened, strengthened. The outer wall had been repaired; masons had piled stones to build more towers. They were seen at a distance, and a cry had gone out; the gates opened as they arrived. Wallace came striding from the castle to the courtyard, even as they rode in. Dismounting, Brendan greeted him, and was greeted warmly in return. Men, warriors turned builders, left their work to hover around. Questions were raised; Hagar wound a story of their accomplishment. Wallace watched gravely, saying nothing, while the others joked, and made much of the deed of saving an English heiress — intended for an English blade.

Corbin, too, had remained silent during the melee of their entry; then, he was noted by the others.

''And we've an English prisoner!'' said Rune MacDuff. ''Did you think the man would wound the maid?'' he demanded, walking forward to study Corbin.

Corbin of Clarin was no laggard. He faced the brawny Rune down. ''Never, sir, would I bring harm to any maid, least one who is my kin.''

''Corbin, Lady Eleanor's cousin,'' Brendan explained briefly.

Wallace and the others studied Corbin. Corbin studied them in return. He shrugged at last. "Not a tail or horns among you. That must be rumor then."

Rune MacDuff let out a loud laugh. He was soon joined by the others.

"He's not a prisoner then?" Jem MacIver, another of the men, demanded. "No ransom?"

"I don't believe I'm worth the shirt on my back at the moment. And I'm not a prisoner. Sir Brendan has given me leave to go. Once he reaches your fortifications . . . oh, your pardon. This pile of stone is your fortification."

Again, the Scots laughed. "Stay with us a spell, Englishman!" someone shouted. It was Lars, who had sailed upon Wallace's ship, and been with them in France. "There's no horn or tail upon him either, can ye fathom!" Lars stepped forward; he had been in the rear of the taller men, and had not seen all who had arrived.

He saw Eleanor, quietly seated on her horse, and he walked to her, bowing. "Welcome to our home, m'lady, though it is not where ye'd yearn to be."

"Thank you," she said softly.

"You'll be an exile now, from hearth and home."

"I will have to return," she said.

"Aye, she's a wealthy countess!" Jem said.

Eleanor shook her head. "It is not wealth. It is my name."

"Well, you'll not be going back this night," Wallace said. He looked at the new arrivals. "Margot said ye'd be back by tonight. There are rooms prepared, poor as they may be as yet, but then, I'm afraid, my lady, we're not known for the elegance of Paris."

"I am thankful for the hospitality of Scottish earth, which seems most elegant, since I fled for my life, sir," Eleanor told Wallace.

Brendan stared at her, still seated atop her horse, her voice, her manner, entirely gracious, her thanks to others sincere. And the men — dozens of them, burly fellows, stalwart, war weary, honed like the sharpest knives, stood in thrall of her. He didn't know why; he was tempted to take her from the horse and shake her.

At that moment, Bridie, who had ridden close behind Eleanor, let out something of a sigh. As all eyes turned to her, she started to slip from her horse in a swoon.

"Sweet Jesu!"

Despite the fact that she had been mounted and the men had not, Eleanor was the first to reach her maid, catching the woman before she could collapse flat upon the earth.

But Lars had been close. He lifted her into his arms. "We'll get her inside, get her water," he said. "By God, though, what ails the maid?"

Eleanor spoke sharply then. "You, sir, should know!"

A sound of laughter rose again from the crowd. Lars, a blond man with a fair complexion and freckled cheeks, blushed. "My lady —"

"Bring her in. She needs water."

Lars started for the inner keep, then up the steps leading to the central stone edifice. Eleanor followed, as did Wallace, Corbin, and several of the others.

Brendan did not. Eric had remained with him. He clapped his horse on the neck. "The horses need feeding, the arms and equipment need unpacking. Shall we leave it to others?"

"No. I'll tend to it. You, cousin, should go see Margot. She surely realizes you've come by now."

Eric smiled. "Aye, then."

Brendan watched him go. His cousin loved the woman, he thought. She was loyal, true, silent through any hardship, and beautiful. He shook his head. Eric was a fool. They had chosen lives as rebels, outlaws. He should marry the woman.

Yet he wondered if his cousin paused not because of Margot's birth—but because of his own acceptance that death could come any time.

He started leading the horses to the stables, joined by some of the younger men, raw youths from lands run over by foreign powers, ready to learn to fight for their land. "So you donned a priest's cowl, and walked straight into an English castle?" a lad demanded.

"It seemed the proper thing to do at the time," he said with a shrug. "Come along, if you lads would give me a hand, do it then, and let's hurry along."

At length, when he came into the great hall, it was to find a fire burning in the central hearth, a dozen hounds scurrying for scraps, and a great haunch of venison roasting. There were women as well as men, wives, mothers, sisters, laundresses earning what meager wages the men could pay, and a few women, of course, who simply followed soldiers, and earned what wages they could at entertainment.

By the time he arrived in the hall, their English "guests" had been shown to their quarters; a quantity of ale had flowed, and news had spread. Hagar could weave an incredible tale in his native Gaelic, and he did so then, describing their antics with the English. Sir Miles Fitzgerald, he told them, had horns and a tail, and his English soldiers had been just starting to sprout such appendages. There was a great roar of laughter, and for Brendan, tremendous applause.

The ale flowed freely. In the company of these men, with no need of the tension brought by being on constant guard, he let himself relax. He drank, ate, and laughed when one of the camp followers fell into his lap while filling his cup. She rolled against his chest, laughing as well, and touched his cheek.

"A handsome hero, eh?" she said.

He grinned, amused, but when he looked up, he saw that Eleanor had come down; she stood at the foot of the winding stairs, her hand upon the iron rail. Her eyes met his. He thought that she would turn, and walk away, but she did not.

She came across the room, and the party sobered. She ignored Brendan, and walked to the large chair where Wallace relaxed before the central fire.

"My lady," Wallace said, and rose, ever courteous despite his reputation for violence.

"Sir William, please, sit. It's evident that this evening is one of leisure for you and your men. I have come only to express my deep appreciation to your men, those who took tremendous risks in coming south in my defense. They owed me nothing; their kindness is a debt I can never repay, and will never be forgotten."

"My lady, I fear I was no part of it, on behalf of the fellows who rode, your life was the prize worth a gamble, and indeed, the exploit adds to the legend of our abilities, despite our sorry state of being. You have been a worthy opponent, madam — there are those who do say your company helped the flow of English valor at Falkirk — "

"Sir, a sorry slaughter, the likes of which I hope never to see again."

"Nevertheless, you have been a worthy opponent — " he broke off, smiling, " — a less than model prisoner, but now, indeed, a very welcome guest."

She bowed to Wallace. "I will excuse you all to your merry-making. And I give you thanks again, for allowing me to be a — guest."

She didn't look Brendan's way, but headed for the stairs.

For a moment the company remained silent as she disappeared. "Cheers!" cried one of the men. "Cheers to a strange breed of English! Those with integrity and valor!"

The room became raucous again.

The woman, frozen there when Eleanor had appeared, smiled

at him. "Aye, hero, you saved a woman of valor. But is she a lass of any warmth?"

" 'Tis time she and I did have a talk," he muttered, and rose, setting the woman aright.

Gregory was watching him. The woman was pretty, with a quick smile, and tender touch. He prodded her toward Gregory. "Entertain Gregory there," he said. "Now there's a lad who's a hero, if there is one among us!" The woman moved forward, and crawled over Gregory. Hooting, cheering, clapping, filled the room. Attention was off Brendan.

Brendan looked at Wallace. "Where would the lady be as our guest?"

"Up the stairs, the ell to the left, last door."

He started to turn away.

"Brendan."

He looked back. Wallace was grave.

"A brave stunt, and well accomplished. But dangerous, indeed."

"I asked none of them to come with me; they chose to do so."

"We may all die, but let it not be for foolishness — or the headstrong wills and desires of one man."

"I have given my all in the pursuit of freedom; I swore it when I held my cousin in my arms as he died as Falkirk. Sir, there is no fault in my ardor for my country."

"I didn't suggest so. I value your talents, Brendan, your abilities, and aye, your valor and your life's blood. As I valued those of your cousin, John Graham, and many other of your kinsmen. I ask you only that you value your own life as well."

"Aye, sir, that I do," he said gravely.

"Go then," Wallace said. "Such valor does deserve its just reward."

He nodded, and headed for the stairs slowly enough, but then took them two by two.

It was time to talk.

Eleanor walked around the room in great agitation, fuming despite herself. She had married another man, and said goodbye to Brendan, in all belief that she would never see him again. Miraculously, he had come for her in a time of deepest danger. She should be grateful, and nothing more, and realize that his life had moved on, as had her own.

"My lady, you must sit and calm yourself. You'll harm the babe," Bridie said.

Eleanor bit her lip, grateful that Brendan knew nothing of her situation. She couldn't help but feel a tremor of pain, no matter what logic she realized within her mind. Nay, it wasn't pain; it was pure bold jealousy, she thought, and aye — anger. And with such a thought she couldn't help but realize again the differences of their lives; aye, he cared for her. But for Scotland more. And this was his way of life; fighting, taking shelter in strongholds held by the Scots despite Edward's heavy hand. And when he had rested, completed one raid, one fight, one battle, there would be another, and he would return to the forests, and seek out the English again. But there was nothing he called home, other than this earth, and the longer she had been away, the greater dishonor it seemed that she had not had a chance to speak her case in court. Had Fitzgerald really meant to see to her death or disappearance on the way to London? It still seemed far too unbelievable.

"My lady, please, sit, you'll be ill."

"I'm not in the least ill. Bridie, you were the one to faint!"

Bridie smiled. She whispered, "Because I saw Lars again."

Bridie had always seemed so slim, and gaunt. Now, she

appeared pretty, very pretty. Her cheeks were flushed, her eyes were alight.

"Does he know?" Eleanor asked.

"Well, aye, my lady, since you apparently explained the situation when I fell."

Eleanor shook her head. "I'm sorry, so sorry, of course—"

"My lady, it's all right." Bridie was silent a minute, and Eleanor came at last to sit across from her. She smiled at Eleanor. "You did suggest that I get to Scotland, and meant to help me do so."

"Aye. However, I had not meant to join you."

"But my lady! He rode for you! Rode into England! He ignored dozens of Englishmen, trained with swords, decked himself in the guise of a priest, and walked right into the castle. He hid his face and dared pretend to be an escort. How could you not be glad to be here?"

"The Scots are fond of daring exploits that rub English noses in the dirt," she said.

"He risked his life."

"I am grateful for that fact."

She started then, for there was a sudden slamming at the door.

It had swung open.

He looked every bit the wild rebel warrior, as savage as any half-civilized highlander from any of the horror stories told to English children.

His hair fell free and dark to his shoulders, his features were tight, jaw set, eyes hard. He wore his plaid, kilt over a linen shirt, and doeskin boots. He hadn't bothered to knock at the door, but had simply thrown it open with purpose and careless determination.

Bridie jumped up as he entered, looking scared. Eleanor came to her feet as well, defensive and wary—and somehow stronger and bolder if she stood.

Brendan stared at Bridie. "So . . . you're to have a child. With Lars?"

Bridie flushed the shade of a rose.

" 'Twill be fine. The lad's a decent enough fellow. Now, if you don't mind, young woman—out."

"Your pardon, Sir Brendan!" Eleanor exclaimed. "Bridie may stay—"

"Out!" he repeated.

Bridie scampered away. The door closed behind her.

Eleanor stared at Brendan. His eyes were somewhat reddened, with weariness—and with drink, she thought. Still, her heart fluttered. He stood as he did when he was angry—and self-righteous. His jaw was squared at a tense angle. The breadth of his shoulders rose and fell with his every breath. Muscles rippled beneath linen and wool. He stared at her a very long while.

"Well?" he said at last.

"Well?" she murmured. "Has the party broken so quickly? How strange, it seems I still hear sounds of revelry from below."

He ignored her question. "Have you nothing to say to me?"

She stared at him uneasily.

"Thank you?" she inquired. "I didn't mean to be so rude; I did, in fact, descend the stairs to express the depths of my appreciation, and I would have addressed you . . . had you not been so occupied. Your hands seemed quite full at that moment."

He ignored the comment, dismissing it. "Thank you?" he inquired. "Is that really all that you have to say to me?"

Her unease increased as he walked around her, arms crossed over his chest. She followed his movement, suddenly as afraid he would pounce when her back was turned. He seemed like a cat, with a definite quarry in mind, or an animal whose territory had been threatened, and would not yield.

"That is all that you have to say to me?" he repeated.

"Thank you . . . very, very, much."

He came to a standstill, his eyes as sharp as blue flame.

She found herself faltering, and speaking too quickly. "I do thank you, truly, with a depth you can't imagine. Except that, you have to see, I must find a way to go back. I am branded a murderess now, and worse. A traitor. A woman who killed her husband, to flee with her country's greatest enemy."

"You won't be going back."

"I am a guest here, not a prisoner, so I've been told."

"A guest — who will remain."

"Brendan, there's a way —"

"There's not a way."

"Am I your prisoner then, not a guest?"

"You may see it however you like. You're not going back."

"Brendan, the fact that Fitzgerald was not an honorable man does not make monsters of the entire English populace. There are those in England who do want the truth, and this is not a matter of war, but of a terrible wrong done to a good and honest man. And it is a matter of my honor. There must be a way to send messengers to someone close to the king."

"No, and it's not something I care to discuss now. Let's return to my original question. Think, my lady. You've nothing more to say to me?"

There was a lot she had to say to him. But not now, not so close to everything that had happened. She needed time. She wasn't sure she knew him anymore. They had been apart for months, and together, amid a sea of others, just a few days' time. She had lived her different life until then; he still lived his very different life now. With men and women who rode hard, fought hard — and reveled with great passion.

He assessed her slowly, shook his head with angry disgust, and took a step closer to her.

"Come, my lady. I'm sure that there is information you're waiting to give me."

Then she realized, *he knew!*

She suddenly brought a hand to her abdomen, worried that her condition had begun to show. She felt blood rush to her cheeks. "I . . ."

"Oh, do come, my lady! You are so seldom without words, and usually so eloquent. Keep going. I . . . am having a child."

She didn't repeat the words, but stood very still in dismay. If she had told him . . . when she had told him . . . she had never imagined it would be like this, while they were strangers, while she was angry . . .

And he was furious.

He shook his head, staring at her. "Let's see, a child. The lady is with child. And my old friend Alain was . . . let's put it delicately . . . simply far too old to be the father, as your cousin-in-law pointed out to Corbin and Alfred."

She would have protested the possibilities of age, but his words created another question and fury in her heart. "My cousin-in-law?" she said, "Isobel? You spoke with Isobel?"

"Ah, yes, well, I listened to her. She is the lovely little schemer married to Corbin, right? I do have her name correctly? Gregory gave me most of the knowledge I have of Clarin, and the people there."

"Indeed, you have the name right. Gregory tutored you well. But if Isobel said anything, it was most likely a lie."

"I don't think so."

"Oh? And what did Isobel say?"

"She wasn't actually speaking to me, but to Alfred and Corbin. And she told them both that you never slept with your husband. That you had a Scottish lover, and meant to claim the child as your husband's own."

"Isobel knew nothing about our sleeping arrangement," she said uneasily.

"Oh, she probably did. She would have made it a point to know."

"Isobel is a grasping bitch." Eleanor couldn't help but blast out, her fingers curled into fists at her sides.

"That is most definitely true — but unimportant at this time. She went on to say that you might have murdered your husband to keep from having to tell him that you were going to have a bastard child — and give it his good name, of course."

She came around to stand behind the chair by the fire where she had been sitting when he entered, gripping the wood in her fury. "You know that I did not kill Alain."

"Did he know about the child?"

"Yes! No — I haven't told anyone that there is any chil — "

"You haven't admitted it, no. But we both know it's true."

"This is not a good time for this discussion," she told him coolly. "You've had too much to drink."

His brows shot up, and he stared at her incredulously, then a small smile curled his lip. "Too much? Never. Have I been drinking? Aye. It is considered something of a feat for six rebels to march into England, rescue an Englishwoman bound for the block from twice their number, and return, unscathed, and with the countess — unwilling though she might have been — unblemished. The fellows were naturally proud and amused."

"Proud and amused — by all your chances. They will not be so amused when it is you on the block."

"You'll not deter me."

"I say again, this conversation would be better at another time."

"You were the one so eager to press your point last night."

"You were weary; it is my turn to be so."

He shook his head. No hint of a smile touched his lips. "You don't get a turn."

"I am exhausted."

"That's a pity. You can rest when we are done."

"I believe that . . . *people* are waiting for you downstairs."

"I am waiting for you, right here."

He came closer to her, reaching across the chair to catch her hand. She would have evaded him; she was not fast enough. His hold was insistent; his eyes like knives, cutting into her. "Come, dear countess, sit!"

"I don't care to sit—"

But she was turned to the front of the chair, and pressed down into it. He didn't leave, or sit himself, but hovered over her.

She was almost glad to be sitting; she couldn't stop the trembling that had seized her, a rage of emotions. Her body had gone weak. She lowered her head. Alain was barely gone. Aye, he had been a friend, not a lover. Not what Brendan had been . . .

Her stomach knotted, and she hated herself for the jealousy she felt, just seeing someone else touch him. She had no rights. Neither did he. She had married another man.

He had come for her.

She didn't want him to see how eager she was just to touch him, nor did her longing sit well in her conscience, for no, she never would have harmed Alain, never, not for any power of love or desire. Yet so many of the things being said were true.

"Damn you, Eleanor, talk to me!" he suddenly roared.

"I'm telling you, Isobel is incapable of the truth—"

"But are *you* capable of speaking the truth!" he demanded. His hands were on the arms of the chair; his face so close to hers.

"Aye, then!" she cried, angry in return. "You want the truth? There *is* a child."

He pushed away. "Mine?"

"I—"

"When is the child due to be born?"

She inhaled slowly. "I'm not certain—"

"I believe you are. When?"

"November."

"Again, I ask you—mine?"

"Suppose I was certain—how could you ever be?" she demanded.

"Because I knew your husband. And I know you. And I know that you didn't kill him. And I will also believe what you tell me. And I listened to Isobel."

"Isobel did not know about my life—"

"Answer me. The child is mine?"

"You have made your own assumptions."

"I want the words from your lips."

Was he so angry that she would be having his child? Or had Alain been right, that to a man like Brendan, the child was his at all costs?

She gritted her teeth. "Aye."

He was very still for a long moment.

"And you did mean to give my child another man's name, to raise it as his?"

"What would you have had me do?" she flared, rising. "I had to marry Alain; I had to! Even King Philip warned me that it would be your death knell if I did not! And to what end? I returned to England—you, to wage your war, against my people!"

"Your people!" he repeated disgustedly. "The ones who now want your throat!"

"The English populace is not all evil, all cunning, all devious!" she informed him passionately. "You saw the men and women of Clarin, coming to my defense—"

"I am not condemning the people of Clarin."

"Clarin is—"

"Land. Nothing but land."

"No! Clarin is my home! Where people work hard, live

good lives, and believe in God, and their moments and season of happiness. But if you would say that Clarin is just land — then it is the same here. Scotland is land — nothing but land!" she returned. "And from France, you returned here, and you fought again, and you'll fight again, and again . . . and every time you win a few steps, Edward will come and hammer you back down. You'll run your glorious raids; you'll roust with your fellows, gamble, drink and take your amusements. Then you'll live your desperate life again — and you'll lose in the end, and you'll die."

"One day, we'll win."

"You'll die."

"Even if I die, one day, we'll win."

"What day? What day will that be?" she cried. "I had a home, a life to give a child — "

"Children grow well in Scotland."

"Aye — they grow to go to war, and be killed."

"While English children do not?"

Eleanor inhaled a deep breath. "Oh! Why can't you comprehend any of this! I was married to Alain. You lived somewhere in the woods in Scotland. What would you have had me do?"

His jaw tightened. If he knew he was being unreasonable, he would not admit it.

"I don't know. But Alain is dead now."

"Aye," she murmured.

"The child will have my name."

The child would have his name. He thought that if he commanded it, it would be so, and the rest of a harsh world would not matter.

"This is far more grave than any disagreements between the two of us! Don't you see? The child will have no name worth having, if his mother remains branded as a murderess. I must find a way to clear my name. I must have a fair trial."

"You'll not return to England."

"But—"

"You married—because you had no choice. Now, you will remain in Scotland, because I am giving you no choice."

She lifted her hands in a futile gesture. "If I remain here ... with you, I give credence to all that they are saying! I turned to the enemy, I betrayed my husband for another. I married one man for his money—while planning to run away with one of the direst foes of my country. What will happen when this child is born? Rumor will haunt the babe's life—"

"If you went back, the child would have no life."

"But things will be whispered—no, they won't be whispered, they will be said as fact—"

"Will it matter, when we know the truth?"

"Aye, it will matter. You know that it will matter."

"I know that you will not go back to England while carrying this child." His voice had an ice-hard edge to it that frightened her.

"There has to be a way to clear my name!"

"And what would that be, Eleanor? We send messengers asking for an audience with King Edward, he agrees, and you explain, and it will simply be all right?"

"You're being absurd!"

"What is your solution?"

"I don't know! I don't have one. There *is* one, though; because I am innocent, and therefore, someone else is guilty. I can't keep running—"

"Why can't you see that there is no choice but to run?" he demanded angrily. "My God, Eleanor! My life is mine to risk, but men rode with me to secure your freedom!"

"I'm grateful! So grateful. Aye, you and your men saved my life! But it doesn't change—"

"It doesn't change the fact that you are a countess, accustomed to wealth and privilege, and the idea that your child should grow up the son of a commoner—"

She leaped to her feet in a raw fury, slamming her fists against his chest. "Stop it! Aye, I grew up with wealth, and it is hard to abandon all that my father loved—that he fought for! But that is not my argument, and you fail to understand that whether we are in Scotland, England, or France, for me to be labeled a murderess will destroy the babe's future!"

He caught her wrists, and pinned them behind her back. She struggled against him in a rage of emotions, yet he seemed made of steel, and her anger only made that steel hotter, more molten. And all she could remember then was his touch, and how good it felt to lean against him, feel the encompassing warmth of his fire, burrow against the strength of his being.

"Let me go, you understand nothing!" she protested, but his hold tightened. Her hair became tangled in his fingers, and her chin was forced up and she met his eyes, and saw the sudden heat of desire within them. She tried to remember that Alain, dear, beloved good friend, had died so recently, tried to remember right and wrong, and all she felt again was the desperate longing to be with him, loved by him. But pride lived within her almost as strong as the desire, and she told him again, "I believe you have *friends* who await you downstairs!"

"Ah, but if a hero deserves his conquest, that conquest lies here!"

"But the pretty lass downstairs is probably not newly widowed, and most probably is more than willing."

"And you are not?" he queried.

She wanted to assure him that she was not, swear that she was not, rail against him with greater anger. But when she opened her mouth, his was upon it, forceful, passionate, hungry. She tried once to twist away . . . yet the consuming thirst of his touch held her still to that desire, the force made her yield, and the strength in her body and arms seemed to slip from her, and fall away, as leaves shed from a tree in winter. When his mouth parted from hers, she was weak, shaking. She tried once again to find words, or truth, or substance of protest as he lifted her, held hard against his chest, her head against the power of that vastness.

"I tell you again—"

"Tell me no more!" he commanded, and walked with her to the bed, and came down upon it with her, as if he'd give her no chance to escape, to think, to find more just reason that this should not be so.

Indeed, no chance.

His hands, his lips, were upon her. She heard a shedding of clothing, and knew it must be her own, for he was adept at discarding the plaid and kilt. She felt the fierce sear of his naked flesh against her own, the fever with which his caress was given. She laid her fingers against him, yet thrilled to the vital muscle and movement they touched, and she matched his kiss next with a passion and fury of her own, molding against him, desperate then for more. Her fingers trembled as she touched his cheeks, tested the richness of his hair, stroked the lean hard length of his back. His body moved against her, the rough texture of his palms moved over her breasts, his mouth moved against her, and she nearly shrieked aloud as the stream of fire and flame that seemed to burst out through her length, rays of a warm sun sent down a cold and barren field, waking it to life. How often, alone at night, she had dreamed . . . and now the flesh, the pulse of blood, the reality again. Her lips fell against his shoulder, and trembling still, she touched him with abandon, his back, buttocks, the rage of muscles within his length. She felt a gentle touch upon her abdomen, a stroke, featherlight, fingertips upon her thighs, calloused, arousing, felt them move, within her, without, and the stream of fire took flight throughout her again, until she cried out, and he was with her. He moved like a tempest, and she clung to each violent sweep and pulse, as if she consumed all of him, and would be consumed as well, and therein, find the source of wind and fire. Time had passed, but she knew him, and the knot of muscle and sinew, and the force of his hunger. Always, always, he would sweep her along, he would read her as if he read her soul, *knew,* and the storm had swept to the highest tor. He would hold her first, feel the tremors that would seize her, and explode then with a sea of searing crystals, liquid fire to fill her, radiate within her, drench her in an aftermath of slow cooling warmth in which to drift back to the world again, and the reality around her. She heard the crackle of the fire at the hearth as a log snapped; felt him adjust to her side, careful of his weight. She was aware of his breathing then, and the still rapid pulse of his heart. He lay by her side, yet his hand rested upon her midriff, and she couldn't help but wonder then if he lay so casually with that restraining touch upon her, or if there was a statement in his touch.

She didn't speak, but lay very still, listening to the fire, trying not to shiver as her body cooled. Seconds later, she realized that his hand moved, that he tested the contour of her abdomen, far more apparent in her bare state than beneath the concealing flow of clothing. She knew his thoughts, and wished she dared draw away, for he remained bitter, she knew, that she would have borne his child in England as another man's own.

But he said nothing.

Dimly, she could still hear laughter, shouts, and music from below.

"They are probably still awaiting you," she said softly.

"I believe they know where I am."

She reached for the tangle of sheets in the darkness, but he stayed her hand. "No," he said, rising to an elbow, his eyes upon her. "I have dreamed too often of such a time when I lay too many nights awake, in too great a blackness."

She bit lightly into her lower lip, eyelashes falling. She shivered, unable not to do so, and it was he who then drew the covers around her.

"You dreamed of me . . ." she whispered. "All night, every night? There were not other such occasions, when there were not flocks of lovely young nationalists, eager to know a hero's touch?"

"What do you want me to say to you?" he inquired. "That I watched you walk down an aisle to swear to love, honor, and cherish another man, and then fell to my knees myself, swearing that I would love you until my dying day in all chastity, loyalty, and valor?"

She would have moved. He rolled, the cast of his knee carefully pinning her to the bed. "Aye, there were others. The blackness remained. Nothing was ever as good, as sweet, as bright, as vibrant, as it had been before you. Is your pride redeemed?"

"It isn't my pride—"

"What else?"

"I expected nothing from you," she murmured.

"Nay, never my independent, ever-strong countess! *Santa Lenora,* you would give battle still! You're safe, my lady, alive, but that isn't enough for you."

"I have explained over and over—"

He eased to her side again, and this time, his palm and fingers spanned the distance of the swelling low in her stomach. "You've known for some time."

"Please, Brendan . . ."

He rose abruptly, regaining his shirt, swiftly forming his kilt. By then, she had started shivering fiercely, and groped again for the covers . . .

Very cold then, with him gone.

He seemed to realize her discomfort; he paused to stoke the fire.

Then he stood by the bed and told her, "I will do what I can to clear your name. But know this, and I swear it, the child will not leave Scotland! If you attempt anything rash or foolish, my lady, I promise you, you'll know what it is to face the savage enemy."

Chapter 18

Brendan woke on the floor, his head pounding. Someone had nudged him. He looked up to find Corbin of Clarin hunched down at his side. Struggling to his elbow, he saw that the rest of the drunken rabble had already risen.

He blinked, wincing, and opened his eyes again, staring at Corbin.

"I thought you'd like to know—there's a messenger outside."

Brendan scrambled to his feet. He left the hall of the fortification, Corbin at his heels. There was almost as much laughter and shouting in the courtyard as there had been in the hall, the night before.

A handsome horse, festooned in the colors of Robert Bruce, stood amid the cheering men; the horse's rider, a diminutive man next to the great horse, stood conversing with Wallace.

Brendan stopped first to duck his head in a basin of icy cold water, threw his soaking hair back, and approached Wallace. He was curious that the horseman had come from the Bruce; both possible heirs to the throne, the question of Comyn and Bruce serving the state together had turned sour, and Bruce had been keeping his activities to the area of Carrick, in the southwest of the country. Since Comyn, whose lands were farther to the north and admittedly not vulnerable to the constant English raids that had ravaged Bruce territory, kept battle alive and sometimes joined with Wallace, their communications with Bruce were not frequent.

But as he approached Wallace, the giant of a man turned. "A truce has been arranged."

"A truce?"

"The king of France has executed a peace between England and Scotland."

"So Philip is a man to make good his word," he said softly. "And Edward will be true to this?"

Wallace shrugged. "Aye, he'll be true to it — for a time. He raised great armies last year and the year before, came north and inflicted great injury, but then bogged down with the weather, the dictates of the pope that we were a sovereign nation with fealty due the Holy See — and the fact that his barons would give more than their two months' feudal service and his foot soldiers deserted in droves. Edward needs time to gather his forces again, to battle the pope, and raise enough money to fight us. I'd say that good King Philip has bought us time to gather our own forces."

"You don't seem as pleased as you might," Brendan said.

"Aye, I'm pleased. But it gives the great barons of Scotland more time for their own petty feuds, and you know as well I do that the raiding in the south will continue. The king will not raise a great army; but his northern nobles are nearly as argumentative as clansmen, so it will be a time for a man to stay wary, whatever fine words are set upon paper."

Many of the men in the courtyard were talking about going home, and Wallace was quick to tell them it was time to do so. Spring planting should be under way, and they should look to their families. There were those who would stay with him, wherever he chose to travel, and those who would keep the fortifications in the name of the guardian, John Soulis, who would still give appointments and commands in the name of King John of Scotland, whether John still tarried, enjoying France, or not.

Brendan knew, as Wallace did, that the fighting might have lulled, but the war was not over.

"What will you do?" Wallace asked him gravely.

"Bide time a bit," he said. "There are sure to be repercussions for the rescue of the lady of Clarin."

"Aye. 'Tis likely the English will call it an abduction."

"This poor fort was your taking," Wallace said. "Comyn had given men here, and already ridden on to his own estates; news will reach him soon of the peace. The government can give you legal writ to make this your home. Man it, build it, and let the fields grow rich again."

Brendan nodded, grinning slowly. "You're giving me the castle?"

"I haven't the power to give you the castle. But you've served your country as few other men, and we have retained some rights, and now gained more freedom to make them good. Who else should be master here?"

"What of you, William? What will you do for the time?"

"Go north," he said quietly. "Rest, as the English build their forces. Live in peace for a short spell."

"I will always be—"

"Ready to ride with me, whatever the battle, large or small? I know." William set an arm on his shoulder. "And I will be grateful of your sword arm, however great the war."

"When will you go?"

"A few days' time." He grinned. "There will be another celebration tonight, with the frightened tenants coming from the hills to reclaim their lands. Spring is a fine time for a truce."

Wallace clapped him on the back, then started through the crowd. At his back, Corbin spoke. "Ah, well there, you've become a great landed knight with the stroke of a pen!" he said.

"The land is not mine so easily. Scotland has a government, and a king, and a proper way to make things so."

"Ah, the king. I'm sure he'll be glad to hear he has a kingdom," Corbin murmured. "But a truce . . . it will make it far easier to go home."

Brendan turned to him. "Your troubles were not with the Scots, Corbin. Your troubles spill from your own land. Y'er a free man, though. You must make your choices."

He left Corbin then, going to the stables. He was eager to ride, to run with the wind, let it clear his head. A truce. Aye, it sounded good. Land. A castle, newly built, a bare fortification. But Hebert, bloody bastard as he'd been, had set good masons to the task, and there was a strong foundation on which to build a home. It was fine enough.

He didn't bother with a saddle, and chose the horse he had called Rye, for his deep coloring, one of the massive horses bred for war that they had taken from the English knights. He started from the stables, and was startled when he found himself met by a group of the fighting men, laborers, children, wives, and farmers.

"Sir Brendan!" came a cry, and a cheer, and he could barely move the horse forward as he looked to the people with confusion.

"Aye, sir, ye'll be laird here now!" a young lad said, walking along with the horse.

"And ye'll train us, sir, aye, for the fighting to come?" asked another.

A truce. And all knew it meant only time before fighting again.

"Eh, lads, we'll have enough to do, eh, dividing land, planting, gathering what cattle and livestock have run to the hills with the good people." He smiled.

"And we'll train for war!" the lad persisted.

"Aye, and we'll train for war."

He found a clearance in the crowd. They were shouting his name, and it felt fine enough. He waved, smiled, and made his way through.

He reached the gates, still open from having admitted the messenger. The people had heard the news quickly, and begun to stream back to land long ago decimated by the English armies. At the gate, he gave the charger free rein, eased to the animal's back, and felt the earth plow up beneath him, the wind take his hair. He rode across the land, and despite his speed, he noted moor and field, and the fine way the castle sat upon a hill, and the way the stream stretched before it.

Land. His land. Won by the power of his sword.

A land a man could leave to a son.

He remembered his words of last evening to Eleanor, before he made his departure. It had been agony to leave, yet tumult to stay, for as yet, there was no peace between them. He had meant to leave her time, for he knew that she was mourning the man she had married, as she might have mourned her father, yet again. He'd meant to be a most decent man, chivalrous in all manner. But it rankled to manage one of the most audacious raids into England — surely of all time — and hear her so passionate to return, to clear her name . . .

To again be able to lay claim to Clarin. He'd had nothing. She'd been an heiress. Aye, now, if Scotland agreed, then the land was his. A home. He had come from the forest.

And now . . .

He desired her as fiercely as he ever had; aye, indeed, he had loved her, and she had married another.

He loved her still.

Yet here he was, and the times had changed, and still, in her mind, she had to do what was right . . .

She'd never leave Scotland now. He meant that. But he had made a promise.

He left the little hillock beneath mighty oaks where he had looked down upon the castle and land. He rode back far more slowly, again assessing the landscape. Sheep would do well here. Aye, hundreds of sheep. They'd be fine, the expert Flemings with their talented weaving of fine cloth, their centers of industry so very near. The forests here were rich and overgrown. The fowl and game would be plentiful.

He gave off his planning as he returned to the castle. The messenger sat in the great hall, talking, exchanging news. Brendan joined the group around the table. Eric was there, along with Hagar, Collum, de Longueville, and Gregory.

He nudged Gregory. "How was your night, lad?" he asked quietly, not wanting to interrupt the questions being placed before the Bruce's messenger.

"Sir Brendan, a haystack has never been so lovely," he replied with a grin.

"That's fine, lad," he said and sat, and listened to the words the messenger was now speaking. He was a young man, who flushed easily, and didn't appear much the warrior, for he was slender and small. Brendan imagined, however, that he served his post well, and could ride with a speed to cover the marshes, lowlands, crags, and heaths of Scotland quite well enough.

"The king of England had sent out a call for men, and then abandoned the quest, in time with the treaty from France. In truth, he was not able to gather the forces he required, I'll warrant, and even though Robert Bruce has made his peace with the English king, I'll warrant good Edward knew not to count on all Scots of Carrick and Annandale to fight for an English banner!''

Eric, in the stark wooden chair at the table next to the seat Brendan had chosen, turned to him. ''Griffin here says that, as yet, there's been no news to Bruce lands regarding your foray.''

'' 'Tis too soon,'' Brendan said, reaching for a pitcher of cold, clear water, He nodded to the young messenger. '' 'Tis too soon, but there's bound to be trouble. Will you take a letter from me to the Bruce?'' he asked.

''Aye, sir.''

''Do you ride on from here?''

''Others have been sent to different factions in the south. I was sent to find William Wallace, for . . .''

''The king's truce will never apply to Wallace,'' Brendan finished. ''Were other men singled out?''

''There's nothing in the writing even regarding Sir William,'' Griffin said. ''Not as yet! The king did not beat the Scots, sir, he agreed to a truce.''

''And if he crushes us again, I'm sure there will be no truces for certain men,'' Brendan murmured.

''There's to be something of a peace, sir, and a sorry time for Sir William to die.''

''Aye, and he plans to travel north for a time. Go home. See what family and friends he has left,'' Brendan said. ''But if you'll excuse me, I'll write my letter, that you may take it to Robert Bruce at your leisure.''

Brendan started up the stairs, and realized his English ''guests'' had places here, while he did not. But upon the landing at the top of the stairs, he came upon a maid setting oil to the wood atop the banister. She smiled at him, and bobbed a curtsy. ''Laird Brendan—''

''Sir Brendan. I am not a laird.''

''Here, ye be laird, sir. Sir William Wallace has said that you will be master here. And there, yonder—'' she inclined her head to the first door to the left of the landing, "there be y'er quarters, if they be to y'er liking, that is. But 'tis fine space." She sniffed. "Laird Hebert meant to rule a little kingdom here, so set himself up a fine enough private palace, so he did."

"Thank you . . ."

"Joanna, sir. I am Joanna."

"Ah, then, thank you Joanna. I need paper, ink, a quill—"

"Aye, sir, and ye'll find them in Hebert's desk."

He nodded again, and left her to her work. He opened the door, and closed it, looking around.

The room was spacious, indeed. The bed within it was enormous, and could sleep four men, even Wallace's size. It sat upon a platform to the far side of the room, and was sheltered by embroidered draperies. The great hearth was to the side of the bed, in the center of the west side of the room. A stalwart desk of carved oak was to the north, set before windows opened to the spring day. Embroidered draperies hung to the sides of the windows, heavy fabric in rich hues of deep blue and crimson, and those, too, were opened to the beauty of the day beyond, held back by thick cords interwoven with silver thread. There was a wardrobe and a large heavy trunk at the east side of the room.

He walked to the windows first, and saw that it led to the north battlements of this, the inner tower, and that it looked far out over the road that led to the castle from the south. The master here, if not warned by men on guard, would know when forces rode from the south — and the dense border forests where so much trouble brewed. Well planned; Hebert had greatly feared the "savages" whose land he had meant to rule. Yet Brendan was glad of it; they would know if the English rode in from the south. The height of the castle would guard it from the western approaches.

He didn't sit at the desk right away, but walked to the giant bed, with its immense, beautifully woven woolen cover. He hesitated, then bounced upon it, and lay back. Firm, soft. A good bed for a man who had slept too often on the open ground.

He sat up again. He had been the guest of the kings of Norway, and France, and the lesser jarls in the out isles. He had seen splendor, and yet, was far better acquainted with dirt. There was much to be done here. He already felt an affinity for the place.

It was his. His.

Aye, *Scotland* must approve it. But a warrior knight was needed here, and he was that, indeed.

He rose, and walked to the hearth, and noted that it was double, leading to a room beyond. Standing, he saw the archway to his right, the curtain there so heavy and dark he hadn't given it note at first. He walked to it, and opened it then. A second room lay beyond, with a more delicate and far smaller bed, and furniture much more gently carved. A lady's room, he thought. To the side of the hearth there was a large barrel structure with dragon heads, adorned with brass and gold, on each side. It was a great, heavy bathtub, he realized, of Norse design. The carvings about it were finely done, and denoted Thor, God of Thunder, casting down lightning bolts, and Odin, lord of all gods, raging across the skies in a dragon-prowed chariot. A bath, he thought, might be in good order, since he had spent the night on the floor with drunkards and hounds — good friends all, but, alas, he must not smell too sweet.

But first, he wanted to write to Robert Bruce. He sat down, found ink, quill, and paper, and set to relaying his thoughts.

When he was done, he rolled and tied the document, and saw the small pot of sealing wax beside the inkpot. He hesitated, then lit a candle with a straw from the fire. He'd never sealed such a document before. But he wore a ring, a gift from his own father before his early death, and it bore an ornate G, and a bird of prey. He melted the wax, sealed his letter, and set the insignia of the ring into it. He studied the document for a long moment, then rose, and hurried downstairs.

The great hall had somewhat cleared; Eric sat by the fire, whittling a piece of wood, still talking with the messenger, Griffin. "I'll see it to the Bruce, my hand to his," Griffin said.

"Aye, then."

"He'll be pleased with the fine gift you're sending him."

"Aye?"

Eric glanced up. His cousin had remembered to send a gift, in his name.

"The hour grows late; you're welcome here, if you've a mind to start by morning."

"Nay, Sir Brendan. With this in hand, I'll be on me way." He rose, touching the leather bag at his side. "A fine ride. Good food from home, and a fine enough meal for the journey to return. God keep you all . . . and Scotland."

"Aye, God keep us all."

Brendan and Eric escorted him out of the great hall, and to the courtyard. A lad and his horse, ready to ride.

They watched him mount and ride. The gates remained open, and would until sunset — there was no danger to be had that day. "He says he's glad you've a correspondence for the Bruce," Eric told Brendan. "He says that Robert admires you greatly, as he does Wallace. Wallace, for being a man truly ready to give up everything for his ideals."

"If he admired him so, he would have fought with him," Brendan said.

Eric shrugged. "Each man does as he must. And every life is a spool of thread; where it ends is determined when his life begins."

"Norse legend. You don't believe that. Men make their own destinies."

"Do we now? Or are we all entwined, and therefore, destiny preordained?"

"You're philosophical today."

"You didn't ask why the Bruce admires you."

"All right. Why?"

"Because you don't betray a trust."

"What makes him certain?"

"He's seen the disdain in which you hold him."

Brendan stared at him, startled. Eric grinned. "You're loyal to Wallace, and fighting for an ideal. I think that Robert Bruce sometimes wishes that he didn't have his family fortunes and holdings. He envies men who see a greater good, fight when they see the battle, and earn the loyalty of the people. He would like to be hailed as Wallace, I think. Such devotion appeals to him."

"Then one day, he'll have to take a stand against the king of England."

"Maybe one day he will. As you say, men make their own destinies." Eric clapped him on the shoulder and walked on, heading for the stables. Brendan looked up at the walls of the castle. For a long while, he observed the strengths, and assessed the weaknesses.

Then, thoughtfully, he returned to the hall.

Eleanor sat by the fire in the room, attempting a letter she could only hope to find a way to get into Alfred's hands. She asked after his health, begged him to take the greatest care, to guard his own health in any way. She tried to remember, step by step and word by word, everything that had occurred with Miles Fitzgerald and his men, and her certainty that he had intended her harm. She assured him she meant to come home, yet knew that he managed all affairs with care and talent. She told him Corbin had been with her, defensive and loyal both to her and to England, through everything. He was concerned to get home. "Send Isobel our deepest regards," she wrote.

She was sure that Isobel was guilty in some way, but Isobel hadn't been with Fitzgerald. Still, it seemed urgent that she warn Alfred against the woman. She didn't know what words to put on paper, should the letter go astray. She studied the letter.

There was a knock on the door, then it opened tentatively.

"My lady."

"Bridie?"

"Aye."

"Come, come."

Bridie swept in. She seemed oblivious to the late hour of the day. She smiled at Eleanor, said nothing, and began gathering up Eleanor's belongings, plentiful enough since they had packed for the journey to London, knowing it would be long.

"Bridie, what are you doing?"

"Why, getting your things, my lady."

"Why?"

"To move them to the other room."

"What other room?"

"Down the hall, my lady."

Eleanor sighed with exasperation. "Why am I moving down the hall?"

Bridie's eyes rolled. "The master of the castle has said so."

"The master of the castle?"

"Sir Brendan."

Eleanor's brow furrowed. "Sir Brendan is master of this castle?"

"Aye."

"And when did this occur?"

"This morning. Haven't you heard, my lady? We are at peace. There's been a truce arranged between the Scots and English, engineered by King Philip of France."

A truce? She felt shaky. A truce between the two nations . . .

Yet, there had been truces called before. They had not ended the conflict.

"No, I had not heard," Eleanor murmured. "I have not left this room this morning." She hadn't left, nor had anyone approached her, other than the serving girl who had brought her water and food, and she had bobbed frequently, smiled a lot, and spoken very little.

She had expected that someone might come.

Someone . . .

Brendan. Corbin, at least.

She hadn't slept when Brendan left. She had listened to the men below, and contemplated her own position in a tumult of emotion. To be with him again . . . she loved him, loved the feel of him, the scent of him, just feeling him at her side. He hadn't remained at her side. He hadn't returned to her, but stayed below. He never would turn his back on his quest; he would die. Yet he had kept her from certain death, so what right did she have to create doom as the destiny for his courage? And still the haunting thought remained that here, in Scotland, she was a refugee, a branded murderess in her homeland.

And in all her thoughts, she had lain awake. She shouldn't be with him; Alain was scarcely cold in his grave. Yet she listened until the sounds of music and laughter and revelry below faded, wondering if then he would return. He had not done so. When she had finally slept, it had been near dawn.

"Bridie—"

But Bridie slipped back out the door, leaving it ajar. Eleanor stood, ready to follow her, but before she could do so, Bridie came back into the room, humming.

"Bridie—"

Bridie looked up at her, eyes sparkling, cheeks flushed, happiness abounding in her. "Oh, my lady! There's going to be a wedding! Can you imagine?"

And once again, Bridie disappeared.

Eleanor felt a cold anger steal over her. A wedding. He had planned a wedding, and not said a word to her. Logic argued that she wanted nothing more than to be his wife; she had yearned and ached for him, dreamed that such a thing could be true.

But the dream was tarnished now; for the life to be good, she had to be innocent, and she could not live with a legend that would grow regarding her as the countess who had lured her lord for money, then slain him to be with a lover.

The master of the castle! He was not *her* master.

"Where is he?" she asked Bridie.

"Why, in the other room."

"Where is that?"

"Just down the hall, the door at the top of the stairs."

Eleanor went marching down the hall. She raised a hand to the door, then felt another surge of anger.

He was not given to knock.

She threw open the door.

Aye, things had changed. Brendan sat before a desk. Eric and Collum were standing by him, and they all pored over a set of building plans.

Brendan looked up, annoyed at her loud entry. The others turned to her, stared at her expectantly.

She hadn't wanted this . . . an audience. She had thought that he would be alone.

But she had come, and she did not intend to slink away. She approached the desk.

"I'd have a word with you, Sir Brendan."

He leaned back, studying her. "I'm sure you have several, my lady. But this isn't the appropriate time."

"Since I've not been informed regarding time, my words seem expedient."

"Eleanor, as you can see, I am engaged."

"Then I will speak quickly. There will be no wedding."

"No?"

Brendan shoved the chair back, staring at her.

"No. I will not marry you."

He was quiet for a moment, watching her. She saw that his color had heightened, his fingers clenched where they lay upon his knees, and a telltale tic against his cheek betrayed his anger.

"Really, madam?" he said at last. "I don't remember asking you to do so."

It was her turn to flood with sudden color. "Bridie just said—"

He turned his attention back to the papers that lay before him. "Bridie will be marrying Lars this afternoon. Father Duff, of the little church down the hill, will join the two of them."

She felt as if cold air surrounded her; she couldn't have been more humiliated. She wanted to lash out, but she couldn't do so with Eric and Collum watching her, she had to gather up what shreds of her dignity she could find—and retreat.

"That is—wonderful," she managed to say with great dignity, then she spun around and quickly departed, her head as high as she could keep it.

In the hall, she once again came upon Bridie, still moving her belongings about. "Bridie, *you* are to be married."

"Aye! Can you believe it!" Bride said with such happiness that Eleanor could find no fault with her, nor chide her for not explaining fully.

"I'm so very happy for you."

"I knew you would be, Eleanor. If only I could be so happy for you—"

"What will you wear?" Eleanor asked. "Something very fine. We'll go through my clothing, find what suits you best—"

"This is the last of it, being moved."

Eleanor hesitated. She had seen nothing of her own in the room where she found Brendan.

"Bring it back," she said softly.

"My lady Eleanor, Sir Brendan said—"

"Brendan is a strong man, and indeed, a brave hero. But he does not dictate where I sleep."

"My lady—"

"Go back for my things."

"Please, Eleanor—"

"Bridie, go back for my things."

Eleanor walked by her, returning to the very fine room that had been prepared for her when she arrived.

She sat down before the fire. She used a slate for a desk, her ink laid out on the small stool before the fire. She tried to forget Brendan, and the burning humiliation she had brought upon herself.

Her cheeks still burned. Her heart beat too fast. She had to concentrate on her task. It was true that she couldn't go riding boldly back into England as if she were again an armor-clad figurehead, spurring men into war. Yet she was very afraid for Alfred.

She started writing again, forgetting for a moment, fighting to keep her thoughts centered. She managed to gather together some of the words she needed. Time passed. The task absorbed her.

In a while, the door opened. She assumed that Bridie had come back. She did not look up, but said, "Bridie, please, 'tis your day. Look through what you will, take what you will."

She managed to put down a few words, with Isobel's name in the sentence, along with the warning that someone there was a poisoner, without actually accusing Isobel. The silence in the room at last distracted her.

She looked up. It was not Bridie.

Brendan had entered, closed the door. He leaned against it, arms crossed, waiting. Startled, she jumped up, barely saving the pot of ink. Blood rushed to her cheeks. She stared at him,

far more alarmed by his sudden appearance than she wished
to betray.

She smoothed back a strand of hair.

"What is this new game of yours?" he demanded.

"This accommodations are quite fine, Sir Brendan," she
said. "Unless, of course, they are intended for use by someone
else. Then, of course, if I am taking up chambers intended for
other guests—"

"The room is not needed for other guests."

"Then I will remain here."

"You will not."

"If I am a guest—"

"You'll be housed where you are invited to stay."

"I am not leaving."

"You are."

"So you are master of the castle now and would become a
tyrant?" she challenged.

"A tyrant, my lady?"

"Indeed, giving orders, demanding—"

"Using force?" he inquired.

He strode into the room and caught her by the arm. She
shrank back, fighting his hold, furious, and still humiliated.
"Don't, Brendan, don't! Please, for the love of God, let me
be, I am not going—"

He caught her up, heedless of her words, leaving the room
and heading into the hall. She struggled against his hold, her
cheeks flaming.

"Will you put me down! You have humiliated me unto the
grave as it is—"

"Then I suggest you quiet down, else you'll draw attention
from below."

"Aye, and they'll see you behaving like a madman—"

"The difference is, my lady, I don't care what they see."

''Brendan, damn you, do you think that this is not wretched enough—''

He stopped in the hall; she felt his tension. She feared some real violence, but his force was all directed at the door he pushed in with a purposeful kick. The heavy wood gave way, and the hinges opened with a small groan.

''This, Eleanor,'' he said firmly, ''is where you'll stay.''

Chapter 19

He strode into the room and kicked the door firmly shut behind him.

She was sure that the sound of it slamming reverberated throughout the castle. He was heedless of the noise, striding firmly into the room.

At last he set her down upon a rich woven carpet before a burning fire. She stared at him, then surveyed her surroundings. The room was beautifully appointed; it seemed to be one of the finished places in the castle. The carpet made the room seem small and warm and intimate. The walls were not covered with flat tapestries, but heavy, embroidered draperies. The chairs were carved, highly polished, Norse in origin. The room contained a handsome bathtub, Norse as well, with intricate carving.

There was water in it; steaming and ready. Heavy linen towels waited by the side. The bath looked incredibly inviting.

She had no intention of going near it!

There was an archway to the far rear corner, draped as well. She walked to it, pulled back the curtain, and saw that it led to Brendan's chamber.

She turned back to face him. "I cannot stay here," she whispered.

"You can, you will."

"Your men heard what you said to me—"

"Aye, and they heard what you said to me. After we rode into England—to procure your freedom."

"I won't stay here, I can't stay here, I never intended to remain here long; as it is, I must clear my name, and if you don't see that—"

"Your pride is worth more than your life?"

She fell silent. "You know—"

"I know all there is to know, and have taken steps to set the matter straight. And you will stay here. The room has been prepared. It could not be more inviting. I know that you are fond of your comfort. The tub is wonderful. I've already tried it out."

"I am weary of you mocking me for the life into which I was born," she told him heatedly. "I am not desperate for comfort. You enjoy the bath. A Scot can always use an extra cleaning."

She started for the door, found herself dragged back.

"You will enjoy the bath."

"Brendan—"

"Clothed, unclothed?" he asked her.

"Have you gone mad with sudden power!" she exclaimed.

Perhaps he had; he lifted her, striding for the tub. She was going in, she thought, as she was. "Brendan! My shoes! I haven't so many here—"

He paused.

"Let them fall."

"Brendan, please, we can talk as civilized human beings—"

"A civilized Scot? I think not. We are far too uncouth and ill mannered!"

Her shoes fell as she stared at the set of his features. "Brendan, I do not have so very many garments with me that I can afford to destroy them. I—"

He set her down. She stared at him, frustrated, and fighting tears. She'd been angry that he would make plans without her; yet she was anguished to find that he did not intend to marry her. The child would have his name. He'd said nothing regarding her. She had made assumptions.

"I cannot do this; you really don't understand."

He remained before her, both angry and amused.

"You cannot do—*this*. What *this* do you refer to, Eleanor? You cannot take a bath? According to the people in Rome, the English are every bit as filthy as the Scots—we have all forgotten everything those ancient ancestors taught us about water. Ah, but it's easy, my lady, one simply sits and soaks, and the bar there is soap—"

"Brendan, excuse me, I am leaving. Sir Brendan, master of his domain, if you will—"

"What *this* do you mean, my lady? *This*—as in remain with me? Lie with me? You had no difficulty in Paris. The great lady, chancing an encounter with a heathen rebel for the sheer carnal danger of it, the sensual pleasure? Ah, but in truth, you can't do *this* so openly, because you are, of course, the great lady?"

She swung out to strike him, but he caught her arm, spun her around, and found the ties to the fine silk tunic she wore.

"Brendan—"

It came free in his hands. She remained in her linen shift and silk hose, but he made no effort to remove those, lifting her as she swore—and found herself seated in the tub, the hot

water splashing around her, her hair soaked and in her eyes.
He hunkered down by the tub.

"Feels good, doesn't it?" he inquired.

She smoothed back a lock of sodden hair. "Why are you
doing this to me?"

"You made a fool of me in there," he told her quietly.

"You made a fool of me!"

"I didn't come into your room ranting that I would not marry
you."

"I—I had thought that . . ."

"That I'd made arrangements for our marriage without con-
sulting you."

She didn't need to answer. The rose in her cheeks told him
clearly enough.

"They were thoughts you might have shared when we were
alone," he told her.

"You refused to give me time alone."

"I had intended to do so, as soon as we finished discussing
the fortifications and the surrounding land."

"So the castle . . . is really yours?"

"The castle is Scotland's. I will man it, aye. Does that make
me marriage material in your eyes? Does it provide a home?"

She doused him angrily with water from the tub. She managed a good strike; one he had not expected. She drenched his
hair, his face, his shoulders. He was still a single moment, then
moved like lightning, drawing her up to her feet, water pouring
from the linen she wore as if she were a human fountain. His
force was such that she cried out with alarm, "Brendan, the
babe!"

He held still, and to her amazement, he began laughing. "My
lady, you are a crafty opponent indeed." Then suddenly his
fingers threaded the dampness of her hair as he cradled her
nape and the back of her head, pulling her against him. They
were both soaked; she tasted the hot steam of the bath on his

lips, tasted the warmth, felt the wet sinking sensation, and trembled as she stood in his arms. When he released her lips at last, she met his eyes.

"I do intend to marry you, you know," he said, his thumb moving over her cheek.

"Alain is barely cold."

"I know that as well."

"I should, in truth, be mourning."

"We both mourn a good man. But we both know as well that is precarious, and time, like life, very precious."

He held her against him.

They both dripped into the tub, and around it.

She drew away from him, pulled the wet linen over her head, and cast it upon the dragon's head to the side of the tub. She sank into the water, grateful that some steam still rose, and peeled her hose from her limbs, depositing them, too, upon the ferocious head of the dragon. She eased back and closed her eyes.

She was startled a second later when he joined her, clothing shed. His weight displaced the water, which sloshed over the rim.

"You don't fit!" she told him.

"I'll manage." His limbs entwined with hers.

"The floor will be soaked; the water will reach the carpet, it will all be ruined."

"Ah, but as of this morning, it is my floor, and my carpet, to ruin."

He reached for her, water sloshing anew, and manipulated their forms so that he rested against the tub, and she leaned against him, her back to his chest. He smoothed her damp hair, cradling her to him.

"Relax, my lady."

"I can't."

"You haven't spent enough time running," he murmured,

smoothing her hair, "you learn to take what moments you can."

"It's not that."

"Then what."

"Your foot—"

"That is not my foot!" he laughed.

She fell silent, and couldn't help the smile that teased her lips. "I could kill you myself half the time!" she whispered, "And still . . . you . . ."

"Tease your senses? Awaken your wildest dreams?"

"Make me laugh."

"Alas, I have amused you? That was not my intent!"

In a second he was up, the water sluicing once again, and he was out of the tub, reaching for her, and wrapping her in the linen towel. And in seconds he had her up, and despite her shrieks, protesting the water he spewed, they were across the room, crushed upon the down-filled softness of the bed. Her words were still; the instant's deep chill she had felt on leaving the water was quickly gone. The soft fire that burned that afternoon laid claim to their skin, warming it, then casting a sheen upon them as they dried, to grow sleek and damp again in the urgency of their hunger, the depths of their desire. And that afternoon, she gave guilt and worry and fear to the flame, and lay beside him, happy only to be where she was, luxuriously warm in his arms, safe in the haven of his strength.

"We will have to rouse soon, and attend the wedding," he murmured, his lips at her hair.

"Aye. And the servants of this new domain you have claimed will come and see the room and see what havoc has been wrought and they will know . . ."

"Ah, that the brave new master spent the day cavorting with his mistress?"

The word stung.

"Aye," she said. "That is what they'll know."

He rolled, looking at her. "Did you think that these men would all believe I rode into England to seize you from your tormenters to set you upon a pedestal? My lady, I can't seem to make you happy. You furiously inform me that you'll not marry me, however, you are going to have my child."

"It's just . . . so soon."

"Soon, aye, but what choice? Did you want me to go about my business, pretending you weren't here?"

"You managed last night."

He smiled. "Ah, so that is it! Brendan, go away, leave me to my pretense of chastity, but take grave care what you do while I stand on my pedestal."

"No," she murmured. "I want to change what has been."

"Change the fact we met on the seas?"

She shook her head. "Change the fact that Alain was killed." She suddenly pressed him back to the pillows, her temper rising. "You, sir, will stop. I do not need luxury, and it isn't possessions I worry about. It's not even the fact that I . . . that I wanted you in France; I knew what I was doing. And it is not the fact of the child now. I don't hate the Scots — good God, how could I? They have saved me too many times. But I don't despise the English for the acts of a single man, or the deviousness of others. And I want to be with you, and there has never been anything in my life to feel so sweet as having moments to remain idly in your arms . . . but . . ."

"But what?" he demanded, brow furrowed, arm behind his head as he studied her features.

"It's too soon . . . and yet, I would marry you. I don't — " Again, she hesitated. "I don't want to live my life like Margot. I want to be a wife, and not — a mistress."

He watched her for a long moment, then reached out, and caressed her cheek. "My lady, the hour, the moment you choose, I will be waiting."

Tears suddenly stung her eyes. She lay against him, her face against his chest. He stroked her drying hair.

"It's a miracle, this," he murmured. "A home to claim . . . and you."

She played her fingers gently, idly over his chest.

"I would have gladly run with you from Paris," she whispered. "I wasn't afraid of the woods, of life on the run. I was afraid that you'd be killed, and your great dream endangered, if I did not wed. In truth, King Philip warned me it would be so."

"I died when I saw you in that cathedral," he said, "I died a little, and I rode away, but I could never ride far enough."

She rose, pressing against his shoulders as she bent to kiss his lips, a touch that was light, tender . . . and then more fervent. Beneath her, she felt every subtle change and nuance in his length, and then each change that was not so subtle, and then she felt as if the fire exploded, rose to heights, melding them together. And she would have dearly loved to lie there again, knowing nothing but the comfort of his hold, easing away the moment half awake and half asleep. But Brendan was too quickly up.

"My lady, there will be no marriage for your Bridie if we do not make ourselves present."

Bridie had chosen one of Eleanor's ochre gowns, with long embroidered sleeves. Her hair was dark against it. She had never been more beautiful.

The two would ride off to a small farmhouse on a lot of land long abandoned by previous tenants; Lars meant to farm, and still fulfill a feudal duty as a soldier, if — or when — war erupted again. Bridie's happiness was contagious, and yet she promised Eleanor, "I'll still be with you. The house is but a short ride from the fortress."

"I'll do well enough; we are both refugees here, Bridie. Be his wife, and don't worry about me. I have managed frequently enough on my own."

Bridie shook her head, smiling. "You made them bring me, my lady. In all the danger you faced, you might have forgotten me. You did not."

They hugged one another, then Lars came over grinning, and claimed his bride. They left the church, Father Duff, a burly, broad-shouldered priest hailing from Eire, along with them. A bonfire glowed. Pipers played, tunes outlawed but retained, and free again in the night with the words of a truce between warring nations.

Eric found Eleanor watching the festivities, and grabbed her hand. "I'm not the new master of the castle, so I need not stand on ceremony," he told her, his handsome features cast in a rueful grin. "Come, these dances are all miraculously easy."

And so, she faltered, stepped on his feet, but laughed her way through the lively music played on pipes and flute. She saw that Brendan was out among the people, laughing, enjoying the night, and dancing with the people from the fields and the castle, families of some men, lovers of others, workers, and warriors. Then she found herself taken by Liam, Collum, and then de Longueville, who told her, "Strange, my lady, what paths we have both taken to find ourselves here."

"Aye," she agreed. "Most strange."

"I like it well enough."

"I'm glad. You left the high seas for peace in France, and left that peace for the life of a rebel in Scotland, and now . . ."

"Now, there is a lady I met riding this great lowland expanse. She lives in a fine manor beyond that northern hill."

"Indeed?"

"I will become a Scotsman, though, bless the Lord, I learned to eat — and cook! — in France."

She smiled and looked about. Her stalwart English cousin

Corbin was dancing with a beautiful young woman with black hair that swirled around her like a midnight cape as she moved. Brendan was standing with Margot, sharing ale, and the two laughed and talked easily, like very old friends. And so they were.

She excused herself to de Longueville, and walked quickly over to Brendan and Margot. Though Margot had come to the castle when Eric rode south to England, and with absolute faith in their return had prepared for them to arrive, it was the first time Eleanor had seen her since France. Margot looked very pleased when she approached, and Eleanor embraced her warmly. "You're safe, and well," Margot said, holding her hands, stepping back to survey her. "A beautiful exile in our presence, though I am sorry for the loss that brings you here. The Count de Lacville was a very fine man."

"You knew him well?"

"Well enough. That wasn't, of course, our first journey to France through the years. We have cultivated Philip's favor, you know, and what better way than for our men to fight for him?" She had a lovely smile. Eleanor wondered how Eric could ever risk losing her. Her hair was as fine as silk, her eyes bluer than any ocean. Her words were always gentle, and there always seemed to be a great calm about her. "William Wallace carries papers on him — right, Brendan? — from the King of France, asking that his 'good friend' always be given safe conduct through his lands."

"It seems that Philip himself has proven to be a good friend," Brendan said. "But he is at peace now; the truce he has maneuvered will benefit everyone — including him. But Edward will not be done with Scotland."

Eric joined them. "Maybe he'll die," he said cheerfully.

"All men will die," Margot informed them.

"Ah, then, we should dance while we live. Lady Eleanor, Brendan, your pardon."

Brendan's arms slipped around her. He did not mind showing his affection before his people; she should not mind that he did. She still could not help worry about what was said about her, and hope that people would not believe she could have killed a man to be with Brendan.

But here . . . there was simple acceptance of her. She was believed, without explanation.

"It was a fine wedding. And a fine gathering. A day of real celebration," Brendan said.

"Eric should marry Margot," she said.

"Aye, he should," Brendan agreed.

"Can't you—do anything?"

"He is my cousin, and a free man, and he fights a battle because of Scottish blood that is a battle he doesn't need to fight. He is not bound to me by any ties, either than that of his choice to win freedom here. I don't ever presume to tell Eric what to do."

"Maybe I will," she murmured softly.

He was silent and she turned to see that he was smiling.

"What?"

"If you cannot solve the dilemmas in your own heart, you will work on others?"

"She is beautiful and wonderful—"

"I agree. And that is between them. Come, it's growing late."

And so she followed him.

The days that followed were filled with joy. Eleanor came to know his men well, and the fortress changed from being a battered tower filled with men who had no function except for war to the center of a community alive with spring planting and a new desire for life. Land was divided; ruined houses were reclaimed; men fell into the work that had been theirs before they had taken to the forests, and the stone tower that was the last defense in war became more and more of a home.

There were nights when she lay with Brendan and they talked, and he told her that he had written to Robert Bruce, who was currently on excellent terms with King Edward, and asked him to intercede in the trouble at Clarin.

"But what can he do?" Eleanor asked.

Brendan hesitated a minute. "An agreement with Robert Bruce is important to King Edward. He has tremendous holdings in the southwest, and if he had ever set his mind to joining in rebellion, he might have created major changes in how many a battle came out. After Falkirk, when Edward launched his marches, Robert Bruce did hold out on his own lands. He and John Comyn were both guardians of the realm at the time, but the feud between them is too bitter—after John Balliol, one of them would be closest to the crown."

"But I thought that Bruce had betrayed the rebellion time and time again."

"Many a good man has signed a submission to Edward over the years. Comyn holds out with vigor and anger when many a man succumbs, but there are those who say as well that John Comyn took his forces from the field at Falkirk with intent to do so, fearing the battle lost, and his own capture. I haven't trusted Robert Bruce often, but William, who has been the one to suffer the brunt of the barons' deeds, still claims that there is a true hero and king in the way, waiting to come out."

"But Wallace has ridden with Comyn again."

"Aye, William will fight the battles he finds to save Scotland. But Comyn has a terrible temper, and he has his bending point as well. That is why it is not beneficial for a man to grow too possessive of his holdings; they compromise his beliefs."

"And now you are a landholder."

He hesitated. "It's good to have the land, to be master here, to build, to reap, to sow; I've known too little of such practices."

"But you are fiercely proud of your name."

"Usually," he said with a grin, and drew a pattern on a sheet. "The surname, though, has spread far."

"From England," she murmured. "Or so I've heard."

He took no offense, but cast her a smile. "Aye. The first of the Grahams came in with King David, when he arrived having grown at the English court. But the king was quick to make Scotland his own, many years ago now. His wife had the blood of Vikings and ancient tribal Scots, and they had sixteen children, so the family legend goes. They dispersed throughout Scotland, and like many other families, they have taken widely different paths throughout the years. I had a cousin who died at Falkirk, and one who set out a cry that everything of Wallace's should be seized when he left Scotland to pursue aid from France, and make plea to the pope in Rome. My father died when I very young, and I grew up in the household of another cousin — whose home was ravaged and wife was killed by English invaders. Aye, a man becomes fiercely proud of his name. And I like the idea of a place of my own . . . belonging."

"Perhaps you'll begin to understand my feelings for Clarin," she said softly.

"Aye, my lady, but I could leave, were it expedient."

"I am not at Clarin."

"Give it time, Eleanor. You must be rational, and not think to solve such a problem by rushing off madly."

"That's what you did."

"I had a life to save."

"And I have only honor."

"Your honor is not questioned here."

And it was not, she knew.

"Sometimes," she whispered to him, "I'm very afraid."

"Why?"

"I can't believe being here with you. In a place where we don't hide, at a time when being together is not . . . wrong. I touch you, I wake and you're beside me, and I look at you, and shake because you are so perfect, and you lie beside me — ''

''Perfect!'' He said, laughing, but pleased. ''Hardly. I am riddled with scars, capable of a horrible temper — and still an outlaw and upstart, I do assure you.''

''Perfect to be with,'' she told him. ''And I'm afraid that the time will come when it will be a dream, that I will not wake in the night, and be assured, because you are there.''

He was silent a moment. ''There will be such nights, but I will always return to you, I swear it. Wherever you may be, my lady, I will return to you.'' He spoke the words with passion and intensity, and at long last she dared tell him, ''I love you, Brendan. I can . . . I can live without Clarin now far easier than I could ever live without you.''

He rolled, rising above her, studying her face. He kissed her, and made love to her, and in the midst of this, whispered again and again, seemed to wrap her in a cocoon of shimmering silver. ''And I love you . . . I love you . . . love you . . .''

Later, as they lay together, the baby moved and she started, and he woke anxiously. ''What is it?''

''Feel, Brendan, feel!''

''I feel . . . your flesh.''

''No, wait . . .''

And then again the ripple, strong enough that she could feel it with her fingers, holding his to her abdomen.

He felt the flutter. He tenderly pressed his lips to her, and pulled her close, and they slept.

The next morning, Brendan was preparing to ride out with Gregory and Lars to find a small herd of sheep that had run into the hills when Collum, on guard at the outer gate, shouted that a messenger was arriving. Brendan left his horse and raced up the steps to the tower. It was Griffin, and he knew that the messenger would be bringing a reply from Robert Bruce.

He retraced his steps, ready in the courtyard to meet the man when he arrived. Griffin rode in, dismounted, and said quickly, "Greetings, Sir Brendan, from Robert Bruce, Earl of Carrick and Annandale!"

"Welcome, Griffin."

The man quickly lowered his voice. "The message I bring you is for your eyes alone, and to be destroyed, and its contents were not relayed by my master."

Brendan nodded gravely. "My thanks. Come into the hall."

Once inside, he summoned Joanna. The woman whom he had first met as she cleaned the banister had proven to be capable and knowledgeable regarding the fortress, and its previous function. The steward who had run the household had gone with Hebert. She had told Brendan he must find a capable man to manage the vast inner working of the place; he had told her that she must take on the task. She had been pleased, but uncertain — she had never been in charge of a household before.

He had told her they would do well together — he'd never needed such a household run before.

In the hall, he needed only to call her name, and she was there, ready with refreshments for the rider, and cool ale for them both. Brendan excused himself to Griffin, and sat before the fire to read the correspondence.

He scanned the opening courtesies and quickly got to the point of the letter. Bruce wrote,

I don't doubt that I can reach the very young French queen now sitting on England's throne, nor do I doubt that she will have a vigorous interest in the proceedings, since it was an old and dear friend of her brother's who so sadly reached such an end. I do think that justice can be discovered. In time. However, word has reached me

*that, despite the truce, Miles Fitzgerald, without the com-
mand of the king, has raised a large company of men.
More so than can be easily combatted at this time by our
own numbers, woefully depleted in the past years, and
now dispersed through a promise of peace. He is not
afraid of the king's wrath at such a gesture, since Edward
would but give him a slap on the hand for seeking personal vengeance for the wrong you have done him, the
humiliation he has suffered in failing the king's business.
I hope that my warnings reach you in time; the Lady
Eleanor of Clarin is in grave danger; it is my suggestion
that she not be available for any form of abduction, should
Fitzgerald bring a large enough force to breach your
defenses.*

Brendan read the letter twice, then cast the message in the
fire. He sat for a long time staring at the flames, then rose.

Griffin sat at the table, having received a plate of fresh
venison from Joanna.

"You'll excuse me? I've urgent matters to attend to."

"Aye, Sir Brendan."

"The Bruce will not fight with me, will he?"

"He doesn't dare; he shouldn't know of this danger, and his
own peace with the English is so new . . . as is his marriage."

"I understand."

He turned and left the hall, riding out to make the arrangements he felt he must before seeking out Eric and the others.

When he returned to the hall, he asked Joanna if she had
seen Eleanor, and he was told that she had just bathed and
dressed, having slept very late. Brendan walked up the stairs,
glad that she was in the room.

He entered to find her brushing the gold of her hair. She
smiled at his entrance, and he grit his teeth against the measures
he felt himself forced to take.

"What is it?" she asked.

"You have to pack. You're leaving this afternoon."

"I'm leaving?" she inquired, startled. "But—"

"Fitzgerald is leading men this way."

"The Scots and English have signed a truce."

"He is not bringing the king's army."

"Then—"

"He will lead an army of his own making, but I doubt if it was too difficult to persuade the northern English barons to join him on a matter of personal vengeance. Everyone on the borders has suffered some loss or insult, Englishman and Scot. Fitzgerald will not underestimate us as an enemy, he will not come without tremendous strength."

"The castle is strong—"

"Eleanor, he is coming for you."

"Aye, but, you seized this place yourself from the English. Since then, you Scots have repaired walls, brought in arms and armor, the castle is supplied—"

"Any castle can be breached. Any man can fall in battle. You're not safe here."

"Then—"

"You're going north."

"But—"

"Collum and Hagar will ride with you, along with Margot, Bridie, and Lars."

"To—"

"My kin just beyond Stirling. You will be safe there."

She was shaking as she stood. "I don't want to go; this raid will be my fault. I should stay here, Brendan—"

"You'll go."

"Fitzgerald can't breach these walls—"

"For the love of God, Eleanor, this has not been an easy decision for me. You will go. You will not risk the life of the child."

She stiffened, lowering her head.

"I don't wish to do this."

"But you will."

"You will force me, against my will?"

"My lady, I will bind you to a horse myself."

She turned her back to him.

"As you — command," she murmured.

"There is one more thing."

"And that is?"

"The choice is no longer yours. You will marry me."

"When, Brendan?" she demanded, spinning around. Her eyes were incredibly bright. She was passionate and angry — and afraid, he thought.

"You're sending me away," she reminded him heatedly. "What if we are parted for a very long time? What if you do fall in this battle that should not be taking place? When then will this marriage take place?"

"Now," he said flatly. "Father Duff waits in the hall below."

Chapter 20

"I don't wish to be sent away," Eleanor protested. But if he heard her, he paid her no heed. "Brendan, please, we're still doing this too soon—"

"It isn't too soon," he said harshly. The he looked into her eyes, "if I die, the child will have my name—"

"If you die, I will be an exile in a land where there will be many who haven't forgiven me for Falkirk."

"There is no time for argument, Eleanor—"

"Then don't send me away."

"I must."

They had arrived downstairs and she fell silent; Father Duff stood by the fire. The hall was filled. She saw Eric, Collum, Liam, Gregory, de Longueville, and others, all gathered quickly, and most of them, she realized, dressed in some form of mail, some with plate armor, some with simple leather mail, over tunics that bore family crests. Margot was there; she came quickly forward, taking her hand, kissing her cheeks. "Don't look so pale!" she whispered. "It is a truly happy occasion."

"Men are riding here to destroy our lives — " Eleanor protested.

"Men are always riding to destroy our lives," Margot replied.

"How do you ever bear it?" she whispered urgently to Margot.

And Margot smiled. "I make sure that I always plan for the end of the battle, the return of my man. I never doubt him. And so I bear it. Come, along, Father Duff stands ready."

She found herself standing before Father Duff, with Brendan at her side. Her knees threatened to give.

She wanted this more than anything in the world. To be his wife. To be the woman who waited for him.

The one to whom he would always return.

She glanced at Margot as Father Duff greeted their assembly. She was startled when he read a document purported to be from the Archbishop of Lamberton, one of the highest churchmen in the country, blessing the union. She glanced at Brendan, and knew that he had probably sent for the archbishop's blessing at her first arrival, and that he had received the blessing of "the sovereign domain of Scotland, sanctioned by right of her king" as well. Brendan had taken care to see that this union would be legal in every way.

She listened, and found strength, and when the large, broadshouldered Irish priest looked her way, asking who gave her in the marriage, she was startled when her cousin walked up beside her. "I, sir, the lady's kinsman, Corbin of Clarin, do give her solemnly to this man."

Corbin didn't look her way. She wondered if he had been coerced. She saw that a man in the colors of Robert Bruce was looking on as well, and knew that Brendan had intended that this service be witnessed, and documented beyond the parish and archdiocese records.

So this would happen. What she wanted more than anything

in the world, and yet against her will, because he would marry her when her first husband had scarcely cooled in the earth — and when he would send her away the moment the vows were spoken.

She glanced away from the priest, and saw Margot, smiling her encouragement.

When the priest took a lull, and requested if any in the company might protest, she suddenly found herself speaking.

"Good Father, I have a word."

He stared at her, a brow shooting up. At her side, she felt Brendan's incredible tension, felt the furious pressure of his hand on hers, and saw the amazement and fury in his eyes.

"You protest your own marriage?" Father Duff inquired, astounded.

She shook her head. "Not in the least. As we all fear the future, and what is right, and what is wrong, and as men fall in battle, and women are left behind, I seek only to share this happy occasion." She tried subtly to free her hand from Brendan's, but could not. Still, she twisted to see the crowd around them. She met Eric's eyes. "Life is fleeting, we have all agreed. Yet most men here will sacrifice it for honor. Such grand emotion lies in our hearts, and is as near to every woman as it is to every man."

Eric stared back. He looked furious for a moment, reddened, as if, indeed, his rugged features, now reddened to crimson, might explode. Then suddenly he shook his head and laughed.

"My lady," Duff was protesting, "we are in the midst of a ceremony — "

"Aye, that's why we must pause," she whispered.

"Eleanor!" Brendan grated in a low, sharp tone, his fingers winding around hers with a pressure that forced her back around. Tears stung her eyes. She had accomplished nothing.

But suddenly, Eric came forward, striding through the crowd.

"Father Duff, I think I know that of which my lady speaks. And if you'd be so good . . ."

He turned, reaching out a hand to Margot, who stared at him dumbfounded. "Margot, since the Lady Eleanor is most eager we make good this occasion as well . . ."

Margot stared at him, incredulous, then stepped forward, taking his hand. "Brendan, with your permission, Father Duff will say the words for us this day as well?"

"Readily granted," Brendan assured him.

Eleanor was jerked down to her knees.

Sir William Wallace came forward to give Margot into marriage.

The ceremony continued. She heard Duff go on. She was asked again to love, honor, and obey. She whispered words of agreement. She heard Brendan's clear harsh tones. Discretely, and with a minor desperation, she removed the band with the escutcheon of Lacville that still wound her finger. The priest touched a band of gold to her first finger, second, and third. In the name of the Father, the Son, and the Holy Ghost. She gazed at the intricate Celtic band on her finger. Brendan had surely had it made for her, for the gold was fine, the size was small, and still, an initial was entwined in the crest, along with a great bird of prey. She was staring at the ring, and hardly heard the priest's words that before God, they were now joined as man and wife, and no man could set them asunder.

She rose from her knees to the sound of tremendous cheering. She felt Brendan's arms, and his lips, and it would have been well . . .

If only she could stay.

The cheering paused as the last of the sacred rite was spoken for Margot and Eric, then once again the cheering rose, and skins of wine were passed. Then another cry went up. "To Scotland, aye, to the sons and daughters of Scotland!"

Men seized her, held her, kissed her cheek. She found herself moved through the hall, receiving the congratulations of all in attendance, not the least of whom was Corbin.

He held her hands and kissed both her cheeks, then embraced her warmly.

"Find real happiness this time, cousin," he told her.

The wish seemed earnest. She smiled.

"And you, Corbin, are you happy here?"

"I will stay and fight Fitzgerald," he told her ruefully.

"Corbin, you risk so much if you do so—"

"The man would have killed me. I only do what it is right."

"You're an Englishman."

He grinned. "Aye . . . but there is something in the battle they fight here, in the passion. It has aroused something in me."

"You have a wife at home."

"Must you remind me, Eleanor?"

She smiled. "We have left Alfred in her hands. I am afraid for him."

"Don't be. My brother is not a coward."

"All the courage in the world cannot save a man from a knife in his back."

"Eleanor, we'll get through this battle first." He smiled, and kissed her cheek again. "Be happy."

"I am being sent away; you will stay."

"Eleanor, you cannot stay. And I must."

She found herself tapped on the shoulder by Hagar, who gave her such a mighty hug it threatened to break her. She kissed his cheek, and found that she was passed on more quicky, and moving again through the hall.

She was back with Brendan when she neared the entrance. In a second he had her hand firmly in his once again. He led her through it, and to the courtyard outside the main tower.

And there, horses waited. His hands were upon her then, they lifted her, setting her atop a handsome roan.

He stepped away from the horse. "God go with you, my lady, until we meet again."

"Brendan, please, don't do this."

"We've received notice already. Fitzgerald has raised a large number of men from the north, and is very close. He lost no time after we left him tied on the road, but raised a hue and cry immediately. My riders have already come back with word that he has crossed the border. Horsemen ride fast. You will not be able to move with such speed. You must be on your way. The castle will soon be under attack."

"I have been in a castle under attack before. I can fight—"

"That is what scares me," he acknowledged.

"Brendan, the fortress is strong—"

"So I pray."

Near them now, the crowd was gathering; Eric and Margot, the two close and intimate and whispering; the mighty Hagar, ready to mount his great, heavy horse; Collum, ready to lead their party north. Bridie was there, with her beloved Lars. She was busy seeing to the pack animals, that nothing necessary had been forgotten.

Eleanor saw them all, and how carefully this had been planned, before he had ever come to her.

"Brendan—"

"You have just sworn to obey me," he reminded her.

"And if I promised to obey, you in turn promised to cherish me!" she whispered.

"I am doing so, sending you away."

Tears stung her eyes. Despite him, she managed to dismount before he could stop her, and come to him, hands upon his chest. "Brendan, please, for the love of God, don't send me away so!"

Something within him seemed to give. His arms came around her, engulfing her; she felt his lips at the top of her head.

"Eleanor, you must go. I have to meet this battle without

you. I never falter in a fight, never. And yet . . . if you were here, my thoughts would not be on strategy, or battle. I would worry constantly about your position. Fitzgerald is a vindictive man. Many northern landholders have deep grudges, and are ready for a fight that the king will say he condemns, but secretly applauds. Eleanor, you must go. I pray that Fitzgerald will quickly be defeated, and that I will come for you soon. But you must go."

"Brendan—"

"Don't you understand that is anguish for me, too?" he whispered, and drew away, and she saw his eyes, the blue depths, the passion . . . the love.

Such things were worth fighting for.

She suddenly understood something about him. He loved the land; his land. Not his property, but his land. Valleys, gorges, great, towering tors, the colors of spring and summer, the ancient histories of peoples long gone. But it wasn't the land that caused his battle; it was the ideal in which he believed, of a people. Different, unique, quarrelsome among themselves perhaps, but with a right to be what they were. His loyalty to the battle was as elusive, but deep and passionate. The same fierce loyalty and passion he gave to her.

He could falter.

For her.

"Brendan . . ."

He held her very close, then lifted her chin, and kissed her lips with a tenderness that seemed to bring the sun into her very being. She felt again the stirring of their child inside her.

"I will keep the babe safe," she swore. "To bear your name."

He lifted her chin, his knuckles brushing her face and his eyes searching its every facet, as if he would engrave a remembrance in his mind.

"You bear it as well now, my love," he reminded her. "I

had meant to give you so much. A ceremony at a grand cathe-dral—"

"I had a ceremony at a grand cathedral," she told him. "Had we been in the woods, in a sty, in the mud, it would have been sacred, and beautiful, to me."

His smile deepened; she was glad of her words, and glad that her pride had not forced her to let him send her away in anger. This was cruel enough.

One last embrace. She felt his heart beat, the power and heat of him.

Then he lifted her again, and set her on the horse once more.

It was time to ride.

"They've a huge siege engine," Gregory reported to Bren-dan. Fast, agile, and wily, he had been sent to observe the movement of Fitzgerald's column.

Brendan had been busy giving commands for the defense of the walls. He had seen that quivers of arrows were counted and dispersed, and oil had been set in cauldrons to be burned, and that the last of the people living on the outer farms and homesteads of the parish were drawn into the relative safety of the outer walls, bringing with them their children, their animals, their most prized possessions.

"A huge engine . . . a catapult?" Brendan queried.

"Aye," Gregory agreed.

Brendan thought for a moment, aware that such a war machine could send flaming missiles into the castle, destroying them from within rather than without.

"The walls are weakest here," he said to Corbin, pointing, "And there."

"Aye, I'll see that the oil is ready for any who would ram the fortifications," Corbin assured him.

"What are you planning?" Gregory asked.

"To dig a few holes. Eric!" he called to his cousin across the field.

Eric, setting up the positions for the longbowmen, came to him quickly.

"I'm riding out, taking a party of men, to destroy the road," Brendan said. "They'll bog down with their catapult, and buy time for us. Wallace has taken a group of men around the eastern side of the forest; they can inflict some heavy damage from the woods, especially if we can create a noose around the English in the road."

Corbin had come to their group as they spoke.

"I might be more useful riding with you. I'm trained for combat, far more deft with a sword than you might imagine, and good in battle; many of your men are not."

He hesitated, watching the man. Corbin of Clarin had proved to be more than a model prisoner; he had chosen to stay. And though he wanted to trust Eleanor's kinsman, he had learned to be wary of even his own countrymen.

But there was no question of Corbin coming with them.

"You're an Englishman," he said. "If the rest of us are caught and taken, we stand some chance of ransom or prison. You would be inflicted with dire punishment; enough to wish that you were dead."

Corbin shook his head. "You think you stand any chance against Fitzgerald, any more than I? No, my friend, they will but cut your bowels with a duller knife, and do it more slowly."

"Still, you're needed here. You have defended such a fortification before."

That he was necessary inside the walls was a lie. He knew the truth, even as Brendan spoke. But the lie was what would be, and Corbin knew it too.

"You will miss my sword arm," he said.

"I believe I will," Brendan agreed.

Corbin turned back to the task he had been assigned, and

soon, Brendan was riding with a group of men from the castle walls. Deep into the south where the road was most heavily surrounded by forest, he called a halt. He thanked God for the spring rains that had already rendered the poor road treacherous and muddy. He called a halt, and his party of twenty men — farmers many, those who knew how to turn the earth, began to dig. Within an hour, they had created a gully that would bog down not just a siege engine, but many a heavy horse and rider as well. The Scots, knowing every small trail through the forests, would not face the same trap as the English, for he sent Gregory in search of Wallace with the new plan, and knew that the wily strategist would bring his forces up behind Fitzgerald's raiders.

The farmers were sent back to the safety of the castle. Brendan left the walls again, aware that the English were very close to the trap. Eric stayed behind, in command of the defenses behind the walls. Corbin would work with him.

Liam rode with Brendan, ready to flank his efforts on left and right.

In time, they saw the English army approaching. From a distance, it appeared that Fitzgerald rode in front. He was heavily armored that day, a helm hid his face, but he wore his colors, and at his rear, his squire carried his standard.

The first horse rode through the woods. From his vantage point in the trees, Brendan watched them near the gully. He calculated the distance between the first riders and the catapult being dragged through the trees by a team of six heavy draft horses. The catapult was a lethal looking weapon, and a merciless one, for properly aimed, a missile sent from it could destroy walls — and flesh and bone. Yet, he thought, it was good that Fitzgerald had thought to bring such a weapon; the transportation of it had surely slowed him down, giving Robert Bruce time to warn them of the attack.

"They're nearly there," Liam said quietly, his voice just

carrying from across the road. He rode the branch as if it were a horse; ready with his bow and arrow.

Brendan nodded. "Aim for Fitzgerald. The throat."

"Aye, Brendan."

The riders came closer. Brendan narrowed his eyes, and saw then that the man wearing Fitzgerald's colors and riding in the position that should justly be his was not the English baron.

Fitzgerald had prepared for an ambush. He had sent another in his stead.

Brendan swore softly to himself.

"Brendan—it's not Fitzgerald."

"I know. Take him down anyway; the horses will soon flounder."

Liam sent out the first arrow. His aim was true, and the man clutched his throat before falling from his horse in such sudden silence that he hit the ground before others realized the danger.

Brendan motioned with his hand. More arrows began to fly in a coordinated rain. The arrows soared, whispered against the wind, and fell.

"Now!" Brendan shouted, and the men chosen to harry the army emerged from the trees, some rushing onto the road with fierce cries, others falling from the trees like spiders skimming down webs. Horses screamed and shrieked; there was a mighty thud as the catapult careened into the deep muddy groove in the road, then Brendan heard little else above the clash of steel that arose around them. He gave his attention to each enemy he faced.

In a copse a good distance from the battle, Miles Fitzgerald stood beside his horse, listening to the sounds of the battle.

One of his men came riding hard to find him.

"There was an ambush?" Fitzgerald said, but it was hardly a question.

"Aye, as you expected, yet worse. We've lost the catapult."

"Lost it?" Fitzgerald inquired in a voice with such a hard edge it was difficult for even the messenger to reply.

"Cracked hard into the mud," the messenger replied. "It would take days to pull it out, and . . . days to repair it."

"A sorry loss," Fitzgerald said irritably.

"We've lost scores of men in the mud as well," the messenger said.

"Thank God, then, that I did not ride at the fore," he murmured. Then he told his man, "Go back; keep your distance. Whatever is lost, see that the horse surrounds the walls. They may keep a distance, but be obvious to those in the castle."

"Aye, sir." The messenger hesitated.

"What is it?"

"The men believed you would take command once the initial fighting was over."

"That had been my intent. The situation has changed. Sir Roger Lawton will lead in my stead; tell him so, and give him my orders that he must be seen from the parapets."

"Aye, sir. And then?"

"And then?" Fitzgerald said irritably. "And then I will return, and he will receive further orders."

"But sir—"

"I will ride north, and capture those who intended to escape our righteous mission," he said. "Go!"

When the messenger had departed, he signaled another man to emerge from the tent he'd erected in the copse. The fellow was Dirk of Pawley. He had served the king for a time, in the tower of London, until too much drink had cost him his work.

No matter. Fitzgerald had known a true artist when he had seen one.

Dirk was nearly as broad as he was tall, but his weight was muscle. He'd lost an eye in a tavern brawl, and a patch of his scalp was missing as well. He was uglier than sin; the broader his smile, the uglier the man. He smiled a lot. He liked his work.

"Bring him out," Fitzgerald said.

Dirk nodded, and returned to the tent, dragging out the man a group of riders had caught in the woods that morning. There had been something familiar about the young man, who seemed to have a talent for talking and charm. He'd spoken poorly, pretended that his French was bad, and that he was a simple farmer, cast from his desolate lands by the extent of warfare, and looking for nothing other than an evening meal.

But Fitzgerald knew he'd seen the man before, among other young men taken from the northern tenant lands to train for battle. His first thought had been to string up the lad from the next available tree. Dirk would have been glad to manage a noose that would strangle the man to death slowly, rather than breaking his neck; a good end to a traitor. Dirk was a good man to have, he knew.

Just as King Edward knew that Fitzgerald himself made a fine sheriff, a servant in the king's name. Edward thought of himself as a great hammer of justice. A hammer of justice needed men who were not afraid to use force themselves.

The captive was not so cheerful and charming now. He couldn't walk; Dirk literally dragged him by the scruff of his neck. The hold must have been painful; the fellow could no longer cry out.

Dirk dropped the man. Fitzgerald stepped forward, picking him up by the hair. "Once again; the lady is no longer in the castle?"

There was no response. Fitzgerald frowned, and kicked the man in the ribs. Again, no response.

He shook his head, looking at Dirk. "You've killed him already," he said with annoyance.

Dirk shrugged. "He talked. He said what you needed to know."

"I would have liked to assure myself that his words were true."

"I promise you; when he spoke, his words were true," Dirk said. "What shall I do with him?"

"Throw him on the road," Fitzgerald said dismissively. "Let him be a warning to any other would-be traitors."

Dirk hefted the man, carrying him through the woods like a carcass. Still south of the action, he threw the man into the mud. Fitzgerald had mounted when he returned. "To horse, man," he said impatiently.

He let out a long whistle.

The ten men he had picked to ride with him gathered from their hiding places within the woods. Two could play at such a game of warfare.

"Northward, and at as fast a clip as we dare. There is open field between the castle and the next passable road. We bypass the ditches through the routes learned from the traitor."

Horses stamped their feet; his men nodded their agreement.

A good lot he had chosen, he thought. They were all from his own holdings; men with much to lose if they betrayed him or faltered in any way, and much to gain if they fulfilled their quest. Some of them had been with him when Sir Brendan Graham delivered his humiliation upon them at the stream on the road to London. They would be thirsting for vengeance as well.

"Speed matters," he said. "Don't fear the open ground; the other flank of our forces will keep the Scots busy at their walls."

He turned, now ready to lead.

He could almost taste a victory that would be incredibly sweet—and rewarding. And he might have lost it all . . .

His reckoning had been wrong.

But now . . .

Now he knew where *she* was. And he could almost see the

stature that her capture would give him, *taste* the importance his name would take on . . .

They fought until the advance troops lay on the road along with the fallen catapult; then, when the rearguard began to swarm around the obstruction, they began their retreat to the castle walls. They could hear shouts of surprise when Wallace's men began attacking from behind, and they made good their hard ride back to the castle.

Eric saw their advance, ordered the gates thrown open, and when the last of their number made it through the gates, they were quickly closed again.

Brendan shouted out orders, racing up the steps to the parapets. They saw the troops advance and disperse around the front of the fortification. Riders surged forward, but as the first hail of arrows rained, a large group fell; those who made it closer were met with the boiling oil. They retreated; hovering at the edge of the forest.

They didn't ride forward again.

The Scots at the castle waited, tense, ready. The riders came no closer.

"What are they doing?" Eric asked. "Awaiting reinforcements?"

"Maybe," Brendan said.

They watched; they waited. The English held their distance. Night fell.

On the parapets, they continued to keep guard. The English seemed to have settled in for the night.

"If this is a siege, it's the most curious siege I've seen," Eric murmured.

"There's something else curious," Brendan said.

"What's that?"

"Fitzgerald has been missing from all this."

Corbin had come to stand with them as they stared out at the line of opposition. The English had lit fires, and appeared to be bedding down for the night at the edge of the forest. They were easy to see; they remained at a distance.

"How can you be certain Fitzgerald isn't there? He isn't wearing his colors; he doesn't want to be seen," Corbin said.

Brendan shook his head. "He isn't there. He wasn't in the lead with his men; we were on foot with the front guard, hand to hand. He was not among them."

"He is cowering behind all those forces," Eric suggested.

Suddenly, Corbin pointed beyond the gates. "Look, there! A lone rider, one of ours!"

It was true; Brendan saw a horseman, dead low against his animal, rushing for the gates. He carried no standard, but Brendan recognized the tunic he wore.

"One of Bruce's men," he said briefly. He was amazed; it had been a feat of true courage for the rider to brazen his way through the English line with speed alone. Indeed, he was followed by an awkward, uncoordinated spate of arrows; each flew, and missed its mark, but struck the ground dangerously near the horse and rider. "The gates!" he roared. "Open the gates!"

A shout had gone up among the English; a group hastily mounted their horses to come in chase, perhaps hoping to rush the gates as well, though it would be a foolish attack, since there was no time for the men to organize.

"Archers!" Brendan cried, running down the ramparts and grabbing a bow and arrow himself, taking aim over the form of the man now spurring his horse desperately to reach the opening gates.

Brendan let his arrow fly. He was not the archer Liam was, but his missile flew true, catching the first of the Englishmen in the chest. The man had opted for speed rather than safety.

He wore no mail or armor. He was lifted cleanly from his horse, and left in the mud.

A hail of arrows flew from the parapets. The night came alive with the sound of screams and shouts of agony.

The rider entered through the gates. The gates closed behind him.

Brendan ran down from the parapets, eager to meet the man who had dared brave such a treacherous ride.

In the courtyard, the man's horse stood, trembling, foaming. The man instantly leaped from his horse. Brendan saw that it was the Bruce's rider, Griffin.

He was breathless, but strode with hurried purpose to Brendan.

"I've news from Wallace," he said quickly.

"Wallace?" Brendan said, startled, frowning. He set a hand on Griffin's shoulder. "He is well? He was to harry the rear-guard, and retreat with his men into the trees."

"Aye, and that he did. Sir William is fine." He drew a breath. "The Bruce gave me orders to observe what I could—" He hesitated, and shrugged, "give what aid possible if needed . . ."

"Aye, but keep the name of Bruce out of this skirmish, eh?" Brendan said quietly.

"I joined with Wallace from the rear, and was with him when he found your man."

"What man?"

"Gregory of Clarin. They came upon him half dead in the road, but he was desperate to speak. He met with some torture at the hands of a talented master and was left for dead. His lips were swollen, his teeth having gone through them, but he was determined to let Wallace know his deep sorrow—he told Fitzgerald everything he knew about your defenses. *And* the fact that Lady Eleanor was not here, but had been sent on with a large party."

Brendan stared at Griffin, feeling as if his life's blood fled from him.

"What?" he demanded harshly, the wind seemed to rush in his ears.

"Fitzgerald has been no part of the attack, and never was. He avoided the front, afraid you'd have an ambush. And when he discovered the truth, he skirted the forest, using the battle to cover his movements. He doesn't care if his men ever take the castle." He hesitated just long enough to catch his breath.

"Sir Brendan, Miles Fitzgerald has gone straight for the Lady Eleanor. And he is now hours ahead of any possible pursuit."

Chapter 21

"We'll stop here for the night," Collum announced.

Eleanor wasn't at all sure where "here" was, for it seemed that Collum had chosen nothing more than a place in the middle of the road, surrounded by trees and darkness. Though distraught at leaving, she had not found the ride unpleasant — the landscape was beautiful. They had ridden for hours once they left the fortification, stopping only once to water the horses, and then riding again, if not at a breakneck speed, with steady determination.

They had passed through beautiful countryside, hills and vales that rolled gently, filled with glorious colors. Heaths had seemed the color of royal purple, carpeted in wild flowers; the forests they passed were heavy and rich with deep greens. They had traveled through mud, as well — sticky black and brown, but in all, the sun had broken through trees, then it had begun to set, and the colors changed all over again, cast into the gentle shades of the coming night.

The twilight seemed to meld the forest now into a wall, but Collum, far more accustomed to riding by twilight, knew the landscape, and seemed able to see in the dark. He continued riding into what appeared a great void, but it was not — a trail broke through the trees.

"Oh, 'tis dark," Bridie murmured.

"Aye, but the copse is just ahead," Margot assured her. "And there, we'll find a shelter, and build a fire."

"A small ride to go," Hagar, riding at the rear, informed them cheerfully.

The trees here were very close; the trail such that it seemed the horses would be too great to pass through it. But in moments more, the growth gave way; they entered a copse.

Collum dismounted. "A moment, my lady."

He dismounted. She saw that there was a structure in the woods, wattle and daub, and covered with thatch. Soon after Collum ducked his way beneath the small, open doorway, dim light appeared from within. Collum reappeared, coming to Eleanor's horse, ready to help her dismount. " 'Tis not much, but a shelter. We'll be out of the weather."

The crude little house had an opening in the front, a low arch Collum had to duck through, and another like it in the rear. The place had long been open to the elements, but there was a pit of stone in the center for a fire, and the walls seemed sturdy enough. Its very closeness made it warm enough, with the front and rear opening allowing for clean air to pass through. A small opening in the roof overhead would help clear the smoke once a fire was built.

"Ah, well, here we are," Collum said, somewhat helplessly, as if he were not accustomed to being the one to make a lady comfortable on a rough journey.

Eleanor set a hand on his shoulder. "It's a fine shelter," she assured him. "A good place to rest for the night."

"Aye, and we'll make it comfortable enough," Hagar said. "We'll get the blankets and the food."

"And I'll be seeing that you don't make a mess of my packing," Bridie said, giving a firm nod to Eleanor, who wondered how Bridie could still have so much energy, when she suddenly felt so exhausted herself.

She stood alone in the shelter with Margot. Margot walked over to her, taking both her hands. "Thank you," she said fervently. "Thank you . . . you made something happen that . . . might have taken a lifetime. No, it would never have happened — "

"He loves you very much," Eleanor told her.

"Well, I've always believed that," Margot said with a small smile. "If not . . . well, I love him, loved him enough just to be with him. But what you managed . . . and taking the occasion of your own wedding . . ."

"I was rather an extreme circumstance as it was," Eleanor murmured.

Margot laughed.

"We're all fighting for what is right, aren't we?" Eleanor asked her.

"Aye, but still . . . thank you. I will never be able to thank you enough."

"Don't forget, you showed me kindness when I was in terror."

Margot laughed. "You? You were never in terror. You were already planning your leap into the sea."

Eleanor smiled, and what answer she would have given remained with her as the others came into the little house in the woods.

"Blankets, my lady," Hagar said to Eleanor, "the floor is not comfortable, I'm afraid — "

"It will be fine," she assured him.

She took her blanket, and noted that what they had given her was a woolen swath of Brendan's tartan. "I will be quite fine," she assured him, and looked across the room to where Margot was taking a place. She smiled at Margot. "I can learn to sleep easily in the woods," she added softly. "Like Margot."

The blonde woman returned her smile. Bridie had been into their packs, producing the loaves of bread and cheese they had brought, along with a basket of wild berries. There was ale to drink, and famished as she was, the food, eaten on the floor in the smoky hut, seemed to be the finest she had ever tasted. The place was warm, the blanket seemed to cradle her. She smoothed out the tartan, and asked aloud, "I wonder how they are faring at the castle."

"They'll be fine, my lady, don't fret," Hagar told her. "We'll hear word from the south soon enough," he told her.

She agreed. Aware that Collum, Hagar, and Lars were dividing the watch, she curled in her corner and lay to sleep. She realized that she was really Brendan's *wife,* and no matter what her circumstances, that fact suddenly thrilled her, though she lay without him on their wedding night. Whatever the future held . . .

He would always come to her.

Corbin was the one to stop Brendan from the madness of fleeing from the front gates of the fortress alone, and risking the movement of the remaining English forces against them when the enemy still retained powerful numbers.

"If you die, and we're all destroyed, you'll be of no possible use to Eleanor," he reminded him, when he vehemently let out the plan that he could ride on his own, racing through the opposition with such speed and surprise that they would not expect him. But Griffin's words warned them that the frontal attack on the fortress had become a ruse only to keep them from knowing that Fitzgerald had ridden northward, aware of the very roads they would take, and probably what safe houses they intended to use along the way.

"There is a way out," Brendan said, looking at Eric. "The rear, by the water, where the wall is still freshly repaired. We can break a section down, and escape up the hill, and they will never know we are gone."

He didn't wait for agreement, but started calling out to men, seeking the masons drawn to service on the walls, and the brawniest of his soldiers. He picked and clawed at the newly set stone himself. The time to create a portal was minimal, but it seemed as if the minutes sped, passing like wildfire.

Yet while he worked at the stone, Eric ordered horses and chose the men to ride.

This time, Corbin insisted he be among their number.

"Eleanor is my cousin; her enemy is my enemy," he told Brendan.

"As you wish," Brendan told him, mounting, "but be prepared to take your sword against your countrymen."

"That I am, I swear."

Both Liam and Eric would ride as well; six others were chosen. Griffin, Bruce's messenger would stay, commanding the castle defense with Rune MacDuff, a veteran of many of Wallace's skirmishes. Jem MacIver, a man long accustomed to hard riding as well, would accompany Eric, along with Tam of Perth, Morgan Anderson, Paul Miller, Jason Douglas, and Axel de Burg. All were expert at quick movement — and hand to hand combat. Liam, as always, was armed with the weapon at which he so excelled, his bow.

The moon was rising high when they rode out through the cavity they had created in the wall. As soon as they were through it, the masons began repairing.

They sped across shallow water and fields, rising on the hill in a silhouette they could not avoid.

Behind them, the English camp remained still; an eerie black shadow in the menace of the night.

Their horses' hooves thundered as they rode.

Each staccato beat seemed to echo in Brendan's heart.

He had never known such fear.

Eleanor awoke feeling very stiff.

It was one thing to claim that she was quite comfortable on the floor, and that she cared nothing for luxuries.

Quite frankly, she realized, she preferred luxuries.

But rising, stretching, she knew in her heart that she'd rather a floor with Brendan, than the softest bed without him. That morning, she had neither, and hugging her knees to her chest, she suddenly realized that that wasn't quite so easy a thing to do as it had been; she felt the growth in her abdomen, rounder now, yet that discomfort gave her a strange sense of happiness until she realized that it might be a long time before she saw Brendan again, or even knew if he had survived the fight with Fitzgerald's men.

She rose carefully. Collum, sleeping nearest the door like a great bear guarding a cave, woke immediately. "Sorry!" she said softly. "It's very early; not full light." He started to rise. "No!" she protested. "There's no danger. I only need . . . to slip outside."

"Hagar guards outside," Collum murmured. "Don't go too far."

"I won't."

She stepped carefully over Lars and Bridie. The pair were sweetly curled together beneath a plaid near the peat fire which had now died to embers.

Outside the arched entrance, she found Hagar awake and

watchful. He had been sitting on an upturned log, whittling, but his hands were still as she went out. He looked up, offering her a nod. His brow was knit in a frown.

"What is it?" she asked.

"Listen."

She did so. "I don't hear a thing," she said softly. Not even the horses, tethered at the front of the house, shifted or moved.

"Not a thing . . ." Hagar whispered, "that's what's wrong. No birds . . . no rustling of leaves as the night creatures move . . ."

He rose slowly.

Feeling no sense of danger or alarm, Eleanor looked around the copse. Hagar had dropped his wood; his hand was tense on his knife.

His warhorse suddenly shuffled its hooves, and let out a whinny of distress.

"There!"

At a sudden whisper of movement in the trees, Hagar let his knife fly. There was a scream to shatter the quiet of the coming dawn, and then a thud as the man fell to his death. Then, instantly, there was a sudden burst of commotion from the trees. The danger awakening in Eleanor like a bolt of lightning striking, she tore for the horses, seeing that one of Hagar's battle swords remained sheathed at his saddle. She caught the sword and spun in time to parry the sudden violent strike of the man who had rushed behind her.

He had meant to kill. There would be no pretense of taking prisoners here.

By then, Collum and Lars had emerged; they were busily engaged with the men who had streamed into the copse after Hagar had killed the first of their number.

The man she faced was pock-marked and lean; his features were hard, cold, and ugly; he was certainly no young lord of English youth, out for a lark, nor was he a fool with his weapon.

She had been taught that she was no match for the real power of a well-muscled warrior, honed to battle; her defense was in movement, and in forcing an opponent to use his own strength against himself. She was afraid that she would fall, and fully aware that neither Collum nor Lars could reach her, when her last sleight of foot brought her opponent swinging his sword and bearing it down to the earth. Desperate for her life, she swung her own sword. She caught the man's back as his great weight and impetus brought him crashing forward. He fell at her feet with a woof of air expelling from him. She danced back quickly, raising her sword.

She heard the whirr of an arrow; then a grunted cry of pain, emerging from between clenched teeth.

Collum leaned hard against the wall of the dwelling, pinned there by an arrow piercing through him, just below the shoulder.

A sudden, slow, clapping of hands brought her anguished gaze across the copse. Collum bore a bleeding wound across his cheek; the sleeves on Lars' shirt was torn, and an angry stain seeped from it as well. Only Hagar was still standing, and he warily now, his eyes upon the enemy.

There were five fallen Englishmen before them, but there, swaggering across the copse, clapping, was Fitzgerald.

"Ah, my lady, so you really can use that sword! You could have skewered your old husband, my lady, rather than reverting to poison."

"I didn't poison him."

"Alas, but so it appears," Fitzgerald said. She thought he was a fool, walking so into the copse, clapping, his hands not even on his weapon. But then she saw that men were aligned behind him, armed with swords and wearing coats of mail beneath their colors. Six of them, including Fitzgerald. And Lars was upon the ground, possibly bleeding to death, and Collum was pinned to the wall.

"You've come for me because you accuse me of murder,"
she said quickly. "Leave them be; I will go with you."

"Leave them be?" Fitzgerald said incredulously.
"Madam—they are rebel Scots, the bastards, among the number who thought to make a fool of me, I do believe. Let them
be? You must be quite mad, my lady. Pity you didn't lose your
senses before! Locked away in tower, you might have lived
out your days."

"He'll not touch you while there's breath in my body!"
Hagar shouted in warning.

Fitzgerald looked him up and down. "Well, good man, that
may not be long," he said softly.

At that inopportune moment, Bridie came flying out of the
house, crying as she rushed to kneel by Lars's side.

"The servant woman again, eh?" Fitzgerald said almost
pleasantly. "Ah, well, perhaps that's good."

He means to kill them all, Eleanor realized. And again, she
clenched her teeth, because Margot had followed Bridie; she
was not about to hide. She walked to where Collum stood in
agony, pinned to the wall.

"Leave him be!" Fitzgerald barked out.

Margot stared at him contemptuously, then turned to Collum,
telling him he must keep consciousness, he had to help her
break the shaft.

"My God, you fools—" Fitzgerald began.

"Sir Miles!" Eleanor interrupted, knowing that Collum was
defenseless, as was Margot, who would take any risk to help
him. "I've a challenge for you."

"A challenge?" He inquired, amazed, but giving pause.

"I'm not intended to reach London for a trial. I never was.
You wish me dead. Make me so yourself. I'm but a woman,
and you . . . you're the king's servant, a brave upholder of
justice. Prove your own worth. Have your men back away.
Take me on."

"You wish to challenge me—with a sword?" He inclined his head, studying her, and the fallen man at her feet. "You think you are so capable? My dear, I am very, very good."

"So you think."

"You risk a great deal here. Your future is decided. But I can give you a painless death. Indeed, my lady, may I say that it is a true sorrow to destroy such beauty?" It sounded as if he really meant the words; there was a note of regret in his tone.

"If that is the truth, sir, it would be a far greater compliment if you would simply refrain from doing so!"

"Alas . . ." Fitzgerald murmured.

"No!" Hagar shouted out furiously. "I will not stand here and watch this dog come after ye, my lady. Back away, Eleanor." He started forward.

She hurried to him, halting him, pushing him back, whispering furiously.

"Hagar! Give me a chance; let me buy some time for Collum to be freed. If you must, if I start to falter . . . then you may come to my aid!"

"My lady—"

"I have a plan," she lied quickly.

She had no plan, but she had to make Hagar believe that she did. She shoved him all the way to the house.

"Please!" she whispered fervently. "Please . . . help may be coming."

She knew that wasn't true. Hagar's eyes told her that he knew the futility of such a plea as well.

"Trust me!" she whispered again.

He stood still, jaw locked.

She left him there, smoothing back her hair with the back of her hand as she approached Fitzgerald, already feeling a tremendous ache in her arm from the weight of the sword she had taken from the sheath strapped to his horse. Great Hagar. Dedicated to the last.

At that moment, she wished that he were not such a powerful man, for his sword seemed to weigh as much as he did.

She halted between Fitzgerald and the others.

"Are you afraid of such a challenge, Fitzgerald? Are you afraid that the helpless woman you've intended to murder — though God alone knows why! — will take you down."

"Not a chance, my lady," he said politely. He paused, and she saw that he was looking around the copse. How had he known that Brendan was at the castle — and that he had sent her north for safety?

She feared the answer. But still, she was curious that he should be looking elsewhere.

She did not have to worry about the question long, for he looked at her politely. "Your cousin Corbin is not lurking yonder in the house, is he, my lady? Cowering there, until the dead lay strewn and he can slip away?"

He wanted Corbin as well, she thought. To what end?

"Corbin? *Cowering*, sir? I think you seriously underestimate my cousin."

She rued her defensive words the instant they left her lips; it would have been best to make him believe that there were others with him.

She looked back to the house. Empty. They had rushed to the sound of danger. If only . . .

Ah, if only there were a dozen Scotsmen in there, men who had learned to fight from the shadows, with their wits as well as their prowess! She realized suddenly that she was staring at the house with such longing, imagining the scene of men streaming from the entrance, that she must have given Fitzgerald the belief that her dreams could be true.

Fitzgerald cleared his throat. "There is no one there, is there, Lady Eleanor?"

"Can you be so sure? You've been tricked before by a wily enemy."

"This time, my lady, it's the Scots who have been tricked."

Despite the way he spoke, she thought that he hesitated. She forced a smile. "You don't know, do you? You can't be sure. Perhaps they are waiting, watching you now, and when your defenses are lowered . . ."

"Any man worthy to carry a sword would have appeared when the fighting began," he said harshly.

"Worthy to carry a sword, or capable of a great strategy?"

"Madam, the hovel wouldn't hold more than a few men."

"If you're certain . . ." she said, forcing her words to be a subtle taunt he could not ignore. His movements would have to entertain such a possibility.

"I've another proposition for you," she added quietly.

"My lady, you are in no position to offer propositions."

"Really?" she said. "I'm not certain that we don't have a position of power here. If Hagar moves, sir, with your numbers, you will likely bring him down. But not until more of your men are dead, and you will be the man he will first kill. Hagar wants you dead. There will be no sending your men in first. And you value your life, don't you?"

Fitzgerald's face took on a mottled hue; she realized that she had struck a blow. He might be willing to fight — but not until his men had cleared the way for him to do so with an assurance of winning.

"Let's hear your proposition," he said.

"The women take Lars and Collum away from here, before the fight begins."

"No."

"Ah, Sir Miles! You're taking a grave chance. First, of there being reinforcements still beyond your vision. Second . . . that Hagar will break your neck before your men are able to kill him."

"They'll be no one leaving you, my lady—" Collum cried out, but she turned on him, giving him a warning look.

"There's no one in that house!" Fitzgerald raged suddenly.

"Perhaps. Perhaps not. One way or the other, Sir Miles, Hagar does stand just feet away. He can kill you before a man could begin to aim an arrow . . . which could wind up in your back."

"No!" Collum tried to protest again. But at that moment, Margot at last caused the arrow pinning him upward to snap. The pain caused even such a seasoned warrior to scream out and fall, grasping his chest. Then . . . he was silent.

She looked at Fitzgerald. "Your men stay where they are. The others leave. Then you face me alone."

"Filthy Scots—" Fitzgerald began, but a look from Hagar stilled him. He stood furiously, thinking over his options.

"The women leave, and they take their injured. They'll die out here anyway," he said harshly. He pointed at Hagar. "And that one—he goes, too."

"Never—" Hagar said.

"Aye!" Eleanor snapped. She turned from Fitzgerald, her heart sinking. Hagar was all that stood between any of them and certain death now. But alone, he couldn't kill all the Englishmen. If they didn't pay her heed, they would all die.

But they would never willingly leave her.

"If you go," she whispered, touching his massive chest again, "there may be . . . God knows, maybe there will be help on the road. Other rebels, men moving north, heading home from the borders . . . perhaps, perhaps there will at least be a chance. Please, Hagar, don't make Margot and Bridie die because of me, I beg you; seize this last bit of hope, there could be someone out there."

She didn't believe it for a minute. But perhaps Hagar did believe that he could double back, and die with her. He could see that the other two men were sorely wounded. They might well die. If they stayed, they would be slaughtered.

And Margot and Bridie would be helpless. Hagar was a big fellow with tremendous power, and a poor French accent. But he was an intelligent man as well.

"Aye, then, I'll go with the wounded and the women," he whispered harshly. Then he made a pretense of shrugging, as if it had suddenly become no great matter to him — not a matter worth dying for. He stared at Fitzgerald and spoke loudly. "Aye, then, you'll let us go, and I'll leave as well. This is not a Scottish battle, as it is. Though . . ." He spat on the ground. "Filthy English. I wouldn't mind dying to bring them down!"

"Hagar, go."

He turned around. Collum was no longer conscious. Lars, even with Bridie's help, could barely stand. Eleanor watched the proceedings, still but furious, as Hagar lifted Collum as if the muscled warrior were a babe, and set him over one of the horses.

"We cannot leave you, Eleanor!" Bridie said miserably.

"You'll bring help," she whispered, never believing it.

"You'll die; there is no help. And after he kills you, he will only come after us. We'll all stay and fight — "

"Collum may be dying. And you can't lift a sword."

"They'll come after us to cut us down."

"No. Lars and Collum will get you out. I am good enough to keep Fitzgerald occupied for a while."

"For a while. This way there is no hope — for you."

"There may be. God is said to work in very mysterious ways."

Margot looked at her with anguished eyes, and hugged her tightly.

"I'll stay with you," she murmured. "I do know how to lift a sword."

"Margot, it's me he wants. If you don't go, Hagar won't. You must go. Keep Collum alive. And . . ."

"Tell Brendan you love him?" Margot whispered.

"Tell him that . . . I was glad of his passion for freedom . . . that I understand. Aye, tell him I love him. But go."

Margot stood in a moment of terrible indecision, then walked away, biting her lip against tears. She helped Bridie drag Lars to a horse.

With Collum thrown over his mount with as much tenderness as Hagar could manage, he moved to help the women get Lars mounted. Margot managed on her own; Bridie, shaking, did not do so well. Hagar had to help her before looking at Eleanor with deep reproach, and mounting his own horse.

"You will let them ride away," Eleanor told Fitzgerald firmly. "Else, Hagar will turn . . . and we will all die, but you with us."

"I am standing here, my lady, without movement," he said politely. "What do I care if these rebels die today at my hand — or tomorrow, still fighting King Edward?" He lifted a hand, indicating that the rebels should go.

They were all silent as the party of Scots moved out. Eleanor held still as long as she could, listening for the sounds of hoofbeats to die away.

In time, they did so.

"There is truly no one in that hovel, is there, Lady Eleanor?"

She looked at the deserted, thatched dwelling, taking as long as she dared with her reply. "What do you think, Sir Miles?"

Fitzgerald stared at her coldly. "Seize her!" he commanded his men.

The order wasn't instantly obeyed. She was amazed to see that his men seemed to shuffle uncomfortably as one.

"Seize her!" Fitzgerald cried again.

One stepped forward. "Sir Miles! You're a man of your word, or so we'd believe. You told the lady that —"

"She is a murderess. Lies to a murderess mean nothing."

"A man's word means everything, Sir Miles!" one young man said.

"You risk your livelihood, you fool!" Fitzgerald said to him.

"If they'll not take her," said another man, stepping around from the rear. "I will do so!" He wore a patch over one eye. His face was twisted in a knot of hatred . . . and anticipation, she thought. She felt weak. He was a man to enjoy the task of killing.

She felt the flutter of life in her stomach again, and the world seemed to pitch and weave precariously. She had never wanted to survive more in all her days. If she died, her child died with her. It seemed an unbearable injustice.

And yet so many had died . . .

At war. Even cruelly at war. The English; the Scots. The fight had become vicious, brutal, and inhuman, surely ever so before the eyes of God.

But this was not due to a war. Or freedom, or ideals, or even the passion of one arrogant king who felt he had the right to rule from coast to coast, sea to sea.

This was some strange intent on . . . murder. Cold-blooded murder.

The strange ugly man with the patch on his eye came toward her. "I don't mind taking on the task, aye, not at all. Cutting such a pretty piece to ribbons, a lady, and all, will be a pleasure. Like taking hold of that fellow in the woods, aye, the good Scotsman who betrayed you. Took some time for the fellow to do so, I'll grant you that. Could you suffer so long for another, Lady, I wonder? Turned out he was a treacherous rat, trained for the likes of Sir Miles, there. We broke four of his fingers and ripped out most of his nails before he began to give . . . beat him to death for the details, aye, that we did."

Her heart pitched. She thought that she would be ill all over the man before either of them could raise a blade.

Gregory. Gregory had been tortured to death—over her.

Some insanity swept through her that not even the prospect of her coming child could curb. She had always been taught *not* to lose her temper, never to lose control, always to remember her weaknesses.

But the ugly fellow was too close. She lifted her sword with uncanny speed and precision, bringing it down on the man's shoulders with a fury and strength that seemed nearly superhuman. She had the sheer pleasure of seeing the amazement on his face before he staggered back and fell.

Fitzgerald stepped forward, staring at her, then at the man bleeding into the earth. He nudged the man with his boot. There was a groan.

Fitzgerald looked from his prone and bleeding servant to her. "Dirk was a good man, aye, and served me well. Another sin you must pay for, my lady."

She stared into his eyes, wishing he were a few steps closer, that she might repeat the feat that so amazed her.

"He is living still," she said, suggesting that he take the time to bandage the man's wounds.

"We can take no injured from here," he said flatly.

"The man is not dead!"

Fitzgerald shrugged. "Do you think that Englishmen are not aware they risk their lives in Scotland? We will be leaving here in some haste, madam."

"And you will leave a man so grievously wounded?"

"How very kind, my lady, for you to show such concern for the man who tortured one of your poor fellows — to death."

"He was loyal to you."

"He was a man who needed sanction and authority for his pleasures."

"And still, he would have died for you."

"He did not intend to die."

"But he will."

"He underestimated you. I will not."

"Indeed. He failed, and now, the battle *is* to you."

He watched her a moment longer, angry, but shaking his head in rueful admiration.

"It is a pity that you must die. And that we met too late. We might have wed, and you'd have no need to rid yourself of an old, decaying, husband."

"I'm not eager for death, but between you and the grave, worms do become all the more enticing."

The last infuriated him. And he did not underestimate her. He'd have preferred to have his men seize her . . . so that he could slay her without danger of injury to himself.

But that couldn't be. He had lost his opportunity to avoid the fight with her. His men would brand him a coward, and he would lose respect in their eyes, and maybe even the authority to force them to allow his intended execution.

"So, madam, you're eager for a taste of eternity, and the crawl of worms about your flesh. Then it is time. My lady, it's time to meet your maker."

"Or you, yours."

"Doubtful. I am good. Give in; I'll end it quick, a thrust to your heart."

"You are good, but a lightning bolt could fall from the sky."

"Say your prayers, my lady."

"Say yours, Sir Miles."

"As you wish. We'll see then, if you can repeat the prowess you exercised on Dirk there. It is time to be finished here."

Chapter 22

Fitzgerald had known exactly where the little party of Scots was headed. Gregory had been tortured into telling all he knew. But Brendan knew the ground better than Fitzgerald, and would not have to search for any trails.

They had ridden through the night, hard, each man aware that time meant everything. He feared what he would find with each hoofbeat that brought them farther north, into the woods, closer to the shelter Collum had intended to reach for the night.

They were grimly certain of their destination, and that they followed behind. They had used the night riding as hard as they had ever learned to do in their pursuit of the English — or in the days when they had been forced to flee.

He lifted a hand when they neared the area of the safe house; in silence, they all slowed their gaits. A gesture from him, and they came to a halt and dismounted, ready to venture the last of the trail on foot.

He looked at the hand he had raised. Shaking. He feared so greatly that he would come to the copse, to the house, and find a field of dead lying there . . .

Eleanor . . .

Fitzgerald had no plan to take her back to England. He would rid himself of any further threat of her, then and there.

He felt a hand on his shoulder. Eric.

Eric motioned to the ground.

He saw a trail of blood, crossing the road from the narrow twist into the woods to an overgrown path on the other side. Few knew of it.

"Collum . . . . Hagar?" he mouthed.

Brendan nodded. He and Eric turned toward the trail.

Then he froze, hearing the unmistakable sound of clashing steel.

From the opposite direction.

Facing Fitzgerald then, Eleanor tried to remember everything she had ever been taught about swordplay — and strategy. She remembered Falkirk. The dead and the dying all around her. She had been in full armor, surrounded at all times, and she had shirked from the horror. She had carried a sword; she had known how to use it. She had never wielded it once . . .

Other than to use the hilt to knock Brendan to the ground.

And now . . .

Her life depended on her skill.

As did her child's.

Fitzgerald drew his sword, raised it, lowered it. Both arms out, he invited her forward.

"Come now, 'tis time. The battle has come to us."

This time, it was she who was taken by surprise. She barely parried his sudden lunge, and felt the furious weight of it through the length of her arm, into her shoulder. She jumped back then, seeking to avoid his next heavy blow, and purchase herself time to regain her strength.

She moved closer to the horses, moving with a speed greater than he, yet without the protection of the heavy mail he wore beneath his tunic. He raised a heavy blow that missed her, and landed in the earth. She tried to capture him there, struggling to retrieve his sword. He moved in time, yet she caught his lower arm below the mail, drawing blood. He paused, then looked up, and the fury in his eyes sent her scrambling behind a tree to avoid his next blow. They had left the center of the copse. Though his men milled into the copse, watching, they kept their distance.

She kept behind the tree, moving back and forth, causing him to follow.

"This is foolish," she told him. "I would willingly face a trial."

"There can be no trial, my lady," he said, feinting quickly to the left.

She flew to the right.

"Why?"

"There can be no trial," he repeated.

"You are about to kill me. What does it matter if I know the reason. You didn't kill Alain, you couldn't have, I'd never seen you before you came to Clarin that day."

" 'Tis true, we never met. But I have known Clarin." He thought he had her still; he swung, embedding his sword in the tree. She tried to strike again while he disengaged his weapon. He pulled out just in time, and what should have been a death blow was deflected. Her sword went flying across the copse. She stared at Fitzgerald, judging the distance, and knew her only hope then was to distract him for a moment.

"I think I understand," she said slowly. "It's true; you didn't kill Alain. But you know who did."

The fact that he didn't answer gave her all the reply she needed.

"Isobel!" she gasped out furiously.

His lip tightened, and she realized, she was right. Isobel.

"Isobel poisoned him," she said aloud. "And you are serving Isobel."

"I serve no woman, my lady."

"Ah . . . but you are with her. You and Isobel . . . are together in this . . . you poisoned a good man, you caused him to die in agony . . ."

"My lady, apparently, he did not wish to go," Fitzgerald said with rueful disregard.

"But you were never at Clarin," she said. "So how . . . ah. . . . you met in London. You were lovers there, planning all this, and when I returned so unfortunately with my husband from France, you had to find a way to rid yourselves of both of us. You sent men to find de Longueville and pay him to seize my ship. But that plan failed. All the better. Clarin was in deep need of funds, and bringing home a wealthy count improved the fortunes of the estate. But then, you had to find a way to rid yourselves of us both. If I were executed for Alain's murder, we'd both be out of the way."

"Aye, lady. You are perceptive. And you may take it all to your grave."

"Wait!" she cried, sidestepping as he took a massive swing, that again missed her.

"What about Alfred. And Corbin?"

"But they were meant to die as well. Alfred is in danger, even now. As to Corbin . . . I will find him."

She wished they hadn't fought their way into the trees; his men should have heard this, should have seen the colors that raged on his face, mottled, red, giving away the truth though he never spoke.

He raised his sword again. "Madam, the lands adjoining

Clarin have become mine through a number of unfortunate deaths in my family. Isobel's child would inherit Clarin."

"And Isobel's child would not be my cousin's," she said. "At least, that's what you'd be told. But I have information for you. Isobel was like a rabbit with Corbin."

He paused, actually smiling at her. "The child . . . aye, well, her first child would have been Corbin's. We are not fools. Alas, so many infants perish . . ."

"If her child died, she would not inherit. She is no blood kin. The land and titles would revert to the king, to be given at his discretion."

"But they would be given to me. The neighboring knight and servant who helped rid King Edward of many Scots — and brought down the murderess of a renowned French lord!"

"The king is fickle."

"Nay, lady, not when rewarding those who destroy his enemies. And now, my dear, Eleanor, you know all, you can die happy, and as to you . . ."

He moved to strike; she went racing for her lost sword, but slid to the ground just short of the weapon as Fitzgerald came flying at her, arms around her lower body, throwing her to the ground.

The sword remained just out of reach.

She looked up. One of Fitzgerald's armor-clad warriors stared down at her.

To her surprise, he nudged the sword into her reach. She rolled over, bringing up her sword. She caught the first blow Fitzgerald cracked down upon her, sending him staggering back, but he was quickly at her again, the blade in the air. Again, and again. She skinned backward on the ground. She was certain that each additional blow would break her arms.

As desperate as she was to fight and save her life, she couldn't help the terror and the pain that filled her heart.

She would die. When she had just begun to know what it was to value her life.

When her child . . .

It was unbearable.

It would happen.

Fitzgerald struck again. Her defense was far weaker. She had all but backed herself to a tree, and there, he would slice her in two.

He raised his sword arm . . .

In seconds, a dozen thoughts filled her mind. She saw the sun dazzling through the branches of the trees overhead. She thought with dismay that her death would allow him to complete his thirst for greater power and land. She thought of Isobel, planning Alfred's death even now . . .

She thought of the man she had come to love. And the way that his fervent passion for the land, his never faltering devotion, had come to be for her, as deep as the steadfast loyalty he gave to his friends, and his country, and his dreams of right and freedom.

She saw, from the corner of her eye, the little hovel in the forest, in which she had spent her last night, ruing the discomfort, yet knowing she would sleep anywhere to be with one man. She imagined movement, the stream of Scotsmen she had warned Fitzgerald might be within, and she thought that she was already dying, for her dream of salvation seemed almost real . . . there was something . . .

There was something.

There was not.

She closed her eyes, and braced herself to die.

But Fitzgerald's weapon never fell. Eleanor heard a sudden, earth-shattering clashing sound. And then, impossibly, Brendan's voice.

''I tend to be a moderate man; after all these years of battle, I believe in the law, Fitzgerald. And it's important to Eleanor that her name be cleared, though it is more important to me to slash you into bloody remnants. Still, I'll withhold my blade. But if my wife is in any way harmed, you'll never see justice. Gregory's mangled face would appear to be that of a sun god, next to all that I will do to you.''

Eleanor's eyes flew open.

The earth-shattering sound had been Brendan's sword, meeting Fitzgerald's. The man had been unarmed; and forced to his knees. Brendan gazed contemptuously at Fitzgerald, then turned to her, his eyes sharper than any blade, his features wrought with tension.

''Eleanor . . .'' he reached for her.

''Brendan!'' she shrieked. Fitzgerald had risen, and pulled a knife from a sheath at his calf. He was racing at Brendan. He turned in time, avoiding the knife that so easily might have pierced his heart. Fitzgerald's impetus brought him crashing into the tree. This time, Brendan raised his sword to sever the man in two.

But Eleanor found the strength to leap to her feet. ''No! Brendan, we must keep him alive! Isobel killed Alain; he is to kill me for her.''

Brendan lowered his sword very slowly and stared coolly at Fitzgerald. ''So . . .'' he said.

''A lie!'' Fitzgerald cried boldly. ''She is lying!'' He turned, looking for his men.

And it was then that both he, and Eleanor, realized that Brendan's men had surrounded the copse and the men, and that the English had knives at their throats, held there by the Scots. They had come from the house in the wood . . .

Not bursting out. But slipping in through the rear, through the mud, then out upon their bellies, into the trees again, where they had surprised the English as Brendan had gone for Fitzgerald. The Englishmen remained held at bay by the silent, slippery Scots.

Except for one, who had apparently been about to protest.

He lay with his mouth open, a stream of blood trailing from his throat. With amazement, she saw that Corbin had been the one to kill him.

Corbin walked forward through the clearing, still wielding the knife with which he had slain the Englishman.

"Let me watch over this one, I beg you, Brendan, while you see to my lady cousin," he said, approaching Fitzgerald with death in his eyes. "If he so much as breathes with too much energy, I will start cutting the extremities from his body. Keep care that he live, of course, to clear Eleanor's good name."

With Corbin watching his back, Brendan once again reached down to take Eleanor into his arms.

She was shaking so badly that she couldn't have stood without him. Tears sprang to her eyes. She almost sank to the ground again.

He cradled her, pulled her close to him.

She felt his heart . . . a thunder against her. She was where she was meant to be.

But she heard Corbin speaking again then, in deep anger. "Actually, I'm afraid that I can't just stand here, looking at this man!"

Brendan drew away from her, ready to stop Corbin from killing the man.

But Corbin hadn't slashed into Fitzgerald.

Instead, he knotted his fist and sent a blow into the man's face that must have cost him several teeth.

Fitzgerald slumped down, unconscious.

For a moment there was silence.

"What do we do with these—English?" she heard, a sentence spat out in Gaelic. Eleanor gave a glad cry, seeing that Hagar was on the English, covered with mud like the rest of the Scots, but stalwart, well, and tall as he handled one of the men, his knife tight at the fellow's throat.

His query was met with a moment's silence. Eleanor knew what the men were thinking. These were Englishmen, enemies who had ridden north to attack not just her, but Scotland. They deserved death.

"No!" she protested, touching Brendan's arm, forcing his attention. "They—they knew nothing about Fitzgerald's real plan, the depths of his service to his king! Brendan, that fellow gave me my sword back when I was nearly down . . . take them prisoners, return them to England."

Brendan looked back to her, eyes hard, muscles tight with tension.

"Collum lies near death."

"Brendan, if you kill them now, we will be no better than the English. We're at a truce—"

"They rode north," he said harshly.

"But the Scots are . . . *civilized*," she said. "And there can be great strength in mercy."

"If you had died—"

"But I did not. I did not."

He looked at her a long while, then to his men. "Secure—the prisoners," he said at last.

One of the young Englishmen suddenly wept.

She didn't think that a man there, Scottish or English, thought any the worse of him for it.

When the men went through the English fallen, though, looking for the dead, and came upon the man Dirk, there was no hesitation.

Hagar went up to the body, and with a sudden, violent blow, severed the head.

The ride back to the castle was slow and laborious, Margot tending to their injured, carried in makeshift carts all the way home.

At one point, Eleanor rode between Hagar and Brendan.

"She knew that you were coming," Hagar told Brendan, something it seemed that he had said before. "She *knew*. I thought that I would bring the others to safety, come back and find her slain, and myself able to bring down only a few in vengeance. But she knew that you would be on the road, somehow . . ."

Brendan looked at Eleanor. "You knew that I would come somehow?"

She lowered her head. "Aye," she lied.

He didn't believe her.

"What faith," he murmured.

"God works in mysterious ways," she said, keeping her lashes lowered.

Brendan pressed no point with her at that time; indeed, on the two days it took them to return to the castle, they had little time together, and none of that alone. Brendan was frequently with Margot, rewinding Collum's bandages. They had removed the shaft of the arrow which had missed his lungs, and his heart, but there was a great danger that infection would take his life. Margot did seem to work magic with her healing; there were times when Collum could talk, a word or two, and there was a prayer that he would make it.

Brendan also wound up in frequent conversation with Corbin. When she approached, they would fall silent.

No matter what she said, if she pleaded, cajoled, or became angry, they pretended that there was no discussion between them of any importance, but when she expressed her concern for Alfred, alone at Clarin with Isobel, they seemed to exchange glances.

The two nights upon the road were dangerous; in the hours when Brendan did not stay awake, keeping guard, he lay down beside her, taking her into his arms with the deepest tenderness.

At last, they came to the hill north of the castle. The English were gone.

Fitzgerald's nose was broken and he had lost a number of teeth. He was a surly and taunting prisoner, and Eleanor kept her distance from him.

When they rode down the hill to the last valley before the castle, the gates opened. And as the horses streamed in, Wallace came out to meet them.

"Santa Lenora!" he said, ignoring Brendan and lifting her from her horse. "So you are home, well and good."

She smiled at him. "Aye. I am home."

Brendan dismounted behind her, slipping his arms around her. "Indeed, sir. My *wife* has come home."

She knew, in the bustle of their return, the quick attention first to their injured and then to their prisoners, that she was home.

Scotland had become her home.

She didn't need her name cleared for Clarin; Clarin should rightfully be managed by Alfred, if only word could reach him in time to save him from whatever fate Isobel might have planned for him. She would assume that both Eleanor and Corbin were dead by now.

This was now her place.

There was no rest for Brendan when they first returned; he made arrangements for the prisoners, including Fitzgerald, to be taken to Robert Bruce, and he spent time assuring himself that Collum and Lars were made as comfortable as possible as they healed. Eleanor wanted to help Margot, but she was ushered away.

"Tomorrow will be time enough for you to be the lady here, and the healer. Today, tonight, heal yourself. You're not ill?

You went through a great deal . . . expecting a babe, as you are.''

Eleanor smiled. "I'd been afraid as well, but . . . feel! Feel him kicking!''

"Him? It could be a her," Margot said, smiling as she felt the life that still fought hard within Eleanor's body.

"Brendan, I imagine, wants a boy.''

"Brendan, I imagine, will want many," Margot said. "Still, you must rest. But, ah, first, there is someone who wants to see you." Margot had turned a long room on the opposite ell of the castle wall from the great hall into a place to tend their wounded.

She brought her to a bed in a warm corner near the fire. At first, Eleanor didn't recognize the swollen and bruised man there. Then she cried out, tears stinging her eyes.

"Gregory!" She lowered herself to her knees by his side. He was swollen from head to toe, so it seemed, bruised, battered, broken.

His lips moved. She saw his eyes in the puffs of his face, saw him try to smile. "The bones will heal," he managed to say. "The fingernails . . . they are no loss. I never meant to betray you.''

"Gregory, poor Gregory! You suffered all this — for me!''

"My lady . . . you killed him.''

"I think I only survived because he talked about what he did to you," she told him. "I . . . I brought him down. Hagar slew him.''

"It's a blessing, to all Scotland," Gregory said.

It was an effort for him to talk. She gently set a kiss on his forehead, on the one point of flesh she could find that wasn't swollen.

"You must live," she told him.

"I will, my lady, I will.''

* * *

That night, when Brendan at last returned to their room, she was waiting. Wine mulled over the fire. Steam rose from the dragon-headed bathtub. She had lain in the tub a long while herself already; she had paced the room a dozen times. She was anxious about Fitzgerald, worried that he'd somehow escape Robert Bruce, and more worried than ever about Alfred.

She was home now. She knew it.

But she needed to make one more trip to Clarin.

At length, as she paced, the door opened, and Brendan came in. He still wore the dust and dirt of mud and travel, his face streaked with it.

Heedless of the clean silk gown she wore, she raced across the room to him, throwing herself into his arms. His arms enwrapped her. She felt him trembling, and knew that she did so herself. She stepped away, biting lightly into her lip, keeping her lashes lowered.

"You will take a bath?"

"Oh?" he queried, arms folding over his chest. "And you're going to make me?"

"I'm quite capable, you know."

With that, he lifted her, gown and all, and despite her shrieks, she found herself deposited in the water once again. And his muddied plaid was cast aside, and he was joining her.

"Brendan! The water, you'll ruin the very structure of the castle, you'll rain upon those below. Brendan—"

"Ah, but I am master of the castle," he reminded her, seating himself covered, and ducking his head and hair, shaking away the dirt, the grime, the tension.

He sat up straight again, flinging his hair back.

"You're soaking me, sir, soaking—"

He reached out, captured her head in both hands, and drew

her to him, kissing her. When his lips broke from hers at last, she fell silent.

"Did you really think that I would come?" he asked her.

"I prayed that you could," she admitted.

"You told the others to go away; you were heedless of your own life."

"There was no choice," she told him. She set her hands upon his chest. "No choice. And Brendan, still, there must be something done. Alfred is at Clarin, with Isobel. She intended to see that we all died. She — "

He pressed a finger to her lips. "I know."

"Something must — "

"I know. But not tonight, my love, my wife."

She felt silent, meeting the deep blue of his eyes.

"Tonight . . . after all this . . . it is the first night that we are here, together, and you are in truth, and before God, my wife. That you are alive," he said tensely, "is by the grace of God. That we are here now, together so, is no less than one of His most benevolent miracles."

He stood, stepping from the tub, reaching for her as well.

"Brendan . . . the water."

He stood back, looking at her. "Ah, yes, the water . . ."

He walked to her, slipped the sodden silk from her shoulders, skimmed it to the floor. Then he stood before her. His knuckles ran down the length of her arms, over a cheek, then down the valley between her breasts, and to her abdomen. He went down upon a knee, laying his face against her abdomen. She let her fingers fall into the dampness of his hair.

"I love you, Brendan, more than . . . anything in the world. More than life," she whispered.

His lips pressed to her flesh, cherishing her. Then he stood, lifting her.

He smiled tenderly.

"And I love you, wife, more than anything in the world."

"More than Scotland?" she murmured.

"Aye, lady," he said after a moment. "More than Scotland."

She smiled, doubting that was true.

It did not matter.

A fire burned in the hearth, creating the patterns upon his flesh that she so loved, rippling muscle, bronzing skin, creating magic.

And in the midst of the flames, he sought to prove how much he loved her.

In his arms, she did the same.

Chapter 23

They were making plans in the great hall, Eleanor realized as she came down the stairs. Many of them were gathered there; Eric, Corbin, Liam, de Longueville, and more. Wallace, she knew, had taken men and departed at dawn. A truce with the English would not last long. He had his followers, but a great army no more. He would take some time, and go home.

There was no peace or justice for him to be found in England.

She knew that they had been talking a long time, discussing the situation. She walked into the midst of them, but addressed Brendan.

"I must go to Clarin. Alfred is in danger."

"Aye, lady — Tonight."

"Tonight?" she said incredulously.

"Aye. Pack what you will," he told her.

She packed; she helped Margot with the wounded.

Toward dusk, Brendan arrived in their room. He closed the door behind him, and walked slowly to the fire.

She watched him. "Isn't it time to be leaving?" she asked softly.

"Soon," he said.

There was a tap at the door. He walked to it, as if expecting the summons. When he opened it, the woman Joanna was there with a tray and two goblets of wine. He thanked her and closed the door, and brought the tray to set on the stool before the fire.

"Brendan, we need to be leaving—"

"Soon," he said softly. "Come here."

He sat in the large carved chair before the fire and when she approached, he caught her hand, drawing her to him. He pulled her down on his lap, and stroked her cheek, his eyes curiously intent as he studied her features.

"Why are we going by dusk?" she asked.

"We needed the day," he said simply.

"Alfred may be dead already—"

"Don't think that way."

He lifted the wine, offering it. She sipped it, studying him. He didn't care much for wine, but preferred ale.

"Brendan, perhaps . . ."

"There's time. We're waiting to see if Robert Bruce will, or will not, ride with us."

"Do you think he will come?"

"I don't know. If he does, we ride with a large number of men, and we are not immediate outlaws the minute we cross the border."

"And if he does not?"

He shrugged. "We make it to Clarin anyway. Finish your wine," he added softly. She did so, handing him the goblet. He studied her intently again, then kissed her, his lips oddly light but coercive.

"I do love you."

"I know. You are riding to Clarin."

A single tie laced the front of her tunic. His fingers wound around it. They brushed her flesh over the soft linen beneath it. She caught his fingers.

"We have to leave."

"There's time."

"Brendan — "

"Time together, alone, is precious. We've learned that." He brushed her hand aside, continuing to tug at the lacing. The hot calloused feel of his fingers brushed her flesh. She swallowed at the surge of warmth that seemed to sweep her so very instantly.

"Brendan — "

"Make love to me," he said intently.

He stood, lifting her with him. A moment later, all her careful dressing preparations for the ride were strewn on the floor by the side of the bed. His plaid lay upon them. The searing arousal of his flesh touched her, yet he rose over her, eyes still so intent as he studied her face, his manner serious, strangely wistful.

"I do love you."

"I know."

"I do what I do . . . because I love you," he said.

She smiled and touched his face.

"I know."

"For your life," he whispered.

"Brendan . . ."

But his mouth downed upon hers then, and his kiss lingered long and hard, with the stroke of his touch, the thrust of his movement. He cradled her gently, yet made love with a fierce vigor. She saw his face, the passion, something else . . .

Stars seemed to dance in the firelight. She rose to meet him, moved with him, clung to him. The sweetness of their climax seemed to wrap around them like a blanket of molten steel; she clung to him, lay down with him . . .

*   *   *

Later, she woke with a start.

For a moment, she was completely disoriented. Then she remembered. They were to leave. She had been ready, but . . .

She rolled over. She lay in bed, naked.

Brendan was gone.

She looked to the side of his bed. The plaid was gone. Her clothing remained.

She leaped out of bed, heedless of her wildly tangled hair, stumbled into her clothing, and raced to the door.

It didn't budge. She was locked in. She stared at it in amazement for a moment, then rushed to the window that led to the balcony and parapets.

It was day.

And the balcony was not unguarded. Thomas de Longueville sat on a bench outside, reading. He looked up when he saw her. "By a Frenchman," he told her.

"Thomas, what are you doing on my balcony?"

"Seeing to it that you don't seek to escape."

"How long have they been gone?"

"Nearly a day."

"Thomas, you should rot in hell for being a part of this."

"Oh, Lady Eleanor! This is one of my good deeds," he said cheerfully. "I'll rot in hell for many others!"

"Thomas, you'll always be a pirate!" she told him angrily.

He smiled. "Thank you!"

She let out an oath of aggravation and returned to the room, furious. How could Brendan have done this to her.

And she knew.

He feared the danger for her in England. She knew . . . she understood . . .

And she was all the more afraid for him, and worried to be with him.

She burst through the draperies to the larger bedroom next to the lady's chamber, thinking perhaps they had not thought to bar her way out from there.

Margot sat in front of the fire, calmly sewing. She looked up at Eleanor.

"They're long, long gone," she said softly.

"But—"

"It's very, very, dangerous for you to go to England now."

"It is my battle, though, Margot—"

"If it is your battle, it is his as well. Let him fight this one for you."

"But what if Bruce didn't ride to meet him? He'll be an outlaw alone in enemy territory—"

"He will come back to you," Margot said.

"How can you always be so certain?" Eleanor cried.

"Practice," Margot told her, and looked serenely back to her task. "And because he loves you," she added softly.

They waited at the juncture of the road from the southwest, their horses pawing the ground, too much time going by.

"Robert Bruce will not come," Eric said. "He has given us all the help he dares—while keeping his position with the king."

Brendan was about to agree; it had been futile to hope that Robert Bruce would come. He was in far too deep with King Edward at this time. Newly married, his personal papers of fealty and truce so newly signed.

But that was just why he *must* come. With him at their side, the pretext of their visit would work, and no man would be in danger.

"There!" Liam cried suddenly. "There! Horses. I see them— the Bruce rides with us!"

Brendan watched as the horses neared them, as he saw the

colors of Carrick . . . and Robert Bruce himself, riding at the fore.

Brendan rode forward to meet him. He was grave. "Thank you for coming."

"We're not going to war; just to pay a visit upon English lands not far from those that belong to my own family," Bruce said.

He had been called a traitor many times.

And many times, he could have turned the tide for the Scottish cause.

But today, he rode his horse in his colors, his banner borne by a squire, and his jaw was set. The same age as Wallace, he was a different leader. Born to be nobility.

Born to be a king? Brendan wondered.

"Aye, Bruce, that is the plan," Brendan explained.

"I've written to the king as you requested, telling of this plot, and to the queen as well, hoping she will intercede. She is very young, grave in her duty, and of course, sister to Philip of France, who holds you in great regard."

"I will be grateful for whatever steps she takes to see that my wife is cleared of any charge of murder."

"She has married a Scottish outlaw; he will never let her hold the property."

"The property is no matter; it is the charge of murder we want set right."

"A just enough cause," Bruce said. "And this charade you've planned . . . I rather like it. Will you don my colors now? Or later, when we come closer to Clarin?"

They approached Clarin by early morning; the blast of a horn announcing the arrival of a rich and powerful man, the train of the troops stretching behind them.

Naturally, a guard rode out quickly from Clarin to greet

them; the colors of Bruce, a great landholder in England as well as in Scotland, were well known — as was Edward's recent, necessary agreement with the possible claimant to the Scottish throne. The gates of Clarin opened even as they rode close.

The horses clattered through the gateway.

From the main entrance to the tower, Isobel appeared.

She was a stunning woman with her dark hair, regal bearing, and delicate features. She walked straight to Robert Bruce, dropping a low curtsy.

"My Lord Bruce — "

"You know me, madam?" he inquired.

"Of course. I am Isobel of Clarin, all who can greet you here, I fear. Still you are welcome. Do you travel to London? I beg of you, quench your thirst in our hall."

She indicated the open door, and followed behind him. Corbin, Brendan, and Eric, clad in mail and Bruce colors, and helms, followed.

Robert Bruce wasted no time. Even as Isobel called to servants for wine and food, he demanded.

"Where is the master of the castle?"

"The master, sir?" she said sorrowfully. "I am afraid we are in woeful trouble here. The lady by right, Eleanor, poisoned her poor dear husband. She was to be taken to London for trial, but the king's man, his sheriff, was seized by — " here she hesitated, then continued, "Scottish outlaws. She has fled to the north, with her lover, I'm afraid. But the sheriff has gone after her even now. And my husband . . ." she pretended a soft, controlled sob, "was taken with her. Alfred, who manages here, was just in a terrible accident. His saddle . . . broke. While he was riding. He lies abed upstairs right now. Ah, the wine and food come."

Servants had come, with a quickly prepared feast. Isobel had truly yearned to be lady here, Brendan mused. She had ordered the repast as soon as she had seen Bruce's colors on the riders, while they were still far away.

"The food will wait."

"Your pardon, Lord Bruce? You are truly welcome here. I know that you have made your peace with King Edward, Lord Bruce, and though I am so nearly mourning . . . I believe that Corbin is dead now. He was surely slain by the outlaws. Sir Miles Fitzgerald has indeed given me hope, and yet Corbin is so honor bound to his kin. He will defend Eleanor, you see, even knowing that she must have been her husband's killer."

"Where is Alfred of Clarin now?" Bruce demanded.

"Upstairs, where I am tending to him. Come."

Their identities still well hidden beneath the Bruce helmet, Brendan, Eric, and Corbin followed Isobel up the stairs. She opened the door to a room.

Alfred was in bed, looking ashen. "His leg is broken, I'm afraid. It was a terrible accident when he was thrown. His horse never frightens, but that day . . ."

"You've been treating him, of course," Bruce demanded.

"I would allow no other one to tend my dearest brother-in-law. If my own poor husband is dead . . ."

"But your own husband is not dead, Isobel," Corbin said, stepping forward and removing his helm. "And if you so much as touch my brother again, I'll skin you alive!"

Isobel stared at him in horror. By then, Brendan and Eric had removed their helms as well. Isobel's cheeks sucked in with the horrified O she made of her mouth.

Then she gathered herself together, backing away from Corbin. "What is this mockery of justice?" she demanded.

"No mockery, madam," Bruce said. "I've come to escort you to London — along with Sir Miles, who has told us all about a very lengthy and lavish plan to rule these lands together."

"Aye, dear wife," Corbin said. "He has told us quite a bit — about the two of you."

Isobel stared at him, and must have realized in terror that she was truly caught.

She argued at first. "Whatever he has said to make you heathens spare his life is surely a lie. The king will never believe the word of a traitor who deserted her country for a Scottish outlaw, against the word of his own sheriff."

"He might just. There are five of his men who will swear to the fair treatment Fitzgerald received at our hands — and the merciless end he meant for Eleanor," Brendan told her.

She made a mad dash across the room.

It was Brendan who sprinted after her, capturing her before she could hurl herself from the window to the pavement below.

She scratched and clawed him.

"Oh, no, madam," he told her. "You will go to London. And answer for Alain de Lacville!"

"You!" she hissed. "You are — the priest, no, the treacherous, filthy Scot, you bastard!" she raged.

She started clawing at him. Corbin pulled her away, drawing her hands behind her back, where he tied them none too gently.

Then Eric came and took her arm. "We do want her to stand trial" he told Corbin. "I'll see that she is taken to the other prisoners, and made ready to ride."

Corbin nodded. "I have some talking to do with my brother," he said softly. He looked at Bruce. "If your physicians will attend him first . . . ?"

That afternoon, they rode from Clarin. Robert Bruce would take his men south. Brendan's party would ride home.

He had thought that Corbin might want to remain at Clarin, but with Alfred in true healing hands, he intended to ride with them.

"This never was my property, and Alfred manages so very well. I'm coming back. To Scotland."

"What of Isobel?"

"She will meet the king's justice. I believe I'll be granted a divorce."

They stayed long enough to eat the meal Isobel had prepared for their coming. Then they departed once again.

Two days later, as they neared the castle, Brendan wondered just what the extent of his wife's fury would be.

He hadn't dared let her come. If Robert Bruce hadn't come with them, there might have been trouble. There would have been no way to find the justice they needed.

The gates opened as they returned. He rode at the head of his men, an able man, a proud warrior, fierce, and ever courageous . . .

Except now. His palms were damp.

He rode in . . .

And there she was. Standing on the steps. Awaiting him. Eleanor of Clarin. Nay . . . Eleanor of Scotland.

She saw him across the courtyard; her eyes met his.

He raised a hand to her in victory. She smiled.

And she raced across the courtyard to greet him. He dismounted, and swept her into his arms . . .

He held her for a very long time. Then, knowing how concerned she must be, he pulled away, studying her features.

"Alfred will survive, so the Bruce's physicians assure me," he told her. "He was badly hurt, but in the few hours in which he was no longer under Isobel's tender care, he improved greatly."

"But he . . ."

"Aye, he will live; he's strong. He spent a long time with Corbin before we left. She looked beyond him, and saw that Corbin had returned as well."

Brendan shrugged. "He has decided to be a Scotsman."

"And Alfred knows . . ."

"He knows that you will not return. He could not speak much. He sends you all his love and his very best wishes."

"Isobel . . . ?"

"Corbin refrained from killing her on the spot, and we restrained her from an easy demise by leaping from the battlements. She is on her way now, with Robert Bruce, to London."

She lowered her head. He raised her chin, drawing her eyes back to his own. "Are you very angry with me?"

"It was a terrible thing to do to me. You drugged me."

"Very carefully, with Margot's help. So . . . are you angry?"

"Furious," she said, but then she smiled, a beautiful smile that touched the sweeping blue-gray of her eyes, "but you've come home. Safe, to me."

"I will always do so," he said softly.

"Then I'll be angry later," she promised him.

He took her in his arms once again.

Victory was indeed theirs.

Freedom remained to be won.

Epilogue

Eleanor's baby was born on November 4th, a girl.

She had expected a boy, but Brendan, who received the swaddling bundle before she did, was delighted.

"Of course, we're in serious trouble with such a one," he told her.

"Why?"

"She could be like her mother, crawling out balcony windows, and such."

She was called Genevieve Margot, the first, for Eleanor's barely remembered mother, and the second, of course, for Margot, who stood as the child's godmother, while Eric was godfather.

Three weeks after the baby was born, the news at last reached them about events in London. Beneath an English judge and through English peers, Sir Miles Fitzgerald was proclaimed guilty of the murder of the French nobleman, Alain de Lacville.

Isobel, too, was convicted. Rumor from Robert Bruce's lands had it that Isobel used her very best wiles on Bruce, but the Scotsman was far too in love with his bride-to-be to so much as notice. She, too, was pronounced guilty. Fitzgerald was granted the mercy of a beheading over hanging; Isobel, distraught at the prospect of either, had ended her days in much the same manner as Alain; she poisoned herself.

Eleanor knew that despite everything that had happened, Corbin could not help but be dismayed at the fate she had brought on herself. Yet he had embraced Scotland with even more enthusiasm than she had. When he heard about Isobel, he rode out, as Brendan often did. When he returned, it was as if he was healed.

That following year was an especially rich time in their lives, but it wasn't to last too long. The following year, the king once again managed to muster the army he needed for a mass invasion of Scotland—the truce, for what it had been worth, had ended. In May of 1303, Edward reached Roxburgh; he went on to ravage Edinburgh, Linlithgow, Perth, Brechin, Aberdeen, Banff and Elgin. In November, he rode on to Dunfermline, where he spent the winter, his young second wife joining them there. The Scots' resistance made no headway in stopping; only at Brechin, where Sir Thomas de Maule resisted from the castle wall—until he was killed there.

The king did not attempt to raze or sack their castle or the village that grew up quickly around it; the land nearly adjoined Bruce holdings, and it was probably for that reason that the English monarch's soldiers kept their distance. Many, many men capitulated to the king. William Wallace was at Menteith then, visiting with his family. A number of men who cared greatly for him urged him to take the opportunity to make peace with King Edward as well. His answer was that he would stand for the liberty of Scotland; he would not surrender. The king ordered Sir Alexander de Abernathy to keep watch at the River

Forth, in case Sir William attempted to cross. He was ordered to give Wallace no terms, other than complete surrender and subjugation. Wallace had no intention of surrendering. In this time, there were still pockets of resistance. In March of 1304, Wallace, Sir Simon Fraser, and their supporters were attacked in Tweeddale, and forced to retreat through Lothian. At Peebles they were defeated, but neither Wallace nor his followers were captured; they were warned that a turncoat had given the English notice of Wallace's whereabouts. The warning had come from a secret source, a man supposedly now a good servant of the king.

Robert Bruce.

Brendan returned home from the skirmishing weary, and yet, still not defeated—and beginning to find a new respect for their powerful neighbor to the southwest. He'd heard that Bruce had been speaking with Scottish churchmen. Balliol was now obviously never going to return as king. The men in contest for the throne remained John Comyn—and Robert Bruce. In February, John Comyn the Red, the Fierce, had signed a truce with Edward.

And Robert the Bruce was beginning to show a far greater understanding of and admiration for Wallace. Brendan thought that Bruce was beginning to believe that with his position and power and Wallace's sway over men, they could truly create a resistance.

Eleanor had learned to listen, to accept the defeats, to live with the hopes.

When Edward departed Scotland late that summer, he ordered that the abbey at Dunfermline be burned, despite the fact that he had stayed there, that it was a magnificent creation, and many kings and queens of Scotland were buried there— including his own sister, Margaret, her husband, Alexander, and their children. At Stirling castle, he employed a siege engine he called the "War-Wolf," despite the fact that the garrison offered to surrender, he wanted to see how his "War-Wolf" worked, and the hurling of missiles at the castle entertained the ladies.

He left Scotland, pleased that all was in place.

That winter, Eleanor gave birth to a son. He was named Arryn William, for the kinsman with whom Brendan had grown up, and for the man he respected above all others.

Margot and Eric too were blessed. Their little girl was as golden as the sun, born with a crop of white-blond hair and eyes as blue as the sky.

Though Wallace moved quickly and frequently in this period, when the king's hand seemed down on them like a leaden hammer, Wallace frequently sent messages to Brendan.

Brendan and many of the men would join him, engage in battle or skirmish, and melt back home. Eleanor took the children and the other women with her to the north at times, and often to a far western isle, where Brendan still had kin. The ancient family fortress was on a rocky isle protected by the sea, safe from almost any attack. Eleanor learned to live with the events surrounding. She had learned from Margot. She never thought of *if* he returned. She always thought in terms of *when*. And he always came back for her. Whether in victory or defeat, his eyes would seek hers out, and he would hold her, as he had when he returned that first time after Clarin, hold her tight, and then, later, they would talk.

She thought that there were times when she might have talked him out of riding, using the children, a profession of her own fear, or some other ruse to keep him home. She knew that she could not do so. If he didn't remain defiant, a free Scotsman, fierce and loyal, he would not be the man she knew, and loved so fully.

It was not battle, but treachery, that finally brought the great

Wallace down. Sir John de Menteith, a Scotsman who had capitulated to the king, was approached by William's man, Sir Aymer de Valence, who promised Menteith the king's highest favor—if he helped to capture Wallace. Menteith had had kin killed at Falkirk. Menteith brought in his nephew, a boy named Jack Short, and Short joined Wallace, keeping track of his movements and his plans.

Robert Bruce had been at King Edward's court, but he was supposedly traveling north to meet Wallace. Whether Bruce knew this or not, no one was certain. But on a night while waiting for Bruce at an appointed field, John Short disarmed a weary, sleeping Wallace, and his very good friend and loyal follower, a man named Kerby. He then signaled Menteith to bring his men in. Kerby was killed. Wallace, disarmed, still fought. Menteith told him they were surrounded by English soldiers and that he was only to be taken to Dumbarton castle for safekeeping.

There were no English soldiers. Wallace discovered that, after surrendering to a fellow countryman. He had been betrayed.

Menteith did not take him to Dumbarton Castle. He avoided any part of the country where he might find patriots loyal to Wallace.

Menteith turned Wallace over to John de Seagrave, the warden south of the River Forth. From there, Seagrave would bring him on to London.

When Gregory, always the messenger, came riding hard through the castle gates, shouting the news, Brendan was infuriated. He raved and stormed, talking about the king's hatred for William, and the traitors who would do such a thing. He swore against Robert Bruce, and every other man—as he prepared to take off in pursuit of the party bearing William south to London.

Terrified of what he might do, Eleanor consulted with Margot.

When he prepared to ride, she sent Bridie to beg him to come to her before riding.

He arrived at the room, anxious, distraught. "Eleanor, my God, they will kill him! We have to move quickly—"

"They are already into England. What will you do to stop them?" she demanded.

"Something. Anything. We will think of something."

She brought him wine from the tray on the stool before the fire. "Brendan, I am really frightened this time. Give me just a few minutes of your time before you ride."

She led him to the fire, drew him down to the fur before it. He drank the wine quickly, and she watched him, then slipped into his arms, and kissed him. "Hold me, for I'm very afraid this time, Brendan. Make love to me before you leave, my love, let me remember . . ."

The flames rose high before them. She would always think of him as a golden, searing flame within a fire. Dark haired, bronzed, golden, scarred, it seemed, a little more here and there every year, yet ever more splendid, passionate, and tender. Such was life, to be lived so passionately . . .

He seemed to understand her fear. He loved her with a slow building tenderness and passion that left her breathless . . . almost forgetting her own purpose.

She rose above him at the end, smiling ruefully.

"I only do what I do because I love you so much."

"Eleanor—" he began, his brow furrowing.

She leaped away. He tried to rise and follow her. He could not. He fell back to the fur, unconscious. She carefully dressed, and arranged for a few days' supply of food and drink to be left in the room. Then she fled.

When he tried to leave the next day, he found his way barred. He shouted with such vigor that the walls of the castle nearly shook.

They all walked about, ignoring him.

Yet, two days later, when she at last told Eric that yes, perhaps they should unbolt the doors, she still didn't quite have the nerve to face him. She was in the courtyard with Margot and the children when Genevieve pointed to the entry. "Da," she said happily, "Da!"

"I'm not so certain that your da wants to see me right now," she murmured to her toddler. "Margot, if you'll watch the children . . ."

She turned, and, walking quickly, hurried toward the stables. She heard his footsteps, heavy at her heels. She slipped into the stable, only to find him after her still, and when she tried to run, she was brought down to the hay, and what she had done was serious, she cried out with alarm, only to find herself pinned, and his face over hers, and his hands on her cheeks. His eyes, steady, grave, and pained on hers.

"Brendan, forgive me, I had to . . . Brendan, you would have died for him. Against impossible odds. Wallace wouldn't have wanted that—"

"I know."

"Please, Brendan, don't be so terribly angry—"

"I am angry."

"I only did it—"

"For vengeance, eh?" he queried, referring to the time he had imprisoned her lest she attempt to go to Clarin.

She shook her head. "Because it was a good plan. It worked on me. I prayed it would work on you."

"He will be killed," Brendan said.

"I know. I'm so sorry. But you can't stop it. Brendan, are you very angry?"

"Furious." Then he smiled ruefully. "But it doesn't matter." He touched her cheek. "Sleep with me in the hay?" he whispered.

"Anywhere," she replied.

They stayed together, alone in the stables, until darkness had long fallen.

The following month, they heard what had happened.

William Wallace, the great hero, had received a sham of a trial in London. He had admitted to charges of attacking England and Englishmen.

He refused to be branded a traitor. He could not be a traitor to Edward I — he had never sworn fealty to him. Never.

And yet, he was condemned to a traitor's death.

Hauled through the streets on a cart, the great man was accosted by the people of London, the target for rotten fruit, spittle, whatever could be found. He was taken to Smithfield. He requested that the priest hold open his psalter for him, and hold it before him, until they were done with him.

He was hanged in a noose, cut down half dead. His genitals were cut off, his bowels were cut out. At last, his head was hacked from his body, and his body then cut into four sections to be sent to the four corners of the kingdom. His head was sent to London Bridge.

Brendan listened when Griffin, Bruce's man, came to them with the dire tidings, bringing Robert Bruce's sworn oath that he had been no way involved in the treachery practiced on Wallace.

Brendan heard him out, but excused himself.

He went riding.

That day, Eleanor rode after him.

She found him sitting high on the next hill, staring out at the landscape.

"It's dead," he said softly. "Valor, courage . . . the heart of Scotland . . . all is dead."

"William died, and he always knew he might die," she said softly. "He was willing to die, for the dream."

"But the dream has died with him," Brendan said.

She touched his cheek, forcing him to look at her. "Brendan,

I know what he meant to you. Once, I had thought him surely a monster, and I learned myself that he was a man, a great man, of true courage and real integrity. But his death will awaken the dream, as I swear we've never seen it before.'' She plucked a sprig of grass and wild flowers from the ground. ''This is Scotland. The hills are Scotland, the wild waves on the rocky shore, the color, the beauty, the people, aye, even the unruly barons and clansmen. Scotland remains, the dream remains.''

He didn't seem to hear her, or really see her. She stood, and left him, taking her horse, walking down to the stream, leaving him be.

She thought that he had cried at the death; Brendan never cried. But his cheeks had been damp, and she feared the depths of his sorrow.

She stood by the stream, watching the water ripple. It seemed to shimmer in the most beautiful way as the sunlight filtered through clouds.

She looked across the rolling hills, to the mountains far beyond.

Aye, this was Scotland.

A moment later, she heard the sound of his horse's hoofbeats. He stared down at her a moment, then offered her a small, pained smile.

''My lady, I am riding to visit our neighbor, Robert Bruce. I believe that you're . . . right. William will become a martyr. His death, as his life, will change men. He told me once that if he died . . . to look to the Bruce. Aye, and so, I will do so. And see if this is true, if he were honest and true to William, if ever . . .''

''If ever he could be a king.''

''Perhaps . . .''

''Aye?''

"Perhaps *we* could visit our neighbor?"

His smile slowly deepened. She mounted her horse. He reached out a hand; she took it. He pulled her to his side and they turned to ride.

The dream remained . . .

Author's Note

According to Blind Harry, the Minstrel, who wrote *The Life and Acts of Sir William Wallace of Ellerslie* during the reign of James IV (1488–1513), William Wallace led more than an adventurous life. Harry is often accused of exaggerating and creating a hero of more than legendary proportions. But many of Harry's claims are borne out by historical documents of the time, and if Harry was fond of his hero, it is easy to understand why. Fact. Wallace was a man who never wavered in his loyalty or conviction to his country; he asked no man to risk more than he did himself. When his strength was broken, he looked to other means to further his cause. When he might have found a safe harbor for himself in Norway or France, he returned to Scotland to continue his fight in any manner open to him, knowing that King Edward wanted him at all costs, and wanted him dead.

Wallace's journeys abroad after the Battle of Falkirk definitely occured; his meeting with the pirate Thomas de Longueville has been related by more than one chronicler. I have probably taken license with dates and places, but the truth behind the myth was too intriguing to ignore. Please forgive what license I have taken; I, like Harry, can't help but see Wallace as a man so heroic that no adventure was beyond his capability.

Chronology

c6000BC:	Earliest peoples arrive from Europe (Stone Age): Some used stone axes to clear land
c4500BC:	Second wave of immigrants arrive (New Stone Age or Neolithic) "Grooved ware," simple forms of pottery found. They left behind important remains, perhaps most notably, their tombs and cairns.
c3500BC:	Approximate date of the remarkable chambered tombs at Maes Howe, Orkney.
c3000BC:	Carbon dating of the village at Skara Brae, also Orkney, showing houses built of stone, built-in beds, straw mattresses, skin spreads, kitchen utensils of bone and wood, and other more sophisticated tools.
c2500BC:	"Beaker" people arrive; neolithic people who will eventually move into the Bronze Age. Bronze Age to last until approximately 700BC.
c700BC:	Iron Age begins — iron believed to have been brought by Hallstadt peoples from central Europe. Terms "Celts" now applied to these people, from the Greek *Keltoi;* they were considered by the Greeks and Romans to be barbarians. Two types of Celtic language, P-Celtic, and Q-Celtic.

c600–100BC:	The earliest Celtic fortifications, including the broch, or large stone tower. Some offered fireplaces and freshwater wells. Crannogs, or island forts, were also built; these were structures often surrounded by spikes or walls of stakes. Souterrains were homes built into the earth, utilizing stone, some up to eighty feet long. The Celts become known for their warlike qualities as well as for their beautiful jewelry and colorful clothing; "trousers" are introduced by the Celts, perhaps learned from Middle-Eastern societies. A rich variety of colors are used (perhaps forerunner to tartan plaids) as well as long tunics, skirts, and cloaks to be held by the artistically wrought brooches.
55BC:	Julius Caesar invades southern Britain.
56BC:	Julius Caesar attacks again, but again, the assault does not reach Scotland.
43AD:	The Roman Plautius attacks; by the late 70s (AD), the Romans have come to Scottish land.
78–84AD:	The Roman Agricola, newly appointed governor, born a Gaul, plans to attack the Celts. Beginning in 80AD, he launches a two-pronged full-scale attack. There are no roads and he doesn't have time to build them as the Romans have done elsewhere in Britain. 30,000 Romans marched; they will be met by a like number of Caledonians. (Later to be called Picts for their custom of painting or tattooing their faces

and bodies.) After the battle of Mons Graupius, the Roman historian Tacitus (son-in-law of Agricola) related that 10,000 Caledonians were killed, that they were defeated. However, the Romans retreat southward after orders to withdraw.

122AD: Hadrian arrives in Britain and orders the construction of his famous wall.

142AD: Antoninus Pius arrives with fresh troops due to continual trouble in Scotland. The Antonine Wall is built, and garrisoned for the following twenty years.

150–200AD: The Romans suffer setbacks. An epidemic kills much of the population, and Marcus Aurelius dies, to be followed by a succession of poor rulers.

c208AD: Severus comes to Britain and attacks in Scotland, dealing some cruel blows, but his will be the last major Roman invasion. He dies in York in 211AD, and the Caledonians are then free from Roman intervention, though they will occasionally venture south to Roman holdings on raids.

350–400AD: Saxon pirates raid from northwest Europe, forcing Picts southward over the wall. Fierce invaders arrive from Ireland: the Scotti, a word meaning raiders. Eventually, the country will take its name from these people.

c400AD: St. Ninian, a British Celtic bishop, builds a monastery church at Whithorn. It is known as Candida Casa. His missionaries might have pushed north as far as the Orkney islands; they were certainly responsible for bringing Christianity to much of the country.

c450AD: The Romans abandon Britain altogether. Powerful Picts invade lower Britain, and the Romanized people ask for help from Jutes, Angles, and Saxons. Scotland then basically divided between four peoples: Picts, Britons, Angles, and the Scotti of Dalriada. "Clan" life begins — the word *clann* meaning "children" in Gaelic. Family groups are kin with the most important, possibly strongest, man becoming chief of his family and extended family. As generations go by, the clans grow larger, and more powerful.

500–700AD: The Angles settle and form two kingdoms, Deira and Bernicia. Aethelfrith, king from 593–617AD, wins a victory against the Scotia at Degsastan and severely crushes the Britons — who are left in a tight position between the Picts and Angles. He seizes the throne of King Edwin of Deira as well, causing bloodshed between the two kingdoms for the next fifty years, keeping the Angles busy and preventing warfare between them and their Pictish and Scotish neighbors. c500, Fergus Mac-Erc and his brothers, Angus and Lorne, brought a fresh migration of Scotia from Ireland to Dalriada, and though the communities had been close (between Ireland and Scotland), they soon after began to pull away. By the late 500s, St. Columba came to Iona, creating a strong kingship there, and spreading Christianity even farther than St. Ninian had gone. In 685AD at Nechtansmere, the Angles are severely defeated by the Picts; their king Ecgfrith is slain, and his army is half slaughtered. This prevents Scotland from becoming part of England at an early date.

787AD: The first Viking raid, according to the Anglo-Saxon chronicle. In 797, Lindisfarne is viciously attacked, and the monastery is destroyed. "From the Fury of the Northmen, deliver us, oh, Lord!" becomes a well-known cry.

843AD: Kenneth MacAlpian, son of a Scots king, who is also descending from Pictish kings through his maternal lineage, claims and wins the Pictish throne as well as his own. It is not an easy task as he sets forth to combine his two peoples into the country of Scotland. Soon after becoming king of the Picts and the Scotia, he moves his capital from Dunadd to Scone, and has the "Stone of Destiny" brought there, now known as the Stone of Scone. (And recently returned to Scotland.)

The Savage Viking raids become one focus that will help to unite the Picts and the Scots. Despite the raids and the battles, by the tenth century, many of the Vikings are settling in Scotland. The Norse kings rule the Orkneys through powerful jarls, and they maintain various other holdings in the country, many in the Hebrides. The Vikings will become a fifth main people to make up the Scottish whole. Kenneth is followed by a number of kings that are his descendants, but not necessarily immediate heirs, nor is the Pictish system of accepting the maternal line utilized. It appears that a powerful member of the family, supported by other powerful members, comes to the throne.

878AD: Alfred (the Great) of Wessex defeats the Danes. (They will take up residence in East Anglia and at times, rule various parts of England.)

1018AD: Kenneth's descendent, Malcolm II, finally wins a victory over the Angles at Carham, bringing Lothian under Scottish rule. In this same year, the king of the Britons of Strathclyde dies without an heir. Duncan, Malcolm's heir, has a claim to the throne through his maternal ancestry.

1034AD: Malcolm dies, and Duncan, his grandson, succeeds him as king of a Scotland that now includes the Pictish, Scottish, Anglo, and Briton lands, and pushes into English lands.

1040AD: Duncan is killed by MacBeth, the Mormaer (or high official) of Moray, who claims the throne through his own ancestry, and that of his wife. Despite Shakespeare's version, he is suspected of having been a good king, and a good Christian — going on pilgrimage to Rome in 1050AD.

1057AD: MacBeth is killed by Malcolm III, Duncan's son. (Malcolm had been raised in England.) Malcolm is known as Malcolm Canmore, or Ceann Mor, or Big Head.

1059AD: Malcolm marries Ingibjorg, a Norse noblewoman, probably the daughter of Thorfinn the Mighty.

1066AD: Harold, king of England, rushes to the north of his country to battle an invading Norse army. Harold wins the battle, only to rush back south, to Hastings, to meet another invading force.

1066AD: William the Conqueror invades England and slays Harold, the Saxon King.

1069AD: Malcolm III marries (as his second wife) Princess Margaret, sister to the deposed Edgar Atheling, the Saxon heir to the English throne. Soon after, he launches a series of raids into England, feeling justified in that his brother-in-law has a very real claim to the English throne. England retaliates.

1071AD: Malcolm is forced to pay homage to William the Conqueror at Abernathy. Despite the battles between them, Malcolm remains popular among the English.

1093AD: While attacking Northumberland (some say to circumvent a Norman invasion), Malcolm is killed in ambush. Queen Margaret dies three days later. Scotland falls into turmoil. Malcolm's brother Donald Ban, raised in the Hebrides under Norse influence, seizes the throne and overthrows Norman policy for Viking.

1094AD:	William Rufus, son of William the Conqueror, sends Malcolm's oldest son, Duncan, who has been a hostage in England, to overthrow his uncle, Donald. Duncan overthrows Donald, but is murdered himself, and Donald returns to the throne.
1097AD:	Edgar, Duncan's half-brother, is sent to Scotland with an Anglo-Norman army, and Donald is chased out once again. He brings in many Norman knights and families, and makes peace with Magnus Barelegs, the King of Norway, formally ceding to him lands in the Hebrides which has been a holding already for a very long time.
1107AD:	Edgar dies; his brother, Alexander, succeeds him, but rules only the land between Forth and Spey; his younger brother, David, rules south of the Forth. Alexander's sister, Maud, had become the wife of Henry I of England, and Alexander has married Henry's daughter by a previous marriage, Sibylla. These matrimonial alliances make a terribly strong bond between the Scottish and English royal houses.
1124AD:	Alexander dies. David (also raised in England) inherits the throne for all Scotland. He is destined to rule for nearly thirty years, to be a powerful king who will create burghs, a stronger church, a number of towns, and introduce a sound system of justice. He will be a patron of arts and learning. Having married an heiress, he is also an English noble, being Earl of Northampton and Huntington, and Prince

of Cumbria. He brings feudalism to Scotland, and many friends, including de Brus, whose descendants will include Robert Bruce, fitzAllen, who will become High Steward—and, of course, a man named Sir William Graham.

1153AD: Death of David I. Malcolm IV, known as Malcolm the Maiden, becomes king. He is a boy of eleven.

1154AD: Henry Plantagenet (Henry II) becomes king in England. Forces Malcolm to return Northumbria to England.

1165AD: Malcolm dies and is succeeded by his brother, William the Lion. William forms what will be known as the Auld Alliance with France.

1174AD: William invades England. The Scots are heavily defeated; William is taken prisoner and must sign the Treaty of Falaise. *Scotland falls under feudal subjugation to England.*

1189AD: Richard Couer de Lion (Plantagenet, Henry's son) now king of England, renounces his feudal superiority over Scotland for 10,000 marks.

1192AD: The Scottish Church is released from English supremacy by Pope Celestine III. *More than a hundred years peace between England and Scotland begins.*

1214AD: William the Lion dies. Succeeded by Alexander II, his son.

1238AD: As Alexander is currently without a son, a parliament allegedly declares Robert Bruce (grandfather of the future king) nearest male relative and heir to the throne. The king, however, fathers a son. (Sets a legal precedent for the Bruces to claim the throne at the death of the Maid of Norway.)

1249AD: Death of Alexander II. Ascension of Alexander III, age seven, to the throne. (He will eventually marry Margaret, sister of the king of England, and during his lifetime, there will be peaceful relations with England.)

1263AD: Alexander III continues his father's pursuit of the Northern Isles, whose leaders give their loyalty to Norway. King Haakon raises a fleet against him. Alexander buys him off until October, when the fierce weather causes their fleet to fall apart at the Battle of Largs. Haakon's successor, Magnus, signs a treaty wherein the isles fall under the dominion of the Scottish king. The Orkneys and Shetlands remain under Norse rule for the time being.

1270AD: *(Approximate date)* William Wallace born.

1272AD: Edward I (Plantagenet) becomes king of England.

1277–1284   Edward pummels Wales. Prince Llywelyn is killed; his brother Dafyd is taken prisoner and suffers the fate of traitors. In 1284, the Statute of Wales is issued, transferring the principality to "our proper dominion," united and annexed to England.

1283AD: Alexander's daughter, Margaret, marries the King of Norway.

1284AD: Alexander obtains from his magnates an agreement to accept his granddaughter, Margaret the Maid of Norway as his heiress.

1286AD: Death of Alexander III. The Maid of Norway, a small child, is accepted as his heiress. Soon after the king's death, Edward of England suggests a marriage treaty between the Maid and his son, Edward.

1290AD: The Maid of Norway dies. With the number of Scottish claimants to the thorne, the Bishop of St. Andrews writes to Edward, suggesting he help arbitrate among the contenders.

1291AD: Edward tells his council he has it in his mind to ''bring under his dominion the king and the realm of Scotland.''

1292AD: November. Edward chooses John Balliol as king of Scotland in the great hall at Berwick. Edward loses no time in making Scotland a vassal of England; King John, he claims, owes fealty to him.

1294AD: The Welsh, led by Madog ap Llewelyn, rise for a final time against Edward.

1295AD: Edward has put down the Welsh, and the principality is his.

1296AD: Not even King John can tolerate the English king's demands that Scotland help him finance his war against France (ancient ally of the Scots). John rises against Northern England; Edward retaliates with brutal savagery at Berwick. King John is forced to abdicate and is taken prisoner. The king of England demands that the barons and landowners of Scotland sign an oath of fealty to him; this becomes known as the Ragman Roll. Among those who sign are the Bruces, who, at this time, give their loyalty to the king of England.

1297AD: September 11. Wallace and de Moray command the Battle of Stirling Bridge, a spectacular victory against far more powerful forces. De Moray will soon die from the mortal wounds he receives during the battle. But for the moment, freedom is won. Wallace is guardian of Scotland.

1297–1298AD: Wallace is knighted. England is invaded, the country of Northumberland is raided of food and supplies for Scotland's population. For ten months Wallace governs his country, his spies informing him of the massive English army being formed by King Edward.

1298AD: July 22. The Battle of Falkirk. It is later argued that the battle might have been won if Comyn hadn't taken his troops from the field. The Scots suffer a brutal loss: Sir John Graham, longtime close friend and supporter of Wallace, is slain. The eight remaining years of Wallace's life, as later recorded by the historian Blind Harry, are full of both legend and myth. Knowing that he hasn't the army he needs to defeat the English, Wallace turns his talent in other directions, seeking foreign recognition and aid. In this time period, he definitely travels to France (probably twice), receives the king's friendship. The French king's favor of Wallace is documented when later, before he is executed, letters from the French king commanding that Wallace be given safe passage to Italy to put his case before the Pope are found on him. More than one historian relates the tale that he did indeed come upon the pirate Thomas de Longueville and find pardon for him. During this period of time, the vacillation in Scotland continues, with certain barons bowing to Edward, while others desperately cling to their dream of freedom. Violence continues during Wallace's time and though he has no army, he is believed to have participated in skirmishes after his return. During the winter of 1303–1304, Edward again invades Scotland, receiving little opposition. At that time, Wallace is in the area; and many men are charged with the job of apprehending him. Relatives urge he submit, but he refuses. King Edward, however, meant to give no quarter. Robert Bruce, for one, was ordered to capture Wallace, yet there is speculation that later, when the king's men were close on Wallace, it was Robert Bruce who sent him a warning to flee. Robert Bruce has learned something important from Wallace: the loyalty of the common man is one of the greatest powers in the country.

1304AD:	Many men, including Comyn and Lamberton, came to the king's peace at Strathord. The king's terms were easy, probably because he intended to besiege Stirling Castle. The king offers terms to many men that bribe them to demand the capitulation of Wallace; to his credit, Comyn, sometimes accused of being a traitor at Falkirk, scorns such a demand.
1305AD:	March. King Edward suffers a seizure. More men rally around Wallace, but, according to Harry, Robert Bruce, in England at the time, arranges to leave London and meet with Wallace on Glasgow Moor on the first night of July. Bruce does not appear. On the eighth night, Wallace is betrayed by Sir John de Menteith and his nephew, Jack Short. His faithful friend, Kerby, is killed immediately. Wallace fights with his bare hands until he is told they are completely surrounded by English troops. He is taken, and only when his hands are tied does he find out that they are not English troops, and he has been betrayed by Menteith. He is turned over to King Edward's men. He is bound on his horse for the long trip to London, surely knowing he is doomed.
1305AD:	August 22. Wallace arrives in London. August 23. Wallace is tried at Westminster. He denies to the end that he is a traitor, for he has never sworn an oath to the king of England. He is brutally executed at Smithfield, being hanged, cut

down, disemboweled, castrated, and finally, beheaded and quartered. His head was placed on a spike and carried to London Bridge. The death of this great patriot creates a legend of mammoth proportions, and in the years to come, many brave men will rally to battle, shouting his name.

Please turn the page for a sample of the next novel in the Graham series,

The Lion in Glory,

coming this July!

Prologue

They were surely madmen.

They flew the flag of Robert the Bruce, self-proclaimed king of Scotland.

From the hill, Igrainia could see the riders coming.

They had to be insane.

She rode with a party of twenty men, carefully selected for their skill and courage—and, of course, the simple fact that they were still alive and well. They wore full armor, and carried well-honed weapons with which they were well adept.

There were less than half that number coming toward them, a sad ragtag band, racing up the hill.

"My lady . . . ?" queried Sir Morton Hamill, head of her guard.

"Can we outrun them?" she asked.

Sir Morton let out a sound of disgust. "Outrun them! They are but rabble; their so-called king runs to the highland while his family is slain in his stead. The Bruce is aware that he is an outlaw to most of his own people. My lady, there is no reason to run.''

"No reason," she said, eyes narrowing, ''except that more men will die. I am weary of death.''

The riders were still gaining on them at a breakneck pace, racing from the the castle, where surely even they had seen that the black crosses on the stone were no ploy of the enemy, but a true warning of the situation within.

Sir Morton was trying hard to hold his temper. ''My lady, I am aware of the pain in your heart. But these are the very renegades who brought the terror to your home, who cost you . . . who cost you everything.''

"No man, or woman, asks for the plague, Sir Morton. And indeed, if you ask Father MacKinley, he will tell you that God sent the sickness in His anger that we should brutally make hostages of women and children, and execute our enemies so freely. We were warned of the sickness; we refused to believe the warnings of our foes. So now, if we can outrun the rene-gades, that is my choice. It was not my choice to leave Langley. I want no more death laid at my feet.''

"Alas. We cannot outrun them," Sir Morton argued then. ''They are almost upon us.''

She stared at him angrily. ''You would fight them rather than do your duty to bring me to safety.''

"My lady, you are beside yourself with grief, and cannot think clearly. I would fight such upstart rebels, aye, my lady, for that is my duty.''

"Sir Morton, I am in my full senses, quite capable of coherent thought—''

"My lady, watch! Your position here on the hill is excellent; you may view the carnage as I take my revenge on these knaves!''

Furious, Ingrainia reined in her horse as Sir Morton called

out an order to his men. He did not intend to await the enemy. He meant to attack first.

"Sir Morton!" she raged, her heart sick as she watched the men spur their horses to his command. In seconds, the liege men of her late lord, Afton of Linley, spurned her order and took flight down the hill.

They seemed to sail in a sea of silver, armor gleaming in the sun. The colors they flew, rich blue and red, noble colors, created a riot of color with the silver stream. Down the hill, a display of might and power . . .

Bearing down upon a sad rabble, scattered horsemen on fine enough mounts, some in tarnished armor, most in no more than leather jerkins to protect their hearts from the onslaught of steel that would soon come their way.

At her distance, she could see their leader. She frowned, wondering what madness would make a man risk such certain death. She narrowed her eyes against the sun, studying the man. A small gasp escaped her.

She had seen him before. She knew, because he rode without protection; no helm covered his head, and the length of his tangled copper hair shone in the sun with almost as much of a sheen as the steel helmets worn by her own people. She had seen him dragged in with the other captured men, in shackles. He had looked like a wild man, uncivilized, a barbarian, yet despite the dirt and mud that caked his clothes, she had seen his eyes. They had met hers, and she had read something frightening in that glance. She had the odd feeling that he had allowed himself to be taken prisoner, though why, she couldn't know. Or perhaps she could. Langley Hall, as her husband's home was called, had just been turned into quarters for the king's men when they had come through, bearing the families of Scottish outlaws to London, where they would be held until their rebel kin surrendered.

Or offered up their own necks to the axeman's blade.

Sir Morton's men were nearly upon the riders. In the glittering sunlight, it was almost a beautiful spectacle, the gleam and glint of steel and color . . .

Until the riders came together in a hideous clash, horses screaming, men shouting, steel becoming drenched in the deep red color of blood. Tears stung her eyes; Afton had wanted no part of this. He had been furious with the order to welcome the king's men, to house renegades who were his own people. He had demanded that the hostages not be treated as animals, even when they had spoken with their highland language and strange burrs, and looked like wild creatures from heathen times. He had stood, a proud voice of reason and mercy, until he had fallen . . .

And neither her love nor her prowess with herbs had managed to save him.

He would be furious at this bloodbath, were he here with her.

But had he had his way, they would never have come to this . . .

She saw that a rebel had met Sir Morton head on, ever ready to do battle. It was the wild man with the tangled blond hair.

Sir Morton's sword never made contact with the rebel's flesh.

Sir Morton's head fell to the earth and bounced as his body continued through the mass upon his horse, until that part of him, too, fell to the ground to be trampled beneath.

Bile filled her throat. She closed her eyes, and lowered her head, fighting the sickness that threatened to overwhelm her. Dear God, she had just left plague victims, nursed the sick, the putrid, the rotting and . . .

With her eyes closed, she could still see the head, bouncing.

The clash of steel seemed to rise in a cacophony around her; she heard more cries, shouts, the terrified whinnies of warhorses. She forced herself to look up.

The finest armor to be found had not protected the men of Langley from the fury of the rebels' wrath. Men lay everywhere.

Armor glinting in the sun, shining against the bloodstained field. Some had survived. Unhorsed, the men milled in a circle. There were shouts and commands; the blond giant was on his feet as well, approaching the eight or so men of Langley who remained standing. Watching, appalled, she didn't realize her own danger. Voices carried on the air.

''Do we slay them now?'' Someone inquired.

The rebel replied, then shouted at the survivors. Swords fell to the ground. One man fell to his knees, either in absolute desolation or in gratitude for his life?

Were they to be executed? Or spared?

She couldn't tell. Others were talking, but they spoke in softer voices.

One of the rebels pointed up the hill.

Then, suddenly, the blond man was staring at her.

She couldn't see his eyes in the distance. She could only remember them.

He started toward his horse.

Only then did she realize that he was mounting to ride once again—after her.

She spurred her horse. She prayed that she knew this region better than he. She prayed that her mare was a fresher mount, ready to take her to greater bursts of speed . . .

For a far longer period of time.

She prayed . . .

There had been a time, not so long ago, when she had wanted to die. When the death and despair had seemed so great that she would have willingly taken Afton's hand, and entered the afterlife with him. That moment when she realized that she had lost, that he had breathed his last, that his laughter would never sound again.

And yet now . . .

She did not want to die at the hands of a furious barbarian, bent on some form of revenge. She thought of how Edward I had killed Wallace, of the horrors that had taken place, of the English furor at the crowning of Robert Bruce . . .

And she rode as never before, flat against her mare's neck, heels jamming the beast's haunches, whispers begging her to ever greater speed. The rebel's horse had to be flagging; their animals had been foaming when they first met with the men of Langley. If she could just evade him for a distance . . .

She galloped over the hill, through the thick grasses of the lea to the north. The forest beckoned beyond the hill, a forest she knew well, with twisting trails and sheltering oaks, a place in which to disappear. She could see the trees, the great waving branches high in the sky, the darkness of the trails beneath the canopy of leaves. She could smell the very richness of the earth, and hear the leaves, as she could hear the thunder of her horse's hooves, the desperate, ragged catch of her own breath, the pulse of her heartbeat, echoed with each thunder of a hoof upon the earth. There . . . just a moment away . . .

She was never aware that his horse's hoofbeats thundered along with those of her mare; the first she knew of him was the hook of his arm, sweeping her from her horse in a desperate gamble. She was whisked from the mare, and left to watch as the horse gained the shelter of the trees. And for a moment, she looked on, in amazement, and then realized that she dangled from the great warhorse, a prisoner taken by a madman.

When she began to twist and struggle and bite, he swore, and dropped her. His horse was huge; she fell a distance to the earth, stunned, then gathered her senses quickly and began to run. She headed for the dark trail, desperately running with the speed of a hunted doe.

Again, she was swept off her feet, this time, lifted up, and thrown down, and the next thing she knew, he was on top of her, smelling of the earth and of the blood of battle. She screamed, fought, kicked, yet found her hands held over her head, and the barbarian straddled atop her, staring at her with a cold, wicked fury.

"You are the lady of Langley," he said.

"Igrainia."

"I don't give a damn about your name," he told her. "But you will come with me, and you will demand that the gates be opened."

She shook her head, "I cannot—"

She broke off as he raised a hand to strike her; the blow did not fall.

"You will," he said simply. "Or I will break you, bone by bone, until you do so."

"There is plague there, you idiot!" she charged him.

"There is my wife there, and my daughter."

"They are all dead or dying within the castle!" she told him.

"So you run in fear?"

"No! No," she raged, struggling to free herself again. Afraid? Of the plague? She was afraid only of life without Afton now.

And of this man. Who would break her, she thought. Bone by bone.

"Good. We will go back, my fine lady, and you will dirty your hands with caring for those who are ill. You will save my wife, if she is stricken, or so help me, you will forfeit your life."

Dirty her hands? He thought that she was afraid to dirty her hands after the days and nights she had been through?

Her temper rose like a battle flag, and she spit at him. "Kill me then, you stupid, savage fool! I have been in that castle. Death does not scare me. I don't care anymore. Can you comprehend that? Are such words in your ken?"

He stood, wrenching her to her feet.

"If my wife or my daughter should die because of the English king's cruelty against the innocent, my lady, you are the one who will pay."

"My husband is dead because of the sickness brought in by your people!" she raged, trying to wrest her arm free. She could not. She looked at the hand vised around her arm. Large, long-fingered, covered in mud and earth and . . .

Blood.

His grip seemed stronger than steel. Not to be broken. She stood still, determined not to tremble or falter. His face was as muddied as his hand and his tangled blond hair. Only those sky blue eyes peered at her, uncovered by the remnants of battle, brilliant and hard.

He either hadn't heard her, or he didn't give a damn.

"If my wife dies, my lady, you will be forfeit to the mercy of the Scottish king's men."

"Mercy? There is no mercy to be had there," she told him.

"Then you had best save my wife."

"I was forced to leave Langley. I did not go of my own volition."

He arched a brow skeptically. "You were willing to serve the plague-stricken and dying?"

"Aye, I would have stayed there willingly. I had no reason to leave."

"You *are* the lady of Langley?"

"Indeed."

He didn't seem to care why she would have stayed.

"Then it will be no hardship for you to return."

"Where I go, or what is done to me, does not matter in the least."

"Then you will save my wife, and my child."

She raised her chin. "And if I cannot?"

"Then you will be right. It will not matter where you go, or what happens to you."

He shoved her forward.

With no other choice, Igrainia walked.

Yet her heart was sinking.

*If your wife is among the women stricken, then I am afraid
that she has already died!*

She had lied. Pain was, at the moment, overwhelming, and
yet something remained in her of survival. As she had thought
before, she knew that she wanted to live.

So he would break her.

Bone by bone.

She stopped dead, turning back.

"I will save your wife, if you will give me a promise."

"You think that you can barter with me?" he demanded
harshly.

"I am bartering with you."

"You will do as I command."

"No. No, I will not. Because you are welcome to lop off
my head here and now if you will not barter with me."

"Do you think that I will not?"

"I don't care if you do or do not!"

"So the lord of Langley is dead!" he breathed bitterly.

"Indeed. So you have no power over me."

"Believe me, my lady, if I choose, I can show you power.
Death is simple. Life is not. The living can be made to suffer.
Your grief means little to me. It was the lord of Langley who
imprisoned the women and children."

She shook her head. "You're wrong! So foolishly wrong!
What care they received was by his order. Those who will live
will do so because he commanded their care. And he is dead
because of the wretched disease brought in by *your* women
and *your* children."

"None of this matters!" he roared to her.

She ignored his rage, and the tightening grip of his fingers
around her arm.

She stared at his hand upon her, and then into his eyes, so brilliantly blue and cold against the mud-stained darkness of his face.

"I will save your wife, if you will swear to let your prisoners live."

Again, he arched a brow and shrugged. "Their fates matter not in the least to me; save her, and they shall live."

She started forward again, then once more stopped. "What if I *cannot?* What if it has gone too far? God decides who lives and dies, and the black death is a brutal killer—"

"You will save her," he said.

They had reached his horse, an exceptionally fine mount. Stolen, she was certain, from a wealthy baron, killed in battle. He lifted her carelessly upon the horse, then stared at her, seeing her, really seeing her, perhaps for the first time.

"You will save her," he said again.

"Her life is in God's hands."

"And yours."

"Which of the women is your wife?" she asked. She wondered if she could kick his horse, and flee. She was in the saddle; he was on the ground.

"And if I give you a name, what will it mean to you?" he inquired.

"I have been among the prisoners."

It seemed he doubted that. "Margot," he told her. "She is tall, slim, and light, and very beautiful."

Margot, Aye, she knew the woman. Beautiful indeed, gentle, moving about, cheering the children, nursing the others . . .

Until she had been struck down herself.

She had been well dressed, and had worn delicate Celtic jewelry, as the wife of a notable man, a lord, or a wealthy man at the least.

Rather than a filthy barbarian such as this.

"Who are you?" she asked him.

"Who I am doesn't matter. Or maybe it does. My name is Eric. I am Robert Bruce's liege man, sworn to Scotland, by birth, and by choice. My father was a Scottish knight, but my grandfather, on my mother's side, was a Norse jarl of the western isles. There is a great deal of *berserker,* or madman in me, lady. So beware. We are not known to act rationally— or mercifully. Does my wife live? You do know her, don't you?"

"Aye. I know her." Igrainia said. "Father MacKinley is with her. When I left, she still lived."

But the woman had been so ill, burning, twisting, crying out . . .

She would die. And then . . .

Igrainia suddenly grabbed the reins and slammed the horse with her heels, using all the strength she had.

The gray warhorse reared straight up, pawing the air. Igrainia clung desperately to the animal, hugging its neck, continuing to slam her heels against its flank. The man was forced to move back, and she felt hope take flight in her heart as the horse hit the ground, and started running toward the trees.

Yet nearly to the trail, the animal came to an amazing halt, reared again, and spun.

This time, Igrainia did not keep her seat.

She hit the ground with a heavy thud that knocked the air from her.

A moment later, he was back at her side, reaching down to her, wrenching her to her feet. "Try to escape again, and I will drag you back in chains."

She gasped for breath, shaking her head. "No one will stop your entry at the castle. Only the deranged would enter there. I cannot help your wife—"

"I have told you who I am. And I know who you are. Igrainia of Langley, known to have the power to heal. Daughter of an earl, greatly valued by many. There will be a price on your head, my lady, and you will save my wife.''

Once again, she found herself thrown onto the horse, which had obediently trotted back to its master.

This time, he mounted immediately behind her.

Even as he did so, he urged the horse forward at a reckless gallop.

She felt his heat and his fury in the wall of his chest against her back, felt the strength of the man, and the power of his emotion.

And more . . .

She felt the trembling in him.

And suddenly understood.

Aye, he was furious.

And he was afraid.

And, dear God . . .

So was she.

GREAT BOOKS, GREAT SAVINGS!

When You Visit Our Website:
www.kensingtonbooks.com

You Can Save Money Off The Retail Price
Of Any Book You Purchase!

- **All Your Favorite Kensington Authors**
- **New Releases & Timeless Classics**
- **Overnight Shipping Available**
- **eBooks Available For Many Titles**
- **All Major Credit Cards Accepted**

Visit Us Today To Start Saving!
www.kensingtonbooks.com

All Orders Are Subject To Availability.
Shipping and Handling Charges Apply.
Offers and Prices Subject To Change Without Notice.

More by Bestselling Author
Hannah Howell

__Highland Angel	978-1-4201-0864-4	$6.99US/$8.99CAN
__If He's Sinful	978-1-4201-0461-5	$6.99US/$8.99CAN
__Wild Conquest	978-1-4201-0464-6	$6.99US/$8.99CAN
__If He's Wicked	978-1-4201-0460-8	$6.99US/$8.49CAN
__My Lady Captor	978-0-8217-7430-4	$6.99US/$8.49CAN
__Highland Sinner	978-0-8217-8001-5	$6.99US/$8.49CAN
__Highland Captive	978-0-8217-8003-9	$6.99US/$8.49CAN
__Nature of the Beast	978-1-4201-0435-6	$6.99US/$8.49CAN
__Highland Fire	978-0-8217-7429-8	$6.99US/$8.49CAN
__Silver Flame	978-1-4201-0107-2	$6.99US/$8.49CAN
__Highland Wolf	978-0-8217-8000-8	$6.99US/$9.99CAN
__Highland Wedding	978-0-8217-8002-2	$4.99US/$6.99CAN
__Highland Destiny	978-1-4201-0259-8	$4.99US/$6.99CAN
__Only for You	978-0-8217-8151-7	$6.99US/$8.99CAN
__Highland Promise	978-1-4201-0261-1	$4.99US/$6.99CAN
__Highland Vow	978-1-4201-0260-4	$4.99US/$6.99CAN
__Highland Savage	978-0-8217-7999-6	$6.99US/$9.99CAN
__Beauty and the Beast	978-0-8217-8004-6	$4.99US/$6.99CAN
__Unconquered	978-0-8217-8088-6	$4.99US/$6.99CAN
__Highland Barbarian	978-0-8217-7998-9	$6.99US/$9.99CAN
__Highland Conqueror	978-0-8217-8148-7	$6.99US/$9.99CAN
__Conqueror's Kiss	978-0-8217-8005-3	$4.99US/$6.99CAN
__A Stockingful of Joy	978-1-4201-0018-1	$4.99US/$6.99CAN
__Highland Bride	978-0-8217-7995-8	$4.99US/$6.99CAN
__Highland Lover	978-0-8217-7759-6	$6.99US/$9.99CAN

Available Wherever Books Are Sold!

Check out our website at
http://www.kensingtonbooks.com